CLASS OF 1983

VICTORIA MAXWELL

Magic Pizza Press

Magic Pizza Press

www.magicpizza.press

Also by Victoria Maxwell

Summer of 1984 | Santolsa Saga Book 2

For anyone who's ever wished they were living in a different place or time.

Prologue

"You are to be hanged tomorrow at dawn." The miserable guard sighed, almost blowing out the candle before him. He had given them their final meal, a small piece of stale bread each and a jug of murky water to share. He tugged at the heavy key, swinging from his waist like a pendulum, and locked the door of their cell. These women would never again know freedom. Never again hold those they loved. Never again would they see the sun set over New England farmland.

"Please sir," came the desperate voice of the young blonde one they called Sister Helena. "I'll do absolutely *anything* if you let us go." She dropped to her knees, sobbing her small heart out as she gripped the iron bars that kept her prisoner. The guard averted his gaze, for he could not show weakness or temptation to these women. This was a dark world they lived in, a world full of spirits, devils and wild accusations made by those in power. To him, these women were no more witches than his own girls who were safely tucked up in their beds less than a mile away. The thought pained him, but he showed no mercy as he tucked the prison keys away beneath his robes.

"It is already to be," said the woman they called Sister Catherine. She had a soft angelic way about her, beautiful hazel eyes that blazed with kindness. It was hard to believe she was anything other than the Godly woman she claimed to be. "We cannot change our destiny," she continued, "we must all make peace with what is to come. We must forgive this man and all those who persecute us. They are not our enemies. They are just pawns in a giant game of chess played by others above them. They know not what they do. He does not mean to harm us, he does not want us dead, but to go against his masters will put his own life, and the lives of his loved ones, in danger."

It was as if she had seen into his own mind. Could they really be what others said them to be? Some sort of witch-nuns the townsfolk had said, praying to a Christian God but playing with witchcraft, the power of something much older.

He pulled the bars with his big rough hands to both check and prove to the women that they were unable to escape. They must meet their fate, whatever it was, what-ever they were. God had decided this. Not him. He *was* a pawn, just as she had said. A lowly pawn whose only busi-ness was to lock up for the night. He would not see these women again on any account.

"May God meet you at the gate," he said with just a hint of compassion before turning to walk back through the dark passageway.

"Who's to decide my fate?" It was the voice of the third woman. She had never uttered a word in his pres-ence, refusing to take food or even look at him. He stopped to listen, for hers was a powerful voice full of conviction.

"Sister Maria," said Catherine softly. "God decides our

2

fate, he decides a destiny for us all, before we've even been born to this world."

"God?" shrieked Helena wildly. "You think God wants this for us? To be accused of causing sickness and death on small children for no other reason than to die ourselves? What kind of a fate do you call that?"

"There are reasons," said Catherine gently, "even if we cannot see what they are. We shall understand all at the heavenly gates tomorrow. Do not be afraid my Helena, for the angels will be with us tonight."

When the conversation turned into nothing but the sounds of Helena's angry sobs he began to move forward again. But it was Maria's strong voice that called him to eavesdrop again just before he reached the steps.

"Never think that you do not have the power to change your own destiny," she said.

"We are trapped in a cell made of stone and earth," Helena cried. "We are deep underground. An iron lock and bars bind us, and we are to die in the early morning. How in Heaven can we change this Maria?"

"Give me your bread," Maria ordered.

"The bread?" squawked Helena.

"For the *salt*," Maria explained curtly.

The guard held his breath as he tried to make out what came next. Whispering, no, not whispering, *chanting*. If they were nothing but nuns praying to God on their last night on Earth, why was he suddenly scared to his bones?

"Join hands," Maria said clearly when the incantation was complete.

"I will join hands," Catherine began, "but if God wants us to die tomorrow then we will die, there is no spell or prayer in all of the world that can change that."

"What if God *wants* us to do this?" asked Helena

suddenly, her voice now full of excitement. "What if *this* is our destiny?"

"It did not work for us in France and it did not work for us in England," said Catherine gently.

"Nevertheless, we must never stop trying," said Maria.

The guard stumbled back as the passageway began to shake. He dropped his candle and gasped. Torn between running towards the women to save them from being crushed in this place and bolting up the steps to save himself, he stood frozen, unable to decide. He raised his hands to protect himself, from what, he did not know, and let out a moan. A bright light lit up the small tunnel, flickering three times like lightning, and then, it stopped.

He ran as fast as he could up the stairs and out through the doors of the town hall.

ONE

Maple Syrup

Magz, as she was called then, was instantaneously transported back to another time and place as she began to think about pancakes. Light and fluffy buttermilk pancakes covered in whipped butter, slices of thin crispy smoked bacon, all drenched in delicious maple syrup. She was sitting at the dining table grinning into a plate of her favorite breakfast, her little legs swinging, unable to reach the floor. Her mother was fussing about the table, making sure everyone had what they needed. Her father was winking a crystal blue eye at her over his newspaper.

"What's that smell?" asked Jack wrinkling up his nose. Magz was hurtled back into the present and into a buzzing colony of lemmings in lemon yellow school shirts, shuffling soullessly towards their lockers. She was no longer playing happy families, she was back at her locker in the hallway of Saint Christopher's High School on the top of a hill at the edge of Santolsa, a small desert town pretty much in the middle of nowhere.

"Maple syrup," said Magz, licking the corners of her pale pink lipsticked lips.

"Uh Magz," said Jack, his brown Converse sneaker letting out a little squeak on the linoleum as he stopped. "I think I know where it's coming from."

"Where what's coming from?" she asked absently.

"The maple syrup." He ran his hand through the front of his messy dark hair and looked down at his feet.

Magz looked down at her brown suede flats, the ones with the bows, and felt something twinge in her stomach.

"Is that…?"

"Maple syrup?" he finished for her.

"Shit," she said under her breath as she looked up at the blue locker which was dripping with her favorite pancake topping. She sighed, grabbed the sticky lock and began entering her combination.

"It could be worse," Jack offered as they peered into her locker together.

"How?" she asked deflated, pulling out a sticky old textbook and a can of hair spray.

"It could actually *be* shit," he said lifting out a syrupy notebook.

"Not really helping." Magz pushed through the crowd to get to the trashcan. She gave a dirty look to a portrait of a mean looking nun, one of the founders of the school who always kind of looked like she was overseeing the trash.

"Or it could be on fire," Jack offered.

"It might as well be," she moaned fishing out half a bottle of 7UP.

"OK, so this looks like a mess Magz, but it was way worse when my locker *was* on fire last month. The message was a lot clearer too. Fire says we wanna burn you at a stake. Maple syrup is more like- we might not like you, but we think you're kind of sweet."

Magz almost smiled.

"I guess you forgot your pancakes this morning," Mindy giggled as she bounced towards them in her way too short for school rules brown skirt with her beef-head boyfriend Jim in tow.

"Well, Jimbo," started Jack, "we do usually bring pancakes to school but today we slept late."

"You two *sleep* together?" Jim frowned, running his thick beefy fingers over Mindy's bad blonde dye job.

"Sure," said Jack shrugging, "don't you and Mindy sleep together?"

"We do it all the time," Jim grunted as Mindy grinned. "But *she's* not a lesbian," Jim pointed his thumb at Mindy.

"Magz is a lesbian?" asked Jack. "Magz, you never told me you were a lesbian!" He faked a gasp, putting his hand to his mouth.

"Don't be a dick Forrester 'cos you know where that'll get you." Jim grabbed Mindy by the waist pulling her close, her red-lipped grin reminding Magz of something out of Stephen King's *IT*.

Magz felt sick.

"*She's* not a lesbian, everyone knows *that*," Mindy said, "and..."

Magz cringed knowing what was coming next.

"...If you didn't, you could just ask Big Mick," Mindy finished.

Magz felt even sicker as she thought about Big Mick and his stupid curly sexy blonde hair and sexy way he convinced her with his fake southern drawl that she was special and that he wasn't just another stupid jock trying to get lucky, when in actual fact, all he was, was another stupid jock trying to get lucky.

"You're a gay," said Jim pointing accusingly into Jack's face with his hotdog fingers.

Jack rolled his eyes. "Gays sleep too," he said. "Not all

gays are Vampires." he hissed at them, showing his eye-teeth.

Magz stood by dumbly as she once again watched Jack get shoved into the locker next to hers.

"You dick," Jim said, sending sour spittle into Jack's face. "If we didn't have a game this weekend, I'd mess you up so bad. Think of this as just a little reminder of what's coming for you if you don't shut up and remember who your superiors are." He sent Jack flying into the locker again causing him to make a noise that was something between a painful sob and a laugh.

Magz dropped to his side as he lay on the cold grey laminate floor. "Are you OK?" she asked.

"Never better," he groaned, closing his eyes.

Magz closed her own eyes as something wet began to drip down onto her head. Maple syrup.

"I've heard maple syrup is really good for dandruff," Mindy said, throwing the bottle down so that it nearly hit Jack in the face before flouncing back down the hallway, cackling as she dragged Jim after her.

"There goes another one of your scrunchies," Jack said opening his eyes.

Magz just shrugged and bit away her tears as the bell rang out signaling the start of another school day.

This was the kind of thing that happened often to Magz and Jack. Magz had pretty much given up hoping for anything to change, but getting your stuff trashed and having to watch helplessly as your best friend gets slammed into lockers on a daily basis just because you liked Phil Collins more than Chris Brown had become kind of soul destroying. Magz could not wait to get the hell out of this hell hole town of Santolsa and start all over.

8

TWO

The Book

Magz was daydreaming about a young John Cusack when her English teacher threw a big old dusty book on her desk - the big old dusty book that would change her life forever.

Magz sneezed.

"Magz!" She looked up to meet a disapproving look from her favorite teacher.

"Have you even heard a word I've said this morning?" Mrs. Willis asked disappointedly.

Magz looked around the room nervously. She quickly scanned the old cracked chalkboard for information. Nothing. She stared at the crucifix above the school motto *Prior Tempore Potior Iure*, but she had no idea what the school motto meant *or* what Mrs. Willis had said. She felt a twinge of guilt. She liked Mrs. Willis. Only just last week Magz had handed in an assignment late and was let off with just a gentle warning. Magz thought Mrs. Willis, with her peppery spiked hair, era-and-age inappropriate affection for heavy handed eyeliner and fire engine red lipstick pretty much rocked.

Magz mumbled an apology as she nervously thumbed

the sticky back of her earring. She was wearing the turquoise and gold triangles. They were her favorite earrings, a gift from Jack one rainy afternoon when she'd awkwardly realized she didn't have any cash on her at a thrift store counter. The cashier wouldn't take a credit card for less than ten dollars and so Jack handed over the seventy-five cents in change.

"Jack, can you fill Magz in on anything she may have missed so far this lesson?" Mrs. Willis threw a similar book on Jack's desk with an unnecessary force that nearly had him jump out of his seat, for Jack had been daydreaming also, although his daydream had very little to do with John Cusack.

Magz looked over at Jack. His similarities to a young John Cusack were really quite remarkable. She sighed as she picked up a pencil which stuck straight to her sticky fingers. She had managed to fix her hair by make-shifting a headband with a pink scarf she'd found in the bottom of her denim backpack, but everything kept getting sticky again, no matter how many times she washed her hands.

Jack turned the dark blue book the right way up, making a face as he flicked some dust off his fingers. "Six more months, Magz, that's it."

"Six more months of getting slammed into lockers? Getting your stuff destroyed? *Hair* destroyed?" Magz hated her fine chestnut hair being a mess and it got into a mess so easily *without* maple syrup.

"I'm just counting the days Magz. Planning my escape. Planning for my future."

"Uh huh," said Magz checking the time on the pink digital watch on her wrist. If every day dragged on like this one six months were going to feel like six years.

"This time next year I'm gonna be driving my vintage sea foam green convertible over to Silicon Valley to pick up my pay cheque and life will be damn sweet. I won't even spare a thought for this place."

"Sea foam green? Really? And I'm pretty sure Silicon Valley pays straight into bank accounts."

"Smart ass," said Jack. Magz felt the corner of her lips raise slightly.

"Hey, I'm going to check out this new vintage store in town after school if you want to come, I walked by on the weekend and saw this cool Van Halen shirt in the window, but it was closed," he said.

"I'm kind of busy tonight."

"Too busy to go vintage shopping? That's not like you. What's up?"

"I just have to do some stuff at home."

Jack looked at her suspiciously. "Please, please tell me you are not seeing Big Mick tonight," he pleaded.

Magz's face turned habanero hot and she turned to face him, her ponytail flicking her painfully in the eye. Trying to ignore the stinging she stared him down. "Really? How could you even ask me that, after everything he put me through?"

"Sorry," he said, shaking his head and pushing his hair out of his face. "I shouldn't have said that. It's just that you would never normally turn down a trip to the vintage store. Not like, ever."

"So, what's this assignment?" Magz asked, changing the subject.

"It's a writing task. Start by comparing and contrasting St C's now and then. Then being when," he tapped on the yearbook cover, "and write a short story about the then. We all got a different yearbook. What year did you get?" he leaned across the space in between their desks.

"1983," Magz said. "You?"

"1984."

"That's the year *Sixteen Candles* came out," she said.

"Yeah? I don't think I've seen that one."

"How is that even possible?" Magz was sure she'd made Jack watch almost every eighties film ever made, at least the good ones. "Come over tonight and we can watch it if you want. No one's home. Again." Magz tried to make a face like *whatever*.

"Again? When do your folks get back this time?"

"Tomorrow."

"Wait, I thought you were busy tonight?" Jack scrunched up his dark eyebrows.

"Yeah, busy *cleaning*."

"So, this invite has more to do with housekeeping than my continued eighties film education 101?"

"You'll really like the movie, Anthony Michael Hall's in it."

"He cracks me up, everyone loves a nerd," said Jack.

"Sure," said Magz, who actually really did prefer jocks and bad boys, much to her detriment.

"Not *everyone*," Jack said giving her a look.

"You don't have to come over," she snapped.

Jack looked at her with concern in his dark eyes, not even bothered she'd just been rude to him.

"I shouldn't have asked you to help me clean anyway," she softened. "It's a real mess."

"Of course I'll help you clean." He smiled and affectionately grabbed her ponytail. She blinked and swallowed away the urge to cry. It wasn't because Mindy and Jim had ruined her stuff, wrecked her hair and slayed her self-esteem that she felt like crying, it was just that Jack was so kind to her. Magz could count all the people who were really seriously nice to her on one chipped pink nail-polished hand. And two of them were in this room.

He gave her a kind look. She smiled back the tears and they both looked back down at their yearbooks.

Class of 1983. The fine hairs on the back of her neck stood up as she ran her fingers over the faded gold lettering, wondering what St C's might have been like in the 1980's.

Magz pretty much lived most of her life in a vintage infused dream world which was far nicer than the real one she lived in. She walked around thrift stores pretending she was in another time. She listened to old records lying on her bed with her eyes closed, imagining that she was somewhere else, that she was someone else, some*when* else. She often hid everything out of view that belonged in her own disappointing decade and pretended for a few hours that her daydream was real.

Staring down at the yearbook, she had that same thrift store feeling. She blurred out everything and everyone else in the room. She even managed to ignore the vibration of an update on her phone going off in her pocket. She was there. For just a few brief moments, for Magz it *was* 1983.

She slowly opened the cover and began her journey through time and space in various shades of blue, black and pencil.

Hello Jell-O, began one message. Magz loved it and couldn't wait to drop it into a sentence at her earliest convenience. The next part of the message included 'O.M.G' and Magz frowned. She would have to Google the history of O.M.G later, it must have been around longer than she'd thought. Some of the messages were super corny. *Have a rad summer* or *all the best for the future.* Magz wondered if she would really stop to think about what she wrote in this year's yearbooks. A hastily, badly scrawled and inarticulate message could outlive her, probably would outlive her. Then again, she'd probably only write in Jack's book anyway.

One message caught her eye and filled Magz with a Déjà vu type of weirdness.

She ran her fingers across the pink penned message and got a rush of goose bumps.

A giggle and a shout brought Magz back to the present and she rubbed at her arms to make the hairs go down.

"Is this you Mrs. Willis?" Anastasia called out. Anastasia was an annoyingly clever pretty girl who always sat in the front row and seemed like a prime candidate for a sticky locker, but never was. Magz suspected that Anastasia was doing Mindy's assignments, they clearly had some kind of deal, Mindy never paid any attention to her.

"Let me see," began Mrs. Willis as she put on the black rimmed reading glasses that dangled from the gold chain around her neck. The class went quiet as they waited for her response.

"Why would you work in this dump for that long?" Mindy mumbled loud enough for everyone to hear.

Mrs. Willis ignored her and grinned instead. "Why, yes, that is me!" She held up the book, smiling as she pointed to the picture. "Gosh, that was some time ago. 1980. I was Miss Bates then."

The memory seemed to take Mrs. Willis somewhere else, her green eyes began to sparkle as she sat on the edge of her desk and flipped through the pages.

Magz giggled when she found Miss Bates' picture in her own book. Mrs. Willis in her younger days had short black spiked hair and a big bright smile. She looked like Pat Benatar and Magz made a mental note to download some Pat Benatar albums later.

"There's a lot of nuns in here," mused Jack.

"Yes, the nuns," said Mrs. Willis who was plenty far enough away from Jack that she really shouldn't have been able to hear his comment. "There were quite a few nuns around in the seventies but by the early eighties we only had a couple left. They've all gone now, and you'd hardly even know we were Catholic these days. Even daily prayers seem to have gone out of the homeroom windows." Mrs. Willis shrugged. "It's a different time."

Anastasia's hand shot up again, but she didn't wait for Mrs. Willis to notice before she spoke. "Have you always worked here Mrs. Willis?"

"Wow," said Jack quietly. "That's over thirty years. I can't *wait* to get out of this place."

Magz nodded in agreement.

"I've worked here most of my adult life. I had quite a few years off during the nineties."

"Why would you come back to this hell hole?" asked Jim.

Mrs. Willis looked at him. "My husband became terminally ill and we wanted to be around friends and family before he went, and when he did go, I just stayed."

The class fell silent.

"Sorry for your loss Mrs. Willis," said Anastasia politely.

Someone dropped a pencil.

"It was a long time ago." She slowly lowered her glasses. "I had so much happiness and joy with my husband that to be sad about his passing would be a dishonor to him and the beautiful, if short, life we had together." Mrs. Willis looked over at Magz. "We had more years together than many couples in love are given."

Magz nodded as she looked into the slightly watery eyes of her teacher. She had no idea how a person who had loved and lost could be so beautifully articulate and wise. She had a warm feeling inside, even though they were talking about something so sad. Like life was worth living after all. Sticky lockers were not a big deal. Magz had her own problems for sure, but no one had *died*. She began to feel a little better about everything. This was the reason she loved Mrs. Willis' English classes. She didn't just learn English here, she learned other stuff too. Life stuff.

"But you," Mrs. Willis went on, rising from her desk and waving the book in the direction of the class. "You have your whole lives ahead of you, so much happiness and tragedy still to come!" She slammed the book closed and threw it back to Anastasia who let out a yelp.

"Is that meant to be inspiring?" Jack whispered.

Magz shrugged. "I don't know, but it kind of is don't you think?"

Mrs. Willis grabbed the 1978 yearbook off Jim's desk and waved it above her head, the sleeves of her black silk blouse billowing out. "These books are a testament to the lives of the people in them, so please don't think of this as just an assignment. These people lived, some of them died. I don't want a report on the facts. I know the facts, I was there." She threw the book back down onto Jim's desk causing him to drop his phone and stop texting Big Mick about how stupid this class was. "Choose someone in your yearbook you can identify with," she carried on, "or someone you find really interesting for no apparent reason. Who do you think you would be friends with? Who would you avoid? What events grab you? I want to know about a night out with your new friends in the sixties, where did you go? What music did you listen to? What did you eat at Dee's Diner?"

"Dee's diner was around in the sixties?" Jack laughed. Jack loved Dee's Diner, he thought the layers of grease just added to the flavor and was always dragging Magz out for a burger.

"Yes Jack, Dee's has been on that same corner of town since the fifties. If those walls could talk, my gosh, they would have some stories to tell. I was a regular there myself in the old days." She smiled mischievously.

"Did you grow up here?" asked Anastasia who appeared to be on some kind of question asking spree and was really starting to annoy everyone. Almost no one could care less about Mrs. Willis' past.

"Well, yes I suppose I did," Mrs. Willis answered. "Let me tell you something," she walked through the desks purposefully. "Teenagers in the past did all the things you do now, they got into all the same trouble you get into now, they just had to plan their misadventures face to face or call each other on landlines."

"What's a landline?" asked Mindy stupidly.

Magz rolled her eyes.

Mrs. Willis raised an eyebrow, ignored her and continued. "I want to know about the auditions for the school production of *Romeo and Juliet* in 1975. That was quite a show, the girl who played Juliet went on to become quite famous, and I can't wait to hear all about the greatest night in history. It was 1982 and the year the Saint Christopher's Chariots last won a basketball game!" The class laughed, Saint C's wasn't exactly known for their Basketball skills. They were the laughingstock of the district.

"Tell me," Mrs. Willis waved an arm towards Magz and Jack dramatically, "about the high school prom of 1983." She stopped suddenly, her face losing all color as she stumbled back nearly bumping into Jim's desk still staring in Magz's direction.

"What happened at the high school prom of 1983?" asked Anastasia.

Mrs. Willis shook her head. "Nothing."

"Nothing always means something," whispered Jack.

After a short moment Mrs. Willis took a breath, stood back up, straightened her skirt and continued. "I urge you though, please do not *Google* anyone." She said 'Google' like it was some kind of made-up word. "And definitely do not contact any of these people through email or otherwise. As far as you are concerned these people are still in the past. Contacting them is completely unnecessary and I'm sure they'd all be very annoyed to know that their personal information is being used for a historical fiction class assignment and I don't want to have to explain that to anyone."

"Can we like, Google the time and the place and stuff?" asked Tom, a dorky guy with glasses who had some level of cute potential but was definitely not living up to it.

"Yes, of course! Do your research on the time period, that's part of the task. Just spare me the phone calls from the kids I taught in the past. I really don't want to speak to them."

She didn't know if he just stood out because someone had drawn a big pink heart around his face, but he certainly did stand out. Drawing love hearts around things, especially photos of cute guys was just so completely juvenile and so something she would do that it seemed like as good a reason as any to pick him. His name was Sammy Ruthven and even though his picture was grey and grainy she could tell he was a good-looking guy. He had light colored, probably light brown or dark blonde, messy longish hair and a relaxed and confident expression, like he was the most popular guy at school and all he had to do was turn up occasionally and he'd pass everything, have all the teachers wrapped around his finger, have any girl he wanted and win any sporting event he put his name down for even without playing. But he probably wouldn't even play sport because he was too cool to sweat. Hell, he probably didn't even sweat. Or did sweat, but just the right amount… Magz blushed and felt completely idiotic. Was she actually crushing on a guy from the eighties? He would be so old and wrinkly right now.

"Did you find anyone to write about, Magz?" asked Mrs. Willis casually leering over her.

"Maybe this guy," Magz said, her cheeks still flushed. She tapped his picture with her own pink pen. "Sammy Ruthven." Oh, it felt nice to say his name.

Mrs. Willis' heavily made-up eyes grew wider and she looked a little like she was in pain.

"Uh, is something wrong Mrs. Willis?" Magz asked.

"Magz," said the teacher grabbing Magz's shoulder, red nails digging into her flesh through her yellow school shirt. "You are, Sammy Ruthven is…" Mrs. Willis raised her other hand to her mouth, stopping whatever information was about to come pouring out. She stood frozen as Magz looked around nervously, and slightly in pain, raising her eyebrows at Jack who also looked a little scared.

"Sammy Ruthven is *what* Mrs. Willis?" Magz asked, putting her own hand on top of her teacher's.

Mrs. Willis looked down at their hands, one on top of the other and then pulled away shakily.

Magz laughed nervously, she was totally weirded out. This wasn't how teachers were supposed to act. Especially Mrs. Willis. She was always so calm and collected. One time, Jim had set fire to her wastepaper basket and she just poured her morning coffee over the side of her desk, putting it out. Then she suggested he go to principal's office on the way to getting her another one. She was fearless, unshakable. Totally dependable.

Mrs. Willis glanced over at Jack. ·

"Uh, I'm still deciding," said Jack. Mrs. Willis nodded, turned and walked back to her desk, sat down and just stared out the window.

"What the hell was that about?" Jack asked Magz.

"I have no idea," said Magz, rubbing her shoulder where she was sure to find nail claw marks later.

Magz shrugged off the bizarre encounter, putting it down to Mrs. Willis getting old before her time, but it was sad that someone as cool as Mrs. Willis was going to lose it that early. She guessed teaching had finally taken its toll, not surprising really.

Magz felt kind of sad as she continued looking through the pages of the book. All these people, where were they now? The sports teams that would never play again, school plays that would never be seen again. As she put her hand on a picture of a painting of Saint Christopher that someone very talented from the Art Club had painted, she felt something hard stuck behind the pages. The bell signaled the end of the lesson, and while the rest of the class hurriedly closed their books and scraped back chairs, Magz was busy, almost totally unnoticed, flipping pages in search of the object, her heart racing wildly at the thought of finding some uncovered little vintage treasure. She found it nestled in between some pictures of students looking down into the Grand Canyon. A key. It was strung on an old yellow ribbon. She stared at it blankly, reached out and rubbed it between her fingers, and then, not quite sure knowing why, she grabbed it and put it in her pocket.

THREE

Chinese

"That was weird huh?" asked Jack as they walked towards the worst sweet sixteen present ever given - Magz's soccer mom SUV. It was parked in the loser section of the student parking lot way at the back. Even the other losers had cooler cars than she did. Magz kicked up dust as she dragged her feet. Only the far back section hadn't been concreted over, so you could tell a loser at Saint C's by the amount of dirt on their shoes.

"Mrs. Willis is getting old," Magz shrugged.

"I guess, but why did she freak out so much when you mentioned that guy in the yearbook?"

"I dunno Jack," Magz said wearily as she unlocked the car. She was so not in the mood for analyzing her teachers. All she wanted was get home and put on some sweatpants and a movie.

"There must be some story there," Jack continued.

"Like what?"

"Maybe something happened to him."

"Uh huh."

"Maybe he was paranormal or something." Jack's eyes

21

lit up making him look like a cute little kid on Christmas morning.

"I can't believe you just said that," Magz laughed as she climbed into the enormous car. She threw her backpack onto the back seat and threw her books on top.

"I wish I was paranormal," Jack sighed. He threw his leather satchel in the back next to hers but kept his books on his lap.

Magz put the key into the ignition, started it up and reversed.

A thump on the car's back window made them both jump. She looked around to see a red sticky liquid sliding down the window.

"What now?" she groaned.

"Fanta," said Jack.

"What?"

"Go!"

Magz put her foot down, churning up dust as a second drink hit the back window.

Magz didn't let out her breath again until they were safely out of the school gates.

"That was crazy, they could've killed us!" Jack wound down the window and shouted profanities back towards the school.

"Or broken my windows. I hate this car, but I don't want it wrecked."

"Six months Magz, that's it," said Jack.

"I can't stand another six minutes of this," she replied.

Magz dropped her bag by the door and slipped out of her shoes. Jack dumped his satchel down next to it and kicked off his sneakers.

"It's not that messy." Jack walked into the cream-colored lounge room and shrugged. Everything in this room was in various shades of cream. The couch, the cushions, the rug. The only exceptions were the black flat screen on the wall and the plates and cups sitting on the glass coffee table. This was Magz's home, but with the exception of her own room, there was nothing homely about it. Jack always referred to her house as 'the show home'. It pissed her off, but it was true. Maybe that was the reason she never put the dishes away. At least with a couple of plates lying around the place it looked lived in.

"Wait until you see the kitchen." She picked up the plates and led the way.

"What happened to your cleaner?" asked Jack as he cleared the mugs from the table and retched a little at something gross growing inside one.

"They cancelled her. They didn't think I was going to make that much mess on my own. They should know better by now."

"You can say that again." He squished up his nose and assessed the damage. "What the hell have you been doing in here?"

"Living?" She rummaged under the sink and brought out some trash bags. Jack grabbed one off her and got to work.

"This is ridiculous, your parents can't just leave you here alone for this long." He shook his head as he threw old food scraps and packaging into the bag.

"They've left me for longer, and it doesn't even make a difference if they are home or not, it's not like they ever eat dinner here anyway." Magz opened the dishwasher and began unloading it as Jack continued throwing stuff in the trash.

"Seriously," said Jack smelling some old containers of

Chinese food. "This is not from last time we had Chinese is it?"

"Probably," she said noisily stacking plates.

"That was a week ago," he said throwing the containers out.

"We can't all have parents who cook and clean for us and actually exist in our lives," Magz snapped at him. "Also, you can recycle those."

Jack fished out the containers and looked at her. "I can't be sorry for having parents who are around, but you know you can come over any time you want a real dinner or some company, and you know I'll come over whenever you get lonely, or bored."

Magz put the plates down and turned to him. "Sorry."

He dropped the containers back in the trash. "And I'm pretty sure you *can't* recycle these," he said.

He grabbed her up in his arms squeezing her tight. It was exactly what she needed. Magz loved the way Jack smelled. He smelled like clean laundry and popcorn. He smelled like home, not home like this house, this house just smelled like rotting dinners for one. She hated that his school shirt was getting damp under her eyes.

She pulled herself together and playfully slapped his shoulder. "Why can't you be straight damn it?" She wiped underneath her eyes with the back of her hand.

"Like you'd be my type anyway," Jack joked.

She laughed weakly.

"Tux!" Jack exclaimed breaking free of the embrace and picking up the black and white tuxedo cat beneath his feet. Magz gave Tux a kiss on the nose, leaving him with a wet cheek. The cat purred and nuzzled his head into Jack's chest. Jack grinned. "The cat loves me!" he boasted as Tux began to meow and wriggled to be let down.

Magz laughed as Jack gently let Tux down on the floor.

She looked at the pile of dishes and sighed. "It's going to take all night."

"You go take a shower then set up the movie, I'll do this." And despite her feigned resistance Jack pushed her out of the kitchen.

"You sure?"

"Yes, I'll even see if I can clean up those containers for recycling and then I'll order more Chinese food," he rolled his eyes playfully.

Jack never bothered with pretending it was going to be OK or giving her some words of wisdom. He was just *there*. He knew tomorrow would bring the same old crap at school, but tonight would bring Chinese food and a movie, and that was enough for now.

Molly Ringwald was on the big flatscreen TV pouting about everyone forgetting her birthday as Magz stuffed a spring roll in her mouth.

"Chinese is so good," said Jack loading his fork with sweet and sour pork and swinging his legs up onto the coffee table in front of the couch.

"How's the pork?" Magz asked with a mouth full of spring roll.

"Awesome," said Jack. "Thanks for dinner."

"Thank the parentals. Thank Mastercard."

"Priceless." Jack slurped on his Pepsi.

"You know, my parents forgot my birthday one year," said Magz.

"Shut up," said Jack taking a spring roll off her plate.

"I was twelve. I guess it was just before we became friends. That night they came home at nearly midnight with a cake and presents. They pretended they hadn't forgotten, like it was all just a joke and it was meant to be a surprise, but it was so obvious. I sat here all night watching the *Back to the Future* trilogy. Alone on my birthday. Doc Brown was just about to turn up with the steam train."

"You were just a kid," said Jack shaking his head. "But still, there are worse ways to spend a birthday."

"Yeah, I guess."

"Remember that first day we met?" Jack asked.

Magz laughed. "Oh sure, that was a great day," she scoffed.

"You were so fiery, remember? You *literally* kicked Big Mick in the pants trying to stick up for me." Jack laughed. "He threw my bag down the hallway and called me a girl for carrying a satchel. What a jerk".

"I *tried* to help you. But I'm pretty sure I just made it worse. And then you got pushed into a locker for the first time."

"And not the last time, but still, it was worth it. To see you stand up to those guys and all."

"You done with that?" Magz asked, changing the subject and pointing to the pork.

He passed her the pork. "Things were better back then," he said thoughtfully.

"Sometimes I don't know what's better or what's worse, the old times or the now times," she said filling up her plate again. "But at least no one's holding a protractor to your throat these days, a bit of maple syrup is really nothing in comparison."

"I just wish we were having a better time," Jack said. "The last year of high school should be something to remember forever, you know? Making awesome memories, getting crazy and stuff." Jack filled up their drinks again.

"It's kind of all been pretty sucky so far," she mumbled with her mouth full. "I'm just hanging out for new times."

"Me too, like getting the hell out of Saint C's and this one-horse town," said Jack.

"Santolsa 'aint so one-horse if you know where The Stables are," Magz grinned.

The Stables was the name of a biker bar just out of town where Magz and Jack had been a couple of times. The music was great, the people were friendly, and it was pretty easy to get a beer. It had a bad reputation but was much safer for Magz and Jack than Sticks, the jock bar in town.

"Did Magz just make a joke?" Jack asked. "Magz Martin just made a joke everyone!" he shouted. Magz threw the last spring roll at him. It bounced off his chest and landed onto the cream-colored carpet.

"That's such a waste and I'm not picking it up," Jack waggled his foot impatiently for a few seconds and then picked it up. He looked at it suspiciously. Magz grabbed it off him and shoved it in her mouth.

"Waste not, want not," she mumbled.

"Two one-liners in one day, what have you done with my sad friend Magz?" he grabbed her by the shoulders and shook her gently. She giggled and the chewed-up spring roll in her mouth landed on his lap.

"Sorry!" she laughed. He made a face and threw it back on her plate.

"It's good to see you laugh Magz." He grabbed her and hugged her awkwardly on the couch.

"I'm glad we're friends," she said quickly before her brain decided it was too soppy.

"Me too." And he put the last piece of pork on her plate.

After giving Jack a ride home to his tiny house filled with

lights and voices, she felt lonelier than ever as she pulled up into the driveway in front of her big empty dark house. Tux greeted her as she stepped inside, she picked him up and held him like he was a baby.

"It's just you and me kitty," she whispered to him as he began to wriggle away. Even the cat didn't want her.

As Magz was getting ready for bed that night she picked her school skirt off the bed and threw it on the back of her chair. Something dropped from her pocket.

"What is this?" she said to herself picking it up. She rubbed her finger over it. It was nothing special, just a regular brass key, like any other regular door key, but what was it doing in some guy's old yearbook? Magz got to thinking about Sammy Ruthven and why Mrs. Willis was acting so strangely when she mentioned him. *"Sammy Ruthven is…"* she had said without finishing, and the look on her face was as if she had seen a ghost. What did it mean?

When she returned from her en-suite bathroom after brushing her teeth she picked up the key again. "It's just a key," she said to herself. "Stop being so weird Magz."

Tux looked up, Magz shrugged at him. "It's just a key," she said again, this time to the cat.

Tux yawned and closed his eyes.

"Isn't it?" she asked herself. She carefully placed it on the bedside table and got under the polka dot covers.

FOUR

The Scrunchie

_____

"So, Stables on Friday?" asked Jack dropping into his usual seat up the back of the English classroom.

"Sure," Magz shrugged as she sat down beside him.

"I could seriously use a drink after this week," Jack said, tapping his blue pen on the desk and seeming a little wired.

"You know it's only Tuesday, right?" Magz asked.

"Magz, why are you doing this to me? I need _something_ in life to look forward to that's a little sooner than six months away."

Magz sighed. It was going to be a long six months if Jack was going to count down the days like this. "I can pick you up at like, seven? Is that too early for The Stables?" she asked.

"It'll be quiet but that's OK, we'll be able to talk."

"Or we could get some food first," she suggested. "I'll get you at six and we can stop by Dee's for a burger."

"Leave the mom-mobile at home. I'll grab a sandwich, take you on my bike."

"I'm not getting on your bike," she said.

"Why not?"

"Because it's too far to ride, or I'll fall off, and how are we going to get home after a few drinks?"

"I can ride better after a few drinks because I'm more confident," Jack said, running his hand through his dark hair.

"That's what drunk drivers say."

"Maybe they have a point."

"I'm going to forget you ever said that because I know you don't mean it." She gave him a look.

"How are we going to get home if you drive? You can't stay sober at The Stables, that won't be any fun," he pouted.

"Taxi?" Magz suggested fluffing up the top of her topknot held in place by a spotted scrunchie.

"A taxi costs way too much, last time it was nearly a hundred bucks there and back," Jack complained. Jack was mostly pretty broke. What he really needed was a part time job, but in Santolsa there was nothing much but the coffee shop where he'd already worked for one unsuccessful week, or the stores in the Mega Mini Mall. But he just could not bring himself to sell jeans to the kids who beat him up at school.

"I'll pay," she said.

"Way to de-masculate me Magz."

"I'm not trying to *e-masculate* you, and I can afford it so I should pay, regardless of my gender."

"This has nothing to do with your gender, *you* can't afford it either."

"Yeah, well, my folks can," Magz shrugged, her body slumping as she noticed her nemeses enter the room.

"Your parents are basically emasculating me then."

"You can discuss that with them if they ever come home."

"Do you promise we'll go to The Stables on Friday? I don't want to get a text from you at like five minutes to six saying you want to just watch movies like you did the last time."

"Jack, I promise I'll go to The Stables with you Friday," she promised.

"Forrester!" shouted Jim as he made straight for them, his thick neck vibrating like a skin tuba.

Jack looked at him but said nothing.

"Answer when I speak to you," Jim said putting his grubby hands on Jack's desk and leering over him. Magz could smell the stale sweat beneath his one-dollar man spray. She stifled her reaction to gag a little.

"I don't answer to you," Jack said confidently, but without making eye contact.

"The fag and his asexual slut of a fag hag!" Jim shouted as if introducing two new contestants to his audience in some sick game show.

Jack rolled his eyes and Magz had to stop herself asking what exactly an asexual slut was.

"Don't look so confused, Margaret. We *know* what you did last Summer," Mindy grinned from behind her boyfriend, and cackled at her own pathetic joke.

"At least she gets the guys she wants," Jack said. It was no real secret that Mindy had wanted Big Mick for herself. She had hooked up with Jim only after being rejected by Big Mick at a house party last Summer. The same party that Big Mick and Magz had first made out at. The first and last house party Magz had ever gone to. Magz sometimes wondered if maybe Mindy was just super jealous and insecure and that's why she acted the way she did. But then again, it was hard to have any sympathy for someone who was so horrible.

"Say what Forrester?" spat Jim, his fat face turning into a beetroot.

Magz rolled her eyes. Not only were they assholes, they were prejudiced and stupid. She had no idea how they were going to live in the world after High School. They would stay in this town, probably pop out a bunch of bully babies who would torment the next generation of nerds and losers at this very same school. It was not the kind of life Magz wanted for herself. She didn't really know exactly what she did want, but it sure as heck wasn't that.

"What is this stupid nineties scrunchie you wear in your hair?" Mindy asked as her black nail-polished hand thrust towards Magz's face. Magz flinched and closed her eyes waiting for whatever was coming. She felt a sharp tug on her hair, the sensitive skin of her scalp pulled way, way too far away from her skull. She was in agony. Magz put her hands to her head to protect herself and squealed, while Mindy tugged furiously. A second later Mindy had a spotty scrunchie and a good chunk of chestnut brown hair in her hand.

Magz opened her watering eyes. As the pain began to slowly subside, anger began to rise in her chest. This was new. Instead of wanting to cry, she wanted to scream, she wanted to tell her to stop being such a bitch, to leave them the hell alone. She wanted to tell Mindy that scrunchies were from the eighties, not the nineties! But she was still petrified of this girl *and* what her boyfriend would do to Jack. She had no power and no voice and no idea where to look for it, except at Jack, who looked just as lost.

Jack gave her a sorry look. He had wanted to help her, shout, grab Mindy's hand, tell them all to go to Hell, but it had all happened so quickly.

"Scrunchies are stupid," Mindy laughed as she pinged the scrunchie across the classroom, ignoring the stares and whispers from the other students filing into class. Magz looked down at her desk, tears of humiliation now stinging in her eyes.

"Go get it," Mindy spat, slapping Magz's desk aggressively with her palm.

Jack jumped out of his seat, unable to witness one more moment.

"It's called having some individuality, but you wouldn't know about that because you just follow, you just do what everyone else does but worse. You are such a ..."

"Disperse!" yelled Mrs. Willis dropping a huge pile of books on her desk.

"You can't call my girl names and get away with it Forrester," Jim growled. Jack raised his eyebrows. It'd be just another punch in the face after school, no big deal, nothing new. Taking punches was easy, having to watch Magz's hair get ripped out of her head was way worse.

"Yeah, well," Jack began, "why don't you just tell your girl to go to a hairdresser," Jack said tentatively.

"What did you say to me?" seethed Jim.

"That's enough!" shouted Mrs. Willis.

"I said," said Jack, standing up a little straighter behind his desk and looking Jim right in his beady little troll eyes. "Tell. Your. Girl. To. Go. To. A *hairdresser*!" A couple of kids who were game enough giggled and some who weren't just gasped.

Mindy's face turned the same beetroot red color that Jim's had been earlier, and her mouth dropped open. Magz put her pink-polished fingers to her mouth to stop a laugh escaping before turning serious again when she imagined the beating Jack was going to get for this.

"Get to your seats... now!" Mrs. Willis stood over the group waiting for them to move.

Jack jogged in slow motion over to the window where

the scrunchie had landed. He walked back with a fake confidence in his swagger, standing behind Magz and putting her hair into a perfect high ponytail.

"My hero," she said smiling and wiping the moisture under her eyes quickly.

"Do you want me to put in a report?" Mrs. Willis asked quietly passing by their desks.

"No," they both said together as their eyes met. Jack shook his head.

"Maybe we *should* report it this time," suggested Jack when Mrs. Willis was out of earshot.

"Are you kidding? If we report them things only get worse, you *know* that." Magz's hands were shaking as she rummaged for her pink pen in her glittery pencil case.

"Mrs. Willis is cool, she'll do it anonymously."

"You still need to go in for interviews, there is no way they won't find out we told. Do you want your head in a toilet again? At least they've stopped doing that to you."

Jack thought Magz had a point.

"When we leave school, we are going to be the coolest cats around, and they're all just going to end up as assholes," Jack pulled out his notebook and wrote the date.

"They're already assholes," said Magz quietly.

"And we *are* cool," Jack reminded her. "Scrunchies are like totally hipster right now."

"Maybe, but in case you didn't notice we don't live in LA and there are no hipsters in about a million-mile radius. This is Santolsa, remember? Little gem of the desert."

"Why do they even call it that?" Jack mused. "There's nothing gem-like about this place, it's just that people put a lot of grass down where there should be desert dust."

"That is *enough!*" shouted Mrs. Willis over the buzz in the room. "You are going to work silently on your assignments today because I've had enough of all of you. Come get your books."

The scrambling for books began and Jack and Magz watched as Mrs. Willis spoke quietly to Jim and Mindy. Mindy sat with her arms folded and a scowl on her face, but Jim nodded studiously. It was so completely fake it made Magz feel sick. He wasn't showing remorse, it was only because he'd be off the team if he got into too much trouble.

Mrs. Willis shushed the class again. "Come on now, get your books out, ready for a little time travel for this sunny Tuesday morning. Sound good?"

"Sounds pretty damn well good," muttered Magz.

"I'll get your book," offered Jack bouncing up from his chair. She nodded thanks.

Magz sat waiting, doodling love hearts on a blank page of her notebook with her pink pen. As stupid as it was, she sometimes wished that she had a name to put in those dumb love hearts she was always drawing. Like everyone did, she just wished she had someone. The last serious crush she'd had was on Big Mick and that was a total disaster. Worse than a disaster. She'd been totally used and had really only just started to get over it. She'd never forget his voice in the hallway the first day back from summer vacation when she'd overheard him say to Jim, "I'm collecting the virginities of the weirdest girls in school".

Magz had been with Big Mick only the night before. They'd slept together and then talked about school and how weird it was going to be going back. He had assured her things would be different. He told her they would have lunch together every day and Jack could sit with them too. But she realized too late it was all lies. Hearing him say that in the hallway, it was the moment she realized Jack had been right about everything, and when he found her crying in the broom closet near the Math department he spared her the lecture and just gave her a hug.

Jack came back with only one book and shrugged. "Yours wasn't there."

"That's weird, I'll go ask." She felt uneasy on her feet. She took a breath and tried to steady herself. *Just keep breathing.* As she walked by Mindy's desk, she heard a whisper of the word scrunchie followed by a scoffing noise.

Mrs. Willis was staring down at her desk. Dressed in a red silk shirt and matching lipstick she looked both ridiculous and fabulous, like she just wore what she wanted and screw everyone else. Magz wished she had the guts to really wear what she wanted. Unfortunately, Santolsa was a town in which you had to toe the line or live in the shadow of disapproval from the normals. But if Mindy and Jim were the normals, she guessed she was happy to be as weird as she possibly could. It seemed to work well enough for Mrs. Willis.

"Yes Magz?" Mrs. Willis asked looking up over her glasses.

"Mine isn't here," said Magz.

"Your what isn't where?" the teacher asked distractedly flipping through a folder.

"My book."

"Hmmmm?"

"1983, it isn't here."

"Oh gosh darn it." Mrs. Willis threw down her pen.

"I can just do something else today if it's not here," Magz shrugged. The last thing she wanted was to make a scene. She'd had enough attention for one day.

"No!" Mrs. Willis said sternly. Magz jumped. She was still a little on-edge. "That's not a possibility," she finished.

"So, what am I meant to do?" Magz asked. She was asking about the book, but her voice came out wavering.

"I must have left it..." Mrs. Willis began, her voice full of understanding for the question Magz didn't even know she was asking. "In the book room."

"I didn't know we had a book room," said Magz.

"I'm the only one that uses it. Just for the love of God, please remember to lock the door behind you when you're finished. The last thing I need is someone going in there and messing up my whole life." It seemed a bit dramatic, but then Mrs. Willis was kind of like that.

"You want me to go get it?" Magz asked.

"That's the idea Magz. I can hardly go and leave this class to fend for themselves, can I?" She looked over at Jim who was showing off to some girls that he could fit his whole fist in his mouth.

"Uh, so where is it?" Magz asked.

"Where's what?"

"The book room?"

"Oh, yes," Mrs. Willis stopped for a moment. Frozen. Again.

"Mrs. Willis?" Magz asked.

Mrs. Willis continued to stare at her, as if she'd forgotten what they were talking about and was thinking about something completely different.

"Mrs. Willis, do you want me to go to the book room or what?"

"Of course I do!" she almost shouted. "I can't even begin to imagine what would happen if you didn't get to go to the book room today."

Magz looked at her with concern. Mrs. Willis' sparkle was still there even if her mind was somewhere else. She had a spark that most other kids in this class didn't have and they had their whole lives ahead of them. But maybe, Magz wondered hopefully, maybe some people got their sparkle later. Maybe there was still time for her to find hers.

The tiny piece of glitter that was all that was left of Magz's spark fluttered inside her and she felt hope, real hope, for the first time in a long time. Everything was going to be OK. And then, just as quickly, the feeling was gone again.

"Turn left down the hall, last door on the right before the fire exit." Mrs. Willis gave her a nod and then went back to looking through the things on her desk. "Off you go then!" the teacher said, waving her off.

"Don't I need a key or something?" Magz asked.

"You have the key," Mrs. Willis said. And without looking up dismissed her with another wave.

Magz stood confused, a little unsure what to do. She put her hand on her skirt pocket and felt, along with her phone and pale pink lip-gloss, the key she had found yesterday. She felt so embarrassed and stupid. Mrs. Willis must have left the book room key in the book by mistake and then seen Magz take it at the end of class yesterday. She rolled her eyes at herself. Why did she take a stupid old key out of someone else's book? Why didn't she just give it back to Mrs. Willis? She wanted to say something to her teacher to redeem her weird actions, but Mrs. Willis had perched herself on a desk near Mindy and her face was very stern.

She shrugged. Whatever. She had permission to get out of class and that in itself seemed nothing less than Heaven-sent.

Jack watched her standing awkwardly at Mrs. Willis' desk and wondered what she was doing. He watched her as she took something from her pocket and he watched as she walked out of the classroom and closed the door behind her, not knowing then, that in that brief moment of time her life, and his in turn, were about to be changed forever.

FIVE

The Book Room
_____

The door to the book room was easy to miss and Magz very nearly missed it. It looked more like a broom closet than a book room. Magz wondered if she was the first student to ever go in there, or at least in recent history. There was no sign on the door, nothing to differentiate it from any other door and she wouldn't have been at all surprised to find it contained only brooms. She been fumbling with the key in her pocket as she'd walked the empty halls, and now she took it from her pocket and examined it in the light. Brass. Regular. A tattered ribbon. Nothing special.

She felt a pull in her hand towards the lock as if someone or something was guiding her hand, and her fingers pushed the key in effortlessly. It clicked into place and as she turned it, an electric shock went straight up her arm. She grabbed her shoulder, letting out a yelp and jumped back, watching the yellow ribbon dance across the dark wood of the door.

She shook her head. This school was a total Health and Safety nightmare.

She tapped the doorknob tentatively with her finger-
tips, and when nothing happened, she turned it and shoved
the door open. She was overpowered with the smell of
musty old books, dust and stale air. It was oddly comforting. It was the same smell of the tingle of excitement at
finding a vintage treasure in a dark corner of a thrift store.
Just last week she'd found a pair of original vintage Ray-
Ban Wayfarers tucked away in a box of buttons and knit-
ting needles. It made her so happy to have something
someone else had owned before her, something someone
else had loved. Someone who she would never know, but
someone she shared something with. It made her feel
connected to the world in the same way that made other
people follow team sport or religion.

Feeling around the wall in the dingy light, she flicked
the switch. A dangling dusty bulb lit up the room and as
she laid eyes on the bounty of books before her, she quickly
pulled the door shut. She didn't want to share this place
with anyone. She stepped into the center of the tiny room
and a flash of light blinded and stunned her, sending her
spiraling into the shelves, knocking books over, and falling
to the ground. Most people who think they've walked into
some kind of electrocution chamber would run straight out
of there, but not Magz. She was actually a little relieved.
Maybe she would get to go to the hospital and get out of
school for a few weeks, maybe even for the rest of semester.
She opened her eyes slowly, hoping for the worst.

The old smell had dissipated, and the air cleared. The
dust flew off the light bulb as it swung in place above her.
Standing up she sighed.

"Not getting out of Prom just yet then," she mumbled
as she dusted herself off.

She began to make a pile out of the books that had

fallen and put them on a shelf next to a brand-new class set of *Romeo and Juliet*s. Weird. Mrs. Willis was always complaining that there weren't enough class sets of anything, but looking around the book room seemed fully stocked. Magz picked up a copy of *Romeo and Juliet*, turning it over in her hands and flicking it open. The last date stamped was from 1981. Magz opened it up and sniffed it before throwing it back onto the pile. There was no smell sweeter than that of an old paperback in good condition.

She caught sight of the yearbooks high on a top shelf and remembered why she was in here. Magz stood on her toes to see. 1955, 1956, 1957... she reached up and patted her hands across the spines all the way to 1982. She thought of Mrs. Willis' warning from only days earlier. *"These are the only copies of these yearbooks we have at St C's, so be careful with them."* Magz frowned. What was Mrs. Willis up to? And why did she send her in here to get a book that wasn't even here?

As she was in no hurry to go back to class anyway, she pulled down the 1982 yearbook. Opening it she wondered if she could find some inspiration for her writing piece if she knew a bit more about Sammy Ruthven. Maybe he was a dork in 1982, that would be a cool story. Dorky kid turns heartthrob. She found him again on the junior portraits page, looking just as hot as he had the year after. He was definitely no dork. She was a little disappointed, she'd kind of liked the dork story. She could just write it anyway, this was just fiction after all. His hair was a little shorter and spikier, and he wore a sort of smirk on his face, as if he was having a private joke with the photographer, or some pretty girl waiting next in line.

Realizing she was grinning at his picture like a complete idiot she snapped the book shut. He was old enough to be her father! Shaking her head at herself she reached up to return the book to its place on the shelf.

She felt like she was in a vintage book paradise and Magz wanted to get a photo of it for Jack. She took a quick picture on her phone and was about to send it straight to Jack back in class when she saw there was no service. Typical. Her phone company totally sucked. She swore to herself when she saw the time. She had gym on the other side of the school next period. Mrs. Klein the Gym teacher was no nun, but she was just about as scary as one.

Magz locked the door behind her, pulling back her hand quickly to avoid any more electric shocks. But there was no shuddering and no shocking and she decided she'd probably just imagined the whole thing.

Walking hastily back towards class, Magz had an uneasy sensation in the pit of her stomach. Something wasn't right. You know that feeling you have sometimes when something just isn't right, but you can't quite put your finger on it?

Something was different. She stopped and looked down at the dark wood floorboards under her feet. She could've sworn the floor was linoleum.

"What the...?"

She looked back up and blinked. A dark figure was gliding towards her. What the heck was it? She squinted and shook her head. The figure continued to float towards her. A big black blob with a little white circle where a face should be. A ghost? It appeared to be hovering above the floorboards. Magz jumped as it began shouting.

"Get to class now, sinful girl!" it shouted.

Magz ran as fast as she could towards her English class. She was seeing ghosts now? Ghost *nuns*?

She took a deep breath to compose herself when she got to the door to class. She was just seeing things, that was all.

Still, she decided it might be a good idea to try and get at least six hours sleep in the future.

SIX

The Elk

_____

Sammy Ruthven was busy daydreaming about a hard-to-get part for an old Mustang when the door to his English classroom opened and in walked a bewildered, naturally pretty girl he'd never seen before. Dazed and confused she looked like she'd just woken up from a killer hangover. Her big blue doe eyes flickered around the room reminding him of a desert elk he nearly turned into roadkill last weekend. The elk had come out of nowhere as he was hurtling down the highway headed out to Salt Valley. The animal had lost the ability to move, and as he made the realization he was going to hit it, the two of them made a connection.

The animal stared into his eyes as the car rushed closer. Too fast. Pleading for help but unable to help itself, it was both pathetic and beautiful. Sammy stepped on the brake, slammed his fist into his horn and at the last possible moment the elk found herself and fled.

"Can I help you?" his teacher asked the girl without looking up from the pile of papers she was marking.

Sammy sort of liked this class, the teacher was young and cool. With her short-spiked hair and knee-length leather skirt she was quite out there for a Catholic School teacher. He respected that. She didn't nag him about skipping class occasionally and the work was easy. An easy A and a bearable period.

"I'm just in the wrong room," the girl squeaked, holding up a shaking hand in front of her face apologetically.

"What class are you looking for?"

"Uh, English. Mrs. Willis."

"You're in the right place," the teacher said, finally looking up. "This is English, but there is no Mrs. Willis on the faculty."

"Huh? Yes, there is, is this some kind of joke?" The girl looked around the classroom frantically, towards the chalk board, the crucifix and school motto above, and then out at the sea of curious faces.

"I wasn't expecting a new student today, but come on in," the teacher said. "I'm Miss Bates."

"Miss… Bates?" the girl whispered to herself.

She was cute, but she seemed kind of crazy, and Sammy had had enough of crazy girls for a while. No more girls. Cars. Just think about cars. He looked back out the window and tried to think about cars.

"She's dead!" screamed Leigh, one of two pretty blondes Sammy had just about had enough of. The classroom turned to chaos. Girls were screaming, and everyone was crowded around something on the floor. Sammy jumped up to see if he could help.

"She's not dead," said Rochelle, an even more troublesome blonde. She rolled her heavily made-up brown bedroom eyes. "Take a chill pill Leigh, she's just fainted."

"Someone help her!" Lacey called out as she stood watching, running her fingers anxiously through her long red hair.

45

"Horace!" shouted Miss Bates. "Go get the nurse!"

Horace seemed an odd choice and Sammy wondered why Miss Bates didn't choose a track jock, or himself to go running for help. But Horace pushed his thick aviator glasses up onto his nose and hurdled over the girl on the floor and ran out of the room like a speeding bullet. Sammy raised an eyebrow. People could still surprise him.

Miss Bates leaned over the girl. "Can you hear me?" she asked. "You're OK, we're getting help. What's your name? Can you tell me your name?"

The girl opened her eyes and began laughing hysterically. A cute girl with a drug problem? Last thing he needed.

"Look at you all!" she exclaimed.

"What's your name?" Miss Bates asked again calmly.

"Look at you Mrs. Willis!" the girl giggled, pointing a finger in the teacher's face. Miss Bates lurched backwards suddenly.

"Did she hit her head? If she hit her head, she's probably got a concussion and we need to keep her awake, so she doesn't totally forget who she is," Lacey said frantically. "This same thing happened on *Dallas* last week!"

Miss Bates stepped forward again. "You're right Lacey, did she hit her head? Leigh, you were right there, did you see?"

"I don't know," Leigh said. "I think she did, yes. I'm not sure, I don't know!"

"You're all here... and look at *hair.*" The girl pointed at June-Belle, a preppy with a poodle perm.

"And your blue eye-shadow is *soooooo* cool." The girl said looking sleepily at Miss Bates.

"Can we give her some space please?" Miss Bates ordered, gently pushing the students aside.

"And you!" the girl said, pointing at Sammy who was

now standing over her with his arms folded looking amused, smirking at the hilarity of the whole thing. It was the first interesting thing to happen at school all year.

"Sammy… Ruth*ven*." Her eyes closed.

Lacey laughed, "I guess your reputation precedes you Ruthven."

SEVEN

The Escort

The sound of heels click-clacking on wooden floorboards woke her from a groggy slumber. Where the hell was she? She was about to open her eyes when she heard voices and decided to play asleep and eavesdrop instead.

"Is she still out cold?" asked a familiar woman's voice quietly.

"She's been in and out of consciousness all afternoon," said a second huskier woman's voice. "She's been talking so much baloney. The only sensible thing she said was that her name was Margaret. I think you need to get her to a hospital Janet."

Janet?

"You think it's that serious?" asked Janet.

"I told Principal Gibson to get you out of class, but he outright refused the son of a... I would have taken her myself if I didn't have to deal with girls coming in all afternoon asking me about STDs and missed periods."

"It's an important job Cindy," Janet said.

"It's in my job description to advocate abstinence and only abstinence. Do you think Gibson would like it if he knew I was referring kids out to the clinic in Salt Valley every second week?"

"You're saving lives Cindy."

"Maybe. But if one more kid comes in here with the clap, I'm gonna scream," said Cindy.

"So, what's wrong with her?" Janet asked.

"Deluded, raving crazy about being from the future."

"The future?"

"My guess is it's just a simple concussion. Says she was sent out of class to get a book, went back in time or some such junk."

"Oh, God," said Janet.

"Quit the blasphemy or we'll both be out of a job before four-thirty."

"Oh, Gosh," said Janet.

"I need you to sign some forms," Cindy said, and the heels clacked away.

She slowly opened her eyes and began adjusting to her surroundings. She was in the sick room at school. A clock above the door told her she'd been out all day and she wondered where Jack was. He should have been here waiting for her to wake up and drive him home. She rolled onto her side, lifted her head off the flat pillow and slipped her hand into her skirt pocket to check her phone. Still no signal. She sat up, head spinning, swinging her legs over the edge of the bed. She put her phone back in her pocket and felt something click against the screen. She pulled it out and frowned. The key.

She began to remember the strangest dream. Walking into class and young Mrs. Willis was there. The kids in class had frizzy hair and blue eye make-up. Sammy Ruthven had been there. She smiled stupidly at the thought of it. She shook her head and sighed deeply as she jumped off the bed and slipped her shoes on.

Grabbing the doorknob, she froze.

She had only been in the sick room a couple of times but she'd sure as hell never noticed a Churches of the World calendar dated 1983 hanging on the back of the door. Her head began to spin, and she backed away falling back down on the bed.

She was still dreaming.

She lay back down, putting a hand over her face and closed her eyes. Opening them again she peered through her fingers at the calendar. Maybe she *was* awake, and it was just a really old calendar?

She closed her eyes again and tried to go back to sleep. She was obviously not well.

"Margaret?" That familiar voice again.

"Mrs. Willis?" Margaret asked blinking her eyes open again. Mrs. Willis was here. Everything was back to normal.

"Margaret, it's Miss Bates," the teacher said.

Margaret bolted upright coming face to face with young Mrs. Willis, only a few fine lines surrounded her eyes and lips, the rest of her face heavily made-up but youthful.

"Miss Bates?" Margaret's jaw dropped.

"Yes, and you're Margaret," Miss Bates said.

"This has got to be a dream," Margaret said, slapping her own face lightly.

Miss Bates smiled through thin lips as a blonde nurse walked in.

"I'm going to take her straight to the hospital Cindy," Miss Bates said standing up and sounding very serious.

"Good, get her out of here. See you at bowling tomorrow?"

"Have I ever missed a tournament?" Miss Bates smiled at the nurse as she put her arm around Margaret's shoulders, helping her off the bed and out the door.

"Why are you taking me to the hospital?" Margaret asked as they walked down the hallway, past the portraits of the nuns and the lockers and the other students who were still loitering about, looking at them curiously.

"I've never been able to lucid dream before." Margaret said as she continued to be half dragged towards the door.

"You're not dreaming," Miss Bates said.

"Of course, you *would* say that, in my dream."

"This isn't a dream," Miss Bates whispered.

"You would say that too."

Miss Bates raised her eyebrows.

"Why are you taking me to the hospital?" Margaret asked again. She really didn't want to spend this dream in a hospital.

Miss Bates pushed open the heavy wooden school doors and ushered Margaret out through them.

"I'm not taking you to the God damn hospital," she said as soon as she was out of the building, her red finger-nails digging into Margaret's bare arm. She yelped, and the teacher loosened her grip.

"That hurt," she said rubbing her arm.

"See, it's not a dream," Miss Bates said pulling her along.

"So where *are* you taking me?" she asked, allowing herself to be pulled through the parking lot.

"The record store," answered Miss Bates.

Margaret laughed. "This is the best dream ever!" she yelled across the lot, which looked different in her dream, dustier but bigger, the sun even seemed to shine brighter.

Miss Bates stopped and grabbed Margaret to face her. "You're not dreaming Margaret. The year is 1983 and you're a time traveler."

Margaret laughed hysterically. "What do you mean, I'm a *time traveler*?"

"I mean," said Miss Bates, "and keep your voice the hell down, you travelled through time today."

Margaret looked down at the dusty earth beneath her feet. The staff lot hadn't been cemented over yet. That made sense. She was dreaming of the past. How did her subconscious come up with this stuff?

"Have you even heard a word I've said?" Miss Bates asked exasperated.

Margaret looked up at her and coughed.

"Get in," Miss Bates said, gesturing towards an old silver Escort that looked brand new.

Margaret walked around to the passenger side door and tried to open it. Miss Bates gave her a funny look. Margaret tried to open it again.

"Just wait," Miss Bates said as she put the key in the door and unlocked the car. Margaret tried again.

"What the…?" she muttered as she continued to flick the silver door handle.

Miss Bates reached over and unlocked the door from the inside, allowing Margaret to finally open it.

"You have to wait until someone unlocks it for you," Miss Bates said.

"Oh sure, no central locking," Margaret shook her head at herself for being so dumb.

"No."

"You got AC?" Margaret asked.

"No."

"It's really stuffy in here, how do you get the window down?" she asked as she clambered with her hands around the inside of the door.

"Are you kidding me?" Miss Bates asked.

Margaret shook her head.

"Wind it down," she leant across and showed her how to wind down the window.

"Oh yeah, I have seen these before," Margaret said, winding the lever up and down as Miss Bates reversed the car, flipped on the radio and turned out of the shiny school gates towards town.

"This is a great dream," Margaret said. "I kind of don't want it to, but I know all of this will go away in a minute, you'll go back to being like sixty years old and I'll go back to having a signal."

"A signal?" asked Miss Bates as she rolled down her window and lit a cigarette.

"Oh, of course, you guys aren't glued to your phones here," Magz said. She thought about how liberating it would be to live life without a phone within reaching distance at all times.

"I'm sixty?" Miss Bates asked. "I live to be sixty, even with the cigarettes?"

"I probably shouldn't tell you too much about your own future and all that stuff, but I don't think you smoke anymore." Magz made a face at the smoke that was curling towards her. "You should probably quit now."

Miss Bates ignored her. "And you called me Mrs. Willis, I'm a... Mrs. Willis?"

"Uh…"

"Am I Mrs. Willis, is that my name now Margaret?"

"I don't know if I'm supposed to tell you that."

"Why can't you tell me? If it's just a dream why does it matter if you tell me?"

"What if it's not a dream?" shrugged Margaret.

"Margaret, please tell me."

"No."

"Margaret!"

"Stop calling me Margaret!" Margaret shouted.

"What do you want me to call you?" asked Miss Bates.

"Peggy," Peggy decided.

"I'm Janet," said Janet. "And you're right, I shouldn't know too much about my own future. I just haven't met anyone from the future before."

"How do you know I'm from the future?" Peggy asked.

"Well for one, you're wearing a future version of the school uniform, see your collar? The collars are rounded now, and the skirts are straighter."

Peggy looked down at the tips of her collar.

"Two, you went into the book room to get a book and came out in 1983."

"How do you know that?"

"You told Cindy."

"Oh."

"Three," she said shifting gear, "you seem to know me in the future."

"Four?"

"Because I'm one too," Miss Bates said.

"One what?"

"A time traveler," Miss Bates replied.

Peggy looked over at her teacher and laughed.

"An English teacher time traveler?" she laughed again.

"What's so funny about that?"

"Aren't time travelers meant to be, like, Science teachers?"

"It's not Science."

"Science Fiction!" Peggy laughed, slapping her thigh.

"Hilarious," said Janet dryly.

Peggy grinned to herself as they drove into town. Santolsa was half the size it usually was, and it seemed twice as bright.

Peggy wished she would never wake up.

EIGHT

Ray's Records

Janet turned off onto a back-street Peggy didn't recognize. On one side was a garage and a row of small white houses, on the other was Ray's Records.

"Well, here we are," Janet said switching off the engine.

Peggy scrambled out of the car, slamming the door behind her. The afternoon breeze blew through her hair gently and she closed her eyes just to really feel it. She'd only been without service on her phone for one afternoon, but she already felt more present than she had in a long time.

"You can't just *close* the door." Janet pushed her gently out of the way, interrupting her perfect moment. She opened the door, pushed the lock down, and then closed the door while holding the handle up.

"That looks complicated," Peggy said.

"Try it."

Peggy tried it. She had to do it a couple of times before she got the hang of it.

"That's so weird," Peggy shook her head.

"You'll get used to it."

Once Janet was satisfied that the car had been locked correctly, she led the way, heels crunching on the sidewalk. She pushed open the glass door and a bell jangled, announcing their arrival.

The store was busy, full of people from every walk of life. Cowboys, preppies, moms and kids. And they were all looking at Peggy as if she was an alien.

"It's so busy in here," Peggy whispered.

Janet shrugged. "It's the only place to get your records this side of Salt Valley."

"Oh right, I forgot you guys actually have to shop."

"You mean, you don't have to shop anymore? How do you get things?" Janet maneuvered through people and shelves straight towards the counter.

Of course, in 1983 you could not just order any old thing you wanted off the internet, from any town in any country in the whole world from your phone right to your door. This was a time in which you had to go out and get things for yourself. Peggy felt the corners of her mouth move up involuntarily. This was so cool.

"Amazon," Peggy said.

"You get your stuff sent from the *Amazon*? Are they using the rainforest as some kind of global storage center now?"

"It's online shopping, the internet," Peggy explained.

Janet shushed her as a man wearing a Jefferson Airplane shirt jumped up from behind the counter. He looked a little like he just came back from Woodstock with his beard, leather vest and various talismans hanging round his neck.

"Janet!" he exclaimed as he tapped the counter confidently with both hands. "You haven't been in for a while, what brings you here?"

"Michael Jackson," Janet said.

Was there a slight blush under the enormous amount of blush Janet was wearing?

"M.J?" he asked. "I thought you'd be more interested in the new Bryan Adams record."

"There's a new Bryan Adams record?" Janet squealed like a thirteen-year-old girl.

Ray laughed warmly. "It's not out for a couple weeks but I'll make sure we keep a copy aside for you as soon as we get it." He opened up a big hard back book and began to write it down. "I'm not going to let what happened last time happen again." He shook his head making a promise with his kind brown eyes.

"It's fine Ray, I wouldn't expect to be able to get whatever I wanted whenever I wanted it in Santolsa," Janet said waving her hand around. Was she... flirting? Peggy cleared her throat.

"Who's your friend?" asked Ray, finally taking his eyes off Janet and noticing Peggy for the first time.

"This is my... niece, Peggy."

"Hi Peggy, nice to meet you," he put out his hand and Peggy shook it.

"You too Ray," Peggy said.

"Uncle Ray," he joked and gave her a wink.

"He's joking," Janet said giggling.

"I'm joking," he said laughing awkwardly.

"Uh, I'm going to go have a look around," said Peggy. She backed away and left them to it.

Looking through the records was just like hanging out in her favorite used record store in Salt Valley. She'd spent so many Saturdays sitting on the floor by the bargain bin pretending she was living in another time, finding a new record to listen to while she got ready for her crush to pick her up for a romantic date to the roller disco or somewhere just as retro.

Billy Joel, Elton John, Judas Priest, they were all here. She continued to flick through the J's and picked up a Journey record she didn't already have.

"Oh my god, it's Miss Bates," squealed a girly voice from the other side of the record shelf. "What's *she* doing here?"

"Buying records?" A nonplussed male voice made Peggy look up. It was him. Sammy Ruthven. She quickly lifted the record she was holding so it covered her face and she pretended to be absorbed in the track listing.

"Old people shouldn't be in here, they should buy records somewhere else," the girl demanded.

"There is nowhere else," he said.

"I don't want to see *teachers* when I'm not at school. It's just not normal."

After a few moments Peggy lowered the record. A stunning blonde girl in a blood red shirt was staring at her from across the shelf. Peggy's hands slipped, and the record dropped to the floor. She dropped on to the floor after it, fumbling like a complete fool.

She sighed and folded her legs beneath her. Even in her dreams she was still an embarrassment to herself.

"Are you getting anything? Because I want to go." The girl stamped a small brown leather boot.

Peggy stayed where she was, waiting for them to move on. She did not want to stand up and have to look at that girl again. That girl was beautiful and sexy and confident and badass, all the things Peggy was not, and all the things Peggy wished she was.

"Nebraska? What *is* that?" asked the girl.

Just as Peggy was about to start crawling towards the

F's and make her escape, he spoke again, stopping her in her tracks.

"Springsteen," Sammy said as Peggy's stomach gave a flip. She had that album. She loved Springsteen.

"Isn't he that guy that like, *working* class people listen to?" the girl asked.

"What, like me and my dad?" Sammy asked.

The girl laughed flirtatiously, her laugh coming scarily closer. Peggy was about to be found crouching on the ground like some kind of deranged insect.

"I'm totally joking Sammy, I just *adore* Springfield."

Peggy rolled her eyes. *Springfield?*

"Oh. My. God," said the girl who was now standing right above her.

Peggy looked up from the floor holding her Journey record. "I dropped it," she said staring up at them. They were so obviously together. The hottest couple she'd ever seen. He was so amazingly good looking even in his school uniform. His desert tan and hair all messed up like he didn't give a damn. Her with her Guns-N-Roses music video model looks.

The girl rolled her eyes. "How embarrassing for the new girl. Twice in one day." She was right. Peggy was a disaster.

Sammy looked down at her, the corner of his mouth raised slightly, it was that smirk that he was always doing in his yearbook picture and in her thoughts.

The temperature in the store suddenly rose about a gazillion degrees and her mouth went dry, and when he put his Springsteen album under his arm and held out a hand to her she didn't know what to do. But when he didn't pull away or laugh or look at her like she was a total idiot she held her hand out in return.

The muscles in his arm tensed as he pulled her to her

feet. She found herself staring at his arm and dropped the record again. She put a hand to her face and cursed under her breath. Sammy bent down, picked it up, looked at what it was and handed it back to her and just as she was about to open her mouth to say thanks, he walked off, the blonde linking her arm around his waist and only turning back to give Peggy a dirty look.

"Peggy?" asked Janet, "are you ready to go?"

"I was going to get this, but I just realized all my money is... at home," she said.

"I'll get it," Janet said. "You can pay me back later."

"No, I can't do that."

"Why not?"

"I feel weird about you buying it for me, I'll just put it back."

"Take it," said Ray overhearing them and ushering them over to the counter.

"I can't just *take* a record," Peggy said.

"I owe your aunt," he said before Janet could protest.

"Ray," Janet said.

"Please, and let me take you out for dinner too, then we'll call it square," he bargained.

Janet giggled and then nodded. "Can't argue with that."

"Thanks Ray," Peggy said taking the record which he had put in a paper bag for her.

Janet grinned, Peggy sighed, and they left the store. Both women reeling from their two separate encounters.

"So, you and Ray huh?" Peggy prodded when they were back on the road.

"He's nice," Janet said casually.

"You luurrrve him," Peggy giggled.

"I've spent a lot of time and money in that store, it's about time he asked me out."

Peggy laughed.

"His last name isn't Willis though, it's Wiley," Janet said.

"Maybe the future can change," said Peggy.

"Maybe," said Janet as she started the car.

Peggy looked out the window as they drove through the town which was so familiar and yet so different, and she thought about a boy. A boy who was thirty-three years too old for her and she wondered if her future could change too.

NINE

Mellow Yellow

Walking into Janet's house was a feast for the senses. The house was full of pot plants, wicker furniture and piles of books and magazines. It was the complete opposite of the show home she lived in.

Peggy caught a glimpse of herself in the mirror beside the front door. She looked like crap. Had Sammy Ruthven actually touched her? Had he touched her looking like *this*? She took a deep breath inhaling the lived-in smell of Janet's house.

"Your room," said Janet pointing through some ferns to the left of the entrance way.

Two red couches sat in front of a fluffy white rug all surrounded by more plants and a couple of glass topped tables. Total wicker overload. In one corner near the window sat the tiniest TV she'd ever seen. It was smaller than her laptop.

"My room?" Peggy asked. "You mean I'm staying here?"

"If you want to stay in 1983 you can stay here." Janet

said hanging her purse on a peg by the door and shrugging off her suit jacket.

"What, for like, *ever?*" Peggy asked.

"Sure, if you want."

"I could stay here forever?"

"It's going to take you a little time to adjust. That's normal," said Janet.

"Adjust?" Peggy asked slipping off her shoes and pushing them neatly under a table by the door which was covered in a mess of letters, lipsticks, cigarette packets and pens. She followed Janet into the kitchen which was about a quarter of the size of the kitchen in the show home. A pale pink counter jutted out in the middle of the small room taking up most of the space, but Janet had still managed to squeeze in a small round dining table and chairs in a corner.

"I'm dying to renovate this kitchen," said Janet leaning over the counter from the serving side. Peggy sat up at one of the bar stools opposite, her feet dangling beneath her.

"I like it like this," Peggy said. The kitchen was crammed with furniture, magazines, pencil pots, notepads, jewelry, make up, it was a total mess. It was the homeliest kitchen she'd ever been in.

"I want it red. Red counter," Janet said running her hands over the pink that Peggy thought was so pretty. "Keep the grey cabinets, red and grey, dramatic."

"No, keep the pink. How about pink and mint green?" suggested Peggy.

"Sounds a little too much like Dee's Diner," Janet said.

"Dee's looks cool," said Peggy shrugging.

"I don't do pastels," Janet made a face.

"I know," said Peggy, "but I do."

Janet gave her a look.

"What?" asked Peggy.

"I only just met you, but I kind of feel like I know you already. Is that weird?"

"This whole thing is pretty weird," said Peggy.

"I know how you're feeling. You probably won't feel normal for a few days. It will take a couple of weeks, hell maybe even months to really get a grip on things. Oh, who am I kidding? I still don't know if I have a grip on things. Do you want a drink?"

"Sure."

Janet placed two wine glasses between them.

"Wine?" asked Peggy.

"Not a chance, I don't drink. And there's no drinking in the house. House rule." Janet grabbed a huge bottle of something yellow from the fridge and grinned.

"We're drinking Mellow Yellow out of wine glasses?" Peggy asked.

"I figure if you're going to drink Mellow Yellow, you should do it in style."

Peggy laughed, lifting her glass to cheers her teacher, new friend, fake aunt, whatever she was.

Janet slid a bag of corn chips over the counter towards her. Peggy hadn't realized how hungry she was and started devouring them.

"Hungry?" asked Janet.

"Starving."

"I'll get a pizza on, is Hawaiian OK?"

"Perfect."

"We need music." Janet ran out to the lounge room, kicking off her heels and leaving them in the middle of the kitchen floor as she went. The sounds of Michael Jackson soon filled the house, asking Peggy if she wanted to be starting something.

"Did you ever hear the story about the Santolsa nuns?" Janet asked when she came back.

"Yeah, sure, something about witches dressed as nuns to escape getting burned at the stake or something?"

"The story goes," began Janet, sitting at the stool next to Peggy and leaning close, as if to share a secret. "That there were once three nuns, they weren't witches exactly, they were nuns with special powers."

"I wish I had a special power," Peggy said sipping on her Mellow Yellow.

"You just time travelled today, and you think you don't have special powers?"

Peggy shrugged.

"There are many stories about the three nuns," Janet went on, "three sisters, all throughout history. In each story they are the same ages, as if they were immortal."

"OK, so what's this got to do with anything?"

"I don't think they were immortal."

"Huh?"

"There are only three reasons that you could keep turning up throughout history looking the same."

"Oh yeah? What are those reasons?"

"Being immortal, being a vampire, *or*," she paused for effect, "a time traveler."

"Right, but vampires *are* immortal, so that's really only two reasons."

Janet ignored her. "I know you still think maybe this is a dream, but you need to understand the basic rules of time travel."

Peggy laughed.

"This is serious," Janet said in her teacher voice.

Peggy felt herself sit up straighter and start paying better attention, just like she would in class when Mrs. Willis noticed her slacking off.

"Just humor me for a minute," Janet softened.

Peggy nodded.

"Let's start with the basics. What happened today was that you time travelled."

"OK," said Peggy.

"If you want to go back to your present you can, but you need to wait until dawn."

"Huh?"

"You couldn't go back right now, but as soon as it's dawn tomorrow, you can travel back, the portal needs to reset, otherwise you'll go too far back. Got it?"

Peggy nodded.

"But there are certain conditions that may mean you can't get back here, or there," Janet explained.

"Like what?"

"If someone gets in the book room between you, which is why it's imperative that you lock the door behind you."

Peggy frowned trying to remember if she locked the door behind her.

"Or if your situation changes."

"What does that mean?"

"This sounds kind of hard to believe, but the book room, it *helps* people," Janet said.

"You're right, that is hard to believe," Peggy said. She could feel a massive headache coming on and put her hands to her head.

"We can talk more about this later, when your head clears. Let's eat." Janet pulled a crispy slightly burnt pizza out of the oven, threw it on a plate and grinned as if she'd just cooked a meal worthy of a prize.

"Come dance," Janet said as she cranked up the sound on the record player which was about ten times bigger than the TV.

Peggy put her drink down on the coffee table and

danced with her teacher. She had never danced with her mother as a child, but if she had, she was quite sure this is what it would have felt like. Fun, silly, like home. They did the twist, the can-can, attempted swing dancing and then fell to the floor laughing.

"When is your present?" asked Peggy staring up at the nicotine stained ceiling.

"I'm from the nineties," Janet said.

"Why didn't you ever go back?" Peggy asked. "To your present I mean."

"Nothing to go back for," Janet shrugged.

"Sorry."

"It's fine," Janet waved her hand away. "I was about to be put into foster care when I found the key. This opportunity to change everything. To find a new life, and I grabbed it with both hands and put it in my pocket, and the rest, as they say, is history. Or future." She shrugged and grabbed her pack of cigarettes off the table.

"Sorry," Peggy said again.

Janet crawled over to a shelf where two unicorn bookends held a small selection of books in place. She pulled one out and handed it to her.

"*The Nuns of Santolsa*," Peggy read, holding the small black leather-bound book in her hands.

"Read it when you've recovered a bit," Janet said.

Peggy held the book and closed her eyes. The sounds and smells of the eighties filled the room. Michael Jackson, Hawaiian pizza, old cigarette smoke and that weird wicker smell. She let herself imagine for a moment that this was real. It was what she had done so many times before in her bedroom at home. Pretending to be somewhere else, some*when* else.

But when she opened her eyes, she was still there. Janet in her electric blue skirt, holding a wine glass full of

Mellow Yellow and dancing around on the shaggy white rug with her eyes closed and a serene smile on her face.

Janet's eyes popped open as she felt some drink spill on her hand.

"Oops!" she giggled.

Peggy had no trouble at all imagining old Mrs. Willis doing the same thing when she thought no one was looking.

And she wondered if Mrs. Willis still lived in the same house in her present.

And she wondered if this was her present now.

TEN

Interlude I

"We should go a little further," said Sister Maria.

The summer sun was setting at the end of another long day of walking through the desert. It had been a long and arduous journey with nothing for comfort but a horse and a small clapped-out wagon which had already been the worse for wear when they began their journey two months previous.

"We *must* stop, we need rest," Sister Helena said coldly. She was tired, not only of walking, but of running, hiding, starving.

"There looks to be a farm ahead," Sister Maria said. "I should think they will give us three nuns assistance if we only ask."

"No," said Helena, her eyes blazing with defiance. "We stop now. This is the place here, on top of this hill."

"We should do as Sister Maria suggests," said Sister Catherine nodding serenely, sweat running down her face. She had been wearing the same habit for some months now and had begun to lose all sense of smell of herself. Her companions on the other hand smelt terrible, but it was not in her nature or her beliefs to think too long about that or ever speak of it out loud.

"Why do you both always get to have the final say?" Helena complained. "I want to stop."

"If you stop, you stop without us," Maria said.

"Just a little further Sister Helena, perhaps they will have bread." Catherine knew Helena would never say no to a fresh bit of bread or anything edible, for much of Helena's difficulty in their quest was due to a lack of enough food. Catherine and Maria were enlightened beyond those cravings, but Helena was more of the body.

"I do not care for bread! Leave me. Leave me!" she shouted.

"Come, Sister Catherine," said Maria, ignoring the young girl before her who was throwing herself onto the burnt orange dust in a tantrum.

"Without our Helena?" Catherine asked. Her big eyes wide with disbelief. They had both at times found Helena to try their patience, but to leave her in the desert alone would be beyond cruel.

"If Helena wishes to be left here, then we shall leave her," said Sister Maria.

"As you say, Sister Maria. Come quickly after us Helena, won't you?"

"Never! I will never go anywhere with you!" Helena wailed after them into the setting sun.

ELEVEN

San Dimas

"Wake up, it's nearly time for school."

She rolled over refusing to believe it, and why was her mother hassling her about school anyway? Her mom was usually gone by six if she was there at all. She reached over to the nightstand for her phone, but the nightstand wasn't there.

"There's coffee."

Coffee? Her mom had made coffee? She continued to feel around for the nightstand. As she began to groggily wake, she frowned. She couldn't feel her own cotton sheets beneath her. She must've fallen asleep on the couch again.

"Wake up!" Her mother was becoming impatient now. "Peggy!"

Peggy? Peggy's eyes flew open.

She looked around the bright room, the pot plants and retro furniture and watched as Pat Benatar, dressed in a red skirt suit and matching lipstick almost disappeared into the red lounge chair across from her. No, not Pat Benatar, *Janet.*

"It's my second favorite mug, so be careful with it,"

Janet said, motioning to the steaming mug on the coffee table.

Peggy sat up and looked at the Bryan Adams 1982 tour mug and blinked. "What... when?" she asked rubbing her eyes and then picking up the mug and inhaling the delicious aroma.

"When do you think?" Janet asked turning on the small wooden box of a TV.

A good-looking man in a tight brown suit with too curly to be natural blonde hair appeared. "Another sunny day in Santolsa today for you folks," he said. "Cooler in the evening again, and overnight it gets damn cold." He pointed to a bad drawing of a map of the area with a long stick.

"If you want more sugar there's some in the cabinet above the kettle, I only put in one," Janet said.

Peggy smiled. "One sugar is perfect" she said. No one at her house had ever made her coffee before, except for Jack when he'd stayed over. Jack was king of cappuccino. It was a shame the manager of the coffee shop at the Mega Mini Mall didn't agree.

"Thanks, I could get used to this," Peggy said sleepily, pushing up the sleeves of spotty pajamas Janet had left for her in the bathroom late last night with a towel, face cloth and offer for her to use anything in the bathroom.

Peggy looked out the window and wondered. "Is this really real?" she asked quietly.

"Yuh huh," said Janet.

Peggy frowned. "My head feels like it's splitting in two."

"That's a side-effect I'm afraid. I'll get you some pain killers."

"Side-effect?"

"Of time travel."

"Oh sure." The pain began to spread.

Janet returned with a bottle of pills and a glass of water. Peggy took two.

"You can hang onto those, but don't take too many."

Peggy nodded and took two. The water tasted different here. Fresher.

"Try not to worry too much about messing things up," Janet said, lighting a cigarette and sitting back down on the chair opposite Peggy. "It will ease the pain a little".

"Messing things up?" Peggy asked, trying not to be grossed out by the cigarette smoke curling towards her.

"You know, like creating time travel paradoxes, destroying the universe, stuff like that."

Peggy's mouth dropped open. "Am I going to create a paradox just by being here?"

"Obviously not."

"What if I run into my parents or something?"

"Are your parents here?"

Peggy thought. "No, they didn't move here until just before I was born. They wanted to get out of the cities to raise me. Although all they ever did when I was growing up was travel to the cities."

"So that's one less thing to worry about, great."

"What if I *do* mess everything up?" Peggy was always messing things up but messing up the whole future of mankind was a pretty big burden.

"There's two schools of thought," said Janet inhaling on her cigarette and then blowing smoke into the air, making Peggy cough. "One, is that everything is predetermined. It doesn't matter what you do at any time because everything happens according to some big destined divine plan."

"And what's the other option?"

"You choose your own destiny," said Janet.

"So, which one is right?"

Janet shrugged. "No one knows".

"Great. So, I *could* mess up everything."

"I've been here a while, and nothing seems to have changed. It sounds kind of crazy, but I feel like I was always meant to come here." Janet stubbed out the cigarette in a dolphin shaped ashtray on the table and stood up.

Even though she'd only been in 1983 for less than a day, Peggy thought she knew exactly what Janet meant.

"Are you ready for your first day?" Janet asked.

"Are you seriously making me go to school on my first day in the eighties?" Peggy took the last sip of coffee and put the mug back on the table.

"I'm your teacher, so yes."

"You're not *really* my teacher."

"I really *am* Peg, and I will be your teacher for the rest of the year if you decide to stay."

Stay.

Stay?

"Stay today, see how you like it. You can go back any time but don't forget time is still ticking in the present, *your* present."

"Huh?" Peggy had zoned out and was watching an advertisement for Kentucky Fried Chicken and missed most of what Janet had just said.

"This is important Peggy," Janet said. "You can't ignore the rules of time travel or else you *are* going to find yourself in trouble. Time doesn't stop moving in the future when you're in the past."

"Yeah, yeah I get it. The clock in San Dimas is always running," Peggy said.

Janet's clutched her heart. "What did you just say?"

"I said the clock in San Dimas is always running. It's from a movie. You probably haven't heard of it yet."

"I know what it's from." Janet reached for the pain killers and took two herself.

"What is it?" Peggy asked.

Janet shook her head, her spiked hair so hair-sprayed it was not even close to moving. She looked close to tears.

"Janet," Peggy got up and put her arm awkwardly around her teacher who was trembling slightly.

"No one has..."

"No one has what?"

"No one has seen that movie yet," said Janet.

"What?"

"Bill and Ted. It's not out yet."

Peggy laughed. "I know!"

"I saw it at the movies with friends," Janet said, her eyes glazing over.

"How did you see it at the movies?"

"Peggy, I'm from the nineties. I'm not from here either." Janet put out her cigarette. "No one knows about me here, Peg."

"About where you're from?"

"About *when* I'm from."

"Well, so now you have me," Peggy said shrugging and giving her teacher a coffee breath smile.

Janet took a deep breath, composing herself quickly. She picked herself and the coffee cups up and returned instantly to her normal self. "Right, so go get ready for school."

TWELVE

Home Room

"My niece, who is from Canada," Janet improvised, "has been through a lot in these recent days and I would really appreciate if you could put her in both my home room and English class."

Peggy stood quietly chewing on the inside of her mouth, catching the sweet taste of her lip gloss. Her pink gloss was the only make-up she had with her and so the rest of her face was totally bare because Janet's make-up was the wrong color for her. She didn't like going out without make-up on and she didn't like lying. She'd just let Janet do this part and be vague about the details.

The grey-haired school receptionist looked up at Peggy suspiciously through her super thick glasses that made her look like a giant bug. She handed over some papers, had Janet sign a form, and it was done.

"She doesn't want to see my ID or anything?" asked Peggy as they walked towards class, students moving out of their way as they went. That had never happened to Peggy before. She guessed having a faculty escort was useful.

"What for? I told her who you were," Janet replied. "And anyway, what *exactly* would your ID say on it? You haven't even been born yet."

Peggy shrugged. "Everyone is pretty security conscious these days. People are kind of freaked out about knowing who everyone is and where they are all the time."

"Like in 1984?" asked Janet looking very concerned.

"I thought it was 198*3*?" asked Peggy.

"But you're saying the future is like 1984, and I thought the nineties were getting bad. What happened?"

"I've never been to 1984, I don't know what happened."

"1984, the *book* Peggy, what am I teaching you in English in the future?" Janet opened the classroom door and ushered her in.

"Oh right," Peggy shook her head. "We're doing creative writing right now. Funnily enough, I'm meant to be researching 1983 for an assignment you gave me."

"Well I'll be," said Janet dropping her bags onto her large desk and standing limply.

"What now?"

"*I* sent you here." Her face paled.

"How could you send me here?"

Janet walked back to the door and pulled it shut.

"I guess you did," Peggy shrugged. "I talked to you when I first saw the book. You warned me about..."

"Stop," Janet demanded perching on her desk as Peggy flopped down in a seat in the front row. "You really can't tell me anything."

"Maybe I'm *meant* to tell you stuff."

"Let's not even go there." Janet looked up at the clock above her desk. "It's nearly nine, you don't want to be sitting in the front row when the bell goes."

Peggy stood up just in time as a couple of nerds wearing thick black frames and their shirts done up to the top buttons sat down in front. In the eighties, the nerds looked like cool hipsters. Like a-bit-less-cool versions of Jack.

She walked past the pre-hipster nerds and headed for her usual seat - the one up the back next to Jack. Jack. Jack would be furious at her for disappearing. Jack would be worried sick. Jack would not be here to keep her safe today.

She dropped the notebooks Janet had given her on the desk and sat down, smoothing out her skirt beneath her. As other girls began to file in, she became aware of how different her uniform was. She felt like that kid who couldn't afford the proper school uniform and had to buy cheap generic shirts second hand.

Life began to move in slow motion as he walked in, holding his notebooks casually under his arm. His shirt was tucked in loosely and he wore a leather belt through the loops of his school pants. Peggy blushed as she realized she had spent far too long looking at that part of him.

"Morning Mr. Ruthven, you're here early." Janet said.

He looked at his watch and then at the clock above him. He threw his books on a desk by the window as the bell went and a cacophony of other students burst through the door.

The gorgeous blonde from the record store strutted straight towards him. Her hair was so fake blonde, a golden yellow color, but it suited her creamy make-up caked complexion. She kissed his cheek with her dark red lips before taking the seat next to him. He looked slightly less bored by her presence but not much. She began talking at him as he opened up his notebook and looked out the window, half listening, half ignoring her.

A stunning redhead eyed Peggy up and down suspiciously and then plonked herself into Jack's seat beside her. Peggy opened her mouth to tell the girl that it was Jack's seat and stopped herself. Jack wouldn't be coming today.

"Good morning class," Janet began as the class became quiet. "I want you all to welcome a new student this morning, Peggy Martin!" She waved her hand as if she was presenting a lounge suite on *The Price is Right*.

Peggy looked up as everyone turned to stare at her. She raised her hand as if to say "hello" and felt her stomach lurch. She hated being the center of attention. She kept her hand up and gave a sort of wave.

"Peggy, do you want to introduce yourself?"

Peggy shook her head.

"Come up the front and tell us a bit about your interests," suggested Janet.

Peggy gave her a deer in headlights look but Janet started clapping. A few nerds up front clapped politely and so she made her way slowly to the front of the room. She took a deep breath and turned around feeling nervous and clammy.

Looking out at the sea of unfamiliar and mostly unfriendly faces, she glanced over to him. He looked at her as if he was actually interested in what she had to say. She felt her stomach flip and she looked down at her feet.

"Peggy?" prompted Janet. "Tell us about yourself, what do you do for fun?"

"Uh, Hi. I'm Peggy," she said with an awkward wave of her hand. She liked saying that, that her name was Peggy. "I like listening to records I guess..."

"Who doesn't?" scoffed a girl with messy black hair and heavy black eyeliner. She was kind of terrifying.

Peggy swallowed. "I like shopping at secondhand shops for retro stuff..."

"Like stuff from the fifties?" asked a boy with frizzy hair in thick aviator glasses. He smiled at her and she felt a little better.

"Yeah sure, like stuff from the fifties." Peggy shrugged, attempting to smile back at him. She guessed her statement didn't really make sense if you were *living* in retro.

"What else?" Janet urged.

Peggy tried to think of something else to say but she had nothing. She *had* no real interests. Movies, music, books, nothing that made her that unique. Except, she guessed, that she was a time traveler. She just stood there trying not to look at him or anyone. Had she already ruined everything? She squinted as if they were all about to throw cream pies at her.

"Peggy is my niece. She's from Canada." A few aaahs and ooohs came from the crowd in understanding. "She's been through a difficult time and it would be really great if you could show her around today."

The nerds looked up at her grinning, clearly eager to show her around.

"Thanks Peggy, you can sit down now," said Janet.

Peggy let out a breath, walked back to her seat and zoned out as Janet did roll call.

"Peggy?"

She didn't realize it was her.

"*Peggy*?" Janet asked again looking straight at her.

"Present." It was the first time she had been called something other than Magz or Margaret during roll call. It was a delight to her ears. It felt like coming home. A weight had been lifted. She *was* Peggy now. Peggy Martin. She was always destined to be Peggy Martin. She was sure of it.

"Sammy Ruthven?"

Peggy felt the fine hairs on her arms fluff up.

"Present."

Peggy knew exactly who he was. He was the boy from the door, the boy with the hair and the eyes. The boy with the smirk. The boy from the book. The boy who'd been kissed by the prettiest blonde in the room.

If Sammy Ruthven was an archer and her heart a bullseye he should be in the Olympics. She couldn't breathe. She couldn't think. She threw her head up closing her eyes, wondering how long it would be until she woke up from this dream, or how long it would be until she would have a conversation with him, how long it would be until she kissed him. How long it would be until...

Stop! She shouted at her brain. He clearly had a girl-friend. Not that a guy like Sammy Ruthven would even consider Peggy to be in the same league as his movie star girlfriend. She wasn't cool enough to ever date someone like Sammy Ruthven. *Forget him, it's stupid*, she told herself. She didn't even have any make-up on.

She concentrated on the daily messages but could not at all repeat any of them back to anyone. Just days ago, she was looking at this boy's picture in a dusty old yearbook, having a crush on him from thirty-three years away, and now she was *here*. *He* was here. He was just there. He was right *there*.

She began to giggle at the craziness of it all. The redhead sitting next to her looked over. Peggy put her hand to her mouth and tried to look like she was fixing her lip-gloss.

She opened her notebook and began drawing love hearts on the inside back cover. She found herself writing the letters SR inside one of the hearts and immediately colored over it. *Stupid*.

Stop it, stop it, stop it, she kept telling herself. But it was no good. Her heart was running away with itself. Sammy

Ruthven had gotten inside of her heart and he would not leave.

When the bell rang, she had never been more both relieved and disappointed to get out of that classroom and off to History.

THIRTEEN

Lacey

────────

Peggy found classes difficult. There were no computers and no Wi-Fi, and she felt more than a little lost without them. Typing class should have at least been something Peggy was good at, but the keys on the typewriters were so damn heavy. She bashed her chipped polished fingers at the keys cursing under her breath as she typed out "*The quick brown fox jumped over the lazy dog.*" for the sixteenth time.

"Have you like, ever done typing before?" asked the stunning redhead from home room who was sitting next to her again and typing about twice as fast as she was.

"Yeah, but not on one of these," Peggy replied, shaking her hands and scowling at the clunky thing.

"Yeah, these are pretty old, it sucks we don't have electric typewriters yet," the girl said rolling her eyes. "I guess school budget is more interested in like, new basketballs or something."

Peggy laughed. "*Electric* typewriters?"

"Have you heard of them?"

"Yeah, I've heard of them," Peggy replied.

83

"We've got one at home, I use it to type up letters to all the guys I'm stalking."

"What?"

"I'm totally joking of course," laughed the girl. "Well, I just did it the once. But, anyway, it's a hell of a lot easier than working on this hunk of junk."

Peggy wasn't sure how to respond. She was unsure of why this girl was divulging this information to her or talking to her at all. She laced her hands together and stretched them out, looking around at the room of clacking keys, for the first time noticing there were absolutely no boys in the room.

"Where are the boys?" Peggy asked.

"Uh, where they always are fourth period, in shop. You think any of them would take typing? No way!" She shook her head. "I'm not even sure they'd be allowed to."

"At my school guys and girls do everything together," Peggy shrugged.

The girl laughed hysterically. "Oh my god, that's the funniest thing I've ever heard, you're totally joking right?" She laughed a bit more. "The last thing in the world I could imagine is like, Ben and Sammy coming in here and typing sentences about foxes! Oh man, that's hilarious."

The mere mention of his name brought a warm scary feeling into her stomach. Peggy wondered if this girl was friends with him.

"Did you used to go to one of those like, hippy schools for free thinkers or something?" the girl asked.

"Kind of, I guess."

"You're not from around here." It wasn't really a question.

"Not really," Peggy replied.

"Where are you from?"

"Canada?" It was more of a question than an answer. "Miss Bates told everyone this morning in home room."

"Oh yeah, I wasn't really listening, home room blows," the girl said. "I'm Lacey by the way." She tossed her thick red hair over her shoulder, revealing a long gold lightning bolt earring dangling from her ear as she twisted her fingers through her hair on the other side. Peggy had a sudden urge to go online and try to find a pair.

"Mag... Peggy," Peggy said.

"Mag-eggy?" asked Lacey making a face.

"It's Margaret, Peggy for short."

"Hi Peggy," said Lacey.

"Hi," said Peggy.

"I can tell you all about this hell hole if you want. Do you have lunch plans? Let's do lunch. I'll meet you in the cafeteria and save you from seven kinds of social disaster. You really don't want to be some kind of freakish outcast on your first day. Like if you are, you'll never escape it. I mean, look at her," Lacey pointed to a girl with frizzy brown hair held in place with a huge pink flower in a high ponytail and huge round rimmed glasses. She was pulling tiny pieces of torn paper out of her typewriter. Peggy thought the girl didn't really look that different to herself. Lose the glasses, invest in a good straightener and a bit of bronzer, she'd be just as cute as any other girl in the room, probably even cuter than Peggy herself.

"That's Awkward Amy. She came here about a year ago and didn't totally assimilate. I swear she was almost hot when she started here. She used to wear contacts and lipstick, I think she just stopped caring because everyone either ignored her or was totally mean to her."

"Unfortunate," Peggy said cringing as she watched the girl scrunch up the paper and walk to the wastepaper basket, two girls laughing at her as she went past.

"Don't get me wrong," said Lacey, "I like Amy, but she's a mess, and if I hung out with her, well, you know."

Peggy did know. She *was* an Amy in the present.

"Why are you being so nice to me?" Peggy asked bluntly. She knew enough about High School politics to have worked out that Lacey was one of the cool kids, or at least something a lot higher up on the food chain than Awkward Amy. Way higher than she herself had ever been.

"I like your earrings," Lacey shrugged.

Peggy put a hand to her earrings, the turquoise triangles she'd had on when she left.

Lunch was gross. All the food looked like it had already been eaten once already. Peggy played it safe by grabbing a salad and a 7UP and put it on Janet's tab. She turned the can in her hand, smiling at the retro design. She'd seen loads of these old cans in antique stores. She'd always wondered if it tasted the same.

She followed behind Lacey quickly, like an obedient lapdog following her to a back corner of the cafeteria. The cafeteria seemed like the only part of the school that had undergone a serious renovation in the last thirty-three years. In her time the tables were silver, long and rectangular, running across the entire space so you always had to sit next to everyone. It was a social nightmare. Magz and Jack had taken to bringing packed lunches and eating in the quad or sneaking out for burgers. There were rules at St C's about leaving school grounds during the school day, but Magz and Jack constantly broke them in order to avoid their nemeses and socially terrifying situations like cafeteria lunches.

Putting her tray down Lacey motioned for Peggy to do the same next to her. In 1983 the tables were white plastic ovals. Lacey was in the middle of the oval and Peggy sat where the oval began to curve out. The chairs were white plastic too, it was just like the outdoor furniture at the swimming pool, only without the umbrellas. It didn't exactly match with the dark wood and stained-glass windows. It was kind of hilarious, and yet very awesome.

"This is Peggy," Lacey waved a hand towards Peggy. "This is everyone," she waved her other hand at everyone. A buff jock looking guy and the dark-haired scary girl from home room looked up at her. Peggy opened her mouth and was about to say hi when she caught the eye of Sammy Ruthven sitting at the other end of the oval, next to the sexy blonde from home room. On his other side sat another blonde, she seemed softer and more natural but just as hot and intimidating. Peggy's mouth went dry and she was unable to utter a word. She closed her mouth again. She felt like a moronic fish. She could've sworn she saw the corner of his mouth move slightly and felt herself make a weird contorted face in his direction as the blonde leaned in close to him and whispered something.

Peggy forced herself to look away, sitting down completely flustered.

"On a diet?" asked Lacey motioning towards Peggy's salad while slurping on a Diet Pepsi.

"No, I just didn't like the look of *that*," she pointed at the slop on Lacey's plate. Lacey just blinked and began pushing it around with her fork.

"Everyone still on for pizza tonight?" asked the scary girl. Peggy didn't really know what she was, or how she'd come to be in this group of friends, but she was kind of intimidated by her. In fact, when she looked around the table, she was intimidated by them all.

"Does the new girl wanna come too?" asked the jock, an attractive, if you were into that kind of thing, tanned and buff guy sitting on the other side of Sammy. She wondered how they ended up being friends. They were a kind of motley crew. It was like James Dean, Joan Jett and Ginny Weasley's sexy older sister had thrown a dinner party.

Lacey nudged Peggy, "wanna come for pizza?" she asked.

"Hells yeah," Peggy replied with perhaps too much enthusiasm, *be cool for god's sake.* Peggy couldn't remember the last time she was invited on a social outing by anyone other than Jack.

"Hells yeah?" asked the beefy jock.

Lacey shrugged. "She's from Canada."

There was an understanding of nods and strange looks.

"Is that a yes then?" asked the scary girl eyeing Peggy up and down.

"Yeah, sounds great," Peggy said coolly, already freaking out that she had absolutely nothing to wear.

"That's Tricia," Lacey said, "she looks a lot tougher than she is."

"I'm tougher than I *look*," said Tricia scowling through layers of thick black eyeliner.

"And that's Ben." The beefy jock gave her the thumbs up and a cheesy grin.

"That's Leigh," Lacey continued on, "with the real blonde hair, and next to her is Rochelle and well, you know Sammy."

"Everyone knows Sammy," Tricia said rolling eyes.

"I don't know Sammy," Peggy said a little too loudly as a sudden silence fell on the table.

"Now you do," Sammy said throwing a paper napkin on the table and vacating his seat, Rochelle following behind.

"Hi Nick," said Lacey as a guy who was like a shorter not as hot version of Sammy joined them, taking Sammy's place.

"What's up Lace?" Nick asked smiling.

"This is Peggy."

"Oh hey, yeah, you're that new girl from Canada, right?" he stood up and shook her hand. He was sweet in that boy next door, wouldn't date him but would make a great friend kind of way, kind of like Jack.

"Hi." Peggy said, unable to say more as she was so overwhelmed by meeting everybody.

"Love to hear all about Canada later but now I gotta go find Sammy about some stuff," Nick looked around. "Where'd he go now?"

"Went out for a smoke with Ro," Tricia said.

Nick's face fell for a moment and then he smiled again. "Well, it was nice meeting you Peggy." He waved and walked off in the same direction as Sammy had.

"I totally cann*ot* wait for pizza," Lacey said stuffing her face with the unidentified lunch slop.

"How do you stay so slim?" Tricia moaned.

"Genes," she mumbled with her mouth full.

"I can't even have a sandwich without getting totally bloated," said Tricia.

"It could be the gluten," Peggy said.

"The glu glu what now?" asked Lacey.

"You could have a gluten intolerance, Tricia," said Peggy.

"I don't even know what you are saying," Lacey said polishing off her plate, obviously able to eat anything with no problem.

"Me neither. I need a smoke," said Tricia taking her tray and leaving just Lacey and Peggy.

"Wanna go for a smoke?" Lacey asked.

"Not really, I don't smoke."

"Well, you better come anyway or else your social life is gonna die right now."

They all sat under a big old tree behind the school but out of view. Peggy was trying to sit a little way away from them without looking too weird and unsocial. Sammy had his back up against the tree and Rochelle had her head resting on his thigh. Peggy found herself looking too long at his thigh. She looked away. A stupid crush, that was all it was. She tried to remind herself he was old, like as old as her dad. Except that he wasn't. He was right in front of her, he was seventeen and he was pretty much perfect.

"Anyone up for the Fire Station after pizza?" asked Lacey pulling another cigarette out of a packet that was being passed around. "It's the best bar in Santolsa," Lacey explained to Peggy.

"It's the *only* bar in Santolsa," Nick said taking the packet next.

"That's not even true, there's the Bowl and McGill's." Lacey said.

"The Bowl is for preppies and McGill's is where the teachers go," Tricia pointed out.

"And," said Ben, who also appeared not to be smoking, "the Fire Station is the only place that doesn't card."

"True, it's not like we even have a choice," Lacey shrugged.

Sammy stubbed his butt on the tree and flicked it onto the grass next to him. Peggy caught his eye and she must have been making a face at him because he reached over and picked the butt back up, just as the bell rang.

"Crap, we're gonna be late!" Lacey dusted the grass off her skirt and picked up her books hurrying the others up.

As they rushed to class Peggy noticed Sammy flick the butt in the trash on the way up the front stairs. He looked back at her and she could've sworn he winked at her. Did he actually wink at her? She totally imagined it. She must have. Boys like Sammy Ruthven did not wink at girls like Peggy.

No, boys like Sammy Ruthven did not wink at girls like *Magz*.

Peggy, she didn't know about yet.

FOURTEEN

Makeover

Janet started throwing clothes onto her king-sized bed. Her bedroom was Japanese style, a giant blue fan adorned the wall above the bed and a floral dressing screen stood separating a section of the room, various abandoned outfits hanging over it.

"What are they like?" Peggy asked, picked up a leopard print shirt. She held it up against herself and made a face in Janet's dressing table mirror.

"Who?" asked Janet.

"Lacey and Ben... *those* guys." She deliberately didn't say *his* name.

"They're the rebels." Janet threw Peggy a pair of green leather trousers.

"Green leather?" Peggy shook her head.

"It's not for everybody," Janet shrugged.

"Not for me, definitely."

"How about black leather?" Janet yanked more clothes from the wardrobe and tossed a short skirt in Peggy's direction.

"Let's stay away from leather."

"You're hanging out with the rebels tonight, they all wear leather."

"Are they really that bad?"

"No one is half as bad as what they think they are."

"What does that mean?" Peggy asked searching through the pile of clothes on the bed.

"It means you shouldn't judge people based on what *I* tell you, or what anyone else tells you. I'm sure what I see at school is very different to what you'll see out tonight. I'm sure they will be much, much worse."

"Lacey seems really nice," Peggy said as she tried a pink blazer on over her yellow school shirt.

"That jacket, yes," Janet nodded. "Hot pink really is your color. And sure, Lacey seems nice enough, Rochelle on the other hand…"

"I met Rochelle, she's dating Sammy Ruthven, isn't she?" Peggy's voice caught on the *th* in Ruthven. So obvious.

"Don't tell me you already have a crush on Sammy Ruthven Peg. Most girls usually wait a week."

"I don't have a crush on him, I was just saying…" How the heck did Janet work that out so quickly? Peggy looked down at the floor.

"I don't know what the deal is with those two. From my home room desk, it looks very hot and cold and on and off again and when it's *on* it seems a little one sided. But who knows? That Sammy," Janet shook her head. "Well, Sammy Ruthven is…"

Peggy's heart skipped a beat. It was exactly what Old Janet had said to her in the future. Peggy held her breath waiting for the end of the sentence.

"…a closed book," Janet finished. Peggy let her breath out. It was not the golden nugget of info she was hoping for.

"It looks like it's on right about now." Peggy flopped down on the bed.

"Watch out for Sammy, Peg. He smokes, he drinks, he drives fast cars, he skips out on school, he breaks hearts, but," Janet shrugged, "I'm sure he's not all bad."

Peggy heard the warning in her ears and felt a thrill in her heart.

"Is he going tonight?" Janet asked curiously as she began throwing clothes on top of Peggy as she lay with her eyes closed, fantasizing about watching him eat a pepperoni pizza and mumbled a positive response.

"Come on then, we have work to do. I'll go see if I can find the hot rollers. I put them away years ago when I cut my hair short, but they'd be perfect for you. You could really use some air in your hair."

Peggy looked at herself in the mirror when her make over was complete. Her hair was big and bouncy, her lips bright pink. She wore the pink jacket over a white top tucked into a short black skirt. Try as she might, Janet did not succeed in getting Peggy to wear a pair of heels. Peggy did not do heels and luckily for Peggy, they didn't share the same shoe size.

"I could text Lacey and get her to bring some shoes for me if I had her number," Peggy said looking down at her brown flats. They so didn't go with this outfit. These were so not the shoes she was going to be wearing when Sammy Ruthven was going to fall in love with her.

"Text?"

"You're from the future, you remember texting."

Janet shook her head.

"Of course, I keep forgetting you're from the nineties. You probably didn't have the internet either."

"Of course we had the internet!"

"On your phone?"

"At the library."

Peggy laughed. "I have internet on my phone, along with my whole life."

"Your whole life is on your *phone*?" asked Janet.

Peggy took her phone out of her pocket and groaned when she saw she had only 2% remaining. She should have turned it off, it was not like she could even use it here.

"It's about to die," said Peggy.

"What's about to die?" Janet asked frowning.

"My phone."

"Die?"

"The battery."

"Show me!" Janet leapt onto the growing mound of clothes on the bed to see the futuristic technology.

Peggy had just enough battery to slide the screen unlocked and touch the internet browser app which came up with the usual error message before it switched off.

Janet sat staring at it, her mouth slightly open.

"It's pretty amazing when you think about it. All my music, photos, camera, diary, shopping, books, everything is on it." Peggy handed it to Janet anyway.

"It's so futuristic." Janet turned the pink glittering object in her hands. "You should definitely not have this here though. What if it fell into the wrong hands?"

"I had it in my pocket when I came here. I thought I was going back to Mrs. Willis' class, how the hell was I supposed to know I was going to come out in 1983?" Peggy shoved it back in her pocket.

"Just keep it out of sight and don't bring it back with you again."

Peggy hadn't really spent much time thinking about the future. She wasn't even sure if she could get back.

"I don't even know if I'm going to go back," she said.

"If you want to stay you can stay with me, but don't you want to go and explain to your family and friends that they're never going to see you again?"

Peggy shrugged.

"You can't just disappear, Peggy. Everyone will think something awful happened to you."

"Or that I just ran away."

"Would you do that?"

Peggy thought of Jack. "I guess I will have to go back, but I don't want to think about that tonight."

"Do I look OK?" Peggy fluffed up her big hair in the mirror. She had never worn it big before and she felt slightly unbalanced.

"You look incredible. Sammy Ruthven won't know what hit him."

Peggy's face blushed under the pink blusher packed onto her cheeks.

"Come on, you're going to be more than fashionably late if we don't get going. And I'm going to be late for bowling!" Janet grabbed the green leather trousers and a white shirt and stood behind the dressing screen to change.

"Janet," Peggy said, starting to feel as if she looked just slightly ridiculous. "Is this outfit too much for pizza? It kind of just feels way too over the top." She tossed a black fringed bag over her shoulder, checking her reflection one more time.

"Peggy," said Janet stepping out from the screen dressed in the green leather trousers. She grabbed a thick black and silver belt and cinched it around her waist before stepping into a pair of black patent stilettos. "This is the eighties, Peggy. If you can't wear your hair big here, where can you?"

FIFTEEN

Super Pan

"Excuse me," Peggy mumbled as she squeezed past some cowboys who were sitting at the bar staring into their beers and watching their cigarettes burn out. She coughed a little. She felt super self-conscious in her totally eighties outfit, but Super Pan was the kitschiest little pizza parlor Peggy had ever seen and she couldn't help but smile a little. The décor was classic with red and white tablecloths over small round wooden tables, matching chairs patiently waiting around for some butts to sit in them. Vintage style posters of Italy adorned the walls. The waiters wore white shirts, and all seemed to be sporting proper moustaches. She nervously fiddled with the strands on her purse as she looked around for her group. It was probably all a joke, a set up for the new girl. Pretend she's invited out with a bunch of cool kids, let her stand around waiting for about half an hour, then when she walks out, realizing she's been stood up, have the whole school out the front laughing at her.

"Peg!" called out a voice and she turned around. It was Lacey waving at her from a booth up the back.

"Hey lady in pink, you look great," Ben said to her as she sat down at the empty seat next to him.

"Thanks, Ben," she said getting a whiff of his beer and olive breath.

"What's your name again?" he asked. "I suck at names".

"Peggy," she said, again loving how it rolled off her tongue.

She looked around the table. Janet was right, she was definitely not overdressed for this. Lacey was wearing a western blouse tied as a midriff with tight black jeans, her lightning bolt earrings falling down to her neck. She looked like a rock star. Peggy felt a small twinge of jealously, she never managed to look anything like either of those things.

Tricia looked a lot less punk out of her school uniform. Dressed in jeans and a red silk top with matching lipstick she looked so grown up. Peggy made an attempt to smile at her, but Tricia just glanced over her and away.

Rochelle was sitting next to Sammy. She looked outrageously sexy in a tight black dress and Leigh wore an almost identical one. They were like groupie bridesmaids in matching outfits on either side of him.

Sammy was dressed in a tight black t-shirt which showed just enough of his biceps to make Peggy even more uncomfortable than she already was. She suddenly didn't care how cool this place was or how awesome it was that she was in the eighties because all she could focus on was that she had the biggest crush on some guy she only just met who was old enough to be her dad in the future, the present, her present. She felt her head pound and admonished herself for not bringing any pain killers. Peggy gave a little wave, but the blondes didn't even look up and neither did he. She felt her shoulders drop and went back to her conversation with Ben.

Conversation with Ben was difficult, and her head was splitting so bad that when the waiter asked her if she wanted a beer, Peggy asked for a screwdriver instead. She was sure she'd seen people drink them in eighties movies. Janet's rules didn't mention anything about alcohol *outside* the house and it was so easy to get served.

"Screwdriver?" asked Ben. "Frickin' awesome, you're my kind of girl Peggy!" He grabbed her around the shoulders giving her a really hard hug, his arm was so hard it felt like being trapped under a fridge. He was way more buff than Big Mick had ever been, Ben could totally beat Big Mick in a fight. The thought reassured her. Peggy laughed awkwardly, and Sammy chose that exact moment to notice her. He looked straight at her, then at Ben's arm around her, then back at her again and then turned back to Rochelle who, Peggy thought, was stroking his thigh under the table. She blushed and put her hand to her ear, rubbing the turquoise triangle.

Lacey's sixth sense for social awkwardness kicked in, she stood up and demanded everyone squash over, sitting herself on the other side of Peggy.

"Hello Jell-O," she said nudging Peggy with her elbow.

"Thanks for saving me," Peggy whispered.

"I see you eyeing up Sammy," Lacey whispered back as she took a sip of her rum and coke.

"He's OK, but whatever." Peggy shrugged with attempted indifference as she thanked the waiter for bringing her drink and immediately took a large sip.

"OK? Sammy Ruthven is not just OK Peg, he's like the hottest merchandise at St. C's."

Peggy looked over to see Rochelle with a cigarette hanging out of her mouth, her mascara all smudged like she'd been crying or making out, or both. She was such a hot mess. Sammy leaned in to take the cigarette off her.

"O.M.G," Peggy exclaimed, "it's so gross that you can smoke in here!"

"Huh? What's oh em gee? You want one?" Lacey asked, looking through her purse.

"God no, especially not with dinner," Peggy coughed.

"Oh Peg, please don't be a square. If you turn out to be a square, I might have to send you back to the typing pool."

Peggy tried not to cause a scene by coughing, but it was hard.

"Just watch your back," Lacey whispered. "Rochelle and Sammy have been kind of together for a while now, if a girl even looks at him she goes nuts, gets totally crazy, does weird stuff like trying to ruin lives, you know, crazy girl stuff."

Rochelle had her arm around Sammy, her breasts pressed up against him. He looked indifferent as he took a swig of his own coke colored drink and she looked miserable. She tried to take his drink, but he moved her hand away.

"Don't even," warned Tricia shaking her head at Peggy as she squished past to get to the bathroom.

"She already hates you," Lacey said.

"Who, Tricia?" asked Peggy.

"Rochelle."

"Why?" asked Peggy looking over towards the three-some, "why would she hate me? She doesn't even know me."

"Because you keep looking at Sammy."

"No, I don't."

"Yes, you do."

"I do not!"

Lacey raised an eyebrow.

Peggy sighed. She looked down at her borrowed black skirt and cringed.

Lacey laughed. "Leigh doesn't hate you though, she just acts how Rochelle acts."

"That's Leigh," said Ben interjecting loudly and pointing to the other pretty blonde girl. "She's cute, but she's a nightmare."

"I *can* hear you," said Leigh exhaling over the table, sending ash into Peggy's drink.

Ben leaned in close and whispered into Peggy's ear. "She's Rochelle's best friend but those three are like a disaster, Sammy doesn't even give a damn, that's the best part. They hang off him like he's some kind of movie star, but any chance he gets he's off with someone else."

Peggy felt sick at the idea Ben had just planted that Sammy slept around.

Ben leaned over Peggy again, just a little too close and offered to buy her another drink. She accepted on the grounds that Janet hadn't given her that much money but worried she was leading him on when he'd started telling her all about his sporting achievements in chronological date order.

The pizza, as amazingly tasty as it was, just made her feel completely sober again and the glares from the blonde girls, advances from Ben the beefcake and complete lack of attention from Sammy had made the night a little less exciting than she'd hoped for. She kept instinctively checking her purse for her phone, so she could text Jack and tell him what was going on before she remembered that she couldn't. She needed something to do with her hands now that she was all out of drinks. She wondered if this was why people smoked. Maybe everyone just wanted something to do with their hands.

"Wanna go for some air?" asked Lacey stumbling

slightly as she stood up. She threw some money on the table, stuck a new cigarette in her mouth and flung her black leather jacket over her shoulders.

Peggy threw some money on top and followed Lacey out.

"Let's go to the bar," Lacey suggested as she lit the cigarette and leant against a streetlight to steady herself.

"I'm getting picked up at eleven."

"What's the time?" Lacey asked.

Peggy checked her watch. She still had an hour to spare. "OK, but just one."

SIXTEEN

The Fire Station

The bar was a total dive. It was dark, dingy and stank of stale smoke, fresh smoke and old beer. The music was loud, guitars blared from scratchy speakers and echoed off the thick brick walls in the space which had once housed old fire engines.

In the present she would have been standing in McDonalds, but here she stood in a sleazy bar watching a woman in a short red skirt gyrating around the old fireman's pole like a stripper, a couple of guys ogling her. Peggy blushed and suddenly felt very prudish. It wasn't that she didn't enjoy dancing, but she could never dance like that.

"It's not much, but it's the only place that doesn't card!" Lacey yelled over the sound of high-pitched male singing as they walked towards the bar.

"I love it!" Peggy shouted back, "it's perfect!"

"What do you want to drink?" Lacey asked flipping her hair over her shoulder and putting on her best flirty smile.

"7UP?"

"You're joking, right?" Lacey leaned over the bar to

shout her order, winking at the barman who reminded Peggy a little of Tom Cruise in Cocktail except this guy was way taller. Another barman caught Peggy's eye. He was kind of creepy looking, his long greasy hair slicked down with a black and white bandana. He gave her a look like he was undressing her with his eyes, and she shuddered.

"I've been trying to get a date with this guy for ages. He won't date me, but only because I'm still at school," Lacey pouted.

"Which one?" asked Peggy.

"On the house, but just this round OK Lace?" the Tom Cruise guy gave them a reluctant smile and two glowing green drinks.

"That one of course, not Jonas, ew! Gag me with a spoon!" Lacey made a gagging sound and handed Peggy her drink. "The *gorgeous* one is called Greg, the gross one is called Jonas. Definitely stay away from him."

"Definitely," said Peggy.

"Stay away from Greg too."

Peggy laughed. "I don't think you have to worry about any competition from me."

Lacey looked confused. "You're like totally cute *and* you're foreign, guys love that."

"What is this?" Peggy asked changing the subject and unable to take the compliment. She looked at the drink suspiciously. "It looks like toxic waste."

"It's called toxic waste!" shouted Lacey looking around for a place to sit.

"What's in it?" Peggy asked.

"No idea," Lacey slurped, "but it's yummy."

Peggy took a small sip, it was delicious even though it looked kind of evil. Lacey took another gulp and led the way to a booth near the door. Peggy sat down on the ripped vinyl seat, removed her blazer and then froze. Sammy Ruthven had just entered the building. *Alone*. Lacey waved him over and Peggy began to play with her straw nervously as she watched him walk in sexy slow motion towards their table.

"Hi Sammy," grinned Lacey. "Where's your other half?"

"What?" he asked shortly.

"Rochelle. Obviously."

Peggy looked up at him and took a huge gulp of the fluro drink.

"Yeah, well, that might be old news," he said holding Peggy's gaze for just a moment too long before turning and heading to the bar.

Lacey wiggled her eyebrows at Peggy. "Av-ail-a-ble," she said sounding out each syllable.

"Tell me about this bar guy," Peggy said, changing the subject but continuing to stare at Sammy from a safe distance.

Lacey's eyes lit up. "He's totally amazing, isn't he?"

"He seems OK," Peggy said watching as Sammy ordered a dark drink in a short glass and was drinking it quickly as he perched himself on a stool at the bar. Why wasn't he coming to join them?

"Just *OK*? He is not just *OK* Peg! He's rad-o-rama. The coolest guy in Santolsa, if not on the whole planet. He used to go to St. C's, but he graduated a couple years ago. I had the biggest crush on him in seventh grade, I still totally do! He must be the one, I never crushed on anyone else for that long before." She sighed looking into her nearly empty glass. "Want another one?" She looked at Peggy hopefully.

"Nuh uh, no way. Janet will absolutely kill me if I go

home smelling of... whatever this is. But finish mine." Peggy slid the drink over.

Lacey rummaged through her purse and handed Peggy a stick of cinnamon gum. "For later," she said. "So, Miss Bates won't know what's up."

"Thanks," said Peggy putting the gum in her purse.

"You probably think we do this every night," Lacey said as she slurped on the ice at the bottom of her drink, trying to capture every last drop of alcohol.

"Don't you?"

"Not *every* night," Lacey shrugged.

"Why is he drinking alone?" Peggy asked.

"Who?"

"Who do you think?"

"Why are you asking so many questions about him?" Lacey grinned.

"I'm not."

"You know it's so good to have a new friend. I'm so over Rochelle and Leigh right now." She rolled her pretty hazel eyes.

Rochelle and Leigh walked past their table just in time to hear Lacey's remark and Lacey spat some of Peggy's drink on the table. The blondes appeared not to even notice them and carried on walking. Nick and Tricia weren't far behind.

"Hey," said Nick warmly, "can we sit?" Lacey shuffled around closer to Peggy to make room.

"Where'd Ben go? He was right behind me," Nick asked. Lacey pointed towards the dance floor. Ben had swaggered straight up to the girl in the red skirt and begun trying to dance with her.

Peggy laughed as she watched Ben's antics for a moment before looking back towards the bar. Rochelle had slipped an arm around Sammy's waist. Peggy blinked, struggling to watch, but when Sammy gently removed Rochelle's arm her heart lurched a little and she wondered if there was hope. Hope that even if he was in no way interested in her at least she might not have to watch him getting touched up by Rochelle every day. Maybe it really was old news. Sammy put his empty glass on the bar and began to walk towards *her* leaving Rochelle folding her arms and pouting behind him.

He perched himself on the edge of the booth right next to Peggy. Her heart began beating wildly and she wished she still had her drink. She grabbed Lacey's and took a sip.

"This is Gina!" Ben yelled over the music, sending some big spit globules flying across the table, completely oblivious to the two massive biker guys in leather waistcoats staring at him from the bar.

Tricia rolled her eyes as Gina, the girl in the red skirt sat down next to Sammy, squashing him closer towards Peggy.

"Move round, move round!" instructed Ben, gesturing wildly with his beefy arms so he could put himself on the end next to Gina, even though it was obvious to everyone else that all Gina's attention was now on Sammy.

Close up, Peggy could tell that Gina wasn't a girl at all, she was practically a cougar.

Gina crossed her legs towards Sammy, hitching up her skirt to show pretty much everything. Sammy's gaze drifted to Gina's upper thighs and Peggy felt ill. She took a sip of Nick's drink by mistake, thinking it was Lacey's.

"Oh god, sorry Nick," she said putting a hand to her lips.

"No problem, I'll grab another round. Trish give me a hand?"

"Do I look like a waitress?" asked Tricia dryly. Even

half-drunk she was still sarcastic and miserable. Peggy wondered what her problem was as she took another swig of Nick's beer.

Sammy brought his eyes back to the table and then looked over at Lacey who was glaring at him.

"She's too *old* for you Sammy. Not to mention that Ben saw her first," Lacey reprimanded.

"Excuse me, I am not too *old* for him," Gina shouted across the table. "Young men like mature women. No strings, no drama." She squirmed even closer to Sammy and ran her fingers across the back of his neck. He ignored her, pulled a packet of cigarettes from his top pocket and lit one.

"May I?" Gina asked, putting one of his cigarettes into her mouth seductively and leaning into him to light it, which he allowed.

"Sammy!" shouted Rochelle who was fuming, standing over the table with Leigh looking bored by her side, like this was just a regular occurrence.

"What?" he asked.

"Come on baby," the woman slurred as she exhaled the smoke between her red lips. "Let's get out of here and leave these *kids* to it."

"Thanks, but no thanks." He blew smoke across the table and Peggy did her best not to cough.

"Two toxic wastes," said Nick passing the drinks over to Lacey and Peggy as he and Tricia sat back down with bottles of beer.

"Thanks Nick," said Peggy taking another large gulp of the new drink. Nick was so sweet. Why couldn't she just like *Nick*?

"Gina! I thought you wanted a piece of the Pepper-corn!" Ben said looking hurt.

"How's about *both* you boys come home with me?"

"Oh yeah!" Ben grinned like an idiot.

"Come on boys," she said placing a hand on each of their legs. "Come to my place and I'll make you both forget about these silly little college girls." She ran a hand down Ben's arm. Peggy could not compete with this. This was a whole different world. Apart from fumbling through one summer of awkward sexual experiences with a boy who was just using her as some kind of creepy jock sex game she really didn't have any idea what she was doing.

"We're not in college," Lacey laughed throwing her head back.

"Student dropouts huh?" Gina scoffed, pressing herself against Sammy.

"They're in high school, *I'm* in high school," said Sammy smirking and sending his hand through his hair, spiking it up at the top, even though it fell straight back down again. God, it was sexy.

Gina sat silently for a moment considering her options.

"No, even I can't go there, sorry kids." She motheringly patted Sammy's knee and squeezed out of the booth.

"What the hell Sammy?" screeched Rochelle when the woman had left.

He finished off his drink and smacked the glass on the table. "What?" he asked, his face twisted in frustration.

"You know what!" Rochelle said as tears began to well in her eyes.

"Let's go," he said, his voice taking on a gentler tone and he led her out of the bar with Leigh following awkwardly behind them like a stray puppy.

"Bye Sammy!" Lacey called out. Sammy gave a wave without looking back.

"What the hell is up with those two?" Lacey asked no one in particular.

"No one knows Lace, and no one really *cares*," said Tricia.

"They're still doing it," said Ben sending a rush of blood to Peggy's face. She didn't want to think about them *doing it*. She'd only known him for a day, but she was quite sure she had never felt this way about anyone, ever. Not in her own time period, not ever, period.

Peggy looked down at her watch and swore. "I need to go," she said.

"Oh, no!" Lacey pouted.

"I'll see you at school tomorrow."

The two girls stood up and before she knew it Lacey's arms were around her tightly, her delicate frame was much stronger than Peggy would've expected. She couldn't remember the last time a girl had hugged her like this.

Lacey let go, grinned and skipped off to the bar.

Peggy smiled. She'd made her first female friend since... she didn't even know.

He was all she could think about as she walked through the crisp night air towards the parking lot where Janet would be picking her up. "Old news" he had said, and then he had looked at another woman's upper thighs right in front of Rochelle, and her. But then they'd left together, and Peggy wondered if they were having sex right now or if, maybe, it was really all over? And if it was all over what was she going to do about it anyway? She didn't even belong here. She needed to go back home. She needed to see Jack and her parents. They'd be worried. She belonged in a different time, she was just here as a visitor, no point getting attached to anyone or anything. She wasn't even meant to be here, she was meant to be in her own time falling in love with someone normal. Someone from her own decade at least. There was still of course the very real possibility that all of this was just a dream anyway.

"Hey," he called out from across the street. He was smoking, leaning up against the coolest car Peggy had ever seen, a blue Pontiac Firebird. He was like a kind of James Dean and Sting mash-up.

"Hey," said Peggy, her heart jumping up into her mouth. Sammy Ruthven was actually talking to her. He was speaking actual words to her, and they were alone. On other sides of the street from each other, but still alone. No one else was around.

Sammy took a drag of his cigarette, not taking his eyes off her for a second.

"I can drive you some place." It was a statement, a fact, not a question. He took a final drag of smoke before throwing the butt to the ground and stamping it out.

"Sure you can," she replied, "you have a car."

He looked back up at her.

"Where do you wanna go?" he asked.

"Home. But I have a ride."

"Where do you live?" he asked, opening the passenger side door for her.

"I have to go with my ride."

Sammy seemed both amused and annoyed as he closed the door and leaned back on it folding his arms.

"Next time," he told her.

"Maybe," she shrugged.

He raised an eyebrow.

"I have to go," she said as she turned and walked away.

She wanted to stand there all night and talk to him. She wanted to get in his car and forget all about Janet and just have him drive wherever he wanted to take her. But she could see Janet's car waiting for her just a few car's down and she was already late. She sighed and said a little silent prayer that she would get to ride in his car one day and that this wasn't her one chance blown.

She heard him start the engine and then she watched him drive off down the road, way faster than he probably should have.

SEVENTEEN

Sober

"A stick of cinnamon gum doesn't hide the smell of alcohol Peggy," reprimanded Janet as she poured Peggy a large glass of water in the kitchen. "I said no drinking. Not only is it completely irresponsible and illegal but I could lose my job."

Peggy inhaled the glass of water feeling way drunker than she had ever intended to be. She'd just been so damn nervous about everything - Sammy, making new friends, not being able to use her phone, her hair being too big – everything.

"But you won't lose your job, because you are still my teacher in the future," she grinned, Dutch courage making her feistier than usual and she put the glass confidently down on the counter.

Janet shook her head. "Help me out here Peggy, I can't be seen picking you up from bars."

"You picked me up at Super Pan, it wasn't *at* a bar."

"We need some ground rules around here." Janet refilled Peggy's glass and handed it back to her.

"Rules? My real parents don't even give me rules."

"It's not my place to comment on your parent's choices, but you need rules. We need rules if this is going to work. That's if you even want to stay, if you are going to go back tomorrow and never come back then who am I to stand in the way. Go get drunk, go do whatever you want with Sammy Ruthven."

Peggy felt her body tighten and then, without realizing what she was even doing, she slapped her hands down on the table in front of her and screamed.

Janet just looked at her blankly.

"I'm so sick of everyone talking to me about Sammy Ruthven. I got here five minutes ago, and everyone is acting as if I'm in love with him!"

"Rule one, no screaming in this house. We have neighbors."

"Rule number two?" Peggy asked folding her arms.

"No drinking. No going out on school nights and a ten o'clock curfew on weekends."

"That is so unfair, you're turning this house into a prison!" She knew it sounded dramatic, but she couldn't stop herself.

"How am I supposed to know if you are going for pizza or going to end up at a bar? What bar did you go to anyway?"

"That one that has a fireman's pole."

Janet looked confused.

"It was dark, and they played what Lacey called heavy metal, but it wasn't really metal, it was more like rock and power ballads and they served these bright green drinks called toxic waste."

"Peggy! I cannot *believe* you were out tonight drinking toxic waste at the Fire Station! Forget the curfew young lady, you're grounded."

"What the hell? You so can't *ground* me!"

"I can *so* definitely ground you, while you are staying under my roof."

"No, you can't. You're not my mother!" Peggy burst into tears and collapsed onto the kitchen floor sobbing into her hands.

"Peggy," Janet said softly as she crouched down and put her arm around the crying drunken mess of a girl.

"I never..." Peggy sniffed.

Janet grabbed the box of tissues from the dining table. "You never what?" she asked gently holding out the box.

"I never got grounded before. I mean, my parents never even knew what I was doing enough to ground me. I just go out and do whatever, I don't even drink much or party or anything, but they don't even know, or care. And now I spend one day in 1983 and I get grounded." Wiping her face on the pink blazer she continued, "I never even had a fight with my parents because I never even see them." She took a tissue.

"I know," said Janet quietly. "I know what it's like to be alone. My dad left before I was born, and my mom was an alcoholic who struggled to look after me. I lived with my Gran for years but when she died, I was left alone. I was about to go into foster care when I found the key."

"Oh my god," said Peggy wiping her eyes with the tissue, "that's horrible, I'm so sorry. My problems just don't compare."

"Just because you live with your parents doesn't mean you don't know the same loneliness I knew. People don't have to be gone to be absent."

"I'm so sorry," sobbed Peggy. "I won't drink again. I won't go out again," she shook her head and blew her nose.

Janet laughed softly. "Peggy, you're seventeen. I know you are going to go out again but not for a little while OK?

But also, I want you to know you can call me any time and I'll come get you, even if I'm mad as hell."

"Call you how? There are no phones here," Peggy blubbered.

"Find a payphone and call the house. Learn the number or carry it on a piece of paper."

Peggy laughed. "Learn a number?"

"Make sure you always carry some change for a payphone too."

Peggy stood up and walked over to put the glass in the sink.

"Go get yourself to bed, we'll go shopping or something tomorrow, we can even take a drive out to the valley."

"I'd like that," Peggy stood up and leaned on Janet to steady herself. "I'm sorry."

Janet nodded, took Peggy's glass from the sink and filled it up for her one more time.

EIGHTEEN

Coffee

Jack groaned as his alarm clock went off and grabbed his phone from the bedside table. He turned off the alarm and checked his messages. Still nothing. He hadn't seen or heard from her in six days now. He had never gone so long without her before. Mrs. Willis had given him some total BS story about Magz having come down with food poisoning. She said she'd found Magz vomiting in the book room and sent her straight home in a taxi. Mrs. Willis had given him Magz's denim backpack to give to her, but when he rode his bike over to her house later that evening it was just as dark and empty as usual. He could have assumed she was in bed sick if he didn't know her so well. Magz was afraid of the dark and always slept with a string of fairy lights on. But the lights were off, and Jack wasn't a complete idiot. He knew something was up, he just had no idea what.

He'd continued to turn up to her house every day after school and knock on her door only to turn around and ride home again each time no one answered.

"She's probably just asleep," Mrs. Willis had said when

Jack told her on Friday that he was moments away from calling the police.

"Why isn't she returning my calls? She can't be asleep all day and all night."

"Maybe she doesn't want you to see her in such a state."

"If she's in a state I really *want* to see her, and she'd want to see me too."

"I'm sure she'll be back at school on Monday," Mrs. Willis had said, totally unphased.

Jack harrumphed his way out of class to his locker. He opened it up looking for his Geography books and Magz's backpack fell out. He sighed.

"What's up dumbass?" asked Jim as he walked past.

"You're the dumbass!" Jack yelled back feeling a fury rise in his chest. Something was seriously wrong, and he didn't know what it was, and he had no way to find out and Jim was such a dick that he didn't want or need to see right then or ever again.

"Who're you calling dumbass?" roared Jim, his face puffing out like a puffer fish.

"You!" Jack yelled back, his own face turning a dark shade of pink. "You are such a dick Jim! No one likes you, you're not cool, people only agree with you because they're scared of you and you're just a total *dick*!" Silence descended across the rows of lockers as the other students in the hallway gasped.

The puffer fish face came towards him with a speed he couldn't beat. He closed his eyes and felt the familiar pain in his back as he was tossed like a salad against his locker and then kicked in the stomach as he fell to the ground.

"What's this? Carrying around a girl's bag now?" Jim picked up Magz's backpack, opened it and poured the contents onto Jack's head. The corner of a book stabbed him in the temple, cutting his face. Jack made a pathetic yelping noise.

"Jim, principal! Now!" shouted Mrs. Willis charging down the hall like a tornado. She bent down to help Jack up.

"No," he said pushing her away, "I'm fine." He touched his face and grimaced as he saw the blood on his fingers. No one else stopped to help, and as the excitement seemingly came to a close everyone went back to their mundane conversations as if nothing had happened.

Mrs. Willis stood over him as he sat up and began to put Magz's stuff back into her bag. He grabbed her keys which were scattered over by her make-up bag and rolled his eyes. If only he'd thought to check her bag for her house keys, he could've used them to get into her house and check if she was there and see if she was OK. But if he had her house keys, how did she get into her house when she went home sick? He picked up the book that had made him bleed and frowned when he saw what it was. Class of 1983. Why was the yearbook in Magz's bag when she'd gone missing looking for it? He looked up to give the book back, but Mrs. Willis was gone.

The school had called Jack's mom to pick him up and take him to see a doctor just in case he had a concussion. He didn't give a damn about a concussion, he just wanted to go over to her house and shout at her for not calling or texting, to get some answers and a hug. But his mom made him go see a doctor and then she woke him up every hour on the hour all night to make sure he was OK. "I'm OK! Get away!" he had screamed at her at around 3:30am. She didn't check back in on him after that.

But on Saturday morning he was on a mission. He called her number again, but her phone was still off. He called her house phone, no answer. He got up out of his bed, walked down the green carpeted hall to use the toilet and washed his face. He styled his hair over his forehead to hide the Band-Aid and was out the door dressed in jeans, a pair of dark grey Vans and a red checked shirt within minutes.

Holding onto the bag tightly he knocked on the door for the sixth time that week. He was about to use the keys when Mrs. Martin opened the door. She shared some of her daughter's features but was shorter and a little rounder and crinklier.

"Is Magz home?" Jack asked nervously. In the whole time he and Magz had been friends there had been very few occasions that necessitated an in-person exchange between himself and one of her parents.

Mrs. Martin frowned. "I think she's still in bed Jack, do you want me to get her to call you when she's up?"

"Is she OK?" he asked, trying to see into the house. It was ironic really, he'd spent so much time in this house, more time than her parents did. He'd even cleaned it for them and now he needed to have verbal permission to enter. He felt like a vampire with no ability to enter a mortal's house without being invited in.

"She's been sleeping a lot, but I'm sure she's fine," Mrs. Martin said. "I'll let her know you stopped by OK?" She smiled sweetly at him as she closed the door.

Walking down her street he began to feel a little sick himself. He kicked an old can of 7UP into the gutter cursing. Everything made him think of her.

He took a right instead of a left, deciding to head to the Mega Mini Mall for some new headphones and a coffee instead of going home. What was he going to do at home anyway?

It was only when he sat down at his favorite window seat waiting for Jen, the barista who trained him during his one week working there, to call his vanilla soy latte that he realized he'd forgotten to give her mom the bag. He looked around the near empty coffee shop and opened it. He felt so bad doing it. Like he was snooping, looking into something personal of hers. This was not who he was. But then she had disappeared of the face of the Earth without calling him and the hurt he felt allowed him to do it. The bag contained two books, her notebook - he refused to look through that and put it back in her bag - and the yearbook. He opened it up and began browsing through the pages. He was looking at a picture of some kids looking out over the Grand Canyon when his latte was called, and the book went back in her bag and was forgotten... for now.

NINETEEN

Ben

Ben waved her over from their table at the back of the cafeteria. She negotiated her way through the preppies, jocks and nerds with her tray of corn chips, salad sandwich and 7UP.

Ben moved over to make room for her. Leigh and Tricia looked absently into their own lunches while Nick tapped his knife on the table. She quickly glanced over in Sammy's direction, immediately wishing she hadn't. He and Rochelle weren't looking so much like *old news* today. She was eating fries off his plate and he was just... letting her. It was so not finished, whatever it was between them. As if you'd let someone eat fries off your plate if it was really over.

"How's it all going?" asked Nick, greeting her warmly while everyone else pretty much ignored her. She wished Lacey was here. She felt so out of place without her, but she was thankful for Nick and Ben. Not for the first time she wished she could have a crush on Nick. He was such a nice guy, what was his story anyway?

"Yeah not so bad," Peggy said popping the top on her

soda. "I got Sister Constance for History which I heard is a bad draw though."

"Oh man," said Ben. "She is the worst, total drill sergeant. I had her last year. She nearly made me cry."

Peggy laughed. "What happened?"

"She read out a paper I wrote in front of the class, it was really bad. I'm not that good at that writing stuff," he shrugged.

"It was so funny," Leigh giggled. "Ben thought we were meant to write about Indians from India when we were meant to be writing about, like American Indians."

"You mean Native Americans," said Peggy.

"Please don't tell me we're going to start talking about what to call Indians," said Tricia.

"We're just talking about Ben's assignment," Rochelle said rolling her eyes. "It's not like, racist to talk about Indians."

"I'm part Indian," Tricia told Peggy. "Not from India, from *America*," she said kicking Ben under the table. He shrugged.

"My best friend back home is part Native American too," Peggy said.

"What are we now, bragging about who knows the most Indians?" Tricia put down her fork and looked like she was about to punch someone.

"I didn't mean it like that," Peggy said, waving her hand around apologetically as Tricia stared at her. "I was just saying."

"Whatever," Tricia said.

"Don't mind her," said Nick cracking open a Pepsi and a smile. "She's part Indian, part Latino, part punk and part new wave. Girl's got problems."

"Shut up Nick," said Tricia.

"I'm part Jewish and part Amish and I go to a Catholic

school in the middle of a desert, you think we don't all have problems Trish?" Nick half-joked.

"A race riot in the cafeteria," Sammy mused, seeming vaguely interested and coming out of his blonde-induced haze.

"All because I screwed up in Sister Connie's class," Ben said lightly, "told you she was tough."

"I'm pretty OK at writing if you ever want me to read over anything for you Ben," Peggy offered quietly as Tricia began a verbal assault on anyone who would listen, and Sammy went back ignoring everyone.

"Peg, that would be the raddest. I have something in my bag actually that I was going to hand in later this afternoon. Did you want to...? Nah, never mind." He shook his head and tossed away the idea.

"I can take a look, I don't mind."

Ben looked at his group of friends and then back at Peggy.

"Did you want to go to the library or something?" she suggested softly.

"You don't have to do that, maybe next one?" Ben smiled as he shoveled in the last bite of a hotdog.

"No really, I'd be happy to help." She looked over at Rochelle. "I don't know how welcome I am here anyway without Lacey."

Ben laughed and punched her on the arm playfully, he was really strong, and it kinda hurt. "You are totally welcome here." He smiled a warm smile and Peggy believed him.

Just as Peggy was finishing her last mouthful of her sandwich which she'd layered with corn chips, she saw Lacey walking towards the table, her red hair flowing behind her and a pair of black Ray Ban wayfarers hiding her eyes. She shoved Tricia over and sat down. She lowered her glasses a little and looked at Peggy, then at Ben raising her eyebrows. Peggy shook her head.

"What happened to you last night?" Peggy asked.

"Just had a couple of drinks with Greg at the bar after you left." Lacey adjusted her glasses and tapped on the top of a soda can.

"Oh yeah? What happened?" Ben asked.

"Dunno, no potato," she said sadly.

"Why don't you just quit this desperate act and wait until you graduate?" sighed Rochelle.

"Mind your own BS Ro," Lacey snapped spraying her drink everywhere.

"BS?" laughed Rochelle, "that doesn't even make sense!"

"Yeah it does," said Lacey straight faced. "BS stands for *business*."

Rochelle laughed. "Are you listening to this Sammy?" she asked, waving a fry around seductively like it was a cigarette.

"Lacey's right, it means business." Peggy said seriously.

"What?" laughed Rochelle. "No, it doesn't. Maybe in *Canada* it does." The way she spat the word Canada was so offensive.

Peggy nudged Ben under the table and was thankful when he got the hint.

"Oh... Yeah, definitely," he nodded, clearly having no idea what he was agreeing about.

"You guys are totally stupid," said Rochelle becoming frustrated at being ganged up on.

Sammy looked over at Peggy and smirked a little, as if thankful that lunch had become entertaining for once.

"It is business," said Sammy holding Peggy's gaze. She blushed and looked down at her empty plate quickly.

"Sammy!" reprimanded Rochelle as she playfully

slapped his arm. Even flustered she was still really beautiful. Peggy hated her. Peggy *actually* hated her. Well, sort of. She hated her in that way that girls hate prettier, more popular teenage girls who get to make bodily contact with their crush.

Sammy lifted Rochelle's red tipped perfectly manicured hand off his shoulder and leaned back in his chair.

Rochelle folded her arms and made a face.

"Fire Station again tonight?" asked Ben changing the subject.

"Sure," said Sammy.

"Totally," said Lacey.

"Can't," said Peggy.

"Didn't you have fun last night?" asked Nick.

"Yeah, but I'm grounded." A silence fell over the usually buzzing table.

"What?" asked Lacey.

"I'm grounded."

"Huh?" asked Ben.

"Like as in, I can't go outside except for school stuff, and stuff with Janet."

"What did you do?" asked Lacey.

"Uh, don't you mean what did *we* do?"

"We did something?" Lacey looked over her glasses, her green eyes just slightly less sparkly than usual.

"Janet was all like - 'a stick of gum does not hide the smell of alcohol Peggy'," she said imitating Janet and then felt bad for doing it.

"Well, she's right," said Nick. "It doesn't." He looked at Lacey.

"How long is this for?" Lacey demanded.

"I don't know. It got emotional and she didn't say."

"Find out," said Lacey. "I'm gonna just go sit under a

tree and maybe even sleep for like twenty minutes before class, this hangover is serious."

"We're going to the library," Peggy said as silence once again fell over the table.

"The library?" asked Lacey.

"The library?" asked Tricia.

"We have a library?" Sammy asked jokingly.

"What's a library?" asked Nick in a stupid voice, making Tricia giggle for the first time since Peggy met her.

"I need to get some books out," Peggy said, saving Ben from certain tormenting. "I'm really behind in History already." Ben looked relieved.

"Later," said Lacey smacking an empty cigarette box on the table as she put the last cigarette in her mouth and walked off. The world seemed to make way for her as she parted the Red Sea of students who she paid no attention to.

Peggy read over Ben's paper for his health class. It was meant to be about the effects of drugs on athletes, but he'd kind of missed the point completely. He'd just made a list of pros and cons on a bit of scrap paper and he had listed way more pros than cons.

"Drugs are pretty bad Ben," said Peggy. "You know that, right?"

He looked sheepish.

"Ben, oh my god don't tell me you are on drugs, like steroids or something?" Peggy whispered to him across the study table.

"Uh, why would you think that?" he asked, folding his arms and looking away from her.

"OK, I don't want to know, but you can't hand in a

paper that is just a list of pros and cons, especially when you've really only put pros on there. When is it due?"

"Last period, can you skip next period and help me?" he asked looking desperate.

Next period Peggy had Math, she hated Math but didn't want to be skipping classes. Janet would freak.

"I can't fail," he said jiggling his leg up and down under the table. "I'm being considered for a couple of scholarships and I need to at least pass this."

"Yeah sure, I guess I'll just tell my teacher I got lost or something," she said resigning herself to helping Ben for the afternoon. She liked Ben and he needed her help.

"Just say they messed up your timetable," Ben offered.

"You're a genius, thanks Ben."

He grinned.

"OK, let's fix this. Where are the computers?"

Peggy looked around but there were no computers. She was sure she'd seen computers at high schools in eighties movies. But then, this wasn't an eighties movie. This was Santolsa in the eighties. They were lucky they even had computers in the present.

"The what?" asked Ben.

"Typewriters?" Peggy asked.

"You want to type it? That will take ages, I'll just hand-write it," Ben said, looking confused. "Just tell me what to write."

"How can we do an assignment without Google?" she asked herself.

"Without what now?"

Peggy let out a loud breath. "OK, books. We need books."

She managed to work out the system fairly quickly and was back at the desk with a pile of books in about the time it would've taken her to finish the whole assignment if she'd had Wikipedia.

"Hey Peg," Ben said as he watched her run a finger down the index at the back of an encyclopedia.

"Mmmmmm?"

"Do you want to come to the next game?"

"Sure, I'd love to see the St C Chariots actually win a game for once."

"What do you mean? We win all the time."

"Nothing, I mean it'll be great seeing you win a game for the Chariots."

"Aw shucks, thanks Peg. It would mean a lot to me, no one else really comes to the games anymore."

"No one? Not even Lacey?"

"She stopped going when everyone else stopped going. She came once on her own, but that's kinda tough, going to a game on your own. It's not really our group's scene you know?"

"If Janet lets me go, I'll try and bring Lacey, but I don't really mind being on my own. I'm pretty used to it I guess."

"Thanks Peg. I'm kinda glad you turned up here."

Peggy smiled. "Thanks Ben, me too."

TWENTY

Back to Reality

Magz walked back out of the book room and into the present during last period on Monday afternoon. She had thought Old Janet might remember this monumental day in her otherwise very average life and be waiting for her at the book room door. It wasn't every day you came back from the past. But there was no one to meet her. The hallway was deserted. She guessed it was probably a big ask for Janet to remember. Magz had seen Janet just a few minutes ago at the end of last period, but for Janet it had been thirty-three years.

She'd only been gone for a week, but it felt like a life-time. While it was true that she had thought about Jack a lot, she had been so caught up in being in the eighties to spend too much time missing him. That made her feel guilty. She should have missed him way more than she had, and now the thought of seeing him and having to explain all this made her just feel really tired. She loved Jack, she really did, but he was the last person she wanted to explain herself to right now.

Magz walked slowly, feeling like she was living in some

futuristic dream. The lights were too bright, and her head was pounding. She began to feel light-headed, another side effect? She pulled her phone out of her pocket and for the first time ever she was relieved when she remembered the battery was dead. She wouldn't have to deal with the present for just a little bit longer.

"Magz!"

Magz grinned.

Balancing a coffee, a pile of books and a shiny black tote bag, Mrs. Willis was clacking her heels down the hallway.

"Get inside," Mrs. Willis whispered, gesturing with her grey spiky head to the classroom and looking the hallway up and down.

Magz did as she was told.

"Well?" asked Mrs. Willis still standing holding everything, about to burst.

"Well... I went to the book room like you said," Magz shrugged. This was a weird conversation to have, she didn't know what to say.

"Did you... *go*?"

"You know I did," Magz said laughing, "look at what I'm wearing!"

"Oh, dear God," said Mrs. Willis falling onto the desk behind her. "That's the uniform I bought you that first week."

"Yeah, it's a little itchier than mine, but whatever."

"There were so many things I wanted to tell you, but I..."

"It's OK, we had that whole conversation about how you can't tell me anything. I get it. I'm not supposed to tell you anything either, but I think I already messed that up by calling you Mrs. Willis."

Mrs. Willis laughed. "Don't worry about that."

"This is so weird," Magz said flopping dizzily into a seat in the front row.

"It's so strange," Mrs. Willis said. "I remember all those years ago, wondering what we would say to each other in this moment, and now it's happening." Her wrinkled face paled.

Magz jumped up and rescued the pile of books before they fell, Mrs. Willis plonked down in the chair at the same time.

"You must have so many questions," said Mrs. Willis.

"Only about a million," Magz said. "I don't even know where to start."

"I think you've met Sammy and Lacey and you've been to Super Pan. Oh yes of course, we had that argument in the kitchen over those *cocktails*, didn't we?"

"You grounded me and I'm still pretty mad about it."

"You'll thank me later."

"I don't know about that Mrs. Willis."

"Oh, for God's sake stop calling me Mrs. Willis."

"Sorry... Janet." Magz rubbed under her eyes, smudging her dark blue liner.

"You can't look them up, you can't meet anyone. You can't *see* anyone. You have to be careful here now." Old Janet looked over at the door.

"I'd be lying if I said the thought didn't cross my mind, like, all the time." Magz thought about Sammy. She knew she wasn't meant to Google anyone, but he was all she could think about. What happened to him? What happened to *them*. Were they ever a *them*? Were they ever *together*? Did she have any effect on his life beyond being the new girl at the cafeteria table? Maybe if she knew they were never going to get together it would be good for her, she could just relax and have fun and enjoy her life without the constant anxiety of having to act cool in front of him because he was so damn gorgeous. And here, in front of her stood the woman who knew all the answers. Old Janet was basically like a God. She knew exactly what was going to happen for the next thirty years.

"I want to know so much, and you can't tell me," Magz said feeling her headache worsen. "You know my whole life for the next thirty years."

"I know what happens if you make certain choices."

"So, there *is* no free will?"

"Don't be so ridiculous Peggy."

Magz's hairs stood on end.

"You just called me Peggy."

"I always wanted to call you Peggy, but you weren't meant to be Peggy until now. Anything you find out about the past needs to stay in the future. Imagine if you knew who you were going to marry, or if you were going to have children or not, or when you were going to die? These aren't things we are supposed to know, and for very good reasons. Just think about that before you go off Googling. You could change everything with a little too much information."

Old Janet was both stern and sad and Magz immediately wondered what she knew about her friends in 1983. Was Lacey still alive and living in Santolsa? She doubted it, if anyone got out it would be Lacey. Would Ben Peppercorn be playing for the LA Lakers? What about Sammy Ruthven, what was he doing? Was he fat and balding and living in the suburbs drinking beer and eating chips on a couch?

Magz didn't want to know if it meant finding that out.

What if she could look herself up? She'd Googled Magz Martin loads of times and also Margaret Martin, but had she ever Googled Peggy Martin. She felt for her phone in her pocket and the yearning for a full battery returned.

"This is just... so crazy," Magz said, shaking her head as she stared at the crucifix above her.

"Life is crazy, whether you have a time machine or not."

"A time machine sure makes it harder."

"So, are you going back?" Old Janet asked.

"You *know* I'm going back."

"Good, I need you to take something for me."

When she bumped into Jack outside her locker as the last bell rang, he was less than impressed. He was mad as hell. He swore at her and Magz thought he was going to storm off and probably not speak to her for at least a couple of days. But he didn't move, he just stood there, fuming, his lips in a thin line and his hands clenching his books.

"...And why the hell are you suddenly here now when you haven't been in class all day?"

"I'm sorry." Magz was totally exhausted, and even though she should've been in awe of the fact that she was one of the only people on the planet to travel through time, she just felt really pissed off and wanted to go home.

"Sorry? All I get is a sorry? Are you kidding me?"

Magz rolled her eyes and sighed. "I was really sick, I didn't think it would be this big of a deal, I'll text you in the future." A promise she knew she would not be able to keep. She frowned at that, she *was* lying to him. She was a jerk. But seriously, she just wanted to go to bed.

"The last time you were doing stuff like this is when you were with Big Mick," Jack accused.

"Oh, for god's sake, when are you going to realize that I am not ever, *never* going to *ever* do anything with Big Mick again? After the way he treated me, do you think I'm that stupid? Really Jack?" Magz couldn't believe Jack was still unable to let this thing with Big Mick go. It was only in that moment as she said it that she realized she was over Big Mick. She stopped herself before she said something about liking someone else. The less she had to explain the better.

"I know you Magz. I probably know you better than your own family and I know something is different with you. You even look different," he said looking suspiciously at her big hair. "How about you just let me know when you're willing to tell me the truth huh?" He stood for a moment waiting for a reply, anything that she could say that would make him stay.

But Magz just looked at him. She knew he was right. Her family didn't know her, and in only a few days Magz had decided where her family would be from now. She wanted Janet to be her family. She wanted Lacey and Sammy and Ben to fill that empty place that had been vacant for so long. She knew that Jack had been filling it for a long time, but something *had* changed. It was like they had snapped apart somehow. He was right. 1983 was home, and it was calling her. Calling her away from him.

When Magz had first met Jack, she thought she was in love with him, but as time passed she'd begun to realize that even though he was cute and lovely and everything she wanted in a boyfriend that he was never going to feel that way about her. Her feelings for him became more about him being funny and generous and everything she wanted in a best friend. He looked after her. He'd been her rock, the light during the darkest nights of her soul.

Her thoughts switched to Sammy. She thought of the unspoken tension between them, whether it was hers or theirs she wasn't sure, but it was something. A feeling she wasn't sure she'd ever really felt before and they had barely even spoken to each other. It was that chemistry people always talk about. That sexual tension. That Soulmate thing. That "the one" thing. She thought it was just something they said in movies before she met Sammy.

She thought of Ben and how he had confided in her. She thought of Lacey and how she had brought a spark of fun back into her boring life. She thought of Janet. She thought about Janet yelling at her when she had come home slightly drunk from the Fire Station and it had been awful and yet it had made her feel so cared for and safe. Like someone actually cared enough to get mad.

Then she thought of Jack again, Jack who she had shared everything with for the past five years. The Jack who knew Magz better than Magz knew herself, but he had no idea who Peggy was. But she *was* Peggy now.

"Whatever," Jack shoved her bag at her and walked off down the hall.

When Magz got home she was not surprised to find herself alone. She put her phone on charge and texts and missed calls started coming through. Jack's began as kind and considerate texts asking how she was, was she OK? And eventually turned slightly crazy, threatening to break into her house or go over to Big Mick's if she didn't reply. She hoped he hadn't done either of those things.

Then there were the ones from her mom who had not even noticed she'd been missing, about getting home late and not wanting to wake her. Getting up early and heading off on some business trip. Something about her dad going to China and her mom staying in the Valley. Why was her mom staying in the Valley? It wasn't like it was that far away. Magz didn't even want to know. Why should she even care when her own family didn't even notice if she was in the house or in another decade? What kind of future did she have here?

But what about Jack? She could just pretend to move away. She wondered if she could continue this charade until the end of the year when she could just tell everyone she was going off to college and disappear. She could delete all her social networking accounts, and no one would be able to find her even if she was still in the present. Working out what to do about her parents was going to be trickier. Sure, they hadn't noticed that she'd disappeared for a couple of days, but surely if she disappeared for the rest of her life it was going to cause some concern eventually.

She'd worry about that later, right now she needed to go to the drugstore to stock up on her favorite mascara that hadn't been invented yet.

TWENTY-ONE

Pajama Party

Magz was a little sad about the fact that she had to drive her SUV to the mall still covered in soda after it had been left at school for a week. She dropped it at the car wash, the guy said he'd have to charge her double. She rolled her eyes, said "fine" and then went to find solace in the aisles of her favorite drugstore. She could not believe how frizzy Janet's shampoo had made her hair. Big hair was one thing, but frizz was out of the question. It seemed kind of pointless though, in a couple of months she'd run out of all this stuff and then what would she do? Janet had tried to explain to her the nonsensical rule about not being able to come back after you chose to stay but Magz didn't really get it. She'd already decided to stay but she'd still gotten back to the present. She still didn't understand how it worked, was it science or magic? She probably should've read the book Janet gave her about the nuns the whole way through, but that whole thing sounded a little crazy. Magz couldn't understand how nuns were connected to time travel.

She stood at the checkout with her cart full of mascara,

tampons, her favorite strawberry shampoo, a bunch of other lotions and potions and tapped her credit card with her pink nails. *Money*. What was she going to do about money when we she went back? She could take some cash with her, things were cheaper in the eighties, so she could make it last a while, but eventually it would run out.

"Can you just wait a second?" Magz asked the girl at the checkout who she'd seen around school but didn't really know.

"Not really," the girl said rudely handing back Magz's tampons.

"Seriously?" Magz pulled her cart out of the line, letting an old lady with a cart full of powdered milk ahead of her, and headed back to the nail varnish section.

Magz jolted out of her time traveler's mind fog when one of their songs came on the radio in the SUV. They had lost count of how many songs they had. They had mix CDs, playlists, almost every song either of them had liked since seventh grade had become *their* song. This one was extra special though. When Magz had been stupidly screwing around with Big Mick, Jack hadn't spoken to her for a few days. It was the longest they had ever gone without speaking. She logged into her Music app one night and found Jack had sent her a track by *The Lumineers* with an apology. She felt her skin prickle at the memory, the lyrics coming out of the speakers as if Jack was saying them to her, telling her that they belonged together. Magz swore. She didn't want to think about Jack. She wanted to get the hell out of this hell hole town once and for all. Forget everything that happened up until a week ago and start her life. Her *real* life. The one she'd been waiting for all this time. The one she was meant to live.

But the thing is, your life doesn't just start one day. You live your life every day. And all the days that have passed make you who you are, and you owe them a hell of a lot more than a wish for them to go away. She couldn't just wish everything she'd had with Jack away.

"Oh, it's *you*," said Jack as he opened the door. He looked like he'd just woken up, his hair was all sticking up on one side.

"Can we talk?" Magz asked, "I mean, *really* talk."

"I guess, if you're not *too sick* or whatever." He opened the door wider and let her in.

Jack's house was nice, nothing fancy, but nice. It was cutesy and comfy and homely. His mother had a thing for bright colors and everything in his house was floral - couches, lampshades, curtains, placemats, coasters. There was colored clutter everywhere, the total opposite of Magz's house. Books, magazines and craft supplies were strewn all over. This house, like Janet's, was actually lived in.

Jack sighed as they walked past the dining table covered with photographs and colored card.

"Mom's been scrapbooking again," he explained as he led her up the stairs to his room.

Jack's bedroom was typical teenage boy. Posters of bands he liked were all over the walls, clothes on the floor, which he quickly scooped up and threw into the closet. There had been some attempt to straighten out the bed sheets, but the bed was not exactly made, and it smelt like boy. Not in a bad way, just in a deodorant and shaving cream, sheets could probably have used changing about a week ago and an old plate with half an old pizza on it kind of way.

Magz thought of all the times they had sat in this room and hung out over the years. She hadn't been over much lately, but she used to come over all the time. She wondered why she'd stopped doing that and felt herself getting teary. She wished she could blame the tears on a side-effect, but she'd always been like this.

"Hey, what's wrong?" Jack's voice softened slightly.

She shook her head as the tears began to fall. He sat on the bed and patted the spot next to him. She slumped down onto it.

"I don't even know where to start... I don't know if I can tell you any of it, or if you'll just think I'm completely crazy even though it's all true!" She began to sob. She just felt *so much*. "Why do I always cry on you?" she cried.

Jack said nothing for a while, he just put his arm around her and let her tears saturate his shoulder.

"I'm sorry," Jack said.

"*You're* sorry? I should be sorry, you have every right to be mad at me." She wiped her eyes with a corner of his sheet.

"I'm not mad now, but you disappeared. I was just so worried. I just want you to be safe, and happy and stuff."

"I went away," she said looking up at him.

"Away, where?"

"When." She wondered if this was the right decision, if he was going to call the guys in the white suits to take her away or if he would just tell her mom and *she* would get the guys in the white suits to take her away.

"When? Well you were gone for days Magz, over a week."

"I mean, I went *when*, not where," she sat up straight, taking a deep breath.

"Huh?"

"I, I time travelled," she said.

141

Jack was silent for a few short seconds and in those seconds Magz thought he actually believed her. They were in on this together, they could work this all out together.

Jack laughed hysterically.

Or not.

"Magz," he laughed. "This is like the worst excuse for not texting someone back I've ever heard. Nice try though. Now tell me what really happened."

"I'm serious, I'm not making this up."

"Magz," he said grabbing her hand to calm her, "I'm not mad, you can tell me anything, even if it's about Big Mick. I promise not to be mad."

"It's not about god damn Big Mick!" she yelled.

"Well what the hell else could it be? I know you still like him." He folded his arms.

"I don't like him. After what he did to me you think I still *like* him?"

"You were crazy about him."

"Well not anymore. Now I'm crazy about someone else."

Jack's sighed. "Great, so who's the lucky dickhead jock this time?"

"He's not a jock *or* a dickhead and I'm so sick of hearing this."

"Where were you?" Jack demanded standing up. All his promises not to get mad coming to nothing.

"I went back in time!" she shouted at him.

"Why would you come here and tell me this BS?" he scowled.

"Because it's *true*," she begged, "and I can prove it to you if you don't believe me."

"How are you going to prove to me that you went back in time Magz? *Seriously*?"

"Look at me! My hair is *big*, and my eye-shadow is *blue*, and my uniform is all *weird*!" she flicked her collar.

"No offence, but it's not the first time you've tried a more eighties look."

"I'll get you a comic," she said as she kicked one of the old milk crates that was peeking out from under the bed. He had loads, all full of comics. One of his nerdy guilty pleasures few people knew anything about.

"You know you can buy old comics on eBay Magz." He shook his head running his hand through his hair. She didn't want to never see him do that again. There was something about it that was so familiar, so *her and Jack*, so comforting. He always did it when he was worried or nervous and Magz loved that she knew him well enough to know that.

"Anything you want, I'm not making it up. I'm going back tomorrow morning, but I'll come back, and I'll bring something for you, and you'll believe me." Magz knew as she said it that this was not the last time she would see Jack. She would come back for him. She promised herself. *He* was the reason she'd be able to come back and forth. She could never fully make her decision when he was still here.

"Sure Magz, bring me a couple of Twinkies that expired in 1983 and if they're good I'll believe you." He rolled his eyes.

"I don't know if it works like that," Magz thought out loud, "like, I don't know if they will just turn old when I come back..."

"If *you* went back in time and then came back again without shriveling up then I would expect dessert snacks to do the same."

Jack had a pretty good point. Did this mean he might believe her?

"Do you want to stay here tonight?" he asked.

"Why, so you know I'm not out with Big Mick?"

"No, it's because I missed you, you big dork."

In all the time they had known each other they had never once spent the night together at his house. Jack had slept on her couch loads of times when she'd been lonely at the show home and wanted him around, but they had never slept at his house before.

"Sure," she said shrugging.

Jack grinned and thrust open the closet. "Pajamas," he said, throwing her a soft grey t-shirt and a pair of way too long blue striped pajama pants.

"Do you want to eat? Or watch a movie?" he asked as she kicked off her brown flats.

"I just want to sleep, I have to get up super early to go home and get my stuff," she yawned, feeling completely exhausted but so comfortable being here in Jack's room. "Won't your parents flip when they find me here?" she asked, turning away from him to take off her shirt.

Jack turned around to face the closet. "Nah, they are out late with crazy uncle Jack tonight and if you head off early, they won't even notice."

"How is crazy uncle Jack?" Magz yawned.

"Still crazy apparently."

"You don't have to turn around, I know you aren't going to be looking."

"A lady needs her privacy," he said in an awkward jokey voice, pretending to fold some shirts.

Magz crawled under his duvet and rested her head on his pillow. Jack got in with all his clothes on and then tried to take his jeans off under the covers.

"Just because I'm not looking at you, doesn't mean you're not looking at me," he said.

Magz laughed. It was kind of weird being here like this with him, but it sure beat being alone with Tux.

"Tux!" she called out sitting up right.

"He's fine, I've been leaving him food round the back next to his cat flap."

"Huh?"

"I went around to your house every day, but no one was there. Tux came up to me on the second day you were gone, meowing like mad. I just put a whole bunch of biscuits out for him, but I stopped when your folks came home."

"Where did you get cat biscuits from?" Magz asked relaxing on the pillow again, knowing Tux was safe and fed.

"I bought them."

"Thanks," she said. "That was really nice of you."

"I love Tux," he shrugged.

"Do you want him?" Magz asked.

"You want me to take Tux?"

"Please. I'm going to be coming and going and I can't trust my parents to look after him. He'll be so much happier with you."

"I'll have to ask my Mom, but yeah."

As their bodies relaxed into the mattress, she felt warm with him being so close. It was the first time she'd slept next to anyone and she felt so content and happy and safe. She smiled softly to herself as Jack switched out the lamp next to the bed.

"Please could you keep it on?" she asked.

"Oh yeah, I forgot." Jack switched the lamp back on but tilted it slightly so that it shed less light into the room.

"So, who's the guy?" he asked getting comfortable again.

"His name's Sammy," she said softly into the pillow that smelled like Jack's hair products. "Sammy Ruthven," she closed her eyes and smiled.

"Is he a jock?""

"No, he's more like a bad boy."

Jack groaned.

"You know," she began, rolling over so that their eyes met across the pillows, "my parents didn't even notice I was gone."

"Huh? But I went over there, your mom said you were asleep."

Magz shook her head, "I wasn't even there."

"Where were you really?" he asked, the light gently lighting up his dark eyes.

"Goodnight Jack," she said, and she fell asleep so fast she didn't even hear him say goodnight back.

Magz woke early to find Jack's arm wrapped around her. She looked down at his slender but muscular arm and frowned. All the nights they had spent watching movies, talking, listening to music or even drinking out at The Stables they had never been this intimate before, and it was confusing. Magz wanted to move. She wanted to just get out of there, pack her duffel bag and get back to 1983 for like, the rest of her life. But she also suddenly felt a little like she wanted to stay. Like this, wrapped in Jack, wrapped in his sheets that smelt like him, so familiar and safe. She listened to his breathing and knew when it changed slightly that he was awake but pretending to be asleep, most probably to avoid the awkwardness of any conversation which would take place in this incredibly comfortable but way too weird position.

Magz felt saliva building up in her mouth, she needed to swallow but she knew as soon as she did, he would know she was awake too. He'd probably keep pretending to be asleep and that would be worse.

She swallowed.

"Morning," he whispered, his warm breath at the back of her neck.

"Hey," she croaked. Why did she feel so nervous? It was just Jack.

He pulled his arm away slowly. "Sorry, I didn't mean to..."

He rubbed his eyes, all scruffy and sleepy looking. She weirdly almost found him attractive.

"I have to go," she said.

"No, so soon?" Jack looked at his phone on the nightstand. "It's so early, sleep some more." He dropped his head back onto the pillow and closed his eyes.

"Keep 'em closed, I'm getting changed." She saw him open one eye.

"It's like you woke up straight or something," Magz accused as she looked for her clothes.

"Don't be ridiculous," he mumbled into the pillow. "Mmmmm young John Cusack!"

Magz grabbed the other pillow and pretended to suffocate him with it.

He pretended to suffocate.

Magz ignored him while she dressed.

"I guess I'll see you sometime soon, I don't know," she said.

"Where are you going?" Jack asked sleepily.

"The eighties."

"Don't forget my snacks."

"Can you do me a favor?" she asked.

"It's before six in the morning and you are already asking for favors?"

"Can you cover for me?"

"Hell no, I'm not covering for you until I see some

evidence of time travel or you tell me the truth about what's going on."

"Just, if my folks call, and you know they won't anyway, but if they do, can you just say that... say that I'm here for some reason?"

"What, forever?"

"For a while, for the next few days at least?"

"OK, so you're staying here because my boyfriend broke up with me and I'm really sad," he pouted.

"Everyone knows you've never had a boyfriend," Magz slipped her feet into her shoes.

"Your parents don't even know if you are in the house or not, I think they'll buy it."

"Fine, whatever works."

"I can try to think of something better. Wait, didn't I just say I wasn't doing this?"

"Thanks Jack," Magz smiled. It was so awkward, she didn't know if to lean down and hug him like that or what. She settled for messing up his hair a bit and attacking him with a pillow again.

"You owe me," he sat up on his elbows. "Come back though, OK?"

"I might be like, fifty, but you'll see me again, I promise."

"I can't wait that long." He pouted.

"It won't be that long," she said.

"Maybe I'll see fifty-year-old you later today. If you're living in the eighties there will be two of you here now. *You* you, and *old* you."

"I didn't think of that..." she said, the headache returning.

"You didn't think of that? Hello, first rule of time travel."

"What do you know about time travel?"

"More than you apparently."

Later that morning, with two suitcases, a duffel bag and a backpack stuffed full of futuristic goods and some favorite vintage treasures, Magz stood at the book room door. There was still a part of her that thought the whole thing was a dream, she was about to wake up somewhere, in her bed, in Jack's bed, on Janet's couch. She was half expecting the book room to be just a book room. That she would go in with her stuff and come out again feeling like the biggest idiot in the history of the world. And then Mindy and Jim would find out she went into a book room with suitcases and her life might as well be over.

She took the key which she'd threaded onto a long silver chain from around her neck and unlocked the door.

TWENTY-TWO

Interlude II

———————

Catherine and Maria continued without Helena for a few miles down the road. As twilight began to return the stars to the sky, they arrived outside a small farmhouse with a stable for horses. Their own horse stopped abruptly, and Sister Catherine stood in silence listening for the animal's spirit to speak to her.

"This is it," said Catherine.

"Yes," agreed Maria.

"No," said Helena who appeared as if out of nowhere.

"There is magic here," said Catherine. "We will be safe now, I feel it."

"I don't feel it," said Helena kicking the dirt and crossing her arms.

"Listen," Catherine whispered, her words riding out into the desert on the soft evening breeze. Helena was just about to open her mouth to complain again but Catherine stopped her by putting a finger to her own lips.

"I feel it," said Maria. "It's an old magic."

"The magic of an ancient people," said Catherine feeling the buzz of energy course through her body.

Elliot the horse snuffed the air gently, stamping his front hoof in agreement.

"There is no magic in this hellish place," Helena said. "This land will bring us nothing but death. We have escaped persecution for mere extra moments of time. We should have stayed in France. We should have stayed in New England." Her eyes became blacker than the sky above them as she carried on. "God should have let us hang after all, it would be better than walking in this desert for all of eternity." The other women gasped, shocked that Helena, tired and weary and hungry as she was would say these things. Helena, speaking only the devil's words continued, "It would have been better than starving. My bleeding feet, my foggy mind, I am myself no longer. We are to die here anyway so it was all for nothing!"

"You stop that right now," said Maria. "There is magic here, if you remember your God and even yourself for once, you will feel it too."

"I feel nothing!" Helena yelled throwing her hands up in the air looking heavenward, waving her small fists at the sky. "Why have you forsaken us?" she wailed falling to her knees.

"God has not forsaken us," Catherine said gently kneeling on the ground next to her. "We still have each other, we have Elliot. We have our lives, the sky above and the earth below. And we are standing in a place of great power."

"You will feel it in time my child," said Maria.

"Stop calling me your child, I am not your child!" Helena folded her arms, her black nun's robes getting all caught up at her elbows.

"Where did you get that?" demanded Maria, taking the girl's wrist and looking at the strange brightly colored object which adorned it.

"I found it," Helena said, pulling away and covering it with her other hand.

"Where?" asked Maria sternly.

"Some miles back down the road, on the top of a hill. I thought it was pretty, so I picked it up. No one is coming back for it in this place. It's not stealing."

"Let me see," Catherine said gently taking her friend's hand. The object was a vibrant pink, like that of a bright pink rose, but much brighter. It almost hurt her eyes. The material was also unfamiliar. Smooth like a thick leather, but she had never seen leather like this before. The Roman letters C A S I and O were etched on the face, as were many numerals. It was the most bizarre thing she had ever seen.

"Did you cast a circle?" asked Catherine as she continued to stare at it.

"Yes, I did. I was tired of all of you and I needed a rest. I've been here for many hours. I don't know why we don't do it all the time."

"Because it's naive, idiotic and dangerous," said Maria angrily. She at once admonished herself for her anger. "I'm sorry my child," she said shaking her head, "but you must be more careful."

"One day you may not come back to us, you may end up elsewhere. You may end up in the pits of hell," Catherine's eyes began to water at the thought of it. She worried so when her friend played this game. Magic was no game, especially the magic that changed time.

"We are only to cast when we are three," said Maria. "I will hear no more of it."

"Do you think..." began Catherine. "No, I'm mistaken."

"What is it, child?" asked Maria.

"Do you think we walked straight past the center of

this place of power without knowing, right where we left Helena? Perhaps she knew somehow when we didn't. Is this artefact a sign?"

"With our lack of food and sleep we may well have made a mistake. We will stop at this farmhouse tonight, and tomorrow we will go back and explore the hill again," said Maria admitting she may have been at fault. Something she found hard to do.

"We *can* make this place our home Helena," said Catherine excitedly.

"Oh?" asked Helena, "and what exactly are we going to do in this forsaken desert landscape with nothing but a hungry horse and each other?"

"What we always do," said Maria.

"Make magic," said Catherine.

TWENTY-THREE

The Preppies

"Are you feeling better?" asked Lacey staring into a plate of brown cafeteria food.

"Better?" Peggy asked through a mouth full of corn chips.

"Yeah, from your migraine or whatever," Lacey stabbed her fork into an unidentifiable piece of meat.

"Oh yeah, I'm OK," Peggy shrugged, vaguely remembering her alibi.

It was just another awkward cafeteria lunch. Sammy was surrounded by blondes, as usual. Nick was perched on the edge next to Rochelle, quite obviously wishing *he* was surrounded by blondes. Ben was stuffing his face with a burger, Tricia was rolling her eyes into her fries every time one of the blondes spoke and Lacey was cheerfully chewing on her cafeteria hot lunch, nodding her head as if to say it was delicious. Peggy took a bite of salad dropping some lettuce out of her mouth. She glanced over, and sure enough he'd chosen that exact second to notice her existence. Her face contributed nicely to the salad by turning into a tomato. She looked down at the lettuce which had very nearly fallen into Lacey's pile of slop.

"Why do you get the hot lunch Lacey?" Peggy asked, trying to detract any attention from herself. "It seriously looks disgusting."

"Huh?"

"It looks so gross. The lunch. But you always get it, and you always eat it, all of it."

"My mom is kind of a health freak," Lacey shrugged. "She's doing this grapefruit diet right now and everything has grapefruit on it. Grapefruit juice for breakfast, salad with grapefruit for lunch *and* dinner. I eat like, nothing for dinner except grapefruit and lettuce, so I eat as much as I can here."

"You should come over and eat with me and Janet," Peggy offered.

"Uh, thanks, but she's my teacher," Lacey said.

"Oh my god," said Leigh butting in. "I totally forgot you were like, Janet's niece or something."

"You don't look anything like her," said Rochelle accusingly, speaking directly to Peggy for the first time.

"Janet's cool," Peggy said to her salad. "Seriously Lace, come for dinner whenever you want." It was the exact same thing that Jack used to say to her all the time when her folks were away. She felt for her earring and thought of his arm around her this morning.

"Sure, sure, I'll come around for one of Janet's frozen Hawaiian pizzas. It'll be good ole' home cookin' at its finest," laughed Lacey.

"I can cook," Peggy shrugged, "I just don't."

"Hi guys!" sang a preppy brunette with a poodle perm and pearl earrings who'd just appeared behind Lacey.

"Why is a *preppy* at our table?" Tricia asked no one in particular.

"Oh, *hey* Tricia!" She smiled a huge fake smile at Tricia who scowled back at her.

"Can we help you with something *June-Belle*?" asked Lacey, putting her fork down on her plate and staring up at her.

"I bet you sure can!" June-Belle grinned, completely oblivious to the fact that no one wanted her there. "I know none of you guys are like, smart enough to be going to college and everything, so leaving school is kind of like, you have to go get jobs now and work all the time and so that will suck *way* more than high school ever did. But I just wanted you to know I'm president of the prom committee." She announced it as if she was president of the world.

"Congratulations," Rochelle said sarcastically as she put an arm around Sammy's shoulder and ran her hand through his hair. Peggy could've sworn he looked slightly uncomfortable.

"Thanks honey," June-Belle said looking away. June-Belle and Rochelle were like chalk and cheese, sex and choir, tattoos and twin sets.

"Was there anything else?" asked Lacey. "My lunch is getting cold and I can't eat with you standing there."

"Well sure, I wanted to tell you I'm going to be accepting ideas for the theme so if you have any you better come find me."

"How about *disco is dead*," suggested Tricia.

June-Belle, who was a fan of disco and refused to believe it would ever die, gasped.

"Prom is still months away," Lacey said.

"I know, but it's going to take so much planning. It's never too soon to start thinking about who you're going with either!"

There was a silence as Sammy gently removed

Rochelle's hand from the back of his neck. Rochelle pouted and looked over at Nick who was practically drooling over her.

"OK y'all, well this was pleasant," June-Belle said as she flounced off to the next table where she could be heard starting her speech over again.

"I hate June-Belle," said Lacey. "Her accent is fake, *and* she's been having a secret affair with Horace."

Tricia spat her Diet Pepsi all over the table.

"Who's Horace?" asked Peggy.

"Horace and *June-Belle*?" shrieked Tricia wiping her mouth. It was the first time she had shown any emotion apart from indifference, sarcasm and annoyance.

"She'd never admit to it, but I definitely saw them under the bleachers last month. No one believes me, but I swear it's true."

"That is so not happening," said Rochelle folding her arms.

"Her reputation would be totally ruined, Horace is like the biggest dork in the school," said Leigh.

"What were you doing under the bleachers anyway Lacey?" asked Nick.

"I was making out with Bruce if you must know," Lacey said, slightly flustered.

"Bruce?" asked Ben putting down his second burger. "Bruce Johnson the quarterback?"

"Yeah, so what?" asked Lacey.

"Well, he's not really your type," said Rochelle. "You hate preppie guys and you hate sports".

"He's cute enough and I was bored," she shrugged, as if making out with the star quarterback was just a blip in her day.

"Horace and June-Belle," Tricia repeated shaking her head. "There's no way."

"Horace is actually kinda OK looking," said Lacey, "if you take away the glasses and that frizzy hair."

"Do you have no standards?" asked Leigh.

"So, what's happening this weekend?" Lacey asked ignoring her.

"It's the weekend again already?" Peggy was getting confused, it was never the same day in the present and in the past. She was losing weeks. Losing weekdays.

"It's Monday," said Rochelle raising an eyebrow at Peggy.

Monday? She was losing weekends!

"Fire Station?" suggested Ben.

"That place is a dive," said Leigh, "I don't like it."

"Well, I love it and *you* don't have to come," said Lacey, reaching over and stealing a fry off Sammy's plate. He pushed the plate towards her, taking one last fry and, hanging it out of his mouth like a cigarette, he looked at Peggy before flipping it into his mouth.

Her heart flipped somersaults as he flipped fries and she held his gaze, watching him chew. She felt her face turning the same color as the sauce on the side but didn't want to look away.

Sammy swallowed, smiled a half smile, the one where his mouth turned up at one corner and then went back to his conversation with Nick.

Peggy let out her breath.

Lacey giggled as she slapped Peggy's arm.

"Fire Station!" decided Ben.

"You up for it Peg?" Lacey asked stuffing the remainder of the fries into her mouth just as the bell went.

"I can't," said Peggy putting her hand on her wrist. She frowned. She couldn't for the life of her remember when she last had her watch.

"You can't what?" demanded Lacey.

"I can't come out, I'm grounded remember?"

"That was ages ago, I'm sure Janet's forgotten all about it."

"She said I can go to the game on Thursday because it's a school thing, but that's it."

Lacey shrugged, "OK, so we'll go to the game."

Ben beamed. "Awesome, so you'll all come?"

Silence.

"We'll make enough noise for all of them," said Peggy smiling. Her first school sports event, and she was actually looking forward to it.

She had no idea who she was anymore.

TWENTY-FOUR

The Game

Peggy, Lacey and Nick walked into the school gym. In the present this was the crappy 'old' gym where the girl's teams would practice, and the new bigger gym would have held this kind of event, but the energy was electric nonetheless. Banners in the Chariots colors of yellow and brown waved through the air, pompoms shook, and people chanted. Peggy had never been to any kind of school sporting event before and she always wondered what the fuss was. She had watched Big Mick practice a couple of times on the field from the bleachers, bored out of her mind, and that was as close as she'd ever been. But she could see it now in this tiny auditorium. It had come alive.

"I can't believe you dragged me here," moaned Lacey, leading them to some empty seats close to one of the baskets.

"It's going to be fun," Peggy said, wondering what was happening to her. She was not and never had been the girl who thought going to the game was *ever* going to be fun.

"It'll be good to see Ben play again," Nick said.

"Yeah, yeah, I wanna support Ben and all, but

everyone else here is a jock or a nerd or a preppy," said Lacey.

"Hey guys!" A voice called out from behind them. It was Awkward Amy who actually looked way less awkward dressed in jeans and a yellow Chariots shirt. Her frizzy mess of a hair was held back with a matching yellow ribbon. Peggy could totally see her cute potential.

"Hi Amy," said Lacey flatly.

"Hi Amy," Nick said pleasantly.

"You're the new girl, Peggy isn't it?" she asked excitedly waving at Peggy.

"Hey Amy," Peggy said.

"What's that thing in your hair?" Amy asked, trying to see the back of Peggy's head.

She put a hand to her high bun and felt the pale pink velvet. "It's a scrunchie."

"What's a scrunchie?" asked Lacey.

"You don't know what a scrunchie is?" asked Peggy.

Lacey, Amy and Nick looked at her blankly.

"I guess they haven't made it here yet," Peggy shrugged.

"It's really cool, I'd love to know where to get one," Amy said.

"I could make you one," said Peggy. Lacey gave her a look.

"Oh really?" asked Amy, looking like she was about to explode. "I'll come down sit with you guys if that's OK?" She started climbing down the bleachers and Lacey rolled her eyes.

"Don't be so mean Lace," nudged Peggy.

Lacey gave a fake smile and squished over to make room for Amy between her and Nick.

"I tried out for cheer this year, but I didn't make it,"

Amy said sadly as she watched the cheerleaders run around the court pumping up the crowd.

"I don't even know why we have Cheerleaders, it's so sexist," said Lacey.

Amy looked down at Lacey's short shorts, black cowboy boots and midriff Laker's shirt.

"I never knew you were such a… feminist Lacey." Amy said, surprised.

"I'm the only feminist in this town," said Lacey running her hands through the ends of her hair.

"I'm sure," said Nick half laughing and Lacey scowled at him.

"Cheerleading looks so fun though," sighed Amy.

"I bet it's really over-rated," said Peggy trying to make Amy feel better.

"But look at them," Amy said pointing to the court.

Peggy watched the cheerleaders parade around in their knee-length skirts and baggy sweaters and wondered what the big deal was. June-Belle was obviously captain, leading the girls into a pyramid formation. She climbed to the top wobbling and looked uncomfortable, not athletic or graceful at all. But the crowd cheered, and Amy clapped her hands in glee.

"They are amazing," she gushed. "What do you think Nick?"

"Uh," said Nick.

"I've seen better," said Peggy, although she'd never been to a game, she'd seen the cheerleaders practicing on the field and even though she hated them, Mindy was one after all, she could tell they were good at what they did. These girls were kind of terrible.

"I came to see the game, not the cheerleaders," said Lacey miserably.

"Oh, but the cheerleaders *are* part of the game," Amy said.

The cheerleaders lined up around the outside of the court and waved pompoms as the team came out. The boys were wearing very short basketball shorts and the crowd went wild. Weird how men's clothes had gotten bigger and women's clothes had gotten smaller. Peggy, Nick and Amy stood up to clap, leaving Lacey in the middle of them pouting, doing some pathetic slow claps. Peggy grabbed her from one side and Nick nudged her from the other and she reluctantly stood up.

"There's Ben," said Peggy waving at him, he waved back and blew her a kiss. The crowd looked over at Peggy. She blushed, embarrassed to be singled out. She wondered if this was how it would've been if Big Mick had let her come to a game. "You'd hate it, you'd be so bored," he'd said, "stay home with your records and movies and stuff." She felt so stupid. She always felt stupid when she thought of Big Mick.

The crowd sat down silently as the other team came out dressed in maroon and white, the Elko Indians. Peggy rolled her eyes. The Elko Indians would win every basketball game against the Chariots for the next thirty-three years. She wondered if tonight was the start of their winning streak.

"Oh my god," said Lacey who was still standing.

"What?" Peggy said following her gaze to the other side of the court.

"It's *Greg*."

"Greg?" asked Peggy. "Greg from the bar?"

"Yep."

"What would he be doing here?" asked Nick.

"I have no idea, but I'd recognize him anywhere."

Lacey tried to squeeze past, but Peggy reached out and grabbed her wrist as the buzzer blared into their ears.

"At least wait until half time."

Lacey slumped down again. "Why is he *here?*" she demanded.

"Who is he?" asked Amy.

"No one," Lacey said folding her arms.

"Just a guy we know," said Peggy as she watched Ben on the court. He was a different person out there, he was confident, strong, powerful and smart. He had the ball, he dribbled effortlessly up the court, took a shot and aced it. Peggy jumped up in her seat and cheered, he looked over at her and gave her a thumbs-up, then forming his hand into a fist he pulled it in close and congratulated himself with a *yes*.

Ben carried on carrying the game, shot after shot, hoop after hoop he was owning the court. The crowd was cheering, "Peppercorn, Peppercorn, Peppercorn!" Peggy couldn't help but get caught up in it all.

But Lacey sat miserably between her friends and a pain in her ass and kept her eyes on Greg, who was cheering just as loud as anyone.

At half time the Chariots were thirty points ahead. It looked like it was going to be a clean sweep. Lacey jumped as soon as the half time buzzer sounded and made a beeline for Greg's side of the gym.

"I'm going to get some popcorn," Peggy said, "do you guys want some?"

"Sure, I'll come with you," said Amy.

"I'll just wait here," said Nick.

"Oh, I might wait here too then," Amy said, smiling at Nick. Peggy gave Nick a look, but he didn't really seem to get what was happening.

Peggy waited in line behind two girls who looked more

like cheerleaders than the actual cheerleaders and accidentally listened in to their conversation.

"Ben is so fine," said a girl with long curly dark hair in
a denim jacket.

"I'd totally ask him out, he's bitchin'," said a girl with
short blonde hair in a very tight Chariots t-shirt.

"But he doesn't date schoolgirls," the first girl said
sighing.

"I heard he was dating some older woman," the blonde
said.

They all took a step forward in the line.

"Two popcorns and a couple sodas," the dark-haired
girl said as they got to the popcorn cart.

"He's cute and all," the blonde said, "but it is kind of
weird he doesn't hang out with the jocks."

"I heard he's got a thing for Rochelle, that's why he
hangs out with those rebel losers," the other one said.

Peggy made a scoffing sound, and the girls turned
around.

"Good game," said Peggy nodding and smiling
awkwardly.

The girls ignored her and grabbed their snacks.

"*Everyone* has a thing for Rochelle," the blonde said
loudly as she stuffed her face with popcorn, glancing at
Peggy like she was something that came off the gym floor
and walked off.

Peggy ordered and then struggled to balance the huge
cup of 7UP in one hand and a massive box of popcorn in
the other as she squinted around looking for Lacey.

"Peg, up here!" she called from the top of the bleachers
where they'd seen Greg sitting. Peggy made her way up
carefully, only spilling a bit of popcorn on a couple of
random people who barely noticed.

"Sit here," she said, moving over to make room.

"Amy and Nick are still holding our seats on the other side, we should go back," Peggy said.

"They'll be fine, these seats are better anyway, this is our basket this half." Peggy couldn't argue with that.

"Greg's here," Lacey said gesturing wildly with her long pale arms at Greg who was sitting next to her.

"Hi Greg, popcorn?" Peggy asked offering the bucket towards him. He shook his head. "What are you doing here anyway?"

"His kid cousin is on the other team," Lacey explained.

"Oh cool, but I thought I saw you cheering for the Chariots?" Peggy asked sipping her drink.

"I'm the only Indian's supporter here so…" Greg said, shrugging.

"Cheer for whoever you want," Lacey said resting her thigh against his.

The teams came out again and Peggy looked over at Amy and Nick. Amy was looking around for them.

Peggy stood up and waved, "Amy! Nick!" she called out as the crowd quietened down.

"Oh jeez, what did you do that for?" asked Lacey.

"We can't just leave them there," Peggy said.

Ben was still on a roll, shooting baskets right in front of them. He looked up into the bleachers after scoring a particularly cool slam dunk and saw Lacey, Greg, Peggy, Nick and Amy all sitting together. He looked confused and gave a half-hearted wave.

His game began to suffer, he missed shots, dropped balls and a few minutes into the second half he took himself to the bench.

"What the hell?" asked Lacey, "he was winning the game for us five seconds ago!"

"I guess he can't compete against my kid cousin," said Greg, clapping quietly when the Indians began to score.

They were losing by ten points and although Ben came back on for the last few minutes, he was unable to score again. By the time the final buzzer buzzed he yelled and threw the ball so hard at the basket the backboard shook violently and silenced the crowd. Ben ran off the court into the change rooms.

"I gotta go," said Greg pushing past them.

"We should go see what's up with Ben," said Nick.

"Yeah," said Peggy wondering if Ben's assignment had given him any crazy ideas which had contributed to his aggression on the court.

"Hey June-Belle," Peggy said stopping the group of cheerleaders who were giggling out the front of the gym, despite their team's loss.

"Oh, I'm good enough to talk to *now*, am I?" June-Belle said putting her hands on her hips.

"Is Ben still in there? We were worried about him is all," Peggy said.

"Nope, he left." She spun around, her not very short skirt flouncing as she ran to catch up with her friends.

"Drink?" asked Lacey, raising her perfectly plucked brows.

"Can't, still grounded."

"But you're already *out*."

"Only because it's a school thing, Janet will flip out and ground me for *life* if I don't go straight home. I'm going to be kinda late as it is."

"So, do you think he's into me?" Lacey asked as they headed through the dark school grounds towards the car. Peggy always liked being at school in the dark. It was kind of exciting, like you weren't supposed to be there, and anything could happen.

"Who?" Peggy asked.

"Greg!"

Peggy was getting as tired as everyone else was about hearing about Greg.

Peggy shrugged.

"I mean he kind of touched my leg at one point, he was getting all stressy and totally cute when Ben missed his shots."

"I dunno Lace, I think he was acting kind of weird."

"He probably just felt weird being back at school."

"Yeah, maybe," said Peggy.

Lacey sighed as she unlocked the red Chevette and slid into the driver's seat, leaning over to unlock Peggy's door.

"Sometimes I think he just doesn't like me you know? But like, why wouldn't he like me? Most guys like me," Lacey shrugged.

"Maybe it's because you are totally conceited," Peggy said only half joking.

"You are totally right, I'm such a bitch sometimes," Lacey looked as if she was about to cry.

"Hey," said Peggy, putting a hand on Lacey's shoulder.

"I wonder what the hell *is* going on with Ben," Lacey said animatedly, completely changing tone in a split second. Peggy withdrew her hand and shrugged.

"Bad game I guess."

"Ben *never* has a bad game, and this time of year is really important for him if he wants to get a scholarship. Hardly anyone from St C's gets a scholarship."

"Maybe it's the pressure of a scholarship that's stressing him out."

"Or maybe he's got such a crush on *you* that he messed up his game."

"O.M.G, Ben is not crushing on me."

"Uh huh, I saw him out there blowing you kisses all night!"

"That would really put another corner in the massive love triangle you guys have going on."

"What love triangle?" Lacey asked innocently, starting the car and navigating through the game traffic, cutting off cars and honking them to get out of her way.

"Nick likes Rochelle, Rochelle likes Sammy, I like Sammy, Ben likes me, you like Greg, Amy likes Nick."

"So, you *do* like Sammy!"

"Fine, yes. Whatever, I do like Sammy."

"So, what we have here is a crazy love hexagon," Lacey laughed.

"It's not quite a hexagon," Peggy said.

"You missed one important bit though," Lacey said as she drove through the school gates.

"What's that?" asked Peggy thinking about all the times she drove home through these same gates with Jack.

"Who does *Sammy* like?"

Peggy shrugged.

"And if Greg doesn't like me, who does he like?" Lacey pouted.

"Leigh? Tricia? *Janet!*" Peggy laughed.

Lacey laughed, "Oh that would be just my damn luck."

TWENTY-FIVE

The Drive

———————

"Hey," he said, flicking a cigarette to the ground. Sammy was leaning up against his blue Firebird in the dusty student lot. It was definitely the coolest looking car in the lot, if not all of Santolsa. It might even have been the coolest car Peggy had ever seen. It was a whole world away from the beige SUV she called her own.

"Hey," she said. There was no way to escape walking passed him on the way to Janet's car in the staff lot.

He took a cigarette packet out of the top pocket of his yellow school shirt, tapped it lightly and put a fresh cigarette between his lips. Peggy tried not to look at his lips, but even though she didn't smoke and thought the whole thing was pretty disgusting, all she wanted in that moment was to *be* that cigarette. She immediately felt stupid for even thinking it and looked away.

"Smoke?" he mumbled as he held the packet out to her, blocking her way. She shook her head and adjusted the denim backpack on her back. "You don't smoke," he said, taking another drag. She shook her head again. She felt like a damn fool, why couldn't she use her words?

"I'll give you a ride."

Peggy's stomach lurched. She wanted nothing more than to get into his car, but the idea of it made her feel nauseous.

"I'd have to check with Janet," she said, reaching in her pocket for her phone. She made a tutting sound at herself, she couldn't just call Janet, she had to go *find* Janet and ask her. Everything took a lot longer in the eighties, but with no social networking and internet to waste all her time on there was also a feeling of having a lot more time to do things like go and find a person and talk to them in person.

"Janet," he said.

"Miss Bates," Peggy explained.

"Your aunt." All his questions came out like statements. It was very hot.

"Something like that," Peggy shrugged.

"Something like your aunt." He took a drag from his cigarette and looked at her with mild curiosity.

"I could go find her, but it might take a while."

"I can wait," he said flipping ash onto the ground.

She took a few steps forward, and then turned to look at him, just to check if he was joking, or leaving, but he was just watching her.

Her feet barely touched the dirt as she walked off to find Janet. Sammy Ruthven wanted to drive her home. It was totally crazy. Her pulse was racing. Her mind was racing. What would they possibly have to say to each other for the whole thirteen minutes it would take to get to Janet's?

"You are still grounded," Janet said as she stood in the middle of the staff lot. She looked over at Sammy in the distance.

"It's just a ride home."

"It's not *just* a ride home, there's no way Sammy

Ruthven is going to just drive you straight home," said Janet.

"I almost forgot," Peggy said, unzipping her bag. She pulled out an LP shaped brown paper bag.

"What is it?" Janet asked.

"It's a present," Peggy said.

"From you?"

"No, from you."

"From me?" Janet frowned.

"Yes," said Peggy. "From the future you. You gave it to me to give to you." She turned to make sure that Sammy was still waiting for her. This whole thing seemed to be taking ages. But he was there, gently kicking one of his front tires and looking down at it.

Janet gasped as she took the record out. "Oh Peggy! What am I going to do with this? I'm going to have to buy a safe to keep it in, what was I thinking sending this to myself? This is far too dangerous, I can't keep it, you have to take it back immediately!" Janet thrust the record towards her, stumbling back into a green Dodge behind her.

"If you didn't want yourself to have it, you wouldn't have given it to me. Old Janet knows that she gave it to you."

Janet looked confused.

"Old Janet is you remember?"

Janet's face softened. "Oh, of course. Sorry this is weird, I've never given myself anything before."

"What is it anyway?" Peggy had been too excited to come back that she hadn't even opened the bag to see what had been so important for her to travel with through time and space for.

"Look!" Janet grinned, her green eyes almost filled with tears at the excitement of her present.

It was Bryan Adam's Greatest Hits. Peggy laughed.

"The date on this is 2005," Janet whispered. "Holy guacamole."

"So?" Peggy asked, looking back over her shoulder to see Sammy leaning on his car in a slightly different position.

"So, that's the future," Janet whispered as another faculty member walked past them. "The future, even for me, I'm from the nineties remember?"

"I always forget that," Peggy said, shaking her head. "Go home and put it on, I'll see you there a bit later?"

"Yes," Janet breathed in and held the record close to her chest. She turned, unlocked the door and got in, placing the record gently on the front passenger seat. "Be back before six," she said, giving Peggy a wave that said she was free to go.

Peggy grinned. Janet had completely forgotten about her grounding and Bryan Adams had just gotten her a ride home with Sammy Ruthven. "Thanks, Bryan," Peggy whispered as she began to walk back towards Sammy's car. She was completely terrified. She nearly turned back and asked Janet to wait.

"Janet said it was cool, she's going home to listen to some record." Peggy stood looking at him but avoiding looking directly into his eyes. Her heart was thumping wildly.

He opened the passenger door for her and walked around to his side, kicking dust softly across the ground. The smell of leather, cigarettes and Sammy overpowered her senses and she had to close her eyes for a moment just to breathe. It was all too much. Just days ago, she was looking at his picture in his yearbook and daydreaming about him and now she was here, and *he* was here, and she was in his car and it was just beyond ridiculous. She began giggling.

Sammy slid into the driver's seat grabbing at something on the dashboard and leaning over her shoved it into the glove compartment.

"A little light reading," he said, putting his cigarette out in the ashtray.

"Is that why you didn't make it to English last period?"

"You noticed."

Of course she noticed! He was all she'd noticed since she got here.

"What are you reading?" she asked.

So, Sammy Ruthven was a reader. There was nothing about him at all that suggested he was into books. She felt bad for judging him. Just because he smoked and had a cool car and skipped school didn't mean he didn't read books. He started the car and she was taken back by how loud it was.

"*Catcher in the Rye*," he said as he put his foot on the gas, spitting up dust. He sped past teachers telling him to slow down and sped right past Rochelle and Leigh who were standing by the gates. Peggy turned around to see the look on Rochelle's face and smiled. Rochelle was pissed, and Peggy was in Sammy's car and there was something just so thrilling about that.

"*Catcher in the Rye*?" she asked raising an eyebrow.

"Yeah," he said, flipping into third gear. "Kind of a jerk book. I mean, the guy is kind of a jerk."

"You don't really strike me as the classics reading type." As soon as the words had left her lips she wondered if she'd insulted him. She was relieved when he just smirked as he turned the car onto the main road.

"Have you read it?" he asked her.

"No," she shook her head. "Aren't you going to put

your seatbelt on?" she asked, fastening her own across her lap.

"*You* strike me as the classics reading type," he said, ignoring her seatbelt question, but buckling up anyway.

"I've read a few I guess." Although Peggy *was* kind of bookish, most of the books she read were more Young Adult romance than literary fiction.

"You can borrow it when I'm done. It's Janet's anyway."

"Oh?"

"She thought I might like it, so you can just give it back to her when you're done."

"Thanks." He was lending her books? Even though it wasn't his book to lend, it felt like he was lending her a book. This felt big.

"Where do you want to go?" he asked.

"Anywhere, as long as I'm home for six."

"What was it?" he asked.

"What was what?"

"The record you gave Janet."

"You noticed?" she asked smiling.

The corners of his lips raised slightly. Peggy couldn't even begin to consider that maybe he had noticed her.

"Bryan Adams Greatest Hits. I like Bryan Adams as much as the next person, but Janet went totally nuts for it!" Peggy laughed.

"Greatest hits?" Sammy looked over at her. Strands of his dirty blonde hair falling gently over his clear blue eyes. He pushed it back and it fell straight back over his face. Hair products obviously weren't that well developed yet. Peggy sighed inwardly. He was so ridiculously gorgeous, no wonder she'd accidentally told him about the Greatest Hits record.

"He's got a Greatest Hits album already?" he asked looking over at her, instead of paying attention to the road.

"It's already out in Canada I guess," she improvised.

"Uh huh."

"Can I wind the window down?" she asked. It was kind of hot in the car and she didn't want to talk about Bryan Adams or Janet or anything. She was too nervous.

"Sure."

Peggy had this. She knew how to wind down windows now. The air felt amazing on her face. She closed her eyes and smiled, not wanting to open her eyes in case she was going to arrive back in the present. She wanted this moment to last forever. The smell of him, the heat of his body next to hers and the feeling deep in her soul that told her this was it. *This* was her destiny.

"Where are we going?" she asked as she opened her eyes looking out at the never changing desert landscape.

"Since you're new in town, I thought we could head out to the lookout across the valley."

The lookout? Peggy almost died right then and there in his blue Firebird.

"You have a really nice car," she said after a few minutes of awkward silence had passed.

"Thanks." He shifted gears, taking the car way faster than the speed limit. Peggy watched the muscles in his arm flex, she liked the way he rolled up the edges of his short-sleeved school shirt. He caught her looking and she looked back out the window.

"I made it myself," he said.

"You made a car?" she asked.

"Well, I put it together."

"Wow, really?"

"Yeah, I've got a thing for old cars, and I found this old

Firebird, a shell really. Me and my dad worked on it for about a year."

"That's so cool," Peggy said, and it was. *So* cool. He made this car? She shook her head in disbelief, who was this guy?

Another awkward silence.

"What else are you into?" Peggy asked. "Apart from fast cars and reading the classics?"

He laughed, his sexy smile lighting up his face. When he laughed, he almost looked like a different person, still sexy as hell, but less cool and brooding and more just, happy. He didn't answer her question though.

"Can we have some music?" she asked.

"There's radio or some eight tracks in the glove compartment."

Eight tracks? She had no idea how to do an eight track. Surely, she could do the radio though. She looked down at the controls but had no idea. She nervously mashed at the buttons and hoped something would happen. He leaned over and began turning a knob to tune in the radio for her.

"Valley FM, rock hits of the seventies and today," an excitable male voice said. "38 Special, Asia and the Stones coming up in the next hour, but first, I think you lovers are gonna dig this one, it's *Foreigner's* big hit from a couple of years ago about finally finding that love you've been waiting for…"

The track started and Peggy knew in that moment that this would be their song. She didn't care how stupid it was to have a song with someone she barely knew. She just *knew* this was theirs.

"I love the desert," he said, lighting up another cigarette and resting his smoking arm out the window. She nodded. She loved it too. Even though she wanted the hell out of Santolsa, she didn't really want to leave the desert. It was her home. As much as she loved the idea of an apartment in Brooklyn, as she looked out at the vast desert landscape before her, she wondered for a brief moment if she could ever really leave. Maybe Jack had the right idea about LA.

The crackly radio continued to play their song and Peggy knew she'd never be able to hear it again without thinking about this moment.

They took the turn to head up Salt Mountain where the lookout was. It was a beautiful view down onto the valley. Peggy hadn't been up there in ages. She wondered why she had never taken Jack and driven up here and talked all night looking down on the only world they knew.

They continued to drive in silence, the tension between them rising as the car rose slowly above the town. She wondered if it *was* between them, or if it was just all in her head. Maybe he just wanted to be friends, he was with Rochelle after all. Or if he wasn't, he was just days ago, but if she was imagining it all, why was she in his car?

When they reached the top, he parked almost too close to the edge, making her nervous.

"It all looks so different from up here," she said looking out over the valley.

Sammy opened his door and got out of the car, a cue for Peggy to do the same. She was kind of scared of heights, so she stood back near the trunk of his car, leaning up against the back door. He slowly walked towards her and with each step he took her heart rate increased. In the car they were in seats, they were close, but they were far enough away that they couldn't touch. Now there was nothing between them, just the dry warm afternoon desert air. She smiled nervously as he came towards her. He leaned up against the car leaving a small gap between them.

"Look." Sammy pointed up into the clear blue sky at an eagle flying low above them.

"Woah, it's so beautiful," she said as she stared up at it. She felt his body move closer to her so that his arm was lightly touching hers. She took a shallow breath. She looked at his arm, the strong defined arm that she'd been staring at for weeks was now touching her own arm. They were so close. Too close. She couldn't breathe.

"Beautiful but brutal," he said. "When two eagles hatch from the same mother the older one kills the younger one."

"Oh gross," said Peggy, looking at the eagle flying powerfully over them. "Do you have any brothers or sisters?" she asked, cringing at herself for making that awful segue.

"A sister, you?"

"No, it's just me."

They stood there for a while just watching the sky together and just as Peggy had finally begun to almost relax, her heart began to race again as she felt his hand reach for hers. Her hand was a limp clammy fish, but his fingers entwined into hers, strong and certain that she was going to return the gesture. Her heart beat hard. What was happening? Was this even real? Her hand was in his and her whole body was turning to Jell-O.

"People are saying all kinds of things about why you ended up here," Sammy said.

"Oh yeah, like what?"

"Lacey thinks you are part of a witness protection. Ben thinks you had some kind of traumatic experience. Rochelle thinks you just moved here to make her life miserable."

"And what do you think?"

He shrugged. "I think you came here because you had nowhere else to go."

"You're right."

"Santolsa's not much, but it's home. And it's not everywhere you get a view like that," he said, looking towards the sun dancing just above the horizon and moving his thumb across the back of her hand gently.

"I do like it here," she said. She'd spent a lot of her life wanting to get out of this town but with Sammy standing here by her side everything felt right and Santolsa suddenly seemed like the most romantic place on the planet.

"Do you know what's up with Ben?" she asked. "He kinda lost it the other night, I'm worried about him."

"I heard about that, I guess he just wasn't on form."

"It seemed like more than that," Peggy said.

"It's Nick I'm worried about," he said, squinting into the afternoon sun.

"Nick? Why?"

"The guy could use a girlfriend that's all." Hearing him say the word 'girlfriend' made Peggy's hand get a little sweatier, but he ignored it, and kept holding it and they stood like that, two sweaty hands holding each other, watching the eagle until it flew away. And when it did they still didn't move, they just stood together in silence, looking out over the valley and the mountains, lost in their own thoughts, watching the sun set over the valley, holding each other's hands until Sammy thought it was time to get her home.

TWENTY-SIX

The Fire Station II

The beefy bouncer took one look at Lacey in a particularly short white lace dress and leather jacket and let them all straight through. Peggy felt much more like herself tonight dressed in her own clothes. She was wearing a sixties style black and white polka dot dress and the vintage velvet heels which she was just starting to be able to walk in. Lacey had looked her up and down and told her she looked like she belonged in a museum. Peggy had looked Lacey up and down in response and told her she looked like she was about to get married to a drunk rock star in Vegas. Lacey had beamed.

"Drinks?" Lacey asked as she flipped her long red mane in front of her shoulder and made a beeline for the bar.

"I need a slash!" yelled Ben over the guitars blaring from the crappy speakers. He walked off leaving Peggy and Sammy standing next to each other, alone, for the first time since the mountain. The evening had not ended with a kiss, but a simple goodbye and "see you tomorrow at school". But school had been the same as ever, Rochelle still followed Sammy around like a bad smell although he now pretty much ignored her. There had been a few knowing looks over plates of fries at the cafeteria table, but nothing more. It was just like Big Mick, she thought. He can hold her hand on a mountain but as soon as there's other people around - nothing.

"Do you want to get a table?" Peggy yelled turning to a complete stranger who had taken Sammy's place. "Sorry!" she yelled again. "I thought you were someone else." She shook her head and looked around. He was back against a wall near the bar looking so cool and confident in his faded jeans, black boots and black t-shirt, smoking a cigarette and ignoring yet another blonde in a tiny black leather dress, giggling, her hand resting on his shoulder. Blondes, he's got a thing for blondes. Peggy put her hand to her own boring brown locks and felt both her ego and hair deflate. She'd need even more hairspray next time. Maybe a bottle of bleach.

"Where's Greg?" Lacey shouted over the bar at Jonas, the gross bar guy, when Peggy finally caught up to her.

"Not here tonight babe," Jonas shrugged, adjusting the red bandanna in his long greasy hair.

"Isn't he working tonight?" she continued, pouting. "He always works Saturdays!"

"Not this Saturday. I heard he's got a date."

"A date?" Lacey squealed.

Jonas laughed. "I'll take you on a date babe, I'd show you a really good time." He leered at Lacey across the bar and she stepped back.

"Gross," she whispered, "can you order?" Lacey handed Peggy a note and walked towards an empty booth on the side of the dance floor.

"What can I getcha sexy?" he asked.

Although he was incredibly disgusting Peggy felt an

involuntary small thrill at being called sexy, stuff like that never happened to her. It was something that probably happened all the time to girls like Lacey, but not to her.

"Two screwdrivers please," Peggy shouted back unable to hide the smile the compliment had put on her face.

"A smile like that'll take you anywhere babe." He began to mix the drinks, throwing in way too much vodka and looking up at her every so often and catching her eye.

"Got another one?" he asked as he put the drinks on the sticky bar.

"Another what?"

"Another smile?" He was so totally lecherous, looking her up and down like a prize pig. "I never saw a smile so pretty, not even your hot red-headed friend has a smile like that."

Lacey was the most gorgeous person Peggy knew and being compared to her physically in any way was stupid, but so flattering Peggy couldn't help but smile again as she held out the cash.

He put his sticky alcohol covered hand over hers and closed it, waving her off with the drinks. Peggy had successfully flirted for free drinks. She felt high, like she'd finally achieved some Cosmopolitan top ten womanhood goal. She floated towards the booth with her free drinks and a new confidence in her step.

Mere seconds later though, she began to feel like nothing but a dirty skank who'd whored out her smiles for free drinks. She sat down next to Lacey and took a swig. She made a face. It was strong. Much stronger than the toxic waste had ever been. But maybe whatever was in a toxic waste hid the taste of the alcohol better.

"Where's Sammy's drink?" asked Lacey.

"I didn't know Sammy wanted a drink," Peggy said looking right at him across the table but speaking as if he wasn't there. Why would she get him a drink when he hadn't even spoken to her all week?

"I'll go get you one Sammy," Lacey said, about to stand up.

"Thanks Lace. I got it," said Sammy, putting a hand on her bare knee. The tiny gesture made Peggy burn with jealousy. Why was he was touching Lacey and calling her "Lace" like they were dating or something when just a few days ago, he was holding her hand? Maybe Sammy and Lacey had dated, Peggy thought. Had they dated? She couldn't keep up with this group, maybe they were all just a bunch of swingers.

"Did you ever like, date Sammy?" Peggy asked, one sip of the strong drink giving her the courage to ask such a loaded question.

Lacey laughed. "What?"

"Were you guys ever... you know? Never mind, I don't even want to know."

"We made out at a party once," Lacey shrugged.

Peggy felt sick and wished she hadn't asked.

"But it was years ago, we were like thirteen. I don't even think about it, Sammy's like my brother now."

Peggy nodded and frowned into her drink.

"Hey!" shouted Nick who was followed in by Rochelle and Leigh who were both dressed in opposites, Rochelle in a red skirt and black top, Leigh in tight black pants and a red shirt. They squeezed themselves into the booth leaving Nick standing up.

Sammy returned from the bar with a round of drinks before they'd barely begun to touch their first.

"Ben's having a good time at least," Lacey said still pouting over Greg's absence as she looked out onto the dance floor. Ben was dancing wildly with a short girl with short black hair. He looked like a giant dancing with her.

"Wanna dance Lacey?" Peggy asked.

Lacey nodded. "Watch our drinks!" she told Sammy.

Sometime later Peggy wondered when her screwdrivers had turned into toxic waste as she absently chewed on the end of her straw back at the booth. Sammy still hadn't really spoken to her, he was at the bar talking to some guys in biker jackets that looked kind of tough. She had lost Lacey to a cute blonde guy on the dance floor who seemed to have made Lacey forget all about Greg for half an hour, and so Peggy found herself in a happy buzz having a deep and meaningful with Ben.

"Sorry about your game," she said. "You were doing so well at the start."

"I'll be back to myself next game."

"I know what's going on," Peggy said whispering.

"What?" Ben took an extra-long swig of beer.

"I know why you screwed up the game."

"No, no I don't think you do Peg."

"I *do* know, it's OK, your secret is safe with me," she tapped the side of her nose like a moron and realized she was actually pretty drunk.

"Uh, OK," said Ben passing her a glass of water that someone had ordered rounds ago and never touched.

"But I think you should stop," Peggy said.

"Stop? How can I stop Peg?" he screwed up his face in frustration as he downed the rest of his beer. He grabbed her arm and made her look at him. "Please," he pleaded, his eyes flickering around the bar. "Please, don't tell *anybody*."

"Of course I won't, I won't tell a soul." Peggy drunkenly zipped her lip. "But you need to stop taking them."

"Peg, what the hell are you talking about?"

"*Steroids*," she whispered.

Ben laughed. "I'm not on steroids!"

"Oh," she made a face at him. "What can't you stop then? If it's not the steroids?"

"So, you and Sammy," Ben gestured towards the bar changing the subject.

Peggy blushed. "Why would you think that?"

Ben raised his eyebrows. "Are you denying it?"

If she had had just one less toxic waste or screwdriver, or if she could even remember how many she'd had, she may have answered differently.

"No, I'm not denying it." She looked into her drink and slurped it dry.

"Just, well, watch out for Sammy Ruthven."

A sip of her drink caught in her throat and she began to cough.

"You OK?" Ben put a hand on her back and began to whack her much too forcefully in the hope he'd dislodge something. She nodded and looked up at the bar while Ben rubbed her back. Sammy was watching with a curious expression.

"Why?" she asked, coughing and putting her hand to her chest. "What do you mean, watch out for him?"

"Sammy is great, Peg. I mean, he's one of my best friends, he's an awesome guy, but he's awesome as a *friend*. I've seen how he is with girls, he's just, he doesn't do it on purpose."

"Do what on purpose?"

"Screw people around. He gets bored. He gets attention, he gets what he wants, then he gets bored."

"Oh, sure." Peggy fumbled in her clutch purse and scowled. No text message was going to help make this awkward conversation come to an end. She threw the purse across the broken leather seat.

"I like you Peg," Ben leant towards her his big brown eyes filled with kindness.

"Oh, what?" asked Peggy pulling away slightly.

"Not like that!" He pulled his hands away and held them up. "I just mean that I think you're rad. Like as a friend, and I don't want to see you get screwed around. You deserve better than that. And if something happens and it goes wrong it'll be all weird like it is with Rochelle, and we were all really good friends before everything went weird with that."

She knew he was right. She should stay as far away as possible from Sammy Ruthven. Future Janet even warned her away from him so no good must come from any of this. But then, if future Janet knew that something was going to happen between Peggy and Sammy then how could she change that? How could she change anything that was destined to happen to her? If the future already knew this was going to happen, she couldn't change it even if she wanted to. Could she?

The headache.

"Do you want another beer?" Peggy asked looking for an escape from this conversation that was hurting her heart and her brain.

"Maybe a Jack and Coke, and could you get me some change for the jukebox?"

Just as Peggy approached the bar the guys in the biker jackets walked off, leaving Sammy on his own at the other end of the bar.

"Hey," she shouted over as she tried to casually lean against the bar.

"Hey," he said.

"Having a good night?" Was this the best she could do? She frowned a little.

"Yeah," he replied.

He was clearly not interested in having a conversation with her, so she went ahead and ordered her drinks.

"He's just so gorgeous I can't even believe he's alive, he must be an angel with like, his wings clipped or something. I mean, not just an angel, but really an *angel*." Lacey was hardly making sense as she wobbled her way towards the bar.

Peggy handed Lacey another toxic waste, although she was unsure if it was a good idea, probably better to cut her off, but Lacey seemed like the kind of girl who could look after herself.

"He's no Sammy Ruthven I suppose," she winked and waved over Peggy's shoulder at him. Peggy turned around to see him engaged in conversation with yet another blonde girl serving at the bar and rolled her eyes, deciding to give up on him right then and there.

"He hasn't said one word to me since we got here. Well, he has said a few words, but not a full sentence." Peggy said quietly.

"Sammy Ruthven doesn't speak in full sentences," yelled Lacey. "He communicates through smirks and subtle eyebrow movements."

Peggy laughed. "Come back when you're done flirting with this guy," she gestured towards the blonde guy that was headed Lacey's way. Peggy was halfway back to the table when she realized she'd forgotten to get change for the jukebox, but it didn't matter. Ben had obviously found some change as he was back on the dance floor dancing like a maniac to the song of the same name.

Peggy nearly dropped the drinks on the table, she was in fits of hysterics watching Ben attempt to climb the fireman's pole. She sat back at the empty booth and watched him for a while, giggling at his antics and the looks on the faces of everyone watching him.

"Hey," said Sammy as he slid into the booth next to her.

"Oh, hey," she said.

Peggy sipped on her drink, trying to ignore him and instead tried to focus her wobbly gaze on Ben's performance on the dance floor.

"You're not really from Canada, are you?" he asked.

"Nope." She had no idea why she had said that. Later she would curse that moment and wish she could go back in time and change it, but time travel didn't work that way.

"Didn't think so." He took a swig of his drink. He leaned in closer to her. He smelt of alcohol and cigarettes, and aftershave and hair gel, and like outside on a summer's day even though they were in a dark bar. And it was completely intoxicating.

"How did you know?" she asked.

"My dad is from Canada. You don't have an accent. Like, at all."

Three sentences. Nearly. This was going very well.

"Oh," she said.

"So?"

"So, what?"

"So, where *are* you from?"

"I'm from the future. But you can't tell anyone. I'm not supposed to talk about it."

Silence.

"You're drunk," he finally said.

"A bit," she said.

"You're different," he said.

"Different?"

"You're different from a lot of girls around here. Wherever you're from, it's gotta be kinda different." He ran his hand through the back of his hair releasing a little more of his scent in Peggy's direction.

189

"That's funny, because I am kind of from here actually…" Peggy began.

"Hey guys," said Tricia appearing out of nowhere. "Did you see Ben on the dance floor? What a fool."

"Hey Trish," Sammy said. "Can you get us some more drinks?"

"I just got here and it's my round already?"

"Looks like it," said Sammy.

"I'm OK," said Peggy waving her green cocktail around.

"I'm so bored," Lacey said returning to the booth.

"Where's angel boy?" Peggy asked.

"Flew away I guess."

"I wanna dance." Peggy stood up and realized again how drunk she was. She steadied herself and stumbled off towards the dance floor, Lacey and Ben following after her.

Ben grabbed Peggy and spun her around, Lacey linked elbows with her and spun her in the other direction. She laughed hysterically and then suddenly felt like she was going to be sick.

"I think I need to sit down!" she shouted at Lacey through the crowd. Pushing through the sweaty smoke screen that was the dance floor she headed to the table to sit. Just to sit. She'd be fine in a minute. Everyone was gone from the table and she stumbled towards it. She just needed a minute.

"Hey sexy," said Jonas as he collected the empty glasses from the table.

"Hi," she managed.

"You OK sexy?" He seemed concerned. It was sweet. He was so sweet, who cared what he looked like? He was so nice to her. He actually talked to her. Sammy never talked to her. Maybe Jonas could be her boyfriend. But no, she loved Sammy. But then Sammy didn't know she was alive.

"I'll be fine in a minute," she told him. As the room spun around her, she tried to see where Sammy was. She couldn't see him anywhere and it made her sad to think he'd gone, she almost had to stop herself from crying. Crying because a boy she liked left a bar early? She *was* drunk. She was a mess.

"You're in a bad way," Jonas said putting his arm around her, the smell of him making her almost retch, didn't this guy shower? He ran his hand across her face, pushing her hair behind her ear. It made her shiver, and not in a good way.

Leaning in closer he whispered in her ear, "wanna go outside?"

She nodded, she needed air. She'd be safe with this guy at least, he worked here. And her friends were around here somewhere, weren't they?

He wrapped his arm around her waist tightly. "You're so hot," he said as he cradled her head in his hands.

She knew something was up, but she was just too drunk to work it out. She had a feeling she needed to get away from him. But how? Go where? So instead, she just stood there, letting him do that to her, even though on some level she knew it was gross and wrong.

The next thing she knew a salty rough tongue was thrusting around in her mouth and making her want to gag. She tried to push him off her, but he was holding her too tight. She struggled but she didn't have the strength to get away.

He loosened his grip suddenly and Peggy was sent flying into the table, bounced off it and landed on the floor. She heard screaming and cheering from above her and looked up just in time to see Sammy Ruthven punch Jonas so hard in the face that he fell onto the ground right in front of her, his face all messed up and bloody. Jonas looked at her, opened his mouth and spat out a tooth.

Peggy screamed.

"Oh my god!" screamed Lacey, running over to her. "What the hell just happened?"

"We gotta go," Sammy said, grabbing Peggy's other arm. "Get her up!"

Sammy took her under one arm, and Ben under the other while Nick, Lacey and Tricia followed behind, out of the bar and across the street to the parking lot.

"Jesus Sammy, you nearly killed that guy!" Tricia said, her voice oozing respect.

"He's a dick," said Sammy fuming.

"No joke," said Nick, "but he's also an Eight."

"I know what he is, and he deserved what he got," Sammy said, unlocking the passenger side door of the Firebird.

"What did he do?" Lacey asked. "What the hell happened? And what the hell is an Eight?"

"Jonas was... kissing her," Sammy said.

"Holy hell Ruthven, you knocked him out for kissing her? He was flirting with her all night!" Lacey said.

"I know what I saw Lace, and it was in no way consensual."

"How do you know?"

"Look at her!" Sammy dropped her as gently as possible into the front seat.

Lacey looked at her new best friend slumped in the car. Her head rolling around on the headrest for a moment before going still.

"She's not breathing!" Lacey screamed. Ben and Tricia came rushing to the other side of the car.

"Don't be an airhead Lacey. She's fine, just passed out drunk," Tricia said.

"Oh," Lacey leaned her cheek against Peggy's mouth just to make sure. "Yeah, yeah. I think she's still alive. OK."

"What are you going to do with her?" asked Tricia.

"Take her home. Do you guys need a ride?" Sammy asked.

"If you guys are cool, I'm gonna go get a burger from Dee's," Ben said. "Unless you need me?"

"Nah, go get your burger," Sammy said.

"I could use some red meat, I'll come with," Tricia said.

"Lacey?" asked Sammy.

"I'll come with you, I wanna make sure you don't try anything," said Lacey sliding into the back seat.

"I don't need to wait until a girl is paralytic before I try something." Sammy got in and started the engine.

"Are you going to tell me what an Eight is or what?" Lacey asked, folding her arms and glaring at him in the rear-view mirror.

"He's a Crazy Eight."

"Well, he's definitely crazy."

"As in the Crazy Eights of Paradise County," Sammy explained.

"The biker gang?" she shrieked.

"The one and only."

"How do you know?"

"I've got friends who are Eights. Well, maybe not anymore."

"If you really punched out an Eight, Sammy, that's not

good. They are going to come after you. They won't rest until they get revenge."

"Don't you think I know that?"

"You should have just let him kiss her."

"Shut up Lacey." Sammy raised his voice only slightly, but it was enough to shut her up.

Lacey had passed out in the back seat by the time he got to Miss Bates' house. These girls were a total mess.

Sammy hated the idea of doing what he needed to do, but ringing the doorbell and getting Miss Bates to come down and see her like this would be worse. Peggy would never be able to go out again, especially anywhere with him, and that was not something he could let happen.

He took a deep breath as he looked in her purse for the house key.

Walking up to the front door he said a quick prayer for her to get in safely and silently before unlocking the door and leaving it slightly ajar behind him.

He lifted her out of the car, being as gentle as possible, but it was hard. She wasn't a big girl, but she was no waif either. He carried her across the threshold, and then stood in the doorway wondering where to put her. He had no idea where she slept, or where Miss Bates slept. Noticing the stairs to his right he sighed, he was not going to get her up those stairs in this state. At least not silently. He checked the room to the left and carried her to the couch, which was perfectly made as a bed, complete with pajamas folded on the edge.

He lifted the blanket and the pajamas and dropped her gently onto the couch. There was no way he was getting her changed, although the thought did cross his mind. Falling asleep in her clothes was something she could explain to her aunt in the morning. This was the best he could do for now.

He tucked her in and pushed the hair away from her face. She was damn pretty. *What the hell*, he thought, and he gave her a slow lingering kiss on the forehead. Panic rose in his chest as she mumbled something. It sounded like a name... Jack? He sighed, swore under his breath, and then he got the hell out of there before his English teacher came downstairs.

TWENTY-SEVEN

The Walkman

_____

The sound of the doorbell rang in her ears, splitting her head into pieces. She covered her head with the pillow, waiting for Janet to come downstairs and answer the door. It rang again. Where was Janet? On the third ring, she opened her eyes. Sun streamed through the curtains which hadn't been closed the night before and blinded her. She lifted the covers. She was still in her dress from last night and now that she thought about it, she had no idea how she'd gotten home.

She slowly got herself into a seated position and managed to push herself to standing as the doorbell rang again. "OK, OK!" she groaned shuffling to the door.

"Peggy!" beamed Lacey, looking as gorgeous and fresh as ever in skintight ripped jeans and a white t-shirt. Her hair was in a braid, falling in front of her right shoulder. She was showing absolutely no signs of what happened last night, except maybe for some smudgy eyeliner around her eyes which Peggy wasn't totally sure was today's. Either way, she looked amazing and Peggy felt like she'd just eaten a sponge.

"What the hell happened last night?" Peggy asked groggily.

"You look like total crap."

"I feel like it."

"Where's Janet?" Lacey demanded walking through the front door as if she owned the place.

"I don't know, but if she sees me like this, I'm so dead."

Lacey whipped a note off the mirror by the door. "Gone to the farmer's market, didn't want to wake you even though I know you would've liked to come. Janet. Kiss, kiss." Lacey waved the note under Peggy's nose. "Like anyone wants to go to the farmer's market."

"There's a farmer's market?"

"Uh, yeah, like every weekend."

"That sounds kind of cool."

Lacey made a face.

"Does it say when she's coming back?" Peggy asked anxiously.

"Nope, but you sure as hell don't want to be looking like *that* when she does."

Peggy caught a glimpse of herself in the mirror. She looked horrible. Her hair was slightly matted on one side and her eye make-up was smudged all over her face.

"I'll fill you in over breakfast, but first you need to go shower."

Peggy did what she was told, fumbling quickly through her duffel bag for some clothes before making her way upstairs.

Lacey headed into the kitchen in search of coffee and was thrilled to see Janet had left a pot before she'd gone out. It was a little bitter, but with four sugars and some milk it was drinkable. Lacey sat at the counter flicking through an old

Vogue. Peggy was taking ages. Lacey had flicked through two more fashion mags and finished her coffee and Peggy still wasn't down. She sighed, and leaving her dirty mug on the table, she went to watch TV.

As she sat down on Peggy's makeshift bed, she felt something hard under her butt. She grabbed it thinking it was the remote control and was about to throw it on the pillow when she stopped.

"What the..." she said out loud looking at the thing. It was about the size of a remote control but a lot thinner. It had no buttons or numbers and it was wrapped in bright pink plastic glitter. She turned it over and over in her hands, trying to work out what the strange object might be. There was a button on the front, a circle with a little square inside it. It felt like it could be pushed but Lacey was scared. She had no idea what it was, was it a bomb detonator?! She freaked out and put it on the table in front of her.

"Oh," said Peggy as she watched Lacey put her phone on the coffee table.

"Peggy?" Lacey asked, confusion and a little fear all over her pretty face.

Peggy, now clean and made-up and dressed in jeans and a blue checked shirt stood dumb.

"Peg?" Lacey asked again. "What is this?"

Peggy sat down next to her on the couch and, taking the phone in her hands turned it on.

Lacey gasped.

"It's my phone," Peggy said knowing she should have lied and made something up. What could she possibly make up though? And she was so over pretending to be from Canada all the time.

"A phone?" asked Lacey, her face all scrunched up.

"It has everything on it. Music, photos, it's a camera too..." she probably should have deleted the photos of the present. Or like Janet said, she shouldn't even have it here at all.

"But what is it?"

"It's a phone, like I said." Peggy turned it on and the light from the screen made Lacey jump backwards.

"A phone with photos and music? Don't you mean it's a camera? Or a Walkman?" asked Lacey.

"It's a phone, camera, Walkman, computer, it does lots of stuff."

Lacey watched dumbfounded as Peggy flipped through the apps. She opened up her music app and clicked on her retro rock playlist. Music came from the speaker at the bottom and Lacey squealed.

"Peggy, how do you have this?"

"I'm not really supposed to tell anyone," Peggy said.

"Are you in like, in the FBI or something? I thought you were just witness protection."

"No," Peggy laughed.

There was a sound at the front door and both the girls jumped. Peggy shoved the phone in her pocket.

"Quick, get your shoes on, we need to go before she realizes how messed up you are," Lacey ordered.

Peggy grabbed her purse and slipped her feet into her black ballet flats, the ones with the silver studs.

"Morning Peggy, oh hi Lacey," Janet called out as she struggled with two large brown bags full of vegetables and fruit.

"Let me help you Miss Bates." Lacey jumped up and carried one of the bags into the kitchen.

"I'm taking Peggy out for breakfast, is that OK?" Lacey asked her teacher.

"Oh sure, I'm going to get started on a new sewing project," Janet said excitedly.

"You sew?" Lacey asked politely.

"I made this dress." Miss Bates put her hands on her hips to model the red striped knee length dress she was wearing. It was cute enough, cinched in at the waist with a chunky black and silver belt.

"That's really cool Miss B. You should totally make our prom dresses," Lacey said.

"Thanks Lacey. Isn't it a bit early to start thinking about Prom though?"

"It's never too early to start thinking about *prom*," Peggy said giving Lacey a look.

"You girls have a good time, I might be out again later though, I think Ray wants to take me out tonight," Janet giggled.

"Ray?" asked Lacey.

"Ray's records," Peggy said.

"O.M.G!" squealed Lacey, "you're dating Ray Wiley?"

"Not dating, just hanging out as you kids say," Janet said, putting the bananas in the fruit bowl.

"Mrs. Wiley," Lacey said. "It's got a ring to it… kinda."

Janet and Peggy exchanged looks.

"I wouldn't change my name anyway, I never liked the idea of doing that," Janet said shaking her head.

"Can I just use your bathroom real quick?" asked Lacey. "That coffee's gone straight through me." She bounded up the stairs without waiting for directions.

"Not even to Willis?" asked Peggy softly.

"I don't *know* anyone called Willis," Janet replied with a shrug. "I can't sit around here waiting for a Willis to show up. I might not get married for years and years. I can't put my life on hold because I know how it ends."

"You don't know how it ends."

"I know who I marry, but I also know that right now, Ray is the one I want to be with, so I'm just going to be with him."

Peggy nodded. She got it. Janet was clever and independent. She knew what she wanted, and she acted on it. Peggy wasn't like that, she would have gotten it into her head she was marrying a Willis and searched the entire country for one, or like Janet suggested, sit in her house until one turned up.

"How do you look so good today?" Peggy asked when they were comfortably seated in a booth table at Dee's.

"I don't know what you mean," Lacey said slurping at the disgusting bottomless coffee.

"We must've had about the same amount to drink last night."

Lacey shrugged.

"I actually hate you," Peggy said as the waitress refilled their coffee cups.

For a moment Peggy forgot where she was. Dee's hadn't changed a single bit. The windows were grubby, the tables were the same laminate grey although they were a little cleaner. The booth seats were still bright red and the walls a pale turquoise blue. It was All-American and hideously garish, and Peggy loved it.

"Tell me what that thing is Peg," Lacey demanded. "Before the others get here."

"What others?"

"Ben, Nick and Tricia are meeting us."

"Oh, I thought it was just going to be us. I really don't feel like seeing people today." Peggy tried to ignore the nauseous feeling in her stomach, washing it down with the awful coffee.

"Those guys aren't *people*. I was going to invite Sammy, but I thought I'd check with you first, but then, he doesn't usually do weekends. What the hell is going on with you two anyway? I know he seems tough and all, but I've never seen him hit anybody like that. Sammy's usually a total pacifist."

The memories of last night came rushing back to her. Seeing Jonas' bloody face on the floor and his tooth and then Sammy grabbing her to get the hell out of there. She flinched. "I don't know," she said.

"Like I never saw him do anything like that for Rochelle, although they were never officially *together* if you know what I mean."

"No, I really don't know what you mean," said Peggy.

"She acts all like she's his girlfriend, but she's totally not. Never has been. She was always just his bit on the side, and she knows damn well he never like, loved her or anything like that."

Peggy nearly spat out her coffee. "Bit on the side of what?" she asked, although she was pretty sure she didn't want the answer.

"The rest of his life, I guess. Cars, his family. They come first to Sammy."

Peggy looked into her coffee.

"I'm sure they wouldn't come first to him after *you* though, if you were like, *together*. So, are you together?"

Peggy shrugged. "I don't think so."

Lacey made a sad face.

"Is it true that none of you guys are going to college?" Peggy asked quickly, thinking of something else to talk about.

"Most of us in this town don't. I'll probably just get a job selling jeans at the Mini Mall while I save some cash, so I can run away and become famous or something. Leigh and Rochelle are talking about moving to Salt Valley and going to dental school. I guess Ben's our only hope, he's still waiting to hear about possible scholarships but after the way he's been playing lately I doubt that's going to happen."

"What about Tricia? She seems pretty smart."

"She's got good grades, sure, but her family can't afford to send her anywhere."

"And Sammy?" Peggy asked casually.

"I should've known you were just asking about Sammy," Lacey said, rolling her eyes. "He's just gonna do what he does, fix cars with his dad. No one around here has any grand plans Peg. You either start dressing like a cowgirl and end up on a ranch, work at the diner or sell jeans at the Mini Mall, and I don't so much like smelling of bacon grease or horse crap, so I know where I'm headed."

"You should leave Santolsa," Peggy said. "Imagine LA or New York, or San Francisco!" What she really meant was - imagine LA, New York or San Francisco in the *1980's*.

Lacey shrugged. "Some people have dreams, some people have responsibilities… or burdens."

"What are yours?"

"My Mom," Lacey rolled her eyes. "She's a pain in my ass but she has no one else. Unless she marries Roger soon, I'm stuck here."

Peggy nodded. "Who's Roger?"

"Her dumb boyfriend. But he's better than most of them have been."

Peggy nodded again.

"So, tell me about that thing, how do you have that? Is it like *war* technology or something? I heard people talking about a World War Three." Lacey looked at her suspiciously.

"It's classified I guess, but it's not for *war*. And there isn't going to be a World War Three so calm down."

"How could you possibly know that?"

"I just know, trust me."

Lacey gave her a look and then glanced over to the door before quickly dipping her head. "O.M.G, don't look," she instructed, which of course made Peggy look. In walked June-Belle dressed in a puffy blue dress and a nerd dressed like a hipster. He was kind of cute Peggy decided, in that Jack/brother/best friend/hipster kind of way.

"That's Horace with June-Belle," Lacey whispered. "I can't believe they are in here together, like everyone comes here, it's hardly secret."

June-Belle looked around the diner anxiously and pulled Horace into a booth up the back. Lacey giggled. "I told you! Didn't I tell you?"

"You told us what?" asked Tricia, sitting down next to Lacey and flicking some ash into the ashtray on the table. Peggy was slowly getting used to everyone smoking all the time but smoking near food was still gross to her and being hungover made it even grosser. It made her want to puke so bad.

"Peggy doesn't smoke, Trish," said Lacey rudely.

"No, it's fine," Peggy said, not wanting to be rude.

"Whatever, I should quit anyway, it's making me jittery." Tricia put the cigarette out and took the ashtray in her dark polished fingers, sliding it onto the next table full of giggling preppy freshman that kind of looked familiar but no one cared who they were.

"Hey, hey, hey!" called Ben, walking into the diner with way more vigor than was necessary. Nick followed behind him and looked a little worse for wear.

"Did you guys order cos I'm starving for those little

pancakes they do here," Ben said, looking around for the waitress as he slid in next to Peggy.

"Little?" asked Nick. "The pancakes here are huge."

"Little to me Nick, I like my pancakes man size, not squirt size."

"Is that June-Belle and Horace over there?" Nick asked squinting.

Tricia's eyes nearly popped out of her head. "Horace and *June-Belle*?"

"I told you guys, didn't I tell you guys?" Lacey gloated.

"I guess you told us," shrugged Nick.

"That's so messed up," said Tricia, shaking her head.

"What'll it be kids?" asked the waitress, blinking her blue eye-shadowed eyes blankly.

"Your number baby," said Ben, looking her up and down.

"Hun, I'm fifty-five. What can I get you to *eat?*" the waitress replied.

"Ben, seriously," said Tricia, "you don't have to do that."

"Do what?" he asked after he ordered his pancakes and vanilla shake.

"You know *what*," Tricia said.

"So, what happened last night?" Ben asked ignoring her.

"I don't even know how I got home so if someone could fill me in that'd be nice," Peggy said.

"What do you remember?" asked Nick.

"I remember being on the dance floor and feeling really sick, so I went to sit down..." The memory of Jonas' tongue down her throat almost brought up the coffee she'd just drunk.

"You remember Jonas kissing you?" Lacey asked.

"It's the only thing I *do* remember, unfortunately."

"Yeah, he was all over you, kissing you and everything. That's what Sammy said," Nick told her.

"I was dancing, but when I saw Sammy jump him, I ran straight over," Lacey said.

"Sammy... jumped him?" Peggy's hands began to shake, spilling a little coffee onto her saucer.

Lacey laughed. "He's got the hots for you Peg."

"I don't think so," Peggy said.

"He put you to bed and everything," said Lacey.

Peggy's face lost some color. "He did what?"

"How do you think you got home? And how do you think you got into *bed*?" Lacey asked. "I sure didn't carry you in there."

"I don't know..." Peggy tried as hard as she could to remember.

She remembered falling to the ground and looking up as Sammy hit Jonas in the face. Sammy's face void of rage or aggression, but full of *something*. She saw Jonas' face on the floor next to her, his yellow tooth rolling towards her on the floor. Sammy and Lacey helping her to the car. That was it.

"He carried you into your house and put you to bed." Lacey said it like it was something that happened every day. Maybe that kind of thing happened to Lacey every day, but not to Peggy.

Peggy swore, staring into the stack of pancakes covered in bacon and maple syrup the waitress had just put in front of her. "I'm so embarrassed," she said putting her head into her hands. Sammy was never going to be into someone who was such a mess.

Lacey ignored her and began talking animatedly about Horace and June-Belle. "Why is she so evil anyway?" She took a bite of her lemon and sugar pancake. "I can't stand her," she said through the pancakes.

"Why do you hate her so much anyway?" asked Peggy. "Like sure, she's a preppy and kind of annoying, but she's doesn't seem that bad."

Silence.

"What?" asked Peggy.

Lacey's face went the same color as her hair, and she looked like she was seconds away from losing it. Peggy had never seen her so mad before.

"Woah, you really went there," said Tricia.

"Went where?" asked Peggy.

"Can I tell her?" asked Tricia. Lacey's face stayed angry, but she nodded and took another bite of her food, looking out the window as she chewed and let her friend tell the story.

"In 1981 Lacey won Miss Teen Santolsa," Tricia said.

"Wow," said Peggy laughing, "that's amazing, I'm sitting here with a bona-fide beauty queen and I never even knew it."

Lacey flickered her eyes towards Peggy and then back out the window.

"And then," began Nick, "the next year, June-Belle won."

"So, you hate her because she won your crown?" asked Peggy.

"No," said Lacey, putting down her fork. "I hate her because she *sabotaged* me." Lacey glared in June-Belle's direction.

"Lacey came out for the finale," Tricia said. "She was going to perform a twirling routine for her special talent."

"But when she went to twirl the baton…" Ben said slowly, checking Lacey's expression to see if it was OK to go on.

"She couldn't hold onto it," Nick said.

"Butter," said Lacey, stabbing another piece of pancake.

"It slipped out of her hand and nearly took out the mayor at the judges table," Tricia said, stifling a giggle.

Peggy laughed, and Lacey threw her a dirty look.

"Where's Sammy today?" asked Nick breaking the tension.

"Probably visiting his mom," Tricia said.

"Where does his mom live?" asked Peggy.

"You should probably ask him about that," said Nick. "He was pretty cut up about last night too, now that the Eights are after him."

"I hardly even remember him being there, God I hardly remember anything." Peggy was suffering severe toxic waste remorse.

"It's fine," said Nick.

"It's totally fine," said Ben.

"We've all been a hell of a lot worse at the Fire Station than you were last night Peg, don't worry about it," Tricia said, hoeing into her own plate of bacon. It could've been the first nice thing Tricia ever said to her.

"It's so not fine, I've really embarrassed myself in front of him, I mean… everybody," Peggy said, tapping the mound of untouched pancakes in front of her with her fork.

"Finally, you admit it to the world, you love Sammy Ruthven!" Lacey accused, pointing her fork.

Peggy shrugged. Trying to deny it was getting too hard anyway.

"Looks like Ro is finally out of the picture so just go for it," said Tricia.

"You are so much cuter than her too Peg," said Ben giving her a nudge. "But just remember what I said, huh?"

"Yeah," said Lacey. "Ro's all make-up and hair. No heart."

"She's actually really great, if you'd take some time to get to know her," said Nick, jumping to her defense.

"Nick don't tell me you are still holding a torch for that girl?" Tricia said, smacking her mug on the table.

"She *used* to be cool, but she's changed," said Lacey, "everyone can see it."

"She was always a pain in the ass," said Tricia.

"She used to be my best friend, like years ago," Lacey told Peggy.

"She's still really cool, she's just been going through stuff," said Nick.

"We've *all* been going through stuff," said Lacey.

"That's the truth," said Ben, staring into his pancakes. "I'm sure these used to be bigger."

"I'm so sick of this shit," said Tricia rudely.

"Woah, what's your damage Tricia?" asked Lacey.

"Come on Trish, eat your pancakes. You're just hungover," said Ben.

"You are all just a bunch of fakes and liars. People think I'm a freak because I wear a lot of eye-liner and I'm the only person in about six million miles who listens to punk music but, Jesus!"

"Liars?" asked Lacey innocently, "I'm not a liar."

"You pretend you're in love with Greg at the bar, but it's only because you can't find a real boyfriend," Tricia said.

Lacey's mouth dropped open.

"Nick is living in Sammy's shadow," Tricia continued. "Peggy can't even admit that she likes Sammy, just admit it Peg. He likes you. Stop making it so hard. It's not hard. Ask him out, if he says no, move on with your stupid life."

Peggy looked at her stunned.

"Come on now," said Ben. "I know you're just hungover and tired, eat something then I'll drive you home."

"You are the worst one!" Tricia shouted, tears welling up in her eyes.

Ben looked around, worried. "Please Trish," he pleaded.

"And now *this*," her arm flailed in the direction of June-Belle and Horace. She pushed past Nick and stood up, throwing some cash on the table. She walked over to June-Belle and Horace's table.

"O.M.G what is she doing?" Peggy asked.

"O.M.G-a-rama," said Lacey, her eyes doubling in size.

"She's just using you," said Tricia to Horace, who looked like he wanted the booth to swallow him whole. "Can't you see it?"

"Just go home Tricia, you're drunk," said June-Belle, giggling awkwardly. "We're just two friends over here having breakfast."

Horace raised his eyebrows at June-Belle. "Friends? Is that what we are June-Belle?" he asked putting down his menu.

"See?" Tricia said. "You are all a bunch of fakers and you can all go to hell."

Everyone in the diner sat silently as they watched her walk out.

"What was that all about?" asked Peggy.

"She's in love with Horace, isn't it obvious?" Lacey said. Everyone stared at Lacey. "Didn't you guys know?"

"Horace and *Tricia*? That's stupider than Horace and June-Belle," said Peggy. Horace was a nerd and Tricia was a punk. That was so not ever going to work.

"I'll go after her," said Ben, throwing some money on the table and running after her.

Horace and June-Belle were having a heated discussion and Horace looked pissed, like a lover scorned.

"Should we go find her?" Nick asked.

"Let Ben talk to her," Lacey said, finishing off her plate and eyeing up the left-over pancakes on the table. Peggy pushed her plate towards Lacey.

"Do you guys really think Rochelle has changed?" Nick asked after a few moments of silence.

"Hell yes," said Lacey.

"I haven't known her long enough to know what she was like before, but she's never been that nice to me," said Peggy.

"I know what Tricia means," Nick said.

"About what?" asked Lacey. "Because I really do love Greg the barman, he's so dreamy."

"About me," said Nick. "I am living in Sammy's shadow." Peggy thought about the day she met Nick, how she thought he was a less attractive version of Sammy. She watched him as he frowned into his plate, toying with a last piece of pancake.

"Nick, Sammy's cool and sexy and all that, but you are the one with the brains," Lacey said.

"Sammy does better than me in most classes," Nick replied.

"Stop trying to be anything you're not and just be yourself," said Peggy.

He looked up at her, his blue eyes sad and searching. "You're probably right."

"What's happening?" asked Lacey as they all looked over at the table where Horace and June-Belle were sitting. Horace had put his brown cardigan over his white button up shirt and stood up.

June-Belle put her hand around Horace's wrist to stop him. She began talking, making the 'crazy' gesture and rolling her eyes around, obviously talking about Tricia. Horace shrugged her off and walked out, leaving her alone and looking very uncomfortable.

Peggy sat silently in Lacey's red Chevette as they drove down Main Street on the way back to Janet's house.

"Slow down," Peggy said urgently.

"What is it?" Lacey asked, slamming on the brakes.

Peggy shook her head, "I just thought I saw someone, but it wasn't him."

"Who?"

"My best friend from home. I think it was just someone in the same shirt he used to have." She heard herself and stopped. 'Used to have'. It probably would have been more correct to say, 'will have'. Future tense. Maybe that was even the exact Van Halen shirt Jack owned. He did get it at a vintage store just down the road, or a store that will be just down the road. Peggy's head began to pound again. It was becoming a constant in her life, these headaches. She couldn't wait to get home and pop a pain killer.

"A *guy* friend?" asked Lacey, grinning as a car behind her honked and she began to drive again.

Peggy smiled and shook her head. "Yeah, the most awesome guy I know."

"Why aren't you with him if he's so awesome?"

"You mean like, *together*?" asked Peggy.

"Yeah, why aren't you together if he's so great?"

Peggy laughed. "Because he's gay!"

"Gay?"

"Yes, he's gay, so he's my best friend, but that's it."

"How do you know he's gay?" asked Lacey.

"Because he is."

"Did he say he was?"

"He didn't have to *say* he was," said Peggy.

"Does he have a boyfriend?" Lacey asked.

"No." Peggy's most recent thoughts about Jack had confused her. Sleeping in his bed. His arm draped around her.

"I never met someone who was gay before." Lacey seemed excited at the possibility of meeting him.

"I'm sure you've met loads of gay people," Peggy said.

"Did he *ever* have a boyfriend?"

"Who?"

"Your friend in the shirt."

"Oh, no, not really."

"Let me get this straight Peg. You have a gorgeous friend who is a boy, who never *said* he was gay and never had a *boyfriend*."

"I never said he was gorgeous."

"He *sounds* gorgeous."

"He is gorgeous, I guess, in a nerdy kinda way."

Lacey made a tutting sound. "I guess he's in like, Canada or whatever anyway, and Sammy Ruthven is right here," she said.

"I should go back and visit soon."

"Back to Canada?"

"Yeah, I need to pick up some stuff, I might not even be in school this week." Peggy didn't want to leave, but she had to sort out her future life before she could fully live in the past and all this talk of Jack was making her wonder how he was, and what was happening back home. Home. Such a strange word to use to describe that place, that *time*. Also, even though she had been warned and had refused to let herself do it the first time, she was dying to Google everyone. Every day the temptation grew. And anyway, what was the worst that could happen?

TWENTY-EIGHT

Chicken

_____

Janet didn't have a rule about shoes in the house like her actual mom did, but Peggy kicked off her studded flats at the door anyway. She was about to throw the vintage purse that she'd bought at a thrift store in the present (which made it vintage, but new, but old so that was weird) on the couch, but it was all tidy. All her bedding had gone and so had all her bags. Was Janet kicking her out? Did Janet know what had happened last night? She walked into the kitchen, anxiety rising in her chest.

"I've got a surprise!" Janet wiped her hands on a tea towel and smiled and Peggy let out a small sigh of relief.

Janet led her up the stairs and opened the door to the sewing room. All the sewing stuff was gone and in its place was a single bed covered in a blanket of pale pink polka dots. A frilly pink lamp sat on a nightstand beside it. There was a small white desk by the window and a matching bookcase against the wall. A few of Janet's books sat on one shelf, including _The Nuns of Santolsa_.

Peggy stood quietly taking it in. It wasn't the huge bedroom with king sized bed and private en-suite she had in her own time, but it felt more like home than her own room had ever.

"Do you like it?" Janet asked nervously. "I know your family has money and I'm sure your room back home is nicer. It isn't much."

"It's perfect," Peggy said as her eyes welled up with tears. It had been a crazy day and she was still feeling a bit hungover, but Janet's kindness was overwhelming. Janet put an arm around her and laughed nervously.

"I really want you to stay, but it's your choice. If you don't want to, I'll just turn it back into the sewing room, so don't feel like you are obliged in any way. I just wanted you to be comfortable while you're here."

"But where will you do your sewing?" Peggy asked.

"I set up a corner in my room, it's kind of nice actually," Janet said. "So, do you like it?"

"I love it," Peggy replied.

"Do whatever you want to it, posters, anything."

"Thanks," Peggy said as she sat on her bed and ran her hands across the clean smelling blankets.

"That's Ray!" Janet jumped as the doorbell rang.

"I thought you looked a little dressed up for moving furniture," said Peggy, checking out Janet's tight black trousers and green silk shirt, a gold belt cinching her tiny waist.

"Ray's taking me to dinner and a movie in Salt Valley, so I won't be home until late. Are you going to be OK? You can come with us if you want?"

"No, no, you love birds go have a good time," Peggy smiled.

"You sure?"

Peggy nodded. She liked the idea of a movie, but she was exhausted.

"OK, well there's a pizza in the freezer or you can have

whatever else you can find to eat."

Peggy looked out her new bedroom window at the peachy pink late afternoon sky and smiled. She wasn't sure how things could get better.

"I nearly forgot to tell you," Janet said as she was walking out the door, "Sammy called."

Peggy's mouth dropped open.

"I wrote his number down by the phone for you to call him back, have a good night!" Janet rushed out of Peggy's room, down the stairs and out the front door, leaving Peggy standing, staring out at Ray's car driving off, heart thumping wildly.

He called. *Sammy had called.* He had called *her*.

She ran down the stairs and into the kitchen to the phone. There was no message, just a number. She looked around frantically and promptly began freaking out. She was way too nervous to call him back, so she grabbed a can of 7UP from the fridge and opened a bag of corn chips. She tried to eat one, but her mouth was so dry she couldn't make enough saliva to chew it. She sipped the drink instead.

She wished she could text Lacey and ask her what to do. It took her about ten minutes to work out that she could look up Lacey in the phone book and that she'd probably be home by now. After all, how did Sammy get *her* number? The phonebook. Duh. She thought about Sammy going through the phone book looking for her number and her heart skipped a beat.

"Hello Fitzgerald residence," answered Lacey, sounding very grown up and professional.

"Lacey?" Peggy asked.

"Who's this?" asked Lacey, sounding all normal again.

"It's me, Peggy."

"Oh, you sound all different on the phone, what's up?"

"Sammy called," Peggy said.

"Oh yeah, what did he say?"

"I don't know, I wasn't home, I was still out with you."

"OK, so did you call him back?"

"No, I don't know what to do."

"O.M.G," said Lacey.

"What should I do?"

"Call him!" Lacey shouted so loud Peggy had to move the phone away from her ear for a second.

"I can't! I'm too nervous!" Why couldn't she just text him or see if he was online and send him a smiley face or something? It was so much easier than this calling stuff. She'd never even called a boy before, well, except for Jack, but he hardly counted.

"You have to," Lacey instructed.

"I don't *have* to."

"Well, you kinda *do*. Because if you don't, then he's going to think you ignored his call and he's not going to call you again."

"Why does he want to talk to me?"

"I don't know Peg, just call him," Lacey said, sounding annoyed.

"Can you call him and find out?" Peggy pleaded.

"*No*, you call him!"

"Can you come over and hold my hand?"

"You're getting ridiculous, go call him, then call me back and tell me everything you said, and everything he said." And then she hung up, leaving Peggy listening to a bunch of beeps.

She stared at the numbers in front of her until they didn't even look like numbers anymore and she started to forget what numbers even looked like. She picked up the phone, put the phone down, sipped her 7UP, picked up the phone, put it down, finished the 7UP, grabbed another one, picked up the phone and put the phone down again.

She screamed.

"I can't do this!" she yelled at herself.

She did deep breathing exercises. She did some yoga poses on the lounge room rug. She had one more 7UP and just when she was starting to feel high on sugar, the phone rang. She went into a panic, heart beating in time with the ringing she lifted the receiver to her ear.

"Hello?" she said, her voice wavering.

"What did he say?" asked Lacey.

"Nothing," said Peggy slumping onto a bar stool. "I didn't call him yet."

"Are you kidding me?" Lacey asked, "it's been like half an hour."

"I'm *going* to call him, I just need some more time to psyche myself up... Hello? Lacey?" the phone was beeping at her again. She replaced the receiver and as soon as she did it rang again.

"Lacey, I *am* going to do it," she began.

"Going to do what?" asked a sexy guy's voice.

"Who is this?" Peggy demanded.

"It's Sammy."

Peggy nearly fell off the chair. She opened her mouth to speak but nothing came out.

"Peggy?" he asked, his voice sounding even sexier from however far away he was calling from.

"Yes?" she croaked as she began twisting the long phone cord around her wrist.

"Hi," he said.

"Hi," she said.

"I just wanted to check you were OK, after last night."

Peggy's shoulders dropped. He was just being a friend

and checking up on her.

"I'm OK, a little hungover I guess." She was suddenly able to speak again, now that she knew he was just calling as a friend.

"Have you eaten?" he asked.

That was totally something a friend would ask, if they were concerned about you. Wasn't it?

"I had pancakes," she said.

"For dinner?"

Why was he asking her about dinner?

"No, I haven't eaten dinner, pancakes were lunch, I guess. The bits I ate."

"Is Janet home?"

"No, she's out on a date."

"Have you *got* dinner?"

Why was he still talking about dinner? Peggy became nervous again and her voice quivered slightly as she said, "I've got a frozen pizza."

"I'll bring you something."

"Uh…" she stammered.

"Do you like chicken?"

"I love chicken."

"Cool. See you soon."

And Peggy was left listening to beeps for the third time that night.

What is happening? She thought.

The answer was that Sammy Ruthven was coming over and he was bringing her dinner and it was the most amazing thing that had ever happened.

She swapped her shirt for a loose-fitting white tank top and threw a blue cardigan with silver buttons over the top. She was about to put some bright pink lipstick on and then settled for light pink gloss. She really wanted to look like she hadn't made any effort, even though she'd been staring at herself for the last twenty minutes. She stared at her reflection in the bathroom mirror, puffed up her hair, and took some deep breaths.

She was in a total state. She felt like she'd consumed a thousand coffees. Her hands were shaking, and she shook herself. She breathed in and out deeply. Nothing helped. Sammy Ruthven was bringing dinner over. Nothing was going to make her cool about that. She began to feel sick, like she was actually going to throw up. She had never felt like this before. Not with Big Mick, not with anyone. She didn't get how people had relationships, how did they ever get past *this*?

She was lying on the hallway carpet trying to breathe normally when the doorbell rang. She swore under her breath and seriously thought about ignoring it. She could just go to bed and never know the anxiety and awkward-ness of what it would be like having dinner with him. Of course, she'd eaten in front of him almost every day at school, but this was different, it was practically their first date. Was it? She silently screamed up towards the ceiling. She'd time travelled through three decades but couldn't cope with a date. Maybe it wasn't a date. Maybe it *was* just a friend bringing food. Heck, who was she kidding? Sammy Ruthven did not bring girls food unless it was a date. Or maybe he did. She didn't even *know* him.

The doorbell rang again, and she wondered how many times he would ring it before he would turn around and go home. It wasn't like he could just text her from out there. It rang once more and in-spite of her head's protests her body jumped up to standing and before she knew what she was doing, she was opening the door.

He stood in front of her, sexy as hell. His dirty blonde

hair was a total mess, his dark jeans clinging perfectly to all his lower-body parts, a plain grey t-shirt, rolled up at the sleeves showing off his subtle tan. He was holding a bucket of chicken under one of his so sexy arms and a brown paper grocery bag in the other.

"Hi," he said.

"Hi," she said.

"Are you going to let me in?" he asked.

"Oh, sorry, yes." She shook her head and opened the door wide enough for him to walk through, brushing past her and making her feel about sixteen different emotions at once.

"Where do you want this?" he asked, gesturing to the bucket and Peggy showed him to the kitchen. He put the chicken down on the small wooden table and started pulling fries, corns and coleslaw from the bag. "I brought a couple 7UPs, I didn't know if you had any."

"It's pretty much the only thing we *do* have apart from frozen pizza," she said, watching him unpack, totally unable to work out what to do.

"Eat out of the bucket or off plates?" he asked.

"Plates," she said. She was way too nervous to eat out of a bucket in front of him. She wondered if she'd manage to eat anything, even though it smelt *so* good. She set a plate and a glass down for each of them and threw some cutlery in the middle. Were they even going to need cutlery? How was she even going to eat a chicken leg in front of him? Eating chicken off the bone was so not sexy.

"Music?" he asked.

She nodded and headed into the lounge and began rummaging through Janet's records. She was thankful for the few moments it gave her to compose herself.

"What do you feel like listening to?" she called out.

"Anything," he said.

The coolest thing she could find was a Foreigner album.

"This is good," he called out over the music.

She walked back into the kitchen and without thinking found herself doing a stupid impromptu dance. It was terrible. Her arms were flapping around, and her hips were swaying in a way which was definitely nowhere near Rochelle-level-sex-appeal. She stopped herself and sat down at the table looking down at her empty plate her face burning.

"Why did you stop?" he asked, grabbing a piece of chicken and grinning.

"That's so embarrassing," she said, staring into the bucket.

"I like the way you dance," he said.

"Thanks." She took a small bite of a chicken leg. It was so tasty and her mouth instantly watered. She wanted to tear the skin off and eat it like she would if she was alone, devouring it in seconds, but she didn't want him to see her do that, so she continued taking tiny little birdy bites.

"You dance like you don't care what anyone thinks."

"Is that a compliment?"

"Definitely."

"Then, thanks." She took another slightly bigger bite.

If she had died right then, listening to Foreigner, chowing down on a crispy leg of fried chicken that Sammy Ruthven had brought to her house, she would've been happy.

"Did you hear about what happened at the diner today?" she asked trying to make conversation.

"No, I was out of town today."

"It was pretty crazy," Peggy said.

"Yeah?"

"June-Belle and Horace were there, on some kind

of date."

"Really?" He didn't seem that interested in the story. He grabbed another chicken piece and ripped the skin off with his teeth.

"Tricia lost it and shouted at everyone. She told us we were all liars and fakers."

"She's got a point. Present company excluded."

Peggy looked down at the chicken bone in her hand. "I'm gossiping, sorry. I'm just... nervous and I can't think of anything to say." She felt herself flush as she put the clean bone down on her plate.

"Why are you nervous?" he asked putting a cob of corn on each of their plates with a small square of wrapped butter.

She shook her head, "I've read this all wrong, haven't I?"

"Read what all wrong?"

"I thought this was like... a date or something." She looked into the bucket of chicken. "And now I don't even know why I'm telling you that I thought that. I'm such an idiot."

All she wanted to do was run away. Go hide in her room. She should've ignored the doorbell. She should never have answered the phone.

"Do you want it to be a date?" he asked, putting down his corn and looking at her intensely.

She held her own cob to her lips and shrugged, trying her best to look like 'whatever'. She took a bite and corn spat out in all directions. She dropped the corn and put her hand over her face not sure whether to laugh or cry, but he just smiled at her, that half-smile smirk that made her melt like the butter on her corn.

They continued eating silently, lost in their own thoughts. Peggy wondering if this was what sexual tension felt like, until half the bucket of chicken was gone and most of the corn and fries.

"What do you want to do now?" he asked her as he wiped his mouth with a napkin and leaned back in his chair.

"I don't know, what do *you* want to do now?" she asked.

He gave her a smoldering look. She tried to hold it for a moment, but it was too intense for her, she broke away by throwing her chicken bones into the paper bag.

"We should clear up," she said. Why, why did she say that? Why didn't she say something flirtatious or sexy or at least witty?

"Yeah," he said, standing up taking the plates to the sink. "Miss Bates won't let me come over again if she sees this mess."

Come over *again*?

Peggy stood up and grabbed the bucket of left-over chicken in both hands. She was about to turn towards the counter when she felt him move around behind her. She stood, frozen to the spot as she felt his hand gently move her hair away from the back of her neck. She turned to marshmallow as he breathed softly against her goose pimply skin, sending her into all sorts of a panic. She gripped the bucket of chicken as he gently kissed her neck. *His* lips were on *her* neck. She was now toasted marshmallow, nothing but a thin crispy coating protecting her gooey center.

He kissed her jaw, her cheek and her cheek again. And then his lips found her lips. The bucket of chicken dropped to the floor as he took her in his arms. Running her chicken greased fingers through his messy dirty hair as they pressed into each other frantically, limbs moving all over the place, chicken legs and wings sliding across the floor in all directions.

They came apart breathless.

"Sorry," he began, "I really shouldn't have done that." But his arms remained around her.

"I'm glad you did," she said, trying to catch her breath.

He released his grip and pushed her hair back from her face. Not the way Jack had always done it. Jack had a tender look in his eye, like he was going to protect her against the baddies or Big Mick, or Mindy. Whichever she was crying over at that moment. Jack was soft and lovely and wore sneakers to school instead of brown leather shoes and that was about as rebellious as he got, apart from the occasional underage drinking antics at The Stables.

Sammy touched her differently. There was a kindness in his touch but there was something more, there was an eagerness, a roughness, a rawness to everything he did that drove Peggy crazy. Jack was the kind of guy you wanted to marry and sit on the couch with. Sammy was the kind of guy you wanted to have take you in the back of his blue Firebird even though you knew you'd spend days and nights sitting by the phone waiting to hear from him. You knew he wouldn't call, you'd never see him again, until one night, months later after you finally felt free of his grasp and began moving on with your life, after days and nights of tears and bad movies, he *would* call. Just casually inviting you out for a drink at The Fire Station or to ask if you wanted to take a drive up Salt Mountain. Or if he could bring you a chicken dinner. Despite everything you would go, and you'd pray to God he was going to take your head in his hands and kiss you hard like that, even if it meant another few months of complete agony, he was the kind of guy it was worth it for.

"I don't usually do this," he said.

"Do what?" she asked, "seduce women with chicken?" She grimaced, of course he was not the kind of guy to need to use anything to seduce anyone. She'd seen him at the bar, he could just walk in and seduce seven girls. He could burp and someone would fall head over heels for him.

"Get involved with friends."

"OK," she said cautiously. They had never exactly been friends, and they were hardly involved.

"I'm not like, a relationship guy," he said.

She nodded, that much was obvious.

"All this stuff with Ro…" he ran his hands down his face, stopping to rub a patch of stubble on his cheek.

"Yeah…" Peggy said, stomach dropping to the floor. He was breaking up with her already and they had only had one kiss. The best kiss of her life, but still. It hardly seemed fair.

"I don't make a great boyfriend, and you seem like the kind of girl that deserves a great boyfriend."

Peggy nodded awkwardly as she tried to get her head around the fact that he had come into her house, brought chicken and kissed her like that and was now giving her the 'I don't make a great boyfriend' line.

"But you know what," he said, putting his hands gently on her shoulders and running them up through her hair to the sides of her face, "fuck it." And he held her face in his hands and he kissed her, softly at first, then harder, then softly again, then he kissed her again and again until both their faces hurt.

"Can you do me a favor?" he asked as they hurriedly picked chicken legs off the floor before Janet got home. "Let's not be too obvious at school."

Memories of conversations she'd had with Big Mick came back to haunt her. Big Mick had said they couldn't talk to each other at school but would still be able to see her after. He had been embarrassed to be seen with her, and so was Sammy. Of course he would be, he had girls like Rochelle and Leigh hanging all over him, what would it look like if he was with Peggy? Her face fell.

"No," he said grabbing her hand and entwining his fingers with hers. "Only because of Rochelle. She's crazy. You don't even *know* how crazy. She'll make your life a living hell, and mine. Just give me time to talk to her before we go… public."

Peggy nodded. Maybe it was a lie, maybe it was true. As long as she got to kiss him again, she didn't even care right now.

"I'll see you at school," he said.

"I'm going away this week. Damn, I totally forgot."

"Canada?" he asked giving her a look.

"Home," she said not wanting to lie again. "I have to tie up some loose ends."

"Give me your number and I'll call you."

"I don't really know where I'm going to be," she said.

"I thought you said you'd be home?"

"I don't know where I'll be staying. It's kind of complicated."

"So, call *me*," he leaned in close and ran his hand down her hair.

"I might not be able to, it's pretty far out near where I'm from, we don't really have good connections."

"So, send me a postcard." He put the bucket of chicken into the trash and walked himself to the door.

"I'll try." She smiled as she opened the door for him. He grabbed her hand and quickly kissed it before walking towards the Firebird, getting in and speeding off down the street. She wished he'd drive a bit more carefully, but apart from that there was nothing she would change about him.

And when she walked back into the house, she knew nothing would ever be the same again.

TWENTY-NINE

The Stables

———————————

Magz handed Jack the retro looking box of Twinkies with the December '83 expiration date marked on the side as they sat in the sun filled quadrangle during their free period. She was holding her copy of *The Nuns of Santolsa*.

Jack looked at her, looked at the box and her book and frowned.

"Try one," she suggested.

He opened the box and pulled one out. He inspected it carefully.

Magz grabbed one of the yellow cakes out of the box, opened the wrapper and took a bite. "Mmmmm, Twinkie delicious!"

Jack lowered his eyes at her and watched her eat the whole thing. He opened the packet and sniffed it. He licked it with his tongue and squeezed it a little with his fingers.

Magz gave him a smug look.

"Come on Magz," he said through a mouthful of Twinkie, "you know these things have a serious shelf life."

"Thirty-three *years* serious?"

Jack kept eating, and when he was done, he ate another one.

"So, do you believe me now?" she asked.

Jack shrugged.

"It's all in this book," she said, pressing the small book into his warm popcorn scented chest. "It's about this group of nuns who kept turning up all over the place in different periods of history. They didn't know whether they were Saints or witches, but I think they were *time travelers!*"

"Sure Magz, I'll uh, give it a read," he said, noncommittally taking the small book from her.

"A night at The Stables. Come on Magz, you owe me. I'll even pay for my own drinks. *Some* of my own drinks."

"I really just want to get back," she said as they walked through the quad together later that day. The tall trees were casting some shade that wasn't readily available in the quad in 1983.

"Are you really going to do that?" he asked, folding his arms.

"Do what?" Magz had no idea what his problem was. She'd proven time travel was real, she'd told him that she was in love with someone in back in 1983, what more did he want from her?

"Just screw me over and say you have to get back?" Jack made air quotes around the word "back".

"I don't want to *be* here Jack."

"You can be such a jerk," he said.

"Why are you being so mean?" she asked, feeling her eyes well up. She didn't want it to be like this. But it *was* like this. Her life was in the eighties now, and what did that have to do with Jack? Nothing. Best just to say goodbye and move on.

"Because you're leaving me here, alone in this hell hole. I've still gotta get through to graduation, do you know how hard that's going to be without you? I mean, god Magz, imagine if it was you. If *you* were staying and I was off on some magical adventure. Would *you* want to deal with Mindy and Jim all alone?"

"No," she said. She couldn't even begin to imagine what it would be like if Jack had left her here all alone.

"You don't even know what's been going on," he said.

"What's been going on?" she asked, pissed at herself for not even asking him before this. She really was a jerk sometimes.

"Jim's off the team."

"What? How did that happen?"

"Mrs. Willis saw him throw me against the lockers. He's in deep. He's lying low, for now. But God knows how long that'll be for."

"Wow. Sorry."

"Just spare a thought for those you leave behind. Stop being a jerk and come to The Stables with me."

She nodded. A night out with her best friend, a few drinks and a bit of dancing was hardly going to kill her.

The taxi pulled up to the curb. "It's an extra five bucks for making me drive so far out of town," the taxi driver said.

"No way," said Magz.

Jack raised his eyebrows. "Magz, are you actually being feisty?"

"No, I'm just not paying for something so stupid. We always get a taxi here and we never have to pay an extra five bucks."

"You are seriously being feisty."

"Jack, I'm not being feisty, I'm just not paying!" Her

skin-tight acid wash denim jeans slid across the leather seat and she slammed the door behind her.

"Sorry man," Jack said as he handed over five bucks, "you did us a favor, so thanks."

The driver yanked the note out of Jack's hand. "Call me for a ride home," he said, replacing the note with his card. Jack made a gun with his thumb and index finger and clicked at the guy with a smile.

"Come on," Magz said, ignoring the exchange.

"It's still really early, what's the hurry? Are you so keen to get our last drink over with?"

"No," she said grumpily, and then looking him up and down her tone changed. "You look nice tonight, different."

Jack laughed. "Why, thank you so much Margaret," he said as he twirled around showing off his new vintage black button up shirt and old faded black jeans. All black was a good choice in a biker bar. "You look good too," he said.

Magz was looking older than usual dressed in a *Whitesnake* tank top, jeans and her black velvet heels. Her hair was out and big, and she looked like a total rock chic.

The Stables bar was not fancy. It was quite literally a bunch of old stables converted into a bar, and not all that much converted.

"Why are all the best bars always converted from something else?" Magz asked as they sat down with their bottles of Bud at an old wooden table covered with drink rings and other stains Magz didn't care to know too much about. At least one was blood. Or sauce. Probably blood.

"Dunno," Jack said, taking a swig and instantly feeling better. "What would the coolest bar converted from something else be?"

"A church?" shrugged Magz.

"Boring, what about a cave?"

"Boring, what about a library? There could be books everywhere, you could drink and read trashy novels all night!"

"No one wants to do that Magz."

"I do!"

"No, you don't, you have like two drinks then you just get stupid and want to dance."

"You think I'm stupid?" she asked pouting.

"Yes. Absolutely. But not yet, you need another few drinks."

"Is this really going to be our last drink Jack?" Magz asked sadly. She couldn't wait to get back to the past, but she couldn't imagine never doing this again.

"You tell me," he said.

"I hope not."

"I didn't want to say this earlier in case you decided not to come but…" Jack took another swig.

"But what?" Magz asked, roughing up the back of her hair, she wondered if it was too big for this century.

"Is my hair too big?" she asked.

"No. It suits you."

"You sure?"

"Yes, can I finish what I was going to say?"

"Sorry, go ahead."

"Hey kids," said the waitress who had just walked over to their table. Her long dark hair hung over her huge boobs and they weren't really all that covered up and her shorts were way too short. Magz looked down at the table.

"What's good?" asked Jack staring up at the waitress.

"You guys want a couple tequilas over here? We've got a special," she suggested.

"No," said Magz at the same time Jack said "Yes." The waitress winked at Jack and strutted back to the bar.

"You *so* looked at her boobs!" Magz accused, pointing her beer bottle at him.

"They were *massive*! How could I not look?"

"Uh, because you are gay," Magz said.

"You're straight and you looked at them."

Magz shrugged. He had a point.

"Anyway, as I was saying…" Jack continued.

"That guy over there, do we know him?" Magz asked as she gestured to an older man with long greasy grey hair standing near the pool table. He looked over at Magz and grinned, a gold tooth catching the light.

"Don't think so," Jack said, "could be one of the regulars we talked to last time."

"Yeah, must be…" she said as she shook her head and looked back over at Jack who was… looking at the waitress. "You are actually looking at her," Magz said.

"I just don't know how she walks around with those things."

Magz rolled her eyes.

"Tequilas," the waitress said, putting the shots in front of them a few minutes later with some salt and lemons. Magz gritted her teeth. She hated tequila.

"You need to do them now, so I can take this stuff back to the bar."

Jack licked his hand like a cat, poured the salt and passed it to Magz. "We only just got here and we're doing shots," she said. "This can only end badly." She licked her own hand and poured the salt, getting it everywhere.

"One, two, three, go!" said Jack as he licked, sipped and sucked the lemon. Magz was a little behind but she completed the process, only feeling a little bit like she needed to vomit.

They ordered some beers to wash it down and the waitress took the stuff back.

"I was going to say," said Jack.

"What?" Magz asked, wiping her hand on her jeans and brushing salt off the table.

"No," he said.

"No what?"

"No, I don't think this is going to be our last drink."

Soon Magz was on the dance floor with two middle-aged women with perms and a middle-aged drunk biker with a balding ponytail. Jack was standing to the side with a beer in hand watching.

"I love this song!" Magz shouted to Jack. "Come dance with me!" She dragged him onto the dance floor, singing loudly and off-key as she tried to slow dance with him.

"How'd you get so wasted already?" Jack asked, trying to keep her upright.

"Tequilas. Tequilas! Bring us tequilas!" she shouted towards the bar. She kept singing along and started acting out the lyrics, running her hands up and down Jack's arms when the lyrics mentioned arms. He pulled away laughing. She grabbed Jack's beer to use as a microphone, leaning in close to him, trying to get him to sing into the beer with her.

"Lucky Sammy Ruthven isn't here to see you like this," Jack shouted over the music.

"Don't shout about Sammy Ruthven!" Magz shouted. "It's a secret! Shhhhhhh!" Magz put her finger to his lip. "I need to pee." And she stumbled off into the ladies' room with his drink.

"Cute girl," said an older guy with greasy grey hair slithering across the dancefloor straight towards Jack. He was the same guy Magz had asked about earlier.

"She's not mine," Jack said.

"Sucks to be you then man," he said looking at Jack a bit too closely for comfort.

"Tell me about it." Jack took a swig of his warm beer and a slight step back.

"She reminds me of someone," he said looking Jack up and down.

"Oh yeah?" asked Jack looking around the bar. He needed another beer.

"Yeah, a girl I knew a long time ago."

"Uh huh." Jack didn't care for this sad story from the past, love lost all that sappy crap.

"I mean she *really* looks like her."

"I don't think you know her dude. We used to come here sometimes though, so you've probably seen us around."

The man kept staring at Jack. He had these dark eyes that were kind of intense, like he'd probably killed someone.

"When I said she's not my girl, I meant, she's not my girl, *yet*. So, like, back off… or whatever." Jack did not want to get into a bar fight. Not with this guy, not with anyone in this place. Big Mick and Jim were one thing, but these guys had knives, and guns. Jack did not need to get stabbed or shot, but he also didn't like this guy.

"If I wanted her, I'd have her," the man said, grinning and showing off a creepy gold tooth,

and with a force he didn't know he was capable of, Jack punched him in the face. But the guy didn't go down, he barely flinched, and then he began laughing. "What's with you guys?" he said, wiping a little blood from his lip.

"Don't move!" yelled the waitress.

Jack threw his hands up, finding himself suddenly looking into the barrel of a shot gun. "Get outta here," the waitress said.

"Isn't this a bit extreme?" Jack asked, trying not to wet himself.

"Come on Jayne," said the man. "He didn't mean any harm. He couldn't *do* any harm," he laughed.

"You know the rules," she said. "No brawling, and this is brawling."

"He threw a punch and I didn't even touch the kid!" the man said.

"You? *You* threw a punch at *Jonas?*" the waitress asked, looking at Jack with a mix of surprise and respect.

"He was being a dick," said Jack, looking at his hand which was already swollen, and really, really sore.

"You still have to leave," she said, shrugging. "Both of you."

"Sure thing babe," said Jonas as he began shuffling his boots across the wooden floor.

"I gotta get my… friend," Jack said, pointing towards the toilets.

"I'll get her," the waitress said. "I'm Jayne by the way." Why was she introducing herself while she was still holding a gun in his face?

"Jack," said Jack.

"Hi Jack," she said, finally lowering the shotgun.

"Hi," he said.

Jonas grabbed his jacket and headed out the door barging past Jack and giving him a creepy golden smile on the way past.

"That was pretty cool," said Jayne.

"What was? Almost getting shot and getting kicked out of my favorite bar?"

"*This* is your favorite bar?" laughed Jayne.

"It used to be. Before I nearly got shot here."

"It's not loaded you nerd." She yanked on the gun and aimed a shot at the floor.

"Jesus!" he said, jumping out of his skin.

"And I meant throwing a punch at Jonas was pretty cool, he's kind of a tough guy."

"I hardly even scratched him."

"Can we get some more tequilas?" Magz asked the waitress as she drunkenly returned to the dance floor.

"I think you guys are going home," said Jayne.

"Going home? It's too early, we just got here," Magz said holding onto Jack's arm to steady herself.

"We gotta go, I got kicked out," Jack said.

"Jack, why does she have a gun?" Magz's eyes went wide.

"It's not loaded," Jayne said rolling her eyes.

"I got in a fight, but don't worry, he didn't hit me back."

"You hit someone? Who did you hit? What's wrong with you Jack?" Magz whined. She just wanted another tequila and some more bad music to dance to.

"This guy, he was talking about you, so I hit him."

"What guy?" she asked.

"That guy that you said looked familiar a few tequilas ago."

"What did he say about me?"

"Doesn't matter," Jack said.

"Jonas is all talk," said Jayne.

"What did you just say?" Magz asked her.

"He's all talk."

"Who is?" asked Magz.

"Jonas," said Jayne.

"Jonas? Oh no," said Magz. "*That's* where I knew him from."

"Who is this *Jonas*?" asked Jack, looking into Magz's unsteady gaze.

"I'll tell you later," said Magz, unable to work out if the

world was spinning because she was drunk or because she'd just created some kind of time paradox.

"Hey Jack," said Jayne.

"Yes Jayne?" he asked, trying to keep hold of Magz and himself.

"Can I call you sometime?" she asked casually.

Magz began to laugh. "She wants to call you!"

"What's so funny about that?" Jack asked.

"It's so cute, but he's *gay*!" Magz said.

"Oh, right," said the waitress. "Well, whatever, you guys need to get out of here." She walked off, shotgun in hand, back to the bar.

"She liked you!" Magz said, grabbing his hand and leading him out the door.

"Jeez, Magz!" Jack shrugged off her hand as soon as they were outside.

"What?" she asked innocently.

"You don't have to announce that… like that."

"I thought you were out? I didn't think it was a big deal."

"Well, maybe I'm *not* out, and maybe it *is* a big deal," Jack said.

"It's not like you were going to *call* her," Magz said defensively.

"It's nice to be asked, when was the last time a girl wanted my number?"

Magz couldn't think of any time a girl had wanted his number.

"Exactly," said Jack. "Now who the hell is this Jonas guy?"

"He's a guy Sammy punched out saving me the other night in 1983."

"You've got to be kidding me," said Jack rolling his eyes.

"Only Sammy knocked him out cold."

"Of course he did."

"He knocked out his tooth." Magz added.

"Well, now he has a gold one, all thanks to Sammy, and not even a light bruising thanks to me." Jack looked down at his hand that *was* going to have a bruising.

"Hey," she said, flinging her arms around his neck. "Sammy's like, the guy I want, you are like, the guy I have."

"What the hell is that supposed to mean?" Jack asked, shoving his hands in his pockets and pushing her off him.

"You are my best friend, nothing is going to change that."

"We can't be best friends any more Magz, you're going away, and it sounds like where you wanna go we can't even call each other, or text or email. Nothing. You won't exist to me."

"Wow, that's harsh," she said sobering up a little.

"Well what did you think was going to happen?"

"Maybe when I'm older, I'll come find you. Like the old me will come hang out with you and watch movies and stuff."

"Cool, I can hang out with the fifty-year-old version of you. Sounds amazing."

"I'll still be *me*," she said, nuzzling her head into his shoulder.

He took his phone out of his pocket and called the taxi.

THIRTY

Google

"Two stops," Jack said to the taxi driver as they slid into the back seats of the car.

"One stop," Magz said.

"Two," said Jack.

"Don't be stupid," said Magz. "It's one stop."

"No, it's *two*," Jack said, finally giving the taxi driver his address, demanding he be taken home first.

"Just stay at my place, I don't want to be alone tonight," Magz said.

"Jeez Magz, it's always about you, and you not wanting to be alone, what about what *I* want?"

"What *do* you want?"

"Maybe I don't want to be alone either," said Jack.

"Stay at my place and you won't be."

He didn't answer her, he just stared out the window into the dark desert night. He wanted to rip her off like a Band-Aid. Feel the pain once, feel it now, just stop being her friend right here and now so that when she left for good, he'd already have started to get over it. He was just lying to himself. He'd probably never be over it. She was his best friend. The one real friend he'd had since he was a kid.

"One stop," Magz said and Jack didn't stop her when she told the driver her address.

Jack resigned himself to another night on Magz's couch, getting paid in taxi fares and drinks to be her confidant.

Walking into her house he kicked off his shoes and threw himself on the couch. "Are you happy now?" he asked.

"I'll be happier if you came to sleep upstairs." Magz didn't know what it was but she felt a little excitement inside of her at the idea of having him in her bed. She silently admonished herself, it had never been exciting to have Jack close to her, it had just always been normal and nice, but tonight felt different somehow. Jack seemed different. She blamed the tequila.

Jack sighed, got up and walked up the stairs. He unbuttoned his shirt lazily and Magz looked away. She heard his jeans drop to the floor and the bed move under him. She switched on the fairy lights and switched off the main light and pulled her own pajamas from under her pillow before taking them to her en-suite to change and wash her face. When she returned, Jack was a drunken snoring mess. His mouth wide open, arms and legs spread out all over the bed. She tried at first to gently move him, then, giving him a big shove, he rolled over and began snoring again.

Alcohol was not Magz's friend on this particular evening, so it was a pretty stupid thing to do grabbing her phone out of her purse and tapping on the browser. She knew she wasn't meant to do it, but a couple of beers, a bunch of tequilas and a fight with Jack later all she could do was go to Google.

Google

"Sammy Ruthven"

She scrolled through numerous results which seemed to be of no relevance.

Google

"Sammy Ruthven, Santolsa"

Her finger wavered over the search button for a moment. Her heart thudding wildly.

"Fuck it", she whispered and hit it.

Sammy Ruthven, 18, student at St Christopher's High School was found dead in the early hours of Saturday Morning. His car was located by Police after it hit a tree at speed on the highway heading South. Police suspect he was driving under the influence on his way home from the Senior Prom...

There was no air.

She could not breathe.

She could not move.

... students from St Christopher's said Sammy was a great guy, always looking out for others.

Looking out for others. She thought of the night he had punched someone out for her, without even knowing her.

Magz tried to get air, heaving it into her lungs, silently screaming before the sobs took over.

Jack woke up immediately and reached over to comfort her.

"What is it?" he asked her softly, all the anger and resentment from earlier in the night gone.

"Sammy's dead," she whispered through heart wrenching sobs.

"Huh?"

She held the phone in her shaking hands and looked at him with terror in her eyes.

"Dead," she said again.

"Maybe it's a mistake," he said, holding her as he read the article off her phone.

She stared at the fairy lights above the window, motionless.

"Magz, this article is from 1983."

"That's where I've been remember? The Twinkies?"

"Oh sure, sure, the time travel thing."

"How can I explain this to you when you don't even believe me?" She made a fist and punched the back of his shoulder while he held her.

"Let's pretend for a minute I *do* believe you and I'm not saying I do, I mean the Twinkie thing was pretty convincing, but you have to admit it's all a bit freaking nuts Magz. But let's say it *is* real... why can't you just change it? Stop it happening?"

"Stop him dying?" she asked, pulling away and looking at his face in the soft twinkling light.

"Sure, if you *can* time travel you can stop it."

"Maybe you're right," she said through her sobs.

He held her a little while longer and soon the two of them were holding each other under the covers, Magz crying herself to sleep and Jack holding onto her tight as he could until they both fell asleep.

THIRTY-ONE

Nightmare

Peggy ran towards the flaming vehicle. She had no sense of time or space, all she knew was that the boy she loved was burning up inside. She sank to her knees in the middle of the highway, completely unaware of cars speeding towards her from the direction he had been heading. A direction towards a destination he would never get to.

She tried to scream but there was no sound. The heat enveloped her, smoke engulfing her lungs as she struggled to her feet. Her vintage heels abandoned on the road as she began running towards him again, oblivious to the burning and bleeding of her feet on the asphalt. She could run no longer. She was held in place by arms. Arms of people who didn't know anything about her, or about him, or about what this meant.

She tried screaming again and a blood-curdling scream rose from her throat, loud enough to wake the dead. But it didn't. It couldn't.

Destiny.

Destiny had a course of its own and it was stronger than the will of any man, woman, or teenage girl.

Kicking and elbowing with an inhuman strength she never knew she had, she managed to break free and she ran. She ran faster than she had ever run in her life.

And she thought she saw his face in the window for just an instant. His once sexy, calm and cool face was full of fear. He mouthed words as he looked into her eyes. She didn't know what he said. What did he say? What were the words? She needed those words more than the air she was breathing. She was stopped again, the arms around her once more, stopping her. She kicked her legs into the air, struggling. And then she dropped like a brick as flames licked the window, licking his beautiful face and then he was gone.

THIRTY-TWO

The Book II
────────────────

Jack woke up early, just as the sunlight began to stream through the gaps between the curtains and the window. Magz was slumped over her desk asleep. The small work light was still on, lighting up her chestnut hair like a halo. His face fell as he remembered the night before. Her sobs had woken him shortly after he'd passed out, and when she'd told him Sammy Ruthven was dead, he didn't know what to think. Sammy Ruthven was a character from a world that he knew nothing about. A world that Magz was convinced was real. The Twinkies had been interesting, and the thing with that Jonas guy at the bar was kind of weird, but time travel?

He pulled on his jeans and buttoned up his shirt before waking her with a gentle nudge on her shoulder.

She lifted her head and wiped some drool from the side of her mouth.

"Sorry, I didn't want to wake you, but you'll get a stiff neck sleeping like that."

Magz nodded sleepily, her red eyes lifeless. She slunk back into the bed and under the covers.

"It's going to be OK," he said, although he didn't really know why he said it. It was just what you said, wasn't it?

"Nothing will ever be OK again," she replied, lowering her head slowly onto the tequila tear stained pillow.

"We can get through this." Whatever this was. "I promise."

She made a soft groaning noise in response.

Jack was about to turn out the light when he saw what she had been looking at. The 1983 yearbook open to a page of portraits. She had drawn a heart around Sammy Ruthven with a pink pen, she was such a dork. He didn't really want to admit it, but the guy was OK looking, Jack couldn't deny that.

He also couldn't deny the picture on the opposite page. Her name was Peggy Martin and she looked a hell of a lot like a girl Jack knew called Magz Martin. She was even wearing the triangle earrings he'd bought for her.

Jack looked over at her asleep beneath the spotty covers.

He turned off the light, took the book and went downstairs to make coffee.

THIRTY-THREE

Making Plans for Sammy

Peggy ran through the hallway, skidding to a stop in front of the English classroom. She peered through the glass window to see Janet, young Janet dressed in a bright yellow skirt suit writing in her scrawling handwriting on the chalk board for a class of Juniors. Peggy rolled her eyes, the one time she really needed her, Janet was teaching.

She knocked on the door and opened it slowly. All heads turning towards her she felt her face growing warm.

"Yes Peggy?" asked Janet, looking over from the board.

"I really need to speak to you." Peggy's heart jumped into her throat at the thought of what she was going to say.

Janet put down her chalk and walked towards her. "Continue questions one to six," she said, waving her hand at the class and following Peggy outside, closing the door behind her.

"What is it?" Janet asked, her face full of worry.

"He's dead," Peggy said as tears slid down her cheeks. She wasn't even crying, tears were just coming on their own now.

"Who?" asked Janet, putting her hands on Peggy's shoulders.

"Sammy."

Janet gasped. "What happened?"

"A car accident," Peggy said through her tears.

"When?"

"The night of the prom."

"Prom? Prom is months away." Janet shook her head in confusion.

"He's *going* to die."

Janet took a step backwards and leant up against the door behind her. She looked both ways down the corridor and then up to the ceiling. "We can't talk about this here."

Peggy looked at her pleadingly. She needed Janet to tell her what to do, to tell her how to fix it. To tell her everything was going to be OK. Now. Not at three-fifteen.

Janet made a waiting gesture and headed back into the classroom, leaving Peggy to stand alone, her face wet with tears, her heart breaking. Two nuns walked past without even glancing at her. Weren't nuns meant to care about other people? Wasn't it their job to come and ask you if you were OK, come and pray over you or something? But they didn't even look. She wanted to scream after them, "Sammy's going to die, don't you even care?!" but she didn't. She just stood there.

"Here," Janet said, handing over her car keys.

Peggy looked up.

"Take the car home," Janet said, putting her hand on Peggy's shaking shoulder. "Go take a shower, I'll get a ride and I'll try to be home early as I can."

Peggy frowned, "Are you sure? Because I don't even have a license here."

Janet tutted. "But you can drive, right?"

"I *have* a license, it's just too current."

"It'll be fine. Just go out the back way, past the book room so the nuns don't see you." Janet's confidence convinced her, and before too long Peggy was hauling her duffel bag and backpack through the rear of the school grounds.

Peggy noticed cigarette smoke curling up into the clear blue sky behind one of the trees and heard giggling.

"Shhhh!" said a male voice.

"Why?" asked a familiar girl's voice. "No one ever comes out here."

Lacey.

"What if someone *did*?" asked the boy. Obviously, he was crapping himself. Lacey should've been in Math and he was clearly meant to be somewhere else too.

"Lacey?" Peggy whispered, not wanting to get too close to whatever was going on behind that tree.

"Oh hell!" the boy panicked.

"Peg?" Lacey jumped up from behind the tree and beamed. "What are you doing here? I thought you were going back to Canada?"

"Yeah, well I'm back. I'm back from Canada."

"Oh cool," Lacey looked back at the tree. "It's OK, it's just my friend Peggy." She rolled her eyes at the tree and a boy stepped out from behind it sheepishly.

"Hi," said a cute, buff tanned boy.

"You can go now Bruce," said Lacey, waving him off as if he'd just finished his shift at Super Pan.

"Can I call you?" he asked all puppy dog eyed.

"Oh my god, you're so cute!" Lacey said giggling.

He looked at Peggy who gave him a pitying look and then walked off, hands in his pocket, dragging his feet.

"So, what's going on?" Lacey asked, leaning against the tree, as if the whole thing with Bruce had never happened.

"I'm going home," said Peggy.

"Home? It's not home time Peg."

"I'm not feeling so good."

Lacey looked at her suspiciously.

"I had some bad news and I really just need to be alone."

"If you had bad news you need a friend. I'll come home with you. We can get a test on the way." Lacey grabbed her bag from the ground.

"A test?" asked Peggy.

Lacey gave her a look.

"I'm not pregnant!" Peggy said as she began to walk towards the parking lot, Lacey trailing behind.

"Oh, what else could it be?"

"Me and Sammy, we haven't even..."

"Are you for real?" Lacey asked, skipping to catch up with her.

"I've had bad experiences and I'm not ready," Peggy shrugged.

"Oh girl, we've all had bad experiences, but if you never did anything because of 'bad experiences' you might as well just stay at home the whole time."

"I wouldn't mind that."

"So, if you're not pregnant what is it?"

Peggy looked around the deserted school lot. "The truth is," she said, "I'm from the future."

Lacey looked at her blankly.

"I came here from the year 2016."

Lacey said nothing.

"And I just found out something about Sammy's future and it's not good."

"Oh," said Lacey.

"Feel free to freak out now," Peggy said.

"Why would I freak out?" asked Lacey.

"Because this is nuts."

"Actually, it explains a lot," Lacey said nodding.

"Wow, I really didn't expect that to go so well," said Peggy.

Lacey shrugged.

"I need your help," Peggy said.

"Help? Help with what?" asked Lacey.

"Help with changing the future."

"So, like, can you *Google* me?" Lacey asked, lying on the fluffy white rug smoking a cigarette, her head partly under the glass coffee table.

"I can, but I'm not going to, not after this." Peggy put her mug down on top of a coaster over Lacey's face.

"Oh please. I want to know what happens to me."

"Why?" Peggy folded her feet up under herself on the couch. "So, I can work out how to save your life too?"

"You think I'm dead?" Lacey asked, frowning and blowing smoke out from under the table.

"Can we just deal with one future death at a time?" Peggy picked the mug up again, she needed something in her hands.

"I hate to break it to you," Lacey said as she crawled out from under the table and sat facing Peggy exhaling more smoke. "But we all have a future death to deal with."

"That's not helping," said Peggy.

"OK, so we need to devise a plan," Lacey said, putting her cigarette out in the dolphin ashtray.

The front door opened, and Janet rushed in. "I got home as early as I could," she called out.

Peggy looked at her wrist forgetting again that her watch was gone.

"Two fifteen," said Lacey, who hadn't appeared to have looked at her watch at all.

"Oh, hi Lacey," Janet said, kicking her shoes into the middle of the living room floor and throwing herself onto a red lounge chair.

"Hi Miss B," said Lacey, "we were just devising a plan."

Janet looked exhausted. "A plan huh? Lacey, shouldn't you still be in class?"

Lacey shrugged.

"Can it even be done?" Peggy asked, taking a small sip of the cold tea in her hands.

Janet shrugged. "I never went back to the present, so I don't know."

"Back to the present?" asked Lacey.

Janet looked at Lacey blankly and then her eyes grew wide as she realized what she'd just done.

"Your secret is safe with me Miss B," Lacey said.

"Lacey, please don't take this the wrong way," began Janet, "but you do have a reputation for knowing all the gossip at St C's."

"Exactly, the *gossip*," said Lacey. "Gossip is when you know who likes who, or who made out with who under the bleachers. Gossip isn't like, about who's a time traveler. Who the hell is going to believe that crap anyway? Oh, hey guys, guess what? Miss Bates is a frickin' time traveler! Do you think so? Really? That would seriously mess up my cred."

Janet shrugged. She was too tired to worry about Lacey right now. "I don't know how much you can change or if you can even change anything," she sighed.

"I don't believe that for a second," said Lacey.

"You don't believe in destiny?" Peggy asked, looking up from her cup.

"No, that sounds stupid. What, I have no control over my life?" Lacey ran her fingers furiously through her hair.

"What do you think Janet?" asked Peggy. "I mean what do you *really* think?"

Janet shrugged. "I'd *like* to believe in destiny, that everything happens for a reason, but there are so many messed up things that happen to people, I just don't know if there can ever be a reason for some things."

Lacey nodded in agreement.

"What do you think Peggy?" Janet asked, tucking her feet up onto the chair under her.

"I believe in destiny," Peggy said. "Even though a lot of crappy things have happened to me, like being bullied and everything at school and my folks never being around. If I was having fun at school, I wouldn't be here right now. If I wasn't so damn sad all the time would Old Janet have given me the key?"

Young Janet looked thoughtful. "So then how do you explain this thing with Sammy? If you believe in destiny, then you have to accept it, and you certainly can't change it."

"I do believe in destiny. But I also know I have to change it," Peggy said, looking into her empty mug.

"That makes no sense at all Peg," said Lacey reaching for her packet of cigarettes and offering Janet one.

"You can't have it both ways," Janet said, taking the cigarette. "If this is *his* destiny you can't change it."

"But what if..." began Peggy, putting down the mug again. "What if it's my destiny to *change* destiny? What if I was *supposed* to come here and save him?"

"Major woah," said Lacey. "I totally just got goosepimples. That's super romantic."

"OK," said Janet, "if that's what we're doing, how are we going to do it?"

Peggy shrugged. "That's the bit I don't know about it."

"It's easy," said Lacey.

"Easy?" asked Peggy. "You think it's easy to go around altering people's destinies?"

"Sure," Lacey said. "He dies in the Firebird."

Peggy and Janet both looked at her blankly.

"Uh, hello?" Lacey said.

"What?" asked Peggy. "What's the big plan?"

"It's not like, rocket science," Lacey looked at everyone like they were stupid.

"Just tell us the plan Lacey," said Janet impatiently.

"To stop Sammy dying at the prom, to change his destiny, to make it so that Peggy and Sammy can live happily ever after, all we have to do…"

"Come on Lacey!" said Peggy.

"Is hire a limo."

THIRTY-FOUR

The Confrontation

Magz slipped out of the book room door before school. She stood in the hallway Googling Sammy to see if their decision to get a limo had changed anything. Other students milled around her, laughing and shouting, grabbing their books from lockers and rushing to their classes. She took a couple of pain-killers and washed them down with a swig of warm 1980's 7UP and marched towards Janet's classroom.

"Janet!" she demanded, storming into the empty classroom.

"Yes?" Old Janet replied, peering over her glasses as she sat marking papers at her desk.

Magz thrust her phone in the teacher's face. "Don't you think you could've warned me about this?" tears welled up in her eyes.

"Darn," Old Janet said, rubbing a hand across her forehead.

"Darn? All you can say for yourself is *darn*?"

Janet sighed and lowered her glasses.

"You didn't think to tell me he was *dead*?"

"It's not my place to tell you anything, you know that." Old Janet calmly stood up and walked over to close the door.

"You didn't think I needed to *know* this?" Tears ran down her cheek and Janet took her in her arms. Magz resisted at first, she wriggled and stomped her feet. She was furious. And yet within seconds she found herself falling into the hug and sobbing into the animal print silk shirt covering Old Janet's shoulder.

There was a knock at the door and the they broke apart. Magz stepped back and wiped her face, her make-up as good as ruined.

Jack's face appeared through a crack in the door.

"It's only Jack," Magz said.

"Jack?" Old Janet asked, looking at him suspiciously.

"Hi," he took a step into the room.

"Why are you here?" Old Janet asked him accusingly.

"Uh, I'm here because my best friend is freaking out." He took a few more steps and rested his books on a desk in front of him.

Janet scowled at him, looked back at Magz, and back at Jack again.

"Magz told me about, you know..." he whispered, checking behind him, "everything. I didn't believe her at first, but then I saw the photos."

"Photos?" Janet asked.

"In the yearbook," said Jack. "Peggy Martin's yearbook photo."

"Oh," said Janet.

"So?" demanded Magz, folding her arms against the eighties version of the school shirt.

"So now you know," Janet said coolly.

"Now I know? That's *it*?" Magz felt the tears of frustration burning behind her eyes again.

"I did *tell* you not to try and find anything out. Did you Google him?" asked Janet, fiercely slapping her hands on the wooden desk.

"Yes, I Googled him," Peggy said, wiping under her eyes with a bright pink manicured finger.

"You Googled him," Janet admonished.

"She Googled him," Jack chimed in.

"I knew you would." Janet shook her head in disappointment.

"I'm sorry, I just, I wanted to know. I had to know!"

"And are you happy now that you do know?"

Magz began to cry again.

"Hey!" Jack scowled at the teacher.

"You stay out of this," she said, pointing at him with a chunky-ringed finger.

"Don't take it out on him, it's all my fault!" Magz sobbed hysterically and Jack rushed to her, putting an arm around her.

"Can she change it?" Jack asked firmly.

Magz looked up expectantly.

"Can she stop him from dying?" Jack asked again.

Janet sighed. "Some things can change, some things can't.

"What the hell does that mean?" Jack demanded.

"Fate is flexible, but there are some fixed points. Some things are destined to happen no matter what choices you make."

"Why did you send me there?" Magz sobbed, "only to have me fall in love with someone that was going to *die*?"

A silence fell in the room.

In love.

"Everything happens for a reason," Janet said. The bell rang, and the classroom began to buzz with students who paid no attention to the three of them stood standing there hopeless. "Even if we don't know what it is yet." Janet finished.

"No offence but that kind of sounds like crap," said Jack.

"I just want to get back," Magz said shaking her head.

"Stay for the lesson, we'll talk at break," Mrs. Willis said.

"What for? So you can tell me more lies?" Magz asked.

"Please stay Magz," said Jack. "Just for today?" He picked her books up from the table. It was the last thing she wanted, but her brain was exhausted and all she could do was follow him to their seats.

"Well, look who's back on the planet," said Mindy, looking menacingly at Peggy. "What's wrong with your uniform? Did you get it at a thrift store or something?"

"Shut up Mindy," said Jack.

"*You* shut up," said Jim quietly as he sat down at his usual seat.

Magz rolled her eyes. "Seriously Mindy, what's your damage?" she said.

"*What* did you just say to me?"

"I asked you what your damage was."

Mindy's mouth dropped open.

Magz continued. She didn't care if she got hit or slammed into a locker. She almost, in that moment, with the thought of Sammy's imminent death lingering over her, didn't care if she lived or died. "Just get a life and stop hassling me, I've got way bigger things to worry about than your bad dye job and matching attitude."

"You little bitch!" yelled Mindy coming at her. Magz

didn't move. She didn't flinch. She just looked into the eyes of her attacker and saw nothing scary. Scary was someone you loved dying. Not this. What was Mindy going to do to her in front of the whole class? In front of Old Janet?

"Get to the principal's office *now* Mindy!" shouted Old Janet.

Mindy screamed, punched Peggy's desk and stormed out.

Magz gnawed on her nails while Jack flicked absently through her 1983 yearbook. They were still working on their assignment. Jack had done a swap with her for the 1984 yearbook, but she couldn't open it. All she could do was sit and stare above the blackboard at the crucifix in front of her.

"Trips to the Grand Canyon huh? They'd never take us there now," Jack said.

"If they took us there now you and me would end up at the bottom of it," she said, glancing out the window at the beautiful clear blue sky. "Or Mindy would."

"And Jim," Jack added, still looking down at the book. "Uh, Magz, have you seen this?"

"Have I seen what?" Magz had read the book cover to cover numerous times, she was pretty sure she hadn't missed anything.

He passed the book to her and pointed at a photo of the backs of two students standing close to each other and looking out over the Grand Canyon. Magz had seen the picture before loads of times.

"So, what about it?" she asked.

"Don't you know who that is?" Jack tapped the caption underneath.

'Sammy Ruthven and Peggy Martin look into the abyss.'

Magz gasped.

"This place hasn't changed a bit, has it?" Magz mused, sliding into a booth seat near the window at Dee's Diner later that day. She had wanted to get straight back, but Old Janet wanted to take her out for coffee and Magz was tired and needed coffee, so she said yes.

"Some things change, some things remain the same," Old Janet shrugged.

It was bizarre hanging out with the Old Janet. In so many ways she was exactly the same. She had the same sense of humor, the same clever twinkling green eyes, the same now outdated way of doing her eyeliner.

Magz looked at the layers of grime around the place and wondered if anyone had even cleaned since the eighties. A middle-aged waitress with frizzy hair came over to their table swinging a coffee pot.

"Janet!" the waitress laughed.

"Amy!" Janet stood up and gave the woman a hug.

"Amy, this is Magz, a student of mine, we're just having a chat over lunch about Colleges."

"Hi Magz," Amy wiped her hand on her apron and then shook Magz's hand with it. The woman was vibrant and cheerful and seemed a lot younger than the lines on her face suggested.

The two women chatted for a while, ignoring Magz completely. They laughed and carried on while Magz stared out the window vaguely, slurping on her 7UP.

"That was Amy," Janet whispered when she sat back down.

"I gathered," Magz said.

"Amy *Brown*."

"Is that supposed to mean something?" Magz looked over at the counter to get another look.

"She's in your typing class," Janet sipped her coffee, made a face and added another sugar. "The coffee here is really terrible."

"Typing class?"

"You used to call her Awkward Amy," she said.

"Awkward Amy?" Magz squealed.

"Keep your voice down!" Janet hushed. "Yes, Awkward Amy. She wasn't even that Awkward. It's so stupid how people get these nicknames. We became friends later on when she started dating John Hardcourt."

"Who?"

"The Math teacher."

"O.M.G! Awkward Amy ends up dating the Math teacher?" Magz leaned forward, excited by the gossip. Lacey would have a field day with this.

"They were dating, but not until after school, well pretty much, and they are still together now so it's not like it was sordid."

"Excellent future gossip, thanks Janet."

"Past gossip, it's all in the past. And don't you dare tell anyone at school. Imagine if there were rumors going around about Amy and John, it could ruin his career and her whole life."

They ate silently for a few moments.

"So how do I change this? Is it just as easy as hiring a limo?" Magz asked.

"I don't know," Janet said. "Maybe everything already set in stone and nothing we do makes any difference". She put her coffee cup down and gave Magz a sad look.

"But I can try, right?"

"You can always *try*. Whatever I think about fate, I know you, and I know you'll do whatever it takes to try and change it, I know you will."

Magz nodded. She *had* to change it.

"I love him," Magz said softly.

"Then you try to move heaven and earth."

THIRTY-FIVE

Sammy's House

Sammy's front yard was tidy, but full of car parts. A shell of an orange-red car sat in the driveway next to where Sammy had parked the Firebird and a garden gnome stood next to a bush. Of all the things she expected to see in Sammy Ruthven's front yard, a garden gnome wasn't one of them. He maneuvered himself around the car parts and took Peggy's hand, leading her towards the front porch which looked like the comfiest, cutest front porch in town. A round table covered in old books and magazines sat in front of an old grey leather couch with two large plant pots on either side. Peggy imagined herself happily spending afternoons here pretending to read magazines while watching Sammy work on cars.

But would she ever have the chance to? She felt the nervousness inside her stir up again. It had been there since she found out, since she had Googled him. A knot in her very center which tightened every time she was with him and knotted even harder every time they were apart.

He unlocked the door looking back at her with his

usual cool expression and she felt a little flutter just below her knot.

He ushered her into the small living room of what was very obviously a guy's house. In front of the tiny TV was a coffee table on a brown shag rug, it was covered in papers, car magazines, a Valley FM coffee mug and an ashtray filled with butts in the shape of a heart.

"Sorry about the mess," Sammy said grabbing the ashtray and the mug and leading her towards the kitchen.

"It's OK," she shrugged.

"Drink?" he asked as she followed behind him.

Peggy shrugged again. "If you're having one," she said politely. She felt as if she suddenly needed to be on her best behavior. Even though they had spent every spare moment of every day of the past few weeks together, being in his house was different. Especially when his dad wasn't home yet. The thought that they were alone rested on her like a heavy cloud and she felt nervous and clammy and scared and excited as hell.

"Tea?" he asked.

Peggy laughed. "You drink tea?"

"Don't tell anyone," he said as he began clattering around in the kitchen.

"Tea and a garden gnome," she said, thinking out loud. "Huh?"

"You drink tea, and you have a garden gnome. All this time I had you picked as a bad boy."

"The garden gnome is my dad's and you know I'd prefer something harder to drink, but he'll be home soon." Sammy lit the stove and placed the kettle on the ring.

"How soon?" Peggy asked, much more confidently than she felt.

"Not *that* soon," he said, his eyes searching hers. She

VICTORIA MAXWELL

felt another little fluttering in a place she didn't know could even flutter and she blushed.

Was today the day she was going to go all the way with Sammy Ruthven? They hadn't done much at all really, except for kiss and hold hands and it had all been just perfect. She didn't want to ruin it. She also didn't know how she felt about doing the deed with a guy who was technically old enough to be her dad in the future and who was going to be dead at the end of semester if she couldn't work out how to change destiny. With Big Mick all she'd worried about was how fat her thighs were going to look and if she'd make the right noises.

When Sammy had made the drinks, he led Peggy up the stairs to his room. It was a large attic room and not so different from what Peggy had imagined. A double bed covered in a brown, white and turquoise colored quilt was nestled in under the slant of the roof. Peggy walked straight to the small bookcase and ran her fingers over the classics and a couple of old Sci-fi novels while Sammy attended to a record player on the floor in a corner. He kicked his boots off into the middle of the room and sat cross legged while he looked through a pile of records. Peggy sat down next to him and picked up the ones he'd discarded.

"Oh, please this one," she said smiling, holding up a Lionel Richie album.

"That's not mine, I don't know how it got in here," he said.

"You listen to Lionel Richie," Peggy laughed. "You're such a dark horse."

"Jessie must have been up here playing around," he said shaking his head.

"Who's Jessie?" asked Peggy trying not to sound jealous.

266

"My sister," Sammy said.

"Where is she now?" she asked.

"She goes to a special school in the valley, she's only home every second weekend."

"Oh," Peggy said. "What's…"

"Wrong with her?" Sammy asked.

"I didn't mean it like that," Peggy said, shaking her head.

"She's deaf."

"If she's deaf how can she listen to Lionel Richie?"

Sammy gave her a look.

"Sorry, I didn't mean that how it sounded," Peggy shook her head.

Sammy put the needle down on the Bruce Springsteen record he bought the day she saw him at Ray's. "She puts her head here," he said lying on his side in front of the record player, his ear to the brown carpet. "She feels the vibration, says she feels the music."

Peggy watched as he closed his eyes. He looked so peaceful, so sweet and cute, not the tough, cool, sexy teenager he usually appeared to be. Not like anyone who was going to go out and get drunk and drive into a tree. The knot tightened.

She lay down next to him, her face just inches away from his and she tried to feel the music. He opened his eyes and looked back at her, the corners of his lips raising slightly. He ran his hand up to the scrunchie at the top of her head and gently slid it down through the length of her ponytail, letting her hair fall softly on the carpet. He took her head in his hand and he pulled her in, kissing her softly, in time with the music playing.

"I feel the music," she said dreamily as she pulled away from him slightly.

"Me too," he murmured, his lips searching for hers

again. He put his arm around her and gently rolled her onto her back, leaning over her. They had kissed quite a few times since that first night in the kitchen with the chicken, but it had never been quite like this before. She gasped a little.

"I'll stop," he said, moving back onto his side.

"No," she said, pulling him back on top of her and grinning.

He grinned back and kissed her again.

"What's this?" she asked, reaching up to touch the silver pendant that had escaped from his shirt and was dangling above her chest.

"St Christopher," he said.

"Like at school?" she asked.

He laughed softly, and she could feel it resonate through both of their bodies.

"Like the saint," he said.

"Why do you wear it?" she asked, letting it go and watching it swing above her.

"My mom gave it to me the first day of school," he said, bending down to kiss her forehead, then her nose, then her lips. "Patron saint of the highway," he continued. "We might be the only Catholic family left in Santolsa."

His hands slipped around her waist and he rolled her over, so she was now on top of him. She hitched up her skirt slightly, and then leant over him, kissing his forehead. Kissing his nose. Kissing his lips lightly.

"If you're so Catholic, why aren't you saving yourself for marriage?" she kissed the side of his mouth.

"I'm Catholic, I'm not dead."

She laughed.

"What's this?" he asked, reaching out to touch the silver object which dangled from her own neck.

"It's just an old key." She quickly grabbed at it, feeling

as if all her secrets were about to be revealed, where she's from, what's going to happen to him. Her face fell and he let go.

"What does it open?" he asked.

"Just an old door."

"It kinda looks like the classroom keys at school."

"You just don't miss a thing, do you?" she asked, shaking her head.

"Not usually."

She looked at him, waiting for him to prompt an answer out of her, but he said nothing, he just looked at her patiently.

"Are you going to ask me again?" she asked.

"Nope."

"Why not?"

"Because you don't want to tell me."

"I *want* to tell you, I just can't right now."

He nodded and then rolling her back onto her side he took her face in his strong hands and kissed her, deeply, sweetly.

He slid his hand under her shirt, exploring the skin of her back and the soft undefined area of her body she hated so much, but he didn't seem to mind it, he just kissed her deeper still.

"I want to," she gasped, "but I don't think I'm ready to," her words muffled by his mouth.

He pulled away, smiling sexily. "OK," he said.

"OK?" she asked.

"OK," he said, shrugging.

"I thought you had like, brought me here for that."

"I brought you here because I wanted to hang out with you."

"Oh," Said Peggy, genuinely surprised.

"I don't let just anyone see my house Peg." He fixed up

her shirt and began to run his hand over her back again, now slightly more covered under the yellow cotton of her school shirt.

"And also, Jonas now has a warrant out for one of my teeth, so I'm laying low."

"What's happened?" she asked.

"I have to raise the money to buy him a new tooth or he's going to take one of mine. Literally. He showed me the pliers."

Peggy's mouth dropped open. "How much is the tooth? I have some money saved."

Sammy shook his head. "He wants a *gold* tooth."

She laughed again. "Of course, he does." Visions of Jonas from the future flashed through her mind.

"You'll find the cash, and it'll all be OK", she said.

"I've got a car I've been working on that I can get a good deal on if I take it down to LA. I can pay for the tooth and have a bit to spare."

Peggy nodded thoughtfully, then lifted her shirt slightly, placing his hand back on her goose bumpy flesh. "I liked it, I want to, with you, but just not right now." This conversation could not have been more awkward, she could feel her heart racing and hoped he couldn't feel it through their school shirts, although she was fairly sure he could. She wanted to be with him more than anything, but she was scared to get too close, scared to lose him. Scared that he was going to die, but stupidly, just as scared that he was going to be talking about her in the halls tomorrow, talking about how she was a bad lay or something equally as nasty. But when she looked into his eyes, she couldn't see any nastiness at all. All she saw was the boy who drank tea, had a garden gnome, a deaf sister and no mother around and in no way tried to get girls to have sex with him if they didn't want to.

Peggy was so in love.

"I'm in no hurry Peg, I know I have this reputation for being a bad boy because I smoke and drive fast cars and drink and I've been with women..."

Peg cut him off, "I don't need details."

"I don't think of you like that, you aren't just some girl from the Fire Station to me."

"You mean woman. Those women at the Fire Station are, like, proper women."

"They're girls pretending to be women. You're more of a woman than any of them, Peg." She loved the way he kept calling her Peg.

She laughed. "Thanks, I think."

"I want to ask you something," he began, almost looking nervous.

"Uh, OK."

He gently brushed her hair away from her face. "Will you go to prom with me?" he asked.

Peggy's heart flipped, and she knew he could feel it too.

"It's OK if you don't want to," Sammy said, moving away slightly.

"I do want to, yes! I want to go to prom with you," she grinned. "But there's something I need to tell you about the night of the prom."

"We don't have to do anything at prom, we can even go as friends if you want."

Peggy laughed. "Oh, that's *so* not it."

"So, what is it?"

"I had a dream," she started. How could she tell him the truth? "I had a dream that on the way home from prom you crashed your car into a tree, and you..." a tear escaped and slid down her flushed cheek and before she knew it she was crying again.

Sammy took her into his arms and held her. He didn't

VICTORIA MAXWELL

ask what was wrong, or offer any dumb advice, he just held her until she could talk again.

"You die, you died," she said, wiping her eyes.

"It's just a dream Peg, I'm fine."

"Will you just promise me," she asked him, "I know it sounds crazy, but will you just promise me you won't drive to prom? We'll get a limo and you won't drive?"

Sammy wiped the mascara from her cheeks. "Sure, I promise."

They heard the front door slam shut.

"Wanna meet my dad?" Sammy asked, kissing her softly on the cheek.

"Sure, I guess I've got a lot to live up to though, I mean how many girls have met your dad?"

"Hardly any," he said, pulling her up off the ground. She tucked her shirt in, and they walked down the stairs, bringing their mugs still full of now cold tea, leaving the record playing.

She would have preferred him to say none, but hardly any would do.

"I'm Sam," he said, holding out a grease-covered hand. He was a fit older man, tanned and sweaty, his long shaggy hair greying and in a tangle.

Peggy shook it politely. "Peggy," she smiled.

"I've gone and greased you," he said, his face falling as she looked at the black grease on her palm.

She laughed. "No problem Mr. Ruthven."

"Sam, please."

"Sam," she said.

"Come into the kitchen and clean up," he said, holding out a hand for her to go first. "We call him Sammy

272

because Sam Junior is kind of a mouthful. He's christened Samuel, but we just call him Sammy."

"Dad," Sammy said, shaking his head and smiling at Peggy.

"Sorry Junior," said his dad giving Peggy a wink.

"Can Peggy stay for dinner?" Sammy asked his dad, leaning casually against the kitchen counter.

Peggy's eyebrows shot up, dinner with his dad? Serious. It was serious. *He* was serious. He was serious about *her*. She dried her hands on a tea towel and tried to calm down.

"I was just going to run down to Super Pan for pizza and ribs, is that OK for you Peggy? We don't really do a lot of proper cooking around here."

"Can we get hot wings too?" Peggy asked.

"And garlic bread," his dad said.

"Do you need to call your aunt?" Sammy asked.

"Call?"

"To tell her you won't be home for dinner?"

"Oh, yeah." Peggy shook her head, she wondered if she'd ever get used to life without her phone. "Can I use your phone?" she asked.

"She reminds me of her," Peggy heard his dad say softly to Sammy as she walked back from the bathroom after three slices of pepperoni pizza, six hot wings, two cans of 7UP. She really wasn't feeling that well. The good news was that she was feeling much more comfortable eating in front of Sammy. *Perhaps a little too comfortable* gurgled her stomach.

"She's nothing like her," Sammy said shortly.

"I don't mean the pills. I mean before that, before Jessie. It's the integrity."

"She's got that."

Peggy didn't want to listen, but she couldn't walk back in when they were talking about her.

"She's not like those other girls Sammy."

"Dad, please."

"Sorry son. Just don't screw this up. Good women don't come along that often."

"I'm gonna try not to, but you know I'm not good at this stuff."

"Well you gotta get good and get good fast."

Peggy walked quietly back towards the bathroom and then walked back again towards the kitchen again noisily, so they'd hear her coming.

Sammy looked up from stacking the plates and smiled at her. Not the half smirk, but a real genuine smile. She grinned back.

"I should get you home," he said.

"Yeah, Janet's pretty heavy on her curfew these days."

"It was so nice to meet you," his dad said, shaking her hand, this time greasing it up with pizza grease instead of car grease.

"Thanks Sam. You too."

Sitting outside Janet's house in the Firebird Sammy tapped the wheel with his hands anxiously. "I'm not that good at this," he began.

"What?" asked Peggy.

"Being with someone, not just for fun."

"This isn't fun?" she made a face at him.

"You know what I mean."

"I'm not that great at it either. Jack always says I'm the stupidest person when it comes to love," the word love hung in the air.

"I need to meet this Jack sometime," said Sammy.

"He probably wouldn't like you," she joked. "He'd say I could do better."

"I'm sure you could," said Sammy leaning over to give her a warm, slow, lingering goodnight kiss. "Now go get inside before Janet doesn't like me either."

She walked up to the door. The knot in her stomach fading away as she thought about how perfect the evening had been. She looked back at his car and smiled.

And he waited until she was safe inside before driving away.

THIRTY-SIX

Road Trip

By the time the school trip came around Peggy was completely, hopelessly, head over vintage heels in love. She was living her life on the edge of a cliff. Constantly teetering between feelings of euphoria and terror. She was flying high as a desert eagle one moment and laying crushed and broken like an old cigarette butt the next.

It was late afternoon when Lacey turned off the engine of the Chevette. Peggy couldn't read a paper map, so Tricia had navigated from the back seat. They'd all been up since stupid-o'clock and it was now taking a toll on them.

"This looks horrible," Lacey moaned, looking out at the camp site.

"If they put the middle of nowhere on a map, this is where it'd be," Tricia said.

"Come on," said Peggy, taking it upon herself to be the optimistic one. "It's going to be fun."

Lacey and Tricia rolled their eyes.

But it had to be fun. This may be the only trip Peggy would ever go on with Sammy. She'd tried to focus on just enjoying the present moment, but she was sinking deeper and deeper into despair. Lacey and Janet were sure they would be able to change his future together and there were moments Peggy felt the same. She *had* to change his future. But there were also times she felt there was nothing at all that could be done.

Lacey struggled with her ridiculously big bright red suitcase across the dirt towards the nuns who were checking everyone in. Tricia and Peggy slumped off after her with their duffle bags.

"You girls are in tent sixteen, over by that tree." Sister Constance growled from beneath her habit. Even the nuns were struggling.

Lacey groaned.

Tricia looked as if she was about to murder someone. "I can't imagine Hell being that much worse than this," she said.

Lacey looked as if she was about to cry. Peggy reached an arm around her, but Lacey quickly shrugged it off. "Don't touch me, what if I get sweaty and I need a shower? I can't go shower in *there*." Lacey pointed to a huge crumbling slab of cement with a shower sign out the front.

"It's probably not as bad as it looks." Peggy said.

"It's worse," said Tricia, pointing to their tent. It was half falling down and looked beyond pathetic.

"I don't know anything about tents," Lacey said, shuddering.

"We'll get through this Lace, I promise," Peggy said unconvincingly.

"At least it's not bear season yet," Tricia said.

"Bears?" squealed Lacey.

"Meet at the campfire at six!" yelled out some peppy preppies dressed in shorts and sweaters who had clearly spent their summers at summer camp while Peggy had spent hers at home alone watching old movies and reading old Sweet Valley High books.

The three girls stared down the preppies and then evaluated their tent. Tricia opened the flap slowly, crouched down and went in.

"It's not so bad once you're in," she said, sticking her head out of the flap.

"It smells!" Lacey whined.

"It kind of does. It smells old and moldy," Peggy said.

"I can't do this," Lacey said, flapping her hands and beginning to flip out.

"Yes, you can," Peggy said, grabbing Lacey's hand.

"No, I really can't." Lacey began to cry. She was kind of an ugly crier, which made Peggy want to laugh a little, but instead she put her arms around her. Lacey cried into Peggy's pale pink shirt and Peggy wondered if this was how Jack had felt most of his life being *her* friend.

"Need a little help?" the voice startled them both.

"Hi Sammy," Lacey said, pulling away from her friend, wiping her face with the back of her hand.

Peggy thought Sammy looked like he'd just stepped out of an old movie. His hair was tousled, and he was wearing a faded pair of jeans, a grey t-shirt and an old pair of sneakers. It was weird seeing him in sneakers.

"Hey," Peggy smiled awkwardly at him. They were still being chill around everyone else and so Peggy never really knew how to act around him. Well, she'd never really known how to act around him anyway, but now it was for different reasons.

"Yes, we need help," Lacey said.

"I've got some spare stuff in my car, I'll go get it."

"It's pretty big, all three of you could probably share it,"

Sammy said when he and Ben had finished pumping up the mattress and had covered it with sleeping bags and some of Sammy's own blankets and extra pillows, that smelled very much like Sammy.

"Sammy, you're so sweet I could almost kiss you!" Lacey hugged him.

"You better not," said Peggy under her breath.

"This tent is terrible, who put this up?" he asked as he began taking out the pegs and putting the tent up for them properly.

"How many pillows did you bring?" asked Lacey as she looked at the massive bed all covered in cushions and blankets.

"I like to be comfortable when I go camping," he said, hammering in a peg.

"You mean you like those girls to be comfortable, because Sammy dude, where's all my pillows?" Ben asked.

"We're men Ben, we can sleep on the floor," said Sammy.

"Then why did you bring all this stuff?" asked Ben.

"Shut up," said Sammy.

Lacey giggled.

"Do you go camping a lot?" Peggy asked as Lacey went inside the tent and fell on the bed with Tricia.

"I haven't been for a while, but yeah. Me and my dad used to go all the time when I was a kid and I go out sometimes on my own, just to get away for a while."

When he was finished, the tent looked like something they could almost sleep in for a night.

"Don't tell Rochelle and Leigh that he did that for you," Ben said as Sammy went to help out with a few other tents that were falling down.

"Are they even here yet?" asked Lacey.

"Nah, but when they do, they're gonna be pissed they missed out on the bed stuff," Ben said.

"Maybe they won't show?" Peggy hoped.

"Sammy Ruthven sleeping in a tent just yards away from where Peggy Martin is sleeping, and you think Rochelle is just going to stay home?" asked Tricia, rolling her heavily made up eyes. "I'm sure."

Rochelle, Leigh and Nick still hadn't turned up by sunset and had managed to miss the preppy campfire that was about the worst thing Peggy had endured in a long time. After a dinner of hot dogs cooked by the nuns the preppies had put on a show. They performed an embarrassingly bad skit pretending to be all the teachers and some of the nuns. It was so cringe-worthy, and no one was impressed except a couple of jocks who cheered like total Neanderthals. Peggy guessed some things were always the same. The show was followed by a guy playing camp songs badly on a guitar while June-Belle sang along loudly and off key, and as soon as it seemed like they had stayed long enough for it to be noted that they had been there at all, they left.

"So tomorrow we're going to the Grand Canyon, that's pretty cool," said Ben, shining his flashlight out in front as they were walking back in the direction of their tents.

Peggy thought about the photo in the yearbook. She wondered if she could change the photo. Maybe if she wore something different or stood somewhere else the picture in the yearbook would change.

"I need a drink," said Tricia.

"Should we be worried about Nick and the groupies?" asked Lacey, flicking her flashlight all over the place.

"I'm sure they'll show up when they want to. They've

probably booked into a hotel around here somewhere," said Tricia.

"Why didn't we do that?" moaned Lacey.

"This could be way more fun," suggested Sammy.

"Oh really, how exactly?" asked Lacey.

"I'll show you, come on," he said.

Before too long they were sitting around a small fire that Sammy had made far enough away so that no one would come out looking for them. The sounds of the night were haunting. Nondescript animal noises, rustling, branches snapping. Everything was making Peggy jump. Her nerves were shot as it was, and this was giving her the creeps majorly. All she wanted to do was snuggle up to him and put her head on his shoulder, but he sat on the other side of the fire from her, pretending to be cool and so she followed his lead and did the same. It was kind of dumb, it was only Ben, Lacey and Tricia round the fire, and they all knew exactly what was going on. Peggy didn't want to miss a moment of touching him or being close to him. She didn't have time to be this far away from him. The knot in her stomach lurched just as Ben handed her a bottle of rum. She took a sip and made a face as it burned her throat.

"We should play spin the bottle," laughed Lacey.

"I'll play!" said Ben enthusiastically.

Peggy and Sammy swapped a look.

"No," said Tricia taking the bottle and taking a swig.

"What about truth or dare?" Peggy suggested, feeling like a total dork as soon as it came out of her mouth. As if people like Sammy and Lacey, especially Tricia, would ever play truth or dare.

"I love truth or dare!" Lacey beamed, the fire light making her face look simultaneously creepy and beautiful.

"Who first?" asked Ben.

"OK, OK, someone ask me a question!" Lacey demanded.

"OK," Peggy began, "who at school would you most like to…" Peggy blushed as she remembered that just inches away from her Sammy was sitting cross legged, drinking rum and staring into the fire. The guy at school *she* would most like to… Afraid she'd get the question back at her she changed it. "Who at school would you most like to *be*?"

"Apart from just staying myself, that's easy, you!"

"Me?" Peggy asked, laughing.

"Yeah sure."

"Why the hell would anyone want to be *me*?"

Sammy stifled a laugh.

"Because you're great. You're a breath of fresh air around this place. Seriously. You are so pretty and really nice. Like you're just kind and nice and sometimes I'm not that nice and I wish I was a bit more like you. Pass the rum." She snatched it off Sammy and took a swig.

"Uh, wow, thanks." Peggy had not been expecting that answer.

"OK, my turn to ask someone…" Lacey looked around. "Sammy."

"Yeah?" asked Sammy.

"Did you ever... kill a man?" Lacey asked quite seriously. They all laughed.

"What kind of question is that?" Sammy asked. "Of course I never killed a man."

"Would you *ever* kill a man?" she re-phrased.

"Depends."

"On?"

282

"I'd do it in self-defense, or in defense of someone I cared about, sure I would. Wouldn't we all?"

Shadows cast on Sammy's face made him look older, he was no longer just a high school kid, he was all versions of Sammy. Ageless. All this time she'd been hung up on him being her dad's age, Peggy realized he may never even live to be her dad's age, not in her present, not ever.

"I'd kill Jonas if he ever tries anything like that again," Sammy said, passing the bottle again.

"You can't just *kill* Jonas, Sammy," said Lacey.

"I might have to if I wanna get the eights to stop following me around."

"I hope you're joking," said Ben.

"Of course, I'm joking," he said, but his voice had an edge to it.

"OK, you have to ask someone now," Lacey said.

"Peggy," he said. Her heart beat wildly inside her chest at the sound of her name spoken from his lips.

"Yes?" she asked.

"What do you want to be when you grow up?"

They laughed. This was the corniest game of truth or dare ever.

"I honestly have no idea. I don't really have any special talents or anything. Everyone seems to have skills or interests and I just, I don't really. So, I don't know." She shrugged, feeling kind of like a loser, but she really didn't know how anyone who was in their last year of school could have it all figured out. She wasn't sure she wanted to have it all figured out.

"You make those cute hair ties," Lacey said. "And you definitely have an eye for fashion."

"Oh, the scrunchies? Sure," Peggy laughed, putting her hand to the pink scrunchie holding her half ponytail in place.

"You have to ask Ben now." Lacey waved her hands around.

"Ben," Peggy began, "how come when you're like a jock and everything and super good at sports and stuff... Well, how come you hang out with us?"

Ben's face became serious and Peggy was kind of sorry she'd asked. But she'd been wanting to ask him this for ages.

"It's like this," Ben began reaching for the bottle. He took a swig before he continued. "We just *get* each other."

Tricia nodded, and Sammy looked thoughtfully into the fire.

"And we've all been through something major," added Lacey.

"Oh," said Peggy, wishing she'd asked something else. Something cheesy.

"My dad," said Ben, taking another drink before passing the bottle to Sammy.

"My mom," said Sammy, taking a drink and then passing the bottle to Tricia.

"My sister," said Tricia before taking a drink.

"I've never been through anything major," Peggy mused as she rubbed her arms to get warmer, it was getting cold.

Lacey looked at her in disbelief.

"What?" asked Peggy.

"You're *here*," Lacey gave her a look.

Sammy took off his sweatshirt and passed it to Peggy. The others cheered and laughed, and Sammy rolled his eyes and told them to shut up. Peggy was sure she saw him blush a little, but maybe it was just the fire. Peggy put the sweatshirt on and felt instantly warm and held, as if he was hugging her.

"What are you going to do after school Ben?" Peggy

asked when everyone had stopped making fun of them.

"Hey!" said Lacey, "that's two questions!"

"I dunno," Ben said, staring into the fire. "I just wanna play ball, but I'm seriously messing up. There was a college scout from LA who was interested but I'm not sure they still will be. I'm not sure how I'd get through college anyway."

"You can always come work for me at the garage," Sammy said.

"Oh sure, and stay in Santolsa for the rest of my days? No way Sammy, I'm getting out. You've always said you wanted to get out too."

"Maybe. I dunno," shrugged Sammy. "We might expand. I kind of like the idea of a shop in Santolsa and one in LA where I can work on really hot cars, just go back and forth between the two."

"Sounds really cool," said Peggy, smiling at him across the flames and creating their whole lives together. They'd live in a super cute yellow and white house near the beach. She'd work at a shop selling scrunchies, he'd work on cars and they'd have two kids. A boy and a girl. The boy would be Samuel Ruthven III, and the girl would be Holly. They'd be the cutest family since sliced bread, and all of showbiz for the next thirty years would know their names and come calling whenever they needed some work done on their cars or a scrunchie.

The few sips of alcohol had given her a buzz for just long enough for her to allow herself to think about their future. Because the reality was that Sammy maybe only had four weeks left to live.

"We should get going," said Sammy as he began putting out the fire. "Before the nuns realize we're gone."

"And drunk," said Tricia.

And Lacey handed out sticks of gum.

THIRTY-SEVEN

The Grand Canyon

Peggy stood looking out across the Canyon. Her fear of heights keeping her clammy hands in her jeans pockets and her feet as far from the edge as possible. She'd decided to play her fate changing game. Instead of wearing a plain sweater she was wearing a check shirt. She wanted to wear Sammy's sweatshirt, but she wasn't sure if it would be weird, so she left it under her pillow in the tent instead.

"Come closer! Look down here!" cooed Lacey as she bounded around, her white sneakers turning orange from the dust.

"I'm OK here," Peggy called out as she contemplated the canyon from a safe distance.

"Words can't describe it," said Sammy, standing next to her. Peggy nodded.

"Have you seen it before?" she asked as Ben and Lacey fooled around way too close to the edge, making her very nervous. Peggy had to look away.

"A couple times, once from down inside, it was… crazy," he laughed gently as if remembering some crazy night at the bottom of the canyon with friends and girls and drinks. "You?"

"Once, with my folks."

"It's a long way from Canada," he said. "Or wherever it is you're from," he added with an edge.

"I'm not very good with heights," she said wanting to avoid the topic of where she was from.

She had been here once before when she was a kid. Her dad who was completely ignorant of her fear of heights had made her step out onto the SkyWalk, a glass bottom structure leaning out into the canyon, which in the future was just near to where they were standing now. Magz had screamed as her dad dragged her to the edge telling her not to be so ridiculous, and her mom had to pick her up kicking and screaming and take her back to the car. She'd been hysterically sobbing, and everyone had stared at her.

Peggy took a tiny step back as she remembered standing off the edge, looking down into the abyss, feeling like she was going to fall. Like she was going to die.

"I'm not that good with snakes," he admitted.

"I bet that makes camping in the desert interesting."

"You have no idea."

Suddenly Sammy was being hurtled towards the edge of the canyon and Peggy screamed. This wasn't how it was meant to happen, they still had weeks together.

Laughter erupted, and Sammy turned around to punch his assailant on the arm.

"You jerk," Sammy said, laughing.

"Sorry," Nick said, looking at Peggy who was a blithering mess, crouched down and covered in dust. He put his hand out to help her up.

"You total *jerk* Nick," she said, brushing herself off, hands shaking.

"Where the hell have you been anyway?" Sammy asked, wiping his forehead with the back of his hand.

"You wouldn't believe it if I told you," Nick grinned.

Peggy didn't want to be standing near anyone who would pretend to throw someone off the edge of the Grand Canyon and so she excused herself and walked away to be alone, away from the boys and away from Lacey and Ben who were still gallivanting around, and she found a nice safe looking rock to sit on.

"Don't get pissed," the breeze picked up Nick's voice and sent it straight over.

"OK," Sammy replied.

"Rochelle," he said.

"Rochelle?" Sammy asked, a hint of surprise in his voice.

"Rochelle," Nick said proudly.

"You have my blessing man."

"Really?" Nick asked.

"Rochelle and me, we had some fun." Peggy's stomach lurched as she thought about what fun they'd had. "But we never... I never totally got her. She never totally got me." Peggy wondered if Sammy thought she got him. She knew he got her. She hoped he knew she got him.

"Oh, I got her. I got her last night," Nick bragged.

"I don't need the details," Sammy said.

"What's up with you and geek-girl?" Nick asked.

"Geek-girl?" Sammy asked. *Geek-girl?* Peggy frowned. Is that what they called her?

"She's not your usual type Sammy, come on, look at her." They looked over at her and she pretended to be suddenly interested in what Lacey and Ben were doing.

"Stop it you guys!" she called out playfully as Lacey and Ben ran over towards her.

"This is so boring," Tricia said, walking over with a can of Pepsi.

"Where'd you get the Pepsi?" Lacey asked.

"I bought it off some family."

"Are you kidding me?" Ben asked.

"No." Tricia cracked open the can and drank.

"I'd kill someone for a Pepsi," Lacey said, looking over the edge. Tricia stepped back.

"Where have you guys been?" Tricia asked as Rochelle and Leigh made their way over, dressed in short dresses and heels and looking like models turned up for a photo shoot, not kids on a school trip.

Peggy looked down at her jeans, t-shirt and check shirt combo and felt very unglamorous.

"We got a hotel," Leigh said, sighing as she noticed the orange dirt on her white heels.

"I only *wish* we'd done that," moaned Lacey.

"You should have come with us Lace," Rochelle said, stepping over a rock with her long-tanned legs.

"Maybe I'll come with you guys tonight," Lacey said, getting all excited. Peggy gave her a look. Lacey had done nothing but bitch about Leigh and Rochelle since Peggy had met her and now, she was talking about going and staying in a hotel with them, leaving her and Tricia alone in the tent. Peggy did not want to be alone with Tricia in the tent. They were starting to get along OK, but not that OK.

"We're staying at the tents tonight," Leigh said. "It was just a one-night thing. We pretended to have car trouble, but the nuns are onto us."

"My life sucks," said Lacey, flicking some dust off her white top and looking like she was about to cry again.

"It's come to our attention," said Sister Constance as they were assembled for cheese sandwiches over lunch, "that some of you think it's acceptable not to sleep in your own tents. Let me tell you that this trip is about survival skills as much as it is about seeing the wonder of the Grand Canyon."

"No, it's not," said Lacey. "They never said anything about survival skills until just then. It's just because the school budget is so totally tight."

"You need survival skills to stay in that camp site," Tricia said loudly.

Sister Constance ignored her. "Tonight, we will be doing checks to see if you are in your tents and if you're not, there will be repercussions."

Ben's hand shot up. "Sister Constance, you can't check the boy's tents!" he said.

Everyone laughed.

"Mr. Harcourt will check the boy's tents," said the nun.

Mr. Harcourt nodded. He was pretty hot for a teacher. Kind of like a young Tom Selleck. He must've been in his mid-twenties. Peggy struggled to imagine him hooking up with Awkward Amy who was watching him attentively through her thick rimmed glasses. Peggy giggled.

"You have a few more hours to explore the canyon then we'll drive back to camp," the nun instructed.

Peggy was almost asleep when she felt something on top of her. She thrashed about thinking she was being attacked by a bear or a ghost or something worse.

"Peg!" whispered Lacey. "Shhhhhh!"

"Get off me!" Peggy squealed

"Shush! You need to get up and be quiet!"

"Is it morning?" Peggy asked groggily.

"Sister Constance just did her check."

"OK, so let me sleep."

"Come on," said Tricia, "we don't have much time."

"What's happening?" Peggy groaned as a flashlight hit her in the face.

"Get dressed," Tricia demanded.

"She can get dressed in the car, let's just get her packed." Lacey said, shoving Peggy's things into her bag.

"Seriously... what the?" Peggy asked.

The flashlight shone in her face again. "Sorry!" whispered Ben.

"Put that thing out," Sammy ordered.

"What's going on?" Peggy nearly shouted.

"We're going to Vegas," Lacey whispered, shining the torch towards her own face and grinning like it was Christmas before putting it out and finishing the rescue mission in the dark.

Lacey's car headlights lit the way, casting shadows across the desert like magic, lighting up glimpses of mountains and trees and other objects that Peggy struggled to make out. It all blurred into one beautiful moment.

She was squished in the back between Tricia and Sammy, while Ben sat up front. She was still dressed in her polka dot pajamas, she wasn't wearing any make-up and her breath was probably gross too. This was not how she wanted Sammy to see her.

"Are the groupies coming too?" Peggy asked sleepily, trying to stop herself from resting her head on Sammy's shoulder and drifting off.

"They went ahead with Nick, didn't wait for checks," Tricia said. "They are going to be so busted."

"You know they'll get out of it somehow," Lacey sighed.

"What time will we get there?" Peggy asked.

"Should be there by four," Lacey said.

"Three thirty if you step on it Lace," said Sammy.

"Step on it Lace!" shouted Tricia, bouncing up and down in the seat like a kid. "I want to get to Vegas!"

"Please don't speed Lacey," Peggy pleaded. "What are we going to even do in Vegas at four in the morning?" she asked, feeling her eyelids getting heavy.

"Party!" said Ben turning up the static and trying to find a radio station.

"Where's your car Sammy?" Peggy asked.

"Horace is going to drive it back," Sammy said.

"Horace?" asked Tricia over the static. "But you don't let anyone drive your car."

"He's going to cover for us in exchange for driving my car back. I trust him."

"If you trust him, I trust him," said Lacey. "I wonder what ever happened with him and June-Belle."

Tricia let out a weird strangled sound.

"You won't find any radio out here," Sammy said but Ben kept trying.

"It's just static," Peggy said, sleepily resting her head on Sammy's shoulder and she began to feel herself drift off.

The bright pulsing lights of Vegas woke her, and she thought she was still in a dream. It was electric, and although she was still half asleep, she was so excited she could burst. Here she was in the eighties, in Las Vegas. It was the coolest thing ever. She looked over at Sammy, maybe it was the second coolest.

"So, what now?" asked Lacey.

"We go hit the casinos," Ben said.

"The strip or old town?" asked Lacey who obviously knew her way around.

"Old town," said Sammy.

"Strip," said Ben at the same time.

"We need a room," said Sammy. "I know a place."

"A room for what?" asked Ben.

"For crashing out later moron," said Tricia.

Peggy felt like she was in a movie. The truth was, in 1983 a small town like Santolsa hadn't really changed that much, but now that she was in Vegas, everything was different. Everything felt *real* somehow. She was no longer just a time traveler who fell out of a book room into the past. This was now her present, her life, her future. As the lights blazed around them and her friends argued around her, she nearly burst out crying because it was all too amazing.

The hotel room was cheap, red and gold and smelt like a bar. Peggy loved it.

"Let's go out, come on! It's getting late, or early," said Lacey. "I'm not waiting another second for you guys. Meet me in the casino downstairs."

"I just need to wash my face and put on some real clothes and make-up," Peggy said, heading into the dingy little bathroom as Lacey walked out without doing anything. Girls like Lacey didn't have to worry about make-up.

Peggy looked at her reflection. She looked rough. Her hair was a mess, and her face looked lifeless. *Urgh.* She changed into her jeans and a tank top, she didn't bring any clothes for Vegas. She slapped on a bit of make-up, fluffed up her hair and shrugged. It would have to do.

When she finally came out everyone was gone. Except Sammy.

"Should we go?" she asked him, feeling tired and puffy but not wanting to miss a thing.

He shrugged.

She gave him a tired look. "But we're in Vegas baby!" she said dropping down onto the bed.

"I don't care about Vegas," he said.

"So why did you plan this whole thing about sneaking out to Vegas?"

"I just," he said as he sat down on the bed next to her and pulled her in close, "wanted," he said, as he pushed her hair out of her face.

"Wanted…?" she asked, resting her hands lightly on his arms. The arms she'd watched in the car that first day he took her for a drive. The way his muscles flexed when he changed gears had driven her wild. And now here they were, these same arms, under her hands, in a hotel in Las Vegas. Life was a funny thing.

"To be alone with you," he said, and he kissed her hard and fast, like he'd been thinking about it all day. He kissed her like she'd never been kissed in her life, she was putty in his hands, weak at the knees and all the other clichés you can think of. It was a perfect moment. It was 1983, and it was Vegas and it was Sammy Ruthven.

"Well, you got what you wanted," she said breathless as he pulled away. But it was only to pick her up in his arms and throw her down onto the bed.

"We can go out if you really want to," he said, leaning gently over her.

She shook her head. Exploring Las Vegas was the last thing she wanted if the other option was exploring Sammy Ruthven.

"We don't have to do anything you don't want to do," he said softly.

"I want to, but I don't want to be just another girl for you," she said nervously, running her hand through the back of his dirty blonde hair. "Just another one of Sammy Ruthven's conquests."

"You would never be that," he said, and he kissed her like he meant it.

And she fell asleep in his arms, there and then. It was the first time Sammy Ruthven had fallen asleep next to a girl and it meant more to him than if they'd done anything else at all.

It was after that night that Sammy started to hold her hand in front of everyone. In front of his friends, strangers, Janet, his dad, Rochelle, everyone.

And if he'd been told he only had a few weeks to live he wouldn't have done any of it any differently.

THIRTY-EIGHT

The Truth

When Magz got back to the present the first thing she did was check the yearbook to see if her shirt had changed in the picture.

She sat on the couch in the show home with Jack beside her and she opened up the book.

They both sat staring at the picture.

"What were you wearing before?" Jack asked.

"A plain sweater. Look, it's changed," she said, adrenaline coursing through her veins, this was proof, she *could* change it. "How do you remember this picture?" she asked Jack.

Jack shrugged. "I can't remember. I remember seeing it, but I can't remember what you were wearing."

"OK, this is good," Magz said. "If I can change a photo, I can change his future."

"Sure," said Jack, putting his feet up on the Martin's coffee table. "But in reality, this changes nothing. There's no big consequence to the future because you wore a different shirt. Stopping someone from dying could create some kind of black hole vortex or something. Wearing a check shirt might not tear a hole in the space time continuum but saving a life could."

Magz sighed, opened a bag of corn chips and offered them to him. The school trip had brought her and Sammy so close, he was actually holding her hand in front of people, like he didn't even care if Rochelle was there or whatever. No boy had ever held her hand in front of anyone before. She needed to stop him dying no matter what.

"I know it sounds kind of selfish," she began, "but I think I would risk a space time vortex paradox-y thing that was going to blow up the whole universe if it meant I could save him."

"If the universe gets sucked into a black hole you haven't really saved him though, have you Magz?"

"Well, I can't just do *nothing*. Imagine if you knew that someone you loved was going to die, wouldn't you do everything you could to try and save them?"

"Of course I would, but you don't even know this guy. You could save him, and he turns out to be some drunk pervert living in someone's mom's basement watching the Gilmore Girls."

"Gilmore Girls?"

Jack shrugged. "It's just an example of the kind of weirdo he could become if you save him. Maybe he's meant to die." Jack ate a chip.

"He's not *meant* to die, you're being such an ass right now Jack."

"How do you know that? You're the one who's always talking about how things are," he made air quotes, "*Meant to happen*, and now you want to go around changing all the things that are meant to happen? You can't have it both ways. There's either destiny or there isn't."

"Yeah well, maybe some destinies are worth trying to

change," Magz said. "Why are you being suck a jerk anyway?"

"I'm not being a jerk."

"You are, you're totally cutting me down, talking crap about the stuff I believe in, trying to make me feel about three feet tall."

"I'm sorry you feel that way," said Jack, taking another chip.

"You're making it *real* easy for me to leave."

"Sorry, you're right," Jack shook his head. "I am being a jerk. I'm just pissed that you have this great new life and I'm still here in Santolsa, gem of hell. And, really, what I'm trying to say is, please don't go."

Magz stared at the packet of corn chips, mentally calculating the differences between this packet and what the packet in 1983 looked like.

"Do you have to decide?" asked Jack. "Like, can't you just keep coming and going like you do now?"

"Janet says it's bad for the soul or something, and that eventually it will just choose for you. I do get these pounding headaches every time I go through the door. It can't be that good for you to live like that."

"Time travel isn't good for your education either. This is your final year of school, what are you going to do? How are you going to get into colleges?"

"I've still been going to school, and I don't even want to go to college anyway."

"You should keep your options open."

"Jack, I'm not coming back."

"What do you mean, you're not coming back? You keep coming back. You're going to *keep* coming back."

"I only came back to check the book, to see you and work out what to do about my parents, but I'm not coming back again after tomorrow. I'm going to live in the eighties now Jack."

Jack's face darkened. "So, you're really leaving me?" he asked, considering the now nearly empty corn chip packet. "Even if this guy dies?"

"I have to," she whispered. "And he's *not* going to die."

"You don't have to go."

"I *do*."

"What about your parents? What are you going to tell them? I know you have your issues with them, but they are your family and they love you, despite what you think about that, it's true. They aren't perfect, but they are the only parents you have. You can't just leave them thinking you're a missing person, worried sick."

"Janet has been more of a parent to me in a few short months than they ever have been."

"Fine, whatever, but what about me then?" Jack's eyes were filled with sadness.

"I'll see you again," she promised.

"See me again? Magz! If you spend the rest of your life in the past, I will *never* see you again!"

"I'll come find you, I'll be older than you, but I'll still be *me*."

"This is insane." He threw the chip packet onto the table and stood up.

"Jack, stop," Magz stood up and grabbed at him.

"I can't lose you Magz!" Jack shouted. His dark thoughtful eyes began to water. She'd never seen him cry before. It stopped her in her tracks.

"How can I stay here just for you?" she asked, putting her hands out for him to take, but he didn't. "You can't ask me to do that!" She began to cry herself, tears of frustration. How could Jack do this to her? How could he stand here and yell at her when she was making a decision that would change the course of her destiny, her future, every-thing for the *better*. Her years of being miserable and hating herself and her life were finally over. Now she liked getting up in the morning and looking into the mirror. She had a reason to exist. She had a reason to keep going. Here, all she had was Jack. And although she cared about him deeply, he just wasn't enough.

"I'm asking you," he said, grabbing her shoulders firmly, forcing her to look at him. "Stay for *me*."

"I can't stay here and spend the rest of my life sitting on this couch waiting for my parents to get home while we share a plate of spring rolls and watch old movies when I could be living my *life*."

"*I* can be your life," he said, pulling her into his arms and holding her like he'd done so many times before.

"I can never have the life with you that I want," she sobbed into his chest.

"Magz," he said, looking up at the ceiling while he held her head against his chest. "I'm not gay."

She laughed through her tears and looked up at him. "Nice try Jack."

He held her shoulders tight and pushed her back to look him in the eyes. They were filled with seriousness. Jack was never serious, and even when he was serious, he was always kind of half sarcastic with it, so you were never totally sure if he was serious, or joking, or joking about being serious.

"I'm not gay," he said again.

She took a step back, shaking her head. He had that look on his face that he had when she told him the stories about her family never being around, or when she told him about the latest prank she was the victim of. He was sincere. He was so seriously sincere right now. But if this was the truth, that meant so much was a lie.

"Magz," he said.

"What do you mean, *you're not gay?*" she whispered

"I'm in love with you," he said.

Magz eyes grew to the size of moons. Stumbling backwards she fell into a lounge chair. He knelt down next to her and taking her face in his hands he kissed her, and she was too shocked to pull away.

His lips were soft, and he tasted like corn chips and soda. He kissed her gently and sweetly, and nervously, and sweaty. He was shaking.

Jack couldn't believe it was happening. Ever since the first day he met her he'd thought about doing this. And now that she was a time traveler and about to leave him for some loser motor-head in the eighties with a sting haircut he'd finally found the courage. All those years of pretending, well, not pretending, just not offering up all the facts, were over in an instant. He'd never actually said he was gay. Not even once. People just assumed, and he'd gotten tired of having to defend and explain himself. He really had done nothing wrong here.

Magz swore at him and pushed him away.

"Sorry, this is a mess," he said, standing up, running his hand through his hair and then shoving his hands in his pockets.

"What am I supposed to do with this? Seriously?" she stood up and moved away from him. "I told you I love Sammy. I'm going back to 1983 to try and save his life so we can be together, and you suddenly turn straight and want me to stay?"

"Yeah, sorry about that. I wish I could've told you sooner." He started to walk backwards towards the door, it was inevitable that she was going to kick him out or kick him in the balls and he knew which one he'd prefer.

"You're just a few years too late," she said, shaking her head.

Jack felt a snap from somewhere deep inside him. Something that had been slowly cracking for all these years had finally broken. Too late. If only he'd told her sooner. If only he hadn't gotten hung up on this stupid lie. If only he'd told the truth, if only he'd been himself. His life was fast becoming full of if only.

"I think you need to go now," she said, shaking her head, "I can't deal with this right now."

"Can I call you tomorrow?"

"I won't be here," she said, staring at the wall behind him.

It could've been worse. At least she was still talking to him. He hoped with everything he had that she would sleep on it and realize that they were meant to be together and that in the morning she would be knocking on his door ready to give herself to him.

"God damnit!" he yelled as he closed the front door behind him. Then he screamed a deep heart-breaking scream out into the night that would wake the dead, wake Sammy Ruthven if he really was dead. Then he thought something for a split second that he wished he could un-think. He wanted Sammy to die. He wanted him to die so that she'd come back to him. Unable to live with the pain, Jack would be there to fix her, make her happy again, wipe her tears, be her shoulder to cry on, the arms that held her when she needed a hug, the one who sat next to her on the couch when she needed company. Then she'd see they were meant to be.

The boy she loved in 1983 was going to be dead in a few short weeks and now Jack was in love with her. No, he'd always been in love with her. She couldn't comprehend it.

"When am I going to catch a break?" she said to herself, suddenly feeling very sad to have given Tux away to Jack.

She fell back down on the couch, phone in hand she tapped on the Google icon and she Googled Sammy Ruthven for the hundredth time, but the results were still the same.

THIRTY-NINE

The Stables II

_____

It was already getting late when Jack had the stupid idea to ride his bike out to The Stables. It was dark and cold and because he hadn't been outside of town at night on his bike before, he was pretty nervous. A couple of trucks had come really close to him which had freaked him out, but by the time he decided he should probably just go back home he was more than halfway there, so he kept going.

He parked his bicycle between two Harleys, quickly switched his sweaty blue t-shirt for a fresh white one he had stashed in his satchel, sprayed some deodorant and ran his hands through his sweaty hair. It would have to do.

"Hey stranger," said Jayne, greeting him from behind the bar as he walked in.

"Hey," he said, trying his best to be cool.

"Didn't think I'd see you around here again. Where's your friend?"

"Gone," he said, making it sound incredibly dramatic.

"Gone where?" she asked sympathetically, grabbing a beer, cracking the top and handing it to him.

"Canada," Jack said, taking a swig. He went to get his wallet out to pay, but she held up her hand, her neatly polished black fingernails stopping him from handing over any cash.

"What's in Canada?" she asked.

"Some guy."

"Last time you were in here she outed you pretty bad."

"Yeah, she was always doing stuff like that."

"I guess she didn't know what she had when she had it." Jayne gave him a look and walked over to the other end of the bar to serve some old bikers.

He watched her, her denim shorts and Stables tank leaving little to the imagination. She was nice to watch. He drank his beer fast and she replaced it just as quickly.

"Better watch out," she warned, looking at the door. "Jonas is here."

"He doesn't scare me," said Jack, throwing back most of the second beer.

"Looks like you could do with something stronger," she said, getting out the tequila tray.

"Damn right I do."

"Hey trouble," said Jonas, taking the bar stool next to him.

"Hey Jonas," said Jayne, grabbing him a beer just like she had done for Jack, but taking his money.

"Hi Jonas," said Jack, rolling his eyes.

"Where's that girl?" Jonas asked.

"Who?"

"The girl you were with last time you were here breaking my balls and getting me kicked out of my bar."

"What's it to you? And you got yourself kicked out, and it's not *your* bar."

"Bullshit," said Jonas.

"You started it," Jack said, cringing at how childish he sounded.

Jonas laughed, took his beer and headed towards the pool table.

"So, is it guy trouble or girl trouble?" Jayne asked.

"Both," said Jack.

"You know it's kind of my job to listen to people's problems."

Jack looked up into her dark eyes. Maybe it was the tequila's idea, but his mouth was going along with it and his brain didn't care and so he told her (mostly) everything.

At midnight, she took a half hour break and took him into the stock room out the back.

Jack had spent a lot of time imagining how he was going to lose his virginity but had not once thought it would be like this, in some back room of a bar, and he'd never really imagined it being with anyone other than Magz.

"Do you want to come to prom with me?" Jack asked, admiring her body as she shimmied back into her shorts when the deed was done.

"Prom? Jack, I'm twenty-one, I can't go to prom."

"Oh."

"Did you just have sex with me, so I'd go to prom with you?" she asked with mock annoyance.

"No, I had sex with you because you're really hot and I like you."

"OK," she smiled, shaking her head. "Sure, I'll come to prom with you."

Jack couldn't decide what made him happier, that he'd just had sex, that he'd had sex with an incredibly hot older woman or that he actually had a date for prom.

And then he thought about Magz and he didn't feel very happy at all.

FORTY

Yearbooks

"Can you guys sign my yearbook?" Lacey asked as she threw her yearbook onto the pile in the middle of the cafeteria table.

"Only if you sign mine," said Peggy, picking up the pile and, with Sammy's help began distributing the books among the group.

"Yearbooks are so stupid," said Rochelle, sitting on the edge of the group.

"You only get to do this once," said Tricia in a rare moment of not being too cool for school.

"We do this every year," Rochelle said, flicking open a cover, tossing her straw mane of hair, scribbling her name, closing it and pushing into the center of the table again.

"We don't *graduate* every year," Lacey said, looking over the messages on the page she was about to sign.

"And we have school dances every year," said Leigh, yawning.

"I've never been to a school dance before," Peggy said.

"Not even in Canada?" asked Nick, who was quickly

put in his place by a dirty look from Rochelle. Apparently, Nick was now not allowed to talk to Peggy.

"We had them, I just never went."

"Well Peggy, tonight you are going to be the belle of the ball," Lacey said. "The dresses Janet made for us are so bitchin' and everything is going to be *perfect*." Lacey gave her a look and passed her another book. It was Sammy's.

"I don't know about that," Peggy said. The knot that had become a part of her these last few months had now consumed her. This was the day. This was the day she had to change destiny. It was a lot of pressure. She knew she could change her shirt in a photo, but she still wasn't totally sure she could save Sammy, or if she was even meant to.

She ran her hand over the cover just as she had done in English class all those years later. This was the book. This was the book that had brought her here. This was the book that had changed her life. Here she was with her new friends, Janet, a boyfriend she couldn't even have dreamed up if she'd tried, and apart from the two girls at the end of the table her life was pretty much perfect. As long as tonight went off without a hitch everything would be wonderful. And so, it *had* to go off without a hitch.

She tapped on his book with her pink pen, trying to remember what she was going to write. She wrote as neatly as she could and signed it *love, Peggy. xxx*

"The limo is going to pick me up first at seven," Sammy said. "So, you guys better be dressed and ready by then."

Peggy was so relieved he'd hired a limo even though everyone else thought limos were for preppies.

"Limos are for preppies," said Leigh.

"Oh yeah?" asked Lacey. "How are you three love birds getting there?"

"My mom's giving us a ride," said Nick. Rochelle made a face and Lacey laughed.

"I've seen your mom's ride," said Tricia. "Isn't it that brown station wagon?"

Rochelle stood up flustered. "Let's go." She motioned for Nick and Leigh to follow and they did.

"Hey!" Amy said, grinning as she perched herself on the vacated seats at the end of the table. "Would you guys sign my yearbook?" She was beaming.

"Of course," said Peggy, giving her a smile and taking the yearbook off her. She opened it up and spotted a scribbled note in one corner from Mr. Harcourt, the Math teacher Amy was going to end up married to. Peggy laughed.

"What is it?" Amy asked.

"Nothing," said Peggy. "I just feel like everything is going to turn out for you Amy."

Amy beamed.

Peggy scribbled her message in Amy's yearbook and said a silent prayer for everything to turn out for all of them.

FORTY-ONE

Limo

Sammy Ruthven stood on the porch under so many hanging baskets of plants he felt like he was in Babylon. He was dressed in a dark blue suit, white shirt, polished black shoes and he was holding a bright pink corsage. He brushed the hair off his forehead, it fell back into his eyes and he took a deep breath and rang the doorbell.

"You scrub up nice Sammy, what a surprise! I half expected you to turn up in jeans," Janet ushered him in.

"Thanks Miss Bates, you don't look so bad yourself." Janet had herself also scrubbed up nicely. Dressed in a red strapless evening dress and matching heels she looked like she was sure to break a couple of hearts as she supervised at Prom.

"Peggy!" she called up the stairs. "I need to get going, are you coming down?"

"Not yet!" Peggy's voice called down. "Just go ahead and I'll see you there!"

"OK, don't forget to lock up," Janet called back. She grabbed her black patent clutch and quickly checked her bright red lipstick in the mirror.

She rushed out the door and down the porch steps, but when she saw the blue Firebird parked in the driveway her heart skipped a beat. She knew changing the future may not be possible, but she had counted on the fact that Sammy would leave his car at home tonight. Surely, they could at least change that. Peggy had changed everything for Janet. Peggy had been the family she'd never had. She felt Peggy's fear as if it was her own. She felt her face begin to sweat, she needed to calm down or she'd have mascara under her eyes in seconds.

"God dammit," she whispered to herself. "When are they going to invent decent waterproof mascara?"

She ran back into the house and straight past Sammy Ruthven and bounded up the stairs.

"He's brought the Firebird," Janet said, panting as she grabbed some toilet paper and blotted her forehead.

Peggy looked at Janet behind her reflection in the bathroom mirror. "No," she said.

Janet nodded.

"What do we do now?" Peggy asked frantically.

Janet shook her head. "I don't know, maybe we just can't change it."

"How can we *not* change it?" Peggy asked. She had been worried sick these last few months, but the thing that had kept her going was a tiny spark of hope. In that instant it was if the hope plughole was opened and hope was rapidly draining out of her. She didn't know how she was going to get through the next few hours without it. Peggy turned around to look at Janet, her eyes glistening with water.

"OK, let's say you can't," said Janet passing Peggy some toilet paper to blot under her eyes. "Let's for a second say that you *can't* change it. And this is the last night you're going to spend with him."

Peggy shakily sat on the edge of the bathtub.

"What do you do?" continued Janet. "Do you go to your room and cry yourself to sleep? Or do you go to prom and freak out about it all night? *Or* do you go to prom and try to have a good time?"

"Have a good *time*?"

"None of us ever know when our time is up. I could die tonight, any of us could, we don't know. But we have to keep living, we have to keep loving, even if we don't know how long it's for."

"I'm still going," said Peggy, taking a deep breath. "Because I love him. And if this is his last night on earth, I want to make it the best night of his life."

"That's all we can ever try to do," Janet said.

Peggy looked back at her reflection and nodded.

"I'm so proud of you," said Janet.

Peggy looked at her blankly.

"You're so strong," Janet said.

Peggy laughed. "Me? Strong?"

"Not everyone could do what you've done."

"What have I done?" asked Peggy really having no clue.

"You came all this way, you started a new life all by yourself with no family, no friends, and look at you now."

"I couldn't have done it without you," Peggy said, feeling her eyes begin to water again.

"Your mascara will run," said Janet sternly.

Peggy looked stunning as she walked down the stairs in her bright turquoise dress. Her hair was in big soft curls around her shoulders, her lips painted fuchsia.

"Wow," he said. "I mean you always look wow, but just... wow."

Peggy smiled. "You look pretty wow yourself."

"I hope the color is OK," he said, presenting the bright pink corsage.

"It's perfect." Peggy's breath caught as Sammy gently took her hand and placed the corsage around her wrist. She turned her hand and looked at it from all angles and a huge smile spread across her face. No one had ever given her flowers before.

But as they walked out of the house and she saw the Firebird sitting in the driveway, the twilight illuminating the perfect blue, Peggy's face fell. She wasn't sure if she could keep it together. She might be stronger than she was, but no one was that strong.

"I know what you're thinking Peg, but I had no choice. The car company called me an hour before they were due to pick us up and cancelled. They'd triple booked."

Peggy was unable to move.

"It's OK Peg, I'll drive us there and if you don't want me to drive home, we can get a taxi or a ride or walk if we have to. I won't drive it home, I promise you."

Peggy stayed frozen.

"Peg, you said in your dream it happened on the way *home* from Prom. Isn't this enough for you?"

She looked at Sammy's pained expression, thinking how gorgeous he looked in his dark blue suit, the glow of the Firebird lighting up like an aura behind him. She looked at her corsage thinking how beautiful it was. She looked at the Firebird again and thought of nothing but flames and death, the end of all this. All she had ever wanted she had right now, in this moment, and it could all be gone in a few hours. She threw herself at him, holding him tighter than she ever had. She kissed him hard, leaving lipstick all over his face.

"When are they going to invent kiss proof lipstick?" she joked, wiping his face and blinking back the tears.

"I won't drive home, OK? I promise you. Hand on heart." He put his hand on his heart and she believed him. And she believed that everything was going to be OK. She had to.

And she took a deep breath and walked towards the Firebird.

FORTY-TWO

Prom

———————

"You guys are late!" yelled Lacey, beaming and rushing to meet them by the door of the gym. She spun around, showing off her short white dress with little black bows down the front.

"You look amazing," said Peggy.

"So do you," Lacey said. "Janet did a good job for us huh?"

Peggy nodded.

Lacey hadn't taken her eyes off Peggy's wrist. "That is not... he did not do that."

Peggy nodded again, casually flinging her wrist about, showing off the corsage as Sammy took her other hand.

"Well I'll be," said Lacey.

"You look great Lace, where's Ben?" Sammy asked.

"Thanks Ruthven. He's over at the refreshments, probably spiking the punch if someone hasn't already done it like five times already. It's gotta be pretty lethal by now."

"I'll go get us some," Sammy said, heading over to the drinks table.

"I can't believe he got you *flowers*," said Lacey. "I

316

don't know what you've done to him, or how you did it, but if you could give me some pointers, I'd really appreciate it. I mean, I'm here with that!" she pointed to where Ben and Sammy were now talking. Ben was dressed in powder blue flares, matching jacket, shirt and a paisley tie.

"I think it's his dad's." Lacey rolled her eyes and stifled a giggle. "I've made it very clear to everyone that we are just here as friends, so please do the same.

Peggy laughed. "It's the best suit I've ever seen, I think he looks amazing."

"Amazing?! It's the *stupidest* thing I've ever seen. But the band is so awesome!" Lacey pointed towards the stage where a band clad in leather and animal print was rocking out. "I can't believe they got a *rock* band, the preppies are so pissed. They actually thought a band called *Turquoise Noise* was going to be pop."

Peggy looked around in awe of the scene before her. She felt like she was in a John Hughes movie. Puffy pink, purple and gold dresses whirled around the floor. A group of preppie guys wearing dark wayfarers were standing suspiciously over the drinks table. June-Belle and the prom committee had outdone themselves with the Paradise theme. The gym was full of pink, green and blue balloons, inflatable palm trees and lawn flamingos. The banner across the stage read "Saint Christopher's High School Prom 1983". It kind of looked like the 3 had been painted over the 2 from the year before, but Peggy didn't care. She closed her eyes and breathed it in. She was home. She was exactly where she'd always wanted to be. It didn't matter that she was still in Santolsa, or that she was in the old gym. She was *home*.

She opened her eyes and looked over at him filling up plastic cups at the drinks table. She was going to stick to him like glue, nothing was going to happen to him tonight. Not ever.

Sammy returned with Ben and enough plastic cups of punch for everyone and they headed to the back of the gym.

"What is Rochelle *wearing*?" giggled Lacey, pointing at the blonde in a plain short black dress who was dancing with Nick but looking around in all directions for someone else. "Like, make an effort, it's prom!"

Sammy rolled his eyes and smirked at Peggy.

Peggy took a sip of the punch, it was potent.

"I like Amy's dress," Peggy said. Awkward Amy looked gorgeous. Her hair was still frizzy, but instead of trying to tame it like she usually did, she'd let it run free and it bounced quirkily around her head as she danced. She was either wearing contact lenses or dancing blind, but in her green fifties style cocktail dress she looked stunning. Even Lacey couldn't argue.

"Susie Collins, what a mess," Lacey said, pointing to a girl who was barely wearing a dress at all. It was skintight, bright orange and hideous. She was getting quite an amount of attention from the boys though, much to Lacey's annoyance.

"This is strong," said Lacey, wrinkling her nose.

"I should probably swap mine for something softer. Janet's around here somewhere." Peggy looked around to see Janet was on photo duty, leading couples through the line to have their photos taken.

"Or go get your photo done before you get too drunk," laughed Ben, reaching out to hold her drink for her.

Peggy looked at Sammy who shrugged.

"You want a photo?" he asked. She nodded and Lacey passed her some gum.

They stood in front of the paradise beach back drop surrounded by cardboard cut-out palm trees. Sammy put his arms around her and she put her hand over his in standard prom pose which she'd seen in so many old photos, but never done herself.

He whispered something into her ear and she grinned. A quick flash immortalizing this perfect moment forever.

A few cups of punch later Lacey had dragged Ben onto the dance floor, no longer caring about his ridiculous suit. The band was good, playing covers of songs they liked and knew. It was kind of like being at the Fire Station but with everyone from school, a lot of balloons and it was a hell of a lot cheaper to get a drink.

"Hey," said Rochelle as she sat down a little too close to Sammy. Nick, who looked quite handsome in his black suit sat down beside her. They did kind of look good together, Nick and Rochelle. Peggy thought if Rochelle wasn't so mean and still in love with Sammy, they'd make a great couple.

"Hey," said Sammy. Peggy tried to give her a smile.

"Lacey sure looks like she's enjoying herself," Rochelle began. "All she did was bitch and whine about tonight."

Her bitchy comment was met with silence.

"Nice dress," she said with a tone Peggy wasn't sure to take as a compliment or sarcasm.

"Thanks," she said anyway.

"You guys got plans for after?" asked Nick, breaking the tension.

"Not sure yet," Sammy said. "I heard there was something happening at the Fire station but I'm not sure if I should show my face around there again just yet."

"I bet *Lacey* wants to go to the Fire Station," Rochelle said. "Like when will she just get a clue?"

"Rochelle, seriously," Peggy said quietly.

"Excuse me, what?" Rochelle leaned forward to look over Sammy at Peggy.

"Leave it Rochelle," Sammy said.

"I won't *leave* it," Rochelle said. She downed whatever drink was in her plastic cup, breathing alcohol into Sammy's face.

"It's Prom you guys," said Nick. "Come on, let's just all get along for once."

"Get *along*?" cried Rochelle. It was obvious now how drunk she was. "Get *along* Nick?" She stood up, arms gesturing wildly. "All I've tried to do these last few months is *get along*. I had a good thing going before this bitch turned up." She pointed at Peggy whose mouth was now hanging open.

Sammy stood up. "Hey," he said calmly, "maybe you should go get a water."

"A *water*?" Rochelle spat. "It wasn't so long ago you'd be getting *me* a water yourself Sammy." It was amazing how quickly her tone changed from drunk and angry to flirtatious and Peggy felt instantly ill. "Remember how we used to..." she put her hand on Sammy's shoulder, leaning in close.

"That's done Rochelle. It's been done for a long time and Peggy had nothing to do with that. We were done because of what *you* did, so if you're looking for someone to blame, that's how it is." He gently removed her hand.

"I'm sorry guys," Nick stood up, clearly embarrassed.

"Sorry?" Rochelle yelled, struggling to stay upright. "No, *I'm* sorry. I'm sorry I had anything to do with you Sammy Ruthven. You asshole, you broke my fucking heart!" She burst into tears, her pretty face contorting.

"Come on babe," Nick said, taking her hand and beginning to pull her away. "I'm so sorry," he said again looking at Sammy.

"You!" she tried to lunge towards Peggy. "You stole him right from under my eyes, you whore!" She tried to grab Peggy, but Sammy jumped in the middle of them. Peggy clung to the back of Sammy's shirt.

"Let's go Rochelle," Sammy said, grabbing Rochelle's arm. "I'll be back," he said to Peggy as he and Nick led Rochelle crying and screaming towards the door.

"O.M.G!" yelled Lacey running over. "What the hell just happened?"

"Rochelle just lost it." Peggy sat back down and took some deep breaths.

"She's totally nuts, I told you," Ben said, shaking his head. "You OK Peg?" he asked her, resting a hand gently on her back.

Peggy nodded as Lacey put an arm around her.

"At Prom and everything, what is she thinking?" Lacey wondered out loud.

"After everything I'm surprised she's held it together for this long." Ben started. Lacey shook her head at him as if to stop him speaking.

"What?" Peggy asked. She was clearly missing something.

"Just tell her," Ben said.

"No way," Lacey said.

"Tell me what?" Peggy demanded.

"Rochelle is crazy," Lacey began.

"I got that, thanks."

"*Real* crazy," said Ben.

"And?"

"They were never really together, like together, together," Lacey said.

321

"She thought they were though," Ben added.

"Yeah, I kind of know all this," Peggy said.

"What you don't know…" said Ben.

"Is that she faked a pregnancy." Lacey finished.

"What?" Peggy couldn't believe no one had told her about this.

"She told him she was pregnant," Ben said.

"It was just before we met you," said Lacey.

"They were talking about what to do," Ben began, "and he even thought about marrying her, for you know, five seconds anyway. He wanted to marry her because he believes in family and looking after your family and all that, not because he wanted to really *be* with her though."

"Oh my god," said Peggy. "Sammy and Rochelle nearly got *married*?"

"Tricia was at her house and saw the pregnancy test in the bin. It was negative, even though she'd just told Tricia it was positive and was crying into a pillow," Lacey said.

"Why didn't anyone tell me?" Peggy shouted over the music which seemed to suddenly get a whole lot louder.

"It didn't really matter Peg," Lacey smoothed down her dress. "We all saw how Sammy looked at you when you turned up, and Tricia ended up telling him that night we all went out to Super Pan, that it was fake and then it was so totally over."

"But she denied it of course," Ben added. "And Sammy didn't want to believe she would do something like that, but he eventually realized it was true."

"It might explain some things," Lacey shrugged.

"You should have told me." Peggy looked at them both.

"Sammy told us not to." said Ben.

"Oh, really?" Peggy raised her eyebrows.

"He didn't want to get you involved in his chaotic life," said Ben. "He didn't even want to date you. I mean his sister, his mom, Rochelle. Things haven't been easy for him."

Peggy nodded. His life was a little more complicated than hers, but she wanted to be a part of every bit of it. She thought about his dad and how sweet he had been when she'd met him, ordering pizza and wings for her. After everything Sam Senior had been through, she couldn't imagine him having to lose Sammy too.

"Hey," Lacey said. "He loves *you*, he just wanted to protect you, and besides, it's Prom. You can't be mad at him tonight. Be mad at him tomorrow."

"If there is a tomorrow," Peggy mumbled under her breath.

"You should have told me," she said softly when he had finally asked her to dance when their song had come on.

"Told you what?" Sammy's breath on the back of her neck was making it difficult for her to stay mad at him.

"That you thought Rochelle was pregnant... and that you were going to marry her."

He laughed. "I was never going to marry her Peg. It seemed like the right thing to do for a very short moment, but when I saw you that day, I knew..."

"What day?" She pulled back to look at him.

He smirked. "That day in class, when you introduced yourself. Then again at the record store."

"*That* day? I was a mess that day."

"You weren't a mess, you were just you. Real. Honest. A little unsure of yourself maybe. But *you*. It was refreshing after spending a lot of time with people who constantly try to be something else."

"You knew what?" she pushed.

"I knew I wanted you." He kissed her neck softly and she melted.

"It was the day I was considering marrying her. That morning I left my house and I thought, screw it, if this is what life has in store, I'll marry the girl, look after my family, work on cars. What's wrong with that? A lot of people get a lot less. I was content with my fate."

"And then?"

"And then I saw you drop that record," he smiled. "And in that moment, it was as if everything I planned for my life was wiped clean. My future was a blank page that I wanted to fill with you."

"I'm not from Canada," she said suddenly.

"I know."

"No, you don't," she had been waiting months to tell him. "I'm not from Canada, I'm from the future," she said seriously.

He laughed, just like she thought he would. But she loved him too much to lie to him.

"I know you are meant to die tonight because I read it online. On the internet."

"On the what?"

"It's where we get our news, it's hard to explain."

Sammy looked confused.

"The story was reported that you died on the way home from Prom, the Firebird hit a tree at speed, and you died on impact."

"Peg, we'll walk home, I don't care, but you're kind of acting crazy. And I've had enough crazy in my life."

She shook her head. "Sorry, I just…"

"Relax, it's prom, and I promise I'm not going to drive the Firebird tonight, OK?"

"OK." And she believed him. And in that moment, she knew, she just *knew* in her heart of hearts that he was going to live and that they were going to end up living happily ever after *together*.

"How awesome was that Prom?" Lacey asked, as if they went to a prom every week. She smiled, taking a sip from Ben's flask they were sharing around under the old tree behind the school buildings.

"Even my date didn't end up being quite so bad," said Ben and Lacey thumped him.

Sammy lit a cigarette. "So, what's the plan now?"

Lacey shrugged.

"There's loads going on," Ben said. "Party down in Salt Canyon?"

"In the *canyon*?" asked Peggy who was resting her head on Sammy lap. She was feeling much more relaxed now that she'd had a couple cups of punch and knew Janet was probably home in bed. But was still a little on edge. She wouldn't completely stop worrying until she woke up tomorrow morning and everyone was alive.

"*By* the canyon," he corrected himself.

"You think drunk people and canyons go together Ben?" asked Sammy.

Nick walked over and threw himself down on the grass next to Sammy.

"Hey, Rochelle get home OK?" asked Sammy.

"Yeah," said Nick, tussling his hair. "I put her in a taxi, I wanted to go with her, but she didn't want me, she only wanted Leigh. I've never seen her so messy."

Sammy looked down at his cigarette.

"Dodged a bullet there Sammy," said Ben who took a swig from his flask.

Nick gave him a look. "It's good though," Nick said, "that she's finally dealing with stuff."

"You guys are cute together," Lacey said.

"We're not together."

"But you *want* to be together," she continued, "and if you *did* officially get together, I think you'd be cute."

Nick shrugged.

"Maybe wait until she's over Sammy," suggested Lacey. "You don't want to be rebound guy. Rebound sucks."

"Yeah, I know." Nick took a drink, finishing the flask. "We need more alcohol."

"And where are we getting alcohol at this hour?" Lacey asked.

"The Fire Station?" suggested Peggy.

"Yes!" said Lacey, "and I have it on good authority Jonas *isn't* working tonight."

Sammy gave her a look.

"I saw Greg at the mall when I ran down after school to get this nail color," she held up her coral nails. "He said there was some Crazy Eights thing happening in Reno or somewhere this week and it's been dead at the bar."

Before she'd even had a response, there was movement. Sammy gently nudged Peggy up and Lacey was skipping towards the parking lot holding Ben's hand.

"How are we going to get there?" Peggy asked nervously allowing herself to be dragged along.

"I can drive, I've only had a few drinks," Sammy said.

"Sammy," Peggy grabbed his arm forcefully and stopped him. "After everything I've said about tonight, you want to drive drunk?"

"No. I just want to get us there. We'll have to wait ages for a taxi tonight and no one wants to walk, and the car is right there," he said pointing towards the lot.

"No," she said, refusing to let him take one more step forward.

"Nick!" Sammy called ahead. Nick stopped and turned around.

"How much have you had to drink?" Sammy asked.

"Man, I've been on Rochelle duty all night. I had maybe two cups of punch hours ago, and one swig of Ben's vodka just then."

"Great." Sammy threw him the keys and they all started heading towards the car.

"What are you doing?" asked Peggy, grabbing his shirt sleeve.

"Was there anything in your dream about a whole group of us in the car heading through town and Nick driving? Or was it just me?"

"It was just you."

"Then I *am* getting us to the Fire Station safely."

Peggy sat squished in the middle of Lacey and Ben in the back, terrified. She wondered if in all her effort to change the future she'd actually changed the future for the worse. Maybe in the future they'd all be dead. Maybe she was going to create an alternative future that was worse. Where Rochelle owned the Fire Station and ran the world.

"Hey guys," she began, alcohol clouding her thoughts. "You know how Marty creates the alternative 1985..."

"What?" asked Lacey.

"Alternative what?" asked Ben.

"You know, when Marty goes back in time..."

"What are you talking about?" Lacey shook her head. "And I thought I was drunk!"

"It's a book I read," Peggy said grimacing. She must've sounded completely nuts when she accidentally said this stuff.

"Peggy has a thing about time travel," Sammy said, raising an eyebrow as he turned to look at her.

"Yeah, I know," said Lacey elbowing Peggy in the ribs. "Shut up," she whispered.

"Time travel is cool," said Ben. "I'd love to see the future, like see if there's flying cars and stuff like in *The Jetsons*. I used to love *The Jetsons*."

"*I* love *The Jetsons*!" said Peggy. "But there's no flying cars in the future," she shook her head.

"I love *The Flintstones*," said Lacey, "I always thought I was Wilma."

"You *are* Wilma," said Ben.

They were only moments away from the main road and Peggy gripped onto her knees and closed her eyes until they were safely parked opposite Super Pan. Peggy let out a massive sigh of relief.

Greg had been right, it was pretty quiet. They had their choice of booths, but they took their usual one anyway.

"I'll get the first round," said Lacey, skipping towards the bar where Greg was throwing around bottles.

"*Now* will you relax?" Sammy asked Peggy as he took her hand under the table.

"Man, I don't even know if I should have left her." Nick folded his arms and leant back.

"Hey, it's not your problem," Sammy started, "what could you do? She's drunk, let her sleep it off. Call her tomorrow."

"That's good advice Sammy. Thanks man." Nick ran his hands over his face.

Lacey returned with a tray of toxic waste and purple shots.

"What is this?" asked Peggy, flicking one of the shot glasses with her bright pink nails.

"Purple people eater, it's Greg's new creation. He's going to come have a drink with us when he gets a break."

Ben looked over at the bar and downed his shot and toxic waste in seconds.

"Looks like someone already drank it and spewed it back up," said Nick, picking one up and then shooting it straight down. He shrugged. "Not bad."

Lacey made a face when she'd finished hers and reached for her other drink.

"Tricia!" she shouted, jumping up and pulling her friend, dressed in skintight black jeans, stilettos and zebra print top to a seat at the edge of the booth.

"Why the hell weren't you at Prom?" Lacey accused.

"Why the hell *would* I be at Prom?" she asked, her dark make-up adding at least five years. She looked like a grown woman and Peggy suddenly felt very young in her puffy turquoise dress.

"Because it was awesome. Rochelle got so trashed and tried to attack Peggy!" Lacey made fists and punched the air.

"Sounds stupid," Tricia said, looking bored.

"You're stupid if you think Prom is stupid," Lacey said.

"I'm going to dance, there's some serious hot stuff here tonight." Tricia got up and headed for the dance floor. Lacey and Ben followed.

"Lacey's cute huh?" asked Nick.

"Don't Nick," said Sammy.

"Don't what?"

"Don't go there," Sammy warned.

"Why not?"

"She's our friend, she's not a *girl*, she's Lacey."

"What about Peggy?"

"What *about* Peggy?" asked Peggy.

"She's a girl. She used to be our friend."

"I *am* your friend," Peggy said.

"It's different with Peggy," said Sammy, lighting up a cigarette and blowing the smoke towards Nick instead of Peggy and offering him one.

"Oh yeah, how's that?" Nick asked, taking a cigarette. "How are you and Peggy any different than Lacey and I would be?"

There was an awkward silence. Peggy stirred her toxic waste.

"Just, seriously man. You like Rochelle. Don't mess around thinking about Lacey."

"Lacey's only interested in one person anyway," Peggy said, looking over at Lacey who had left the dance floor and was dancing by the bar for Greg who was finding her only mildly amusing.

Nick slammed his drink on the table and walked over towards the bar. He began dancing suggestively with Lacey, putting his hands on her waist and trying to dirty dance with her.

Sammy began to get up, but Peggy grabbed his wrist to pull him back.

"She's not interested in Nick," she said, "so, don't worry."

Sammy looked at her. "I know. I'm kind of done protecting people anyway. Mom, Jessie, I spent so long trying to protect Rochelle, now I've got to protect Nick from this stupid crush on Rochelle? Why can't I just worry about myself for once?" He looked defeated. Exhausted. Peggy knew how he felt. The last few months had felt like years. She had never loved harder or been more terrified in her life. Every day was taking the energy of a year. She was exhausted too.

"Do you wanna get out of here?" asked Peggy.

"Where do you wanna go?"

"Anywhere," she shrugged.

"I can do anywhere, he said.

"Ben!" shouted Peggy over the music as she put a hand on his strong shoulder. "Look after Lacey, we're going."

"Oh sure, you lovers go do your thing," and he waved them off.

Peggy and Sammy walked past the Firebird which was still very much in one piece. Peggy ran her hand across the shiny blue paint.

"I'll come back for you later," Sammy said, tapping the car's roof gently.

"Do you ever wonder where everyone is going to end up? Like after school?" Peggy asked him as they strolled through the deserted streets.

"Sometimes."

"What do you think will happen to Lacey?" she asked.

"Lacey's a loose cannon. She's completely unpredictable."

"If you had to predict?"

"A stripper, or a nun... or a soccer mom."

"A soccer mom?" Peggy laughed.

"A rich housewife?"

"I can't believe you just said that."

"What's wrong with being a housewife?"

"Nothing, but, you know, this is the... eighties. Women can do a lot more than clean your house."

"My mom was a housewife," Sammy said.

"Sorry, I... I'm sorry. I just, I don't know, that was just a stupid thing to say."

"No, I get it, you want to do more with your life than be a housewife. But being a housewife could be great. Your life is your family and your home, and you don't have to go to work and slave away doing something you really hate for someone else. It's a pretty cool job when you think about it. Hard, but good."

"My parents are highflyers. Literally. I don't even know what they do really. They own things. Property, businesses. They go to meetings. I don't even know. But they are never home. I don't even remember the last time we all sat and ate dinner together, I think it might have been when I was twelve."

"What happened?" he asked.

"I honestly just think they never wanted to have children, I know I was never planned. I was just an accident."

"You were serendipity."

"Serendipity?"

"A happy accident."

She laughed. "Not for them."

"Well, for me." He brought her hand that he was holding up to his mouth and kissed it gently. Then he dropped her hand and kissed her nose, and then he looked into her eyes for a moment.

When he didn't kiss her, she reached up and ran her hands through the back of his hair and pulled him towards her, kissing him hard and urgent.

When she eventually pulled away her senses were so heightened that the pain in her feet became unbearable. She slipped off her shoes and stood barefoot on the pavement. Sammy slipped off his black dress shoes and offered them to her.

"I'll look ridiculous."

"Maybe a little, but you'll thank me in the morning."

Slipping on his shoes they began to walk again, him stepping carefully in his socks, holding her shoes in one hand and her hand in the other as she shuffled along.

"Would it be OK if I asked you about your Mom?" she

asked. His mom was one of the final Sammy Ruthven secrets.

"She lives in Salt Valley."

"Oh, I thought something had happened to her."

"She's a drug addict," Sammy said.

"Oh," said Peggy.

"She lives in a rehab facility, well, she lives in and out, and she stays with my aunt when she's out."

"I'm sorry," she said.

Sammy shrugged. "She couldn't handle it."

"What?"

"Jessie, being a mom, me, my dad, life."

"Do you see her?"

"I try to go see her a couple of times a month. Dad goes when he can. Jessie comes with me occasionally, but it's hard for her."

"I had no idea. I don't know what to say," Peggy said.

"You don't have to say anything. Just be with me." He took off his jacket and put it over her shoulders.

"Always," she said. And she wouldn't have wished she was anywhere else than walking through the night, through the streets of Santolsa with Sammy Ruthven's hand in hers.

When they finally reached her front door, he kissed her gently again, sending warm shivers of heat through her body. She slipped off his shoes and jacket and took her heels back from him.

"I had a pretty good time tonight," she said.

"Me too. I don't want to sound lame," he began.

"Sound lame, please," she said.

"I think it might have been the best night of my life."

She grinned like a total idiot.

"I'll call you tomorrow," he said.

She nodded and as they kissed again, she could already feel the stubble on his chin starting to come through.

He slid his shoes back on and began to walk away. As he did, he looked back to see her still looking at him.

She blew him a kiss and he caught it with his hand and put it in his pocket.

FORTY-THREE

The News

"Peggy." Janet's wavering voice woke her from her love-drunken slumber.

Peggy groaned.

"You need to wake up." An urgent hand was on her shoulder, nails digging in, shaking her.

She tried to open her eyes, but they were stuck together with last night's mascara.

"*Peggy.*" The voice was insistent, and too loud for her this kind of morning. She needed a water. Or a coffee. Or to just be allowed to sleep longer.

She opened her eyes slowly and frowned at Janet who had blue mascara tears running down her face. Peggy frowned and lifted herself up on her elbow. "What is it?"

"It's Sammy." Janet sat down on the edge of the bed and took Peggy's hand in hers.

"Sammy? No," Peggy rubbed her eyes some more. "Sammy's fine. We walked home."

"Peggy, no. He didn't."

Peggy shook her head, sitting up. "He promised he wouldn't drive, he walked me home."

335

VICTORIA MAXWELL

"I'm so sorry Peggy." Fresh tears ran down Janet's face as she gripped Peggy's hand in hers.

"Janet," she said, rolling up the sleeves on her polka dot pajamas. "Sammy didn't drive, he *promised* me he wouldn't drive."

Janet took a breath. "Then why did they find his car this morning wrapped around a tree just off the highway?"

"Janet, stop this isn't funny. I know he's OK, he's at home, I... he walked me..."

"And *then* where did he go?" Janet asked. "Where did he go after he walked you home? How did *he* get home?"

"Home. He walked, I guess."

It hit her like a wrecking ball. His voice saying the word *later* to the Firebird. He had gone back, later that night. He thought she was stupid, and her dream was stupid, and her talk of time travel was ridiculous, and he went and got the car anyway.

"No, it can't be, how do you know?"

Janet walked over to the boom box on Peggy's desk, tuning into Valley FM. She sat in silence as she heard the last few bars of their song dance fuzzily across the room and into her ears. The song that had been playing on that first car ride together. The song they had danced to at prom. Peggy froze, the memories flashing before her eyes with so many others of him. The yearbook, the first day of class, the afternoon at the lookout, the fried chicken, the dinner at his house, the night of the Prom, him catching her kiss and walking away...

"We're getting a lot of calls this morning about the tragic incident that was called in early this morning," said the DJ over the fade out of their song. "Everyone seems to be grieving in the Valley area today..." Peggy dug her fingers into her own arms as she listened. "Even those who didn't know the boy have been affected by the news of the eighteen-year-old being killed when his car, which was a classic blue Firebird, nice ride by the way, hit a tree at speed and he was tragically pronounced dead at the scene..."

Peggy's heart stopped. But it was OK, because she no longer needed it.

"We've been unable to get in contact with the family, but everyone in town sends out their prayers…"

Janet came closer again crying, arms out to hold her but Peggy pushed her away.

"No," she said, feeling for the key on the chain around her neck. "No," she said again as she stood up, throwing the polka dot covers off her.

"Peggy, I'm so sorry. But we'll be OK. We can get through this. Together."

"Get through this?" she asked numbly. "Get *through* this?" She clutched at the key. "Why did you even give me this key?" Her body was trembling, something was taking over. Grief, fear, anger, love, it was everything. "Damn you Janet!" she yelled, and the tears began to fall. Hot tears of rage.

"OK," Janet said trying to calm her. "I *didn't* give you the key, OK? I *won't* give you the key in the future if that's what you want," Janet said.

"How can you *not* give me the key? I have the key right here!" She held it out, hand shaking. "You gave me the key!"

"I don't know why I did Peggy, but you were obviously meant to come here."

"Come here for what Janet? Come here to find the love of my life and have him ripped away from me in a matter of months? What could possibly be the purpose of *that*? Why would *that* be my destiny?" she yelled through sobs. "Even as horrible as my life was in the present, I never had

337

to deal with anything like this. It was endless suburban monotony, bullying and loneliness, but it was never anything like this pain I feel right now." Peggy thumped her center, the place where the knot had been all this time, it now held a pain so strong she thought she might die from it.

"I don't know Peggy," Janet said, wiping her tears onto the back of her hands. "I don't know why anybody has any destiny, I don't have the answers, but some things are just meant to happen. I don't know why, but I do know that you can't know joy without tragedy."

"God, you're always talking crap like this. *Tragedy walks hand in hand with joy?* What kind of bullshit is that Janet? It's just what people who have tragedy in their lives tell themselves to make it seem OK. Well it's *not* OK, the Universe has given me very little joy in my life and I'm sick of trying to find reasons for why bad things keep happening to me." Peggy jumped up and began throwing things into her bag.

"Peggy, please."

"No. No Janet, I'm not going to stay here without him."

"What about your other friends? What about Lacey and Ben?"

"They'll be fine without me."

"What about me?" Janet looked at her, pleading. It was the first time Peggy had seen her look vulnerable.

She couldn't think about it. Peggy would miss Janet more than any of them. Janet was the mother she'd never had, the big sister that she never knew she wanted, she was family.

"I'll see you when I get home," she finally said.

"Home?"

Peggy slipped on her white canvas shoes.

"At least get changed," Janet said.

Peggy shook her head. "I just want to go home." Tears burst from her eyes all over again as she rushed down the stairs, Janet following on her heels.

Peggy put her hand on the doorknob before Janet stopped her. "*This* is your home."

"I can't," Peggy said.

"At least let me drive you," Janet said grabbing her keys. "And take this," she took one of the keys off her keyring. "It's the key to the school, it opens the back door near the book room."

Peggy slammed the door to the book room behind her, locking herself inside and closing her eyes from the flashing lights as she travelled back to her present. She dropped to the floor and sobbed until she could sob no longer. Her pajama sleeves were soggy from tears. She didn't want to leave but how could she stay without Sammy? She wished for a moment she had gone to see his dad, to see Lacey, Ben, Tricia even Nick. To tell them she was going. To see if they were OK. But how could they be OK? Sammy Ruthven was dead. She wondered how anyone could ever be OK again.

When the tears had slowed and she was able to catch her breath again, she stood up. She opened the door, walked out and locked the door behind her. She placed the key back around her neck, but this time it felt like a noose.

She walked slowly down the corridor. She had lost track of the days and had forgotten they correlated differently. It was a school day.

She didn't care. She walked without thinking, she had no destination. Nowhere to go now. She walked to the door of Mrs. Willis' English class and opened it, not caring that she was dressed in pajamas, or that her hair and face were a mess.

Old Janet looked up from her desk, her eyes widening in shock at the sight before her. Laughter rose from the class, but she couldn't hear it, she could only see their mouths gaping open like ugly fairground clowns. She began to cry again, she didn't even know she was crying until the tears felt hot and salty against her cheeks, as she gasped for air.

Old Janet stood up in what looked like slow motion and ran to her, pulling her into the corridor and wrapping her arms around her. They cried together, Janet cried the same way as she did when she was younger, softly, shaking. Peggy cried as if her chest had been cracked open, her internal organs taken out by some sick invisible surgeon.

They stood there until the bell rang, sending the clowns into the hallway to gawk.

"So, I heard you turned up at school today in your pajamas," Jack said, taking a seat next to her on the couch.

Peggy was still in her pajamas, she hadn't even made it upstairs. She had collapsed on to the couch and done nothing expect cry, think, agonize over her faults and guilt in the situation, Google Sammy, and Google *how to fix a broken heart*, *how to change the past* and *time travel.*

"Nice pants," he said.

"They're Janet's," she said, feeling a little regret for leaving Janet like that earlier this morning. It felt about thirty-three years ago already. But what was she supposed to do? She could not bear to live life in a 1983 version of Santolsa that did not contain Sammy Ruthven. She could not bear to live life in any version of Santolsa, and even the thought of not living at all had crossed her mind for a few very brief moments.

"Can I feed you?" Jack asked, kicking off his Vans and then kicking them towards the door.

She shook her head.

"When did you last eat?"

"Before Prom."

"You need food. I'll make you something, what do you feel like?"

"Sammy died Jack, he's *dead*. He is no longer living. I'll never see him again. How can you talk about food?" she began to cry again, but even though her body made the motion, no tears came, just a bit of noise and an inability to breathe.

Jack knelt next to the couch and put his hands to her face, wiping her tears. He kissed her on the forehead. "That's just as friends," he said.

Peggy looked at him and, in that moment, felt so much regret for the way she had treated him these last few months. She was glad he'd come over when she'd texted him.

Before she knew it, her lips were on his and the taste of his beeswax lip balm was in her mouth. He kissed her gently, not passionately and hard like Sammy did, softer, he was gentle. If Sammy kissed like a Firebird, then Jack kissed like a bicycle. She stopped herself, pushing him back hard.

"I don't know why I did that." She rubbed her eyes and picked at the mascara still attached to her lashes, she rubbed it between her thumb and finger, analyzing it, thinking of the moment she put it on, the anticipation of prom. Sammy standing downstairs with the corsage, and how very, very different that moment was from the present one.

"It's OK. You don't have to explain anything. I can't even begin to understand Magz."

"Peggy," she said.

"Peg," he said. Sammy had always called her Peg. She flinched at the sound of it.

"Peggy," she said again.

"OK, Peggy. Now I'm going to make you dinner, whether you like it or not. Folks expected home?"

"I have no idea."

"Doesn't matter," he said. "I'll go see what there is, why don't you go take a shower?"

Peggy shook her head.

"A bath?" he suggested.

She thought about it, but nothing she thought about sounded good, or like anything she wanted to do. She didn't want anything, she didn't want to do anything.

"I'll run it," he said, "and if you want to go in you can." And then he busied himself with cooking dinner and simultaneously keeping an eye on the bath upstairs.

Peggy took one look at the bath full of bubbles, turned around and got straight into bed without even getting changed.

Jack brought up a small plate of pasta and placed it next to her bed and he hoed into his own dinner while sitting at the edge of her bed, trying to eat quietly, but failing.

"Come to bed," she mumbled sleepily.

He felt like complete crap getting into bed with a girl when she was crying over some other dead guy, but you had to take what you could when you could. Jack wondered if he'd ever have another chance, so he took his t-shirt and jeans off and got in between her crispy clean smelling sheets and tried not to think about Jayne and how he was supposed to be meeting her at the bar tonight.

He nuzzled up to her, not too much, but enough for her to know he was there.

She reached for his arm and pulled it over her. She began to cry again, and he held her until she had cried herself to sleep.

FORTY-FOUR

Burger Barn

"Are you coming to school?" Jack asked as he replaced her untouched bowl of cold pasta with a fresh mug of coffee.

She made a groaning sound.

"It's the last day."

She opened her eyes and looked blankly at the sliver of light coming in between the curtains.

"And prom." He thought of Jayne and felt a nagging feeling in his chest. He wanted to go to prom with Jayne, he really did. But if he got to choose… "Do you want to come to prom with me?" he asked, folding his arms in front of him.

"My boyfriend died at the last prom I went to, so no. Thanks." Her voice was hard.

"I might still go, if that's OK with you." Jack shrugged.

"Do whatever you want."

"I brought coffee."

She looked at the mug. "Sorry."

"It's OK."

She closed her eyes again.

"Should I come over after prom?"

She shrugged, but it sounded like a yes to Jack.

A few days later, still dressed in the polka dot pajamas Peggy made it back downstairs again. She flicked through channels until she found something that didn't remind her of him. *The Breakfast Club*, no. Classic MTV? No way. Food Network, yes. Food Network had nothing to do with anything. As she watched some pretty blonde woman sautéing a bunch of prawns, she began to feel hungry for the first time in nearly a week.

"Hi honey! I'm home!" Jack called from the front door. The sound of his sneakers banging against the door frame almost making her feel something.

"I'm hungry," she said, her blurry red eyes still on the screen.

"Thank God. I thought you might fade away Magz. Peg... Peggy. I was worried."

"I'm OK, and I was carrying a few extra pounds anyway."

"Don't be stupid. You were perfect, you still are perfect, you just need to eat a burger."

"A burger?" Peggy's stomach rumbled like a volcano about to erupt.

"Great idea, we can run down to the Burger Barn. Burgers, fries, slaw, corn. I haven't been to Burger Barn in years."

"We went there a couple of weeks ago, Jack."

"I'll ride over and grab something."

"Take the car," said Peggy, finally looking up at him.

"The car?"

"Yeah, that thing with the wheels on it out there," she said.

"Peg," he said, and she gave him a look. "*Peggy*, I can't drive."

"You have a license."

"Yeah, but I haven't driven since, like the day I got it."

"Take Mom's car, it's easier to drive. The keys are hanging by the door."

"You sure about this?" Jack looked excited, but not very confident.

"What's the worst that could happen?" she asked.

When her phone rang ten minutes later, she wished she hadn't asked.

"Hey, it's me," he said.

"What's up?" she asked, hoping he was just calling to ask if she wanted mayo or hot sauce, but he should have known she wanted both.

"I had an accident."

Peggy felt panic rise in her chest. The accident. The flames, the Firebird. "No," she said.

"No, no, I'm OK, everyone is OK, but the car is just slightly dented. It's just a little scratch really. OK, it's more than a little scratch, what do I do?"

"OK, calm down, don't get hysterical."

"I'm not getting hysterical," he said, sounding hysterical.

"Where are you?"

"Still in the parking lot next to Burger Barn."

"You didn't make it out of the lot?"

"Not exactly, but I got the burgers!" he said.

Peggy sighed. "I'll come get you."

The last thing she wanted to do was get in a car, but Jack needed her, and so did her Mom's car so she threw on a cardigan and some shoes and left the house.

"What the hell happened?" she asked, looking the car over. One taillight had been smashed in and there was a very large dent in the back of the car.

"I have burgers!" He held up a paper bag and slurped a drink with his other hand.

"Just get in and eat," she said, pointing to the back seat of the car. He handed her a 7UP and a burger and fries. She bit into the burger and remembered for the first time in a week that she was alive. Chicken, hot sauce and mayo. She inhaled it and then stuffed in the fries, her fries and then most of his as she listened to what happened.

"So, I just tried to back out and I didn't see there was a pole there. I was turning like this," he used his burger to show how he was turning. "And because I turned just a little too much, I went into the pole instead of *past* the pole."

"A *little* too much?" she asked, her mouth full of the delicious salty potato-y fries.

"I just turned all wrong, I didn't go straight out before I turned. Are your folks gonna kill me?"

"No, but only because they're not here. We should have a few days at least to get it fixed. It's not an issue."

Jack looked relieved.

"Hey, I forgot to ask you, how was prom?" She asked, slurping on her drink and stealing some more of Jack's fries.

"You wanna talk about prom?" he asked.

She shrugged.

"It was OK."

"Who did you go with?"

"Jayne."

"Jayne? Who's *Jayne*?" A touch of jealousy in her voice.

"The girl from the bar."

Peggy's face dropped. The girl from the bar. The girl she'd accused him of checking out before she knew he was straight. She looked at him. Maybe, if she was honest with herself, she'd always known he was straight, somewhere deep down.

"Can you drive the car back?" she asked, changing the subject.

"Uh, yeah I guess, I'm kinda scared though."

"Follow me, stay close. I'll drive slow." She had a feeling she'd be driving slow for the rest of her life anyway. "Come on." She tossed her burger wrapper into the bag, leaving the corn on a cob untouched in the bottom.

FORTY-FIVE

Clean

_____

Later that night Peggy finally managed to wash herself.
She was even able to throw Janet's rank spotted pajamas
into the washing basket. Not because she didn't want to
stay in them; there had been something so comforting
about wearing Janet's pajamas. The ones she had put on
after saying goodnight to Sammy. But it didn't matter, did
it? They were now nothing but a set of stinky pajamas and
a bad memory.

The keys to the book room and the back door of the
school hung dangled from their long chain, hooked onto
the back of the bathroom door. She stared at them for a
long time as she let the warm water wash over her. She had
no thoughts about them really. She just stared until the
dull, deep wound in her chest reopened and the water
went cold. She wrapped herself in a towel and sat on the
cold bathroom floor, hands holding her heaving chest, she
felt tears again for the first time in days.

When she finally stood up and dressed herself, she
dropped the chain around her neck, the keys now heavy
with guilt, death, blame and grief. She didn't want to keep

the keys, she didn't want to wear them. But she wanted to feel it. She wanted to feel the pain, it was all she had left of him.

She should have stopped it. She could have stopped it, and she didn't. It was all her fault.

Jack's presence was beginning to suffocate her. She loved him in a way, and she had appreciated him being around, and the burgers and everything. But now she just really wanted to be alone.

When he draped an arm around her that night in her bed, she gently pushed it away.

"You OK?" he asked softly, breathing into her hair.

"I just... I need some space tonight."

"I can go downstairs."

"I just need you to not touch me. I'm sorry if that's weird. I do want you here, I just... I don't even know what this is, that we're doing, and it's too much right now."

"I'm just trying to be a friend, be here for you," he said softly as he moved away from her slightly. "I want to help you through this Peg."

In the dark the name 'Peg' was like a dagger in the heart for it was Sammy's voice she heard, not Jack's. It would always be Sammy's voice.

"I do need you here," she said, but her voice was full of confusion.

Jack knew she wasn't there before he even opened his eyes. The morning light had woken him, but she was already gone. And all she left was a note.

FORTY-SIX

Road Trip II

She turned off the GPS and just drove. It didn't matter where she was going, it just felt good to be going somewhere, and to be driving away from Santolsa. She only realized a few hours later she was heading towards the Grand Canyon. Only this time she was alone, and she was thirty-three years too late to see him here, but she decided to keep driving anyway.

She walked slowly, trance-like, kicking the orangey dust up with her black ballet flats, the ones with the studs, the same ones she had worn here so many decades before. She stood in the same place she had stood next to Sammy and she breathed him in. She could still smell him, still feel him next to her, almost as if his ghost was still with her here. Goosebumps raised on her arms. She closed her eyes, stopped the tourists, the chatter, it was only him and her. She knew she was meant to come here. She opened her eyes as a soft breeze caressed her face and she looked down into the abyss below. She knew it was the right thing to do. To end it all. Her toes were so close to the edge, she felt as if she was standing on the edge of two worlds. Standing on the edge of a choice. Her fear of heights still very much present and whispering to her, asking her if she was really ready for it to end?

She grabbed at the chain around her neck, pulling the keys out from beneath her t-shirt where it had been kept safe for so many months. She ran her fingers over the key to the book room and replayed in her mind those first few moments with the key, looking through the yearbook, his picture, the comments, reading the notes to Sammy.

She took the chain from around her neck, holding on so tight that she gave herself an indentation of the key in her sweaty palm.

She had some kind of romantic idea about this being the big grand gesture. She would throw the key over the edge in a fit of rage, screaming his name and exhausting herself with sobs in a Scarlett O'Hara level display of heartbreak until a mob of strangers had to come and remove her from the edge, kicking and screaming. They would escort her back to her motel room where the manager would be asked to check on her every few hours, so she didn't do herself in. They would tell her they'd have to call her parents, but of course her parents wouldn't answer, they wouldn't even know she was out of the state.

In reality though, it was all quite pathetically normal. She just kind of dropped it, just like she had dropped her car keys earlier that day at the gas station. The keys simply slipped away, no slow-motion special effects or screaming. Just another object dropped in the world.

She had expected to feel relieved, like it was the end, or to at least feel something, the first stitch sewn into the cut that sliced through her entire body. She wanted to feel more than just the same sadness. The same blankness. She wanted something different, worse, anything, just some-thing *different*. It wasn't different. It was exactly the same, only now she had taken away her chances of ever seeing Lacey, Ben, and Young Janet again.

She cursed herself, kicked some dirt into the canyon in frustration and headed back to the car, and no one around her had even noticed a thing.

FORTY-SEVEN

Las Vegas

After spending a couple of weeks holed up in the very same Las Vegas hotel she'd stayed in with Sammy, Peggy finally turned on her phone. She had only left the hotel, which had hardly changed at all over the years, except become a bit grungier, to get coffee. She'd had Chinese food delivered to the room once a day and had watched MTV classics between taking long showers and drinking until both the mini bar went dry and hot water went cold. She was never leaving. She felt him here. More than in Santolsa, more than in her own stupid broken heart, more than anywhere. He was in every video clip, every sip of rum, he was in these sheets.

Messages began to bleep through, mostly from Jack wanting to know where she was and pleading for her help with fixing the car. She rolled her eyes at herself. She'd completely forgotten she'd just left Jack there with her Mom's car all dented in. There were also a couple texts from her mother saying they were coming back next week.

She threw her phone onto the other side of the painfully large king-sized bed. She looked back over and grabbed the phone again. She sent a text to her mom telling her where she was and that she was fine. It was summer, her parents would hardly care that she went to Vegas. Then she sent a text back to Jack telling him she was OK.

The phone rang immediately. Jack.

"Hello?" she answered, as if she didn't know who it was.

"I thought something horrible had happened to you," he said.

"I'm fine, I'm just in Vegas."

"You went to *Vegas* without me?"

"It's not like that Jack, I just needed to come here. It's the only place I can be right now."

"When are you coming back?"

"I don't know if I am coming back."

"What?"

"I don't know what I'm doing," she sighed. "Come down if you want, I guess." She didn't know where the invite came from, loneliness, missing him? But the sound of his voice did make her feel less alone and she had been alone for weeks. Maybe it was time to start talking to people again.

"How am I going to get to Vegas Peg?"

Peg, why did he always have to call her Peg?

"Get Mom's car fixed and drive it down. They aren't coming back until next week."

"But I can't even drive. And pay for it how?"

"I'll send you some money."

"OK, so let me get this straight. You've been in Vegas for the last few weeks with your phone switched off. Now you want me to come join you and you want me to drive your Mom's car to Vegas that I *crashed* in the parking lot after I get it fixed with your mom's money?

"I don't know what's going on with me, or what's going on with us, but I could use a friend if you still want to be friends."

"Always," he said.

Jack had no idea how to get a car fixed. He knew nothing about cars. He was the complete opposite of Sammy Ruthven in all ways, and didn't he just know it. He didn't even really know anything about bikes if he was honest. He knew how they worked, but not so much that he could do more than put the chain back on.

He Googled garages and tried to find a quote, but they all asked for specific information about make, model and registration. He knew it was an SUV and it was a grey kind of silver color, but that was it.

"Mom?" he called as he bounded down the stairs.

"Yes darling?" she asked, pushing her dark hair behind one ear and looking at him attentively.

"Do you know a good garage?"

His mother looked confused and put down the scissors she was holding over her scrapbooking book.

"A garage Jack, what for?"

"Yeah, it's for Peggy, I mean, Magz."

"*Peggy*?" she asked.

"I meant Magz, but she's gone on this weird thing where she's asking everyone to call her Peggy. But yeah, it's for her, she needs to get her Mom's car fixed before they get back."

"Can't she just take it where her mom goes?"

"I dunno Mom, she just asked me for help."

"This all sounds a little suspicious," she said, lowering her eyes.

"It's not, much."

She smiled and her soft brown eyes crinkled. "I go to Sam's."

"Sam's?"

"It's a couple blocks past the diner. I can get the address for you." She was about to get off the couch when Jack stopped her.

"I'll just look it up," he said, grabbing his phone out of his pocket.

He found the number and called, but he got all flustered when the guy answered.

"Yeah hi, this is Jack." He sucked at calling people. "I've got a question for you about a car," Jack really had no idea what he was saying.

"Uh huh," said the guy.

"I accidentally drove into a pole in the parking lot and it doesn't look good."

"Just bring it in with your insurance certificate and we'll take a look."

"See the thing is, I was driving it for a friend..."

"So, bring cash," the guy said.

"How long do these things take to fix? I kinda need to be in Vegas as soon as possible."

"Vegas?" the guy asked.

"Yeah, I have to drive to Vegas to meet my girlfriend." The word 'girlfriend' was spilling out of his mouth before his brain could catch it.

"What did you say your name was?" asked the man.

"Jack. Jack Forrester."

There was a pause on the line.

"Hello?" asked Jack.

"OK Jack, bring it in, I'm here until six tonight."

Driving up to the garage in the totaled car Jack felt much more confident. If he had an accident again it wouldn't even matter, because it was already wrecked, and he was on the way to getting it fixed. He had the radio cranked up and the window down and he was feeling very cool, driving was so fun. He should really get a car, and a job, and a real girlfriend.

He parked badly out the front, walked into the office and dinged the bell on the counter. A middle-aged man was working on something out the back and held up a hand, gesturing for Jack to wait. Jack looked around at the walls which were covered in framed pictures of nice looking cars, certificates, old newspaper articles praising the service at the garage, that kind of stuff. Jack tapped his fingers on the counter impatiently. He wanted to get to Vegas dammit. He didn't want to have to deal with these boring admin tasks of life.

The man walked over, stood behind the desk and gave Jack a dark look. Jack took a step back.

"Jack," said the man, raising his eyebrows. He was about the same height as Jack, maybe a little shorter, but he was packing some pretty good muscles for a middle-aged dude. Much better than Jack's. Jack looked down at his arms.

"Going to Vegas huh?" the man asked, wiping his hands on a greased-up cloth.

"Uh, hopefully, once I get this fixed," he thumbed outside towards the car.

"Sure, sure, girlfriend in Vegas," mumbled the man.

"Not really," Jack admitted, shrugging.

The man looked mildly interested.

"No, I don't know why I said that. I used to want her to be my girlfriend, but she met someone else, but then he died, it's a mess, a long story. I don't really know why I'm telling you this."

The man said nothing.

358

"So, uh, how long will it take to fix because I really want to be in Vegas by tonight."

"There's no way you'll be in Vegas tonight with this car."

"But Peggy's waiting for me," Jack complained.

The man said nothing, but just kind of stared him down.

"Look old man," said Jack, "I can just take it to somewhere else if you're going to be so weird."

The phone rang, and the man picked it up, motioning for Jack to wait. Again. Jack rolled his eyes. "Sam's," the man said. "No, it's Sammy not Sam, I'm sure I can help you… yes ma'am, Sammy Ruthven."

Jack's face paled, his body lost its ability to stand and he fell over his own foot, landing on a small table. "Sammy Ruthven?" Jack whispered.

Sammy shot him a look as he carried on with the phone call. "You just bring it into us, and we'll sort it out in no time, don't you worry." Sammy hung up the phone and folded his arms, smirking at the boy in front of him perched on a table.

"You're Sammy Ruthven," Jack said, pointing to the man.

"And you're Jack Forrester."

"I thought you were…"

"What?"

"Dead."

"Do I look dead to you?" he asked.

"Where the hell is Peggy?" Jack demanded.

"In Vegas, apparently."

"You should go straight down there and see her, she's a complete mess," Jack said accusingly as he scrambled back onto his feet.

"I can't go down there," Sammy said.

"Why not?"

"I'm not the Sammy Ruthven she wants to see."

"What do we do then?"

"*You* have to go down there."

"How? My car's wrecked."

"Take mine." Sammy threw Jack a set of keys. "The red Mustang out front."

Jack sat in the driver's seat of the red Mustang and almost died himself. It was the most beautiful car he'd ever seen.

"Drive safe, and bring her back in one piece," Sammy said through the window before tapping the roof gently. Jack didn't know if he was talking about Peggy or the car. But it didn't matter. What *did* matter was that Sammy was still alive, and that meant that he was no longer competing against a dead guy. Sammy was back in the running, but Jack was driving his car.

FORTY-EIGHT

The Rescue

———————————

"He's *alive*," Jack panted. It was just after midnight and he
was standing in a seedy hotel room doorway in Vegas.
Driving the Mustang through town, he got lost for about
an hour, but nonetheless, he felt like the King of the world.
Girls were *looking* at him. And all because of a *car*. Jack was
going to get a car immediately. As soon as he worked out
how to pay for it.

"What?" she asked groggily as she ushered him inside.

Jack rested his hands on her shoulders gently. He
wanted to lean in and hug her, kiss her, but instead he just
said, "Sammy."

She looked up at him blankly. She was a total mess.
Her hair was greasy, her face was pale, she had dark circles
under her eyes, and she smelt like liquor.

"Sammy Ruthven is…" Jack said, "…*alive*."

"Why would you say that to me?" she asked angrily.
She flopped back down on the unmade bed, her eyes
returning to the TV where an old-school rock star was
gyrating wildly.

"I saw him," Jack said as he finally caught his breath.

"Stop it," she said, putting her hands over her ears like a child, and then dropping them to take a sip out of one of the many travel sized alcoholic beverages on the nightstand.

"I saw Sammy," Jack said. "He works at the garage, *Sam's* Garage."

"That must've been his dad." She shook her head and offered him a miniature bottle of vodka.

He shook his head and sat on the edge of the bed. "No, it was *him*, he was like fifty, but it was him."

"Yeah, that's his dad."

"You're not thinking Peg. I saw him *here*, in this time. So, he *would* be about fifty. He told me to come get you."

"Why didn't he come get me himself if he's so alive?" She crawled back under the covers.

"He said he was going to freak you out because he was all old, something about it was my job to get you. But he gave me his car."

"What car?"

"A Mustang. It's downstairs, come see."

She stood in front of the Mustang in her sweatpants and dirty hair with her jaw on the floor.

"He's alive, Peg. I don't know how, but he is. There's no way in hell I would make this up. Why would I?"

She ran back through the casino of the hotel and up the stairs with him right on her heels.

"What are you doing?" he asked.

"Packing."

"You can't drive, you've been drinking."

"As if I care about that," she stopped herself and shook her head. "No, you're right. You'll drive me." She was like a whirlwind, grabbing everything and packing it all into her duffel bag within minutes.

"And what will happen to your car?"

"You'll get the bus back to Vegas. I'm paid up for the week, so you can stay here if you want, bring Jayne. You can pick it up then," she said, zipping up the bag.

"And then what?"

"Keep it."

"I'm not driving that thing."

"Sell it, whatever, I don't care."

Jack picked up her bag and walked to the door.

"Let's get lattes to go," she said, instantly returning to her usual self.

He wanted her to be happy. He loved her enough to want that for her and it made him want to cry, but he couldn't cry in front of her, so he just nodded at her and carried her bag to the coffee shop.

"I'm not sure we're meant to drink these in the car," she said putting her massive drink in the cup holder.

"Sammy Ruthven doesn't always lend me his car, but when he does I put soy lattes in the cup holders."

Peggy laughed.

"So now what?" Jack asked.

"Let's go home."

FORTY-NINE

The Parentals

In a strange twist of fate, Peggy's parents were home when they got back early the next morning.

"Magz, is that you?" called her mother from the kitchen.

Jack and Peggy exchanged looks. She could hardly remember the last time she'd seen her mom.

"We were just talking," her mom continued, leaning on the door frame between rooms. "We're going to take you out for lunch today."

"Seems like ages since we've done that," her father chimed in, appearing from the kitchen with two coffee cups. "Jack, you are welcome to come too of course," her father added, noticing Jack standing slack-jawed behind Peggy.

Peggy said nothing. What was there to say? *I'm a time traveler and I have to go back to 1983 today and I won't be back again?*

"We have to be back by two though," her mother said. "I've got a conference call."

Peggy rolled her eyes, of course her mother had a

conference call. Even lunch out with her parents for the first time in years would have to be cut short as, once again, work takes priority in their lives.

"I can't," said Peggy, "I've got plans."

"I think you can cancel your plans Magz. It's rare we get to do this." Her father was not *asking* her to change her plans, he was making a demand.

"No," she said, taking a step backwards.

Her mother's eyebrows shot up.

"Don't say no to your father Magz," she tutted. "We never get to see you, make an effort."

"You never get to see me because you're never *here*. You're always at work, on a trip or just away somewhere. Why should I change my plans, so I can spend two hours of your precious time out at some fancy restaurant listening to you both talking BS?"

Her mother looked horrified and her father was dumb-founded.

"I meant business, not bullshit," Peggy said softening her tone. She thought of Lacey and took another step backwards.

"I don't know who you've become Magz, but I'm not sure I like this new you," her father shook his head. "We'll go without you, we don't want to lose our reservation."

"Of course you don't," she said.

"And do you mind," continued her father, "explaining exactly where your mother's car is?"

"It's at the garage, I crashed it," Peggy said bluntly.

"*Magz*, I don't believe this is you!" said her mother.

"You don't even *know* me, either of you."

"That's not fair." Her father didn't even look up from his coffee.

Peggy felt the stinging frustration behind her eyes again, but this time she would not let it come. These people weren't worth her tears. They were like paper-doll versions of her family offering a short lunch in exchange for months and months away at a time. A complete lack of knowledge about her life, her interests, how she spent her days, they knew nothing about her. She had raised herself while they had been worried about losing their reservations. Then she had met Janet, who in days had taken her in and shown her what a real family was.

"It's getting fixed," Jack added.

"Well, as long as it's getting fixed. But you could have told me." Her mother didn't know quite what to say. She had never had to reprimand her daughter for anything before.

"We can talk about it at lunch," her father went on.

"I'm not *going* to lunch, Dad," even the word *dad* sounded foreign coming from her lips, she so seldom said it. "You don't even listen!"

"Don't expect us to do anything nice for you again then, if this is the way you're going to be," he finished.

"I never expected you to do anything for me. That's just it."

Peggy walked towards the stairs, Jack following behind, ready to hold her while she cried, tell her everything was going to be all right, but when they walked into her bedroom, she burst out laughing.

"Are you OK?" he asked, standing by the door as he watched her throw her bag on the bed and start throwing everything around.

"Never better."

"I, I don't really know what happened down there," Jack shook his head.

"They aren't my family Jack," she said, rooting through the bag for something, tossing around clothes and books.

"Well, yeah, they kinda are."

"Janet is my family."

"Janet is your teacher."

"She's the closet thing I've got to a Mom, Jack," she said grinning, catching the Nevada keyring and Janet's house keys... no, *her* house keys in her hand.

And then she realized.

"Oh no," she said, dropping to the bed.

"What is it?" Jack dropped down next to her.

She looked up at him, her eyes filled with terror. "The key."

"What about it?"

"I threw it in the Grand Canyon."

"Well that was stupid."

"What am I going to do?" She grabbed at her chest and looked at him pleadingly. "What do I do?" Now tears *did* begin to well in her eyes.

"We go see Mrs. Willis," Jack said, rubbing her back, "and," he continued, "the key just opens the door. That's all right? They key isn't magic, it's the *room* that is."

"But how do I get in without it?"

Jack shrugged. "We'll work it out."

"Does she even still live here?" asked Jack, pulling up outside Janet's old house in the Mustang.

"I don't know," said Peggy. "I never thought to ask. It looks like it, the plants are still here." The hanging baskets were a lot wilder and more unkempt, but the house didn't really seem all that different.

She knocked lightly on the door, and when there was no answer, she tried her key and it worked. She pushed open the door and the familiar smell of home reached her nostrils as she smiled. She pushed the door open further and stepped inside.

"She's gone," said Peggy, looking around the empty house. She looked down at the empty space where the table used to be and ran her foot across the floor where she used to keep her shoes. She walked into the empty lounge room where she had slept all those nights before she'd moved upstairs. Where she'd spent all those nights with Janet and Lacey planning how to save Sammy.

"I just, never thought..." said Peggy.

"Maybe we can call someone, get a forwarding address."

Jack kept talking but Peggy wasn't listening. She walked up the stairs towards her bedroom as if on autopilot. It felt so much like home, it was exactly the same, although the carpet was worn, and the paint chipped in places. She felt so much as she walked into her old bedroom and looked out the window and down to the street. She thought of the times Sammy had come to pick her up and dropped her off and parked in the driveway, and she looked down at the red Mustang and wondered if it had all been a dream after all, and she was so busy wondering what was real anymore that she almost walked away without seeing it. Almost.

Her hand brushed the window ledge and she heard something fall to the floor. An envelope. She tore it open in a heartbeat. A key fell into her hand and she held it to her pounding chest. And then she unfolded the yellow paper.

My dearest Peggy,

I'm sorry I never told you he was alive, but I couldn't. You had to go on your own journey. I knew the path you had to take was the right one for you because I knew exactly what was going to happen. Remember, I've seen how it all works out. You were supposed to come back here. Jack was supposed to meet Sammy for reasons I can't even fully explain now, but it just had to be this way.

I couldn't take away all the pain Peggy, because that wouldn't be letting you live. No one can tell you how to live, or what to do. Not even someone who knows, because, despite everything, I still think things can change. And maybe we did change it. Maybe Sammy was meant to die. Maybe we did stop it, but at what cost? I still wonder about that sometimes. But if we changed it, maybe it was our destiny to change it. Remember that, it might give you some comfort when you are questioning it all.

It still gives me a headache.

So now we come to the answer to the big question that everyone has been waiting for - is it all pre-determined or is it fate?

I think it's both. We are like magnets attracting and repelling events and people in our lives, but at any moment we can still choose.

If you choose something else, if you choose not to go back, I don't know what will happen to me. I don't know if I will forget everything that's happened over the last thirty-three years. Maybe my memories will be replaced, maybe the me who's writing this letter will no longer exist, I don't know.

But I hope you choose us. I hope you choose 1983. I hope you come back to live with me and that you continue to be the daughter I never knew I wanted, the little sister I never had and my best friend.

We are all there waiting for you.

Hope to see you soon.

But remember to choose your own destiny, Peggy.

All my love,

Janet

xxx

Peggy stumbled down the stairs into Jack's arms. He swung them around her.

"All good?" he asked.

"Better than good," she said, smiling and wiping her eyes.

He saw the key in her hand and knew this was it, she was gone. Out of his life forever.

"What does this mean for us now?" asked Jack as he drove the Mustang and Peggy straight to school.

"It means we have to break into school. If you don't want to be part of it, I'll understand."

"Are you crazy? After everything we've been through together, you think I won't help you break into school?"

She grinned.

Jack took a deep breath.

"I don't want to leave you, Jack. All I know is that my life isn't here anymore."

"Yeah yeah, I know. You don't fit in here in Santolsa, no one gets you, you can't wear your scrunchies without getting your face punched in, but you have options. Move to LA or New York or something. There are other people out there like you Peg, in this century."

"I know, because you are one of them."

"Doesn't this seem a little extreme to you? Can't you just keep coming and going? Do you have to stay there forever?"

"Coming and going has been a disaster Jack, and if what Janet says is true, I could get stuck forever there or here. I hope it hasn't been too long already."

"What are your parents going to think? Like, you go into the book room and never come out? Some questions are going to be asked. There could be investigations. People will think you died!"

"So, cover for me."

"How can I cover for that? How can I cover you for thirty-three years?" He stopped the car in the staff lot, all empty except for one security car.

"Tell everyone I went to Canada," she said.

"On a whim?"

"Sure."

"For a boy?"

"Even better, makes total sense." She threw her duffel bag over her shoulder. She turned to Jack. "Bye Jack." she said shrugging.

"Oh God, no. Don't do this goodbye BS." Jack looked away.

"If not now, when?"

He looked up at the passing clouds in the never changing bright blue sky and then looked down at her. "Well, crap." He threw his arms around her and let some of his own tears fall onto her shoulder for a change.

FIFTY

Back to her Future

Breaking into school had been easier than they'd antici-
pated. Jack had made up some story about leaving a
thumb drive in a school computer and could he come and
check because it had some important college stuff on it.
The security guard had let them in, escorting them to the
library. Cue Peggy pretending she needed to use the
bathroom.

After a few minutes of checking around the backs of
computers in the computer lab Jack pulled out a thumb
drive from his pocket and shouted, "Found it!"

The security guard looked solemn and asked Jack
about the girl. Jack mumbled something about meeting her
back at the car and he walked out of the school doors
without her, walked towards the Mustang and got in, and
that was it.

She was gone.

There was no security guard waiting for her outside the
girl's toilets in 1983 and she'd had to climb out of a

window in the typing lab to get out. But she was back. Back where she belonged, and the musty old school hallway had never smelt better.

Peggy ran as fast as she could through the school grounds, down the hill and out of the gates. She lost steam about halfway down the hill and carried on speed walking, until what seemed like hours later, she finally reached Sammy's street. She stood standing outside his house, puffed, dirty, sweaty, exhausted. But she was here. And he was alive. She burst out laughing, *he was alive*!

The door opened, as if welcoming her home, and just as she was about to go running into his arms, she saw him with… *Rochelle*? They were embracing on the porch, she was saying something into his neck. And then she walked to a slick white car in his driveway. Peggy's mind raced at a million thoughts per second as she struggled to work out what was going on. Could he have so quickly fallen back into Rochelle's arms? Surely, he wasn't that stupid, after everything. He didn't even *like* Rochelle. She waited until Rochelle had driven away before slowly emerging from the bushes.

Peggy lifted her hand to knock on the door, her hand shaking, her stomach churning. She'd never felt so nervous, excited, confused and angry all at the same time.

When the door opened, Peggy frowned. A blonde girl of about eleven or twelve looked up at her confused.

"You must be Jessie," Peggy said.

The girl just kept looking at her.

Peggy rolled her eyes, of course, Jessie was deaf. Peggy waved and smiled at the girl who looked even more confused.

"Is Sammy home?" Peggy asked. "Sammy?" she asked again slowly.

The girl ran away, leaving the door wide open.

She could hear him talking inside the house and her insides flipped. He was alive, it was true. She gasped when she saw him, standing in front of her, he looked tired, older. His hair was a mess and he was dressed in a dirty old t-shirt and a pair of sweatpants. He was a much lesser version of himself.

"What are you doing here?" he asked.

"You're alive," she gasped, throwing her arms around him.

But he didn't move. "You noticed?"

"I thought you were *dead*," she said, letting her arms fall. Why wasn't he hugging her back?

"You thought I was dead huh? So, what? You ran off back to Canada or wherever it is that you're from without even telling anyone?"

This was *so* not how this was meant to go.

"As soon as I found out, I came straight here," she said shaking her head in disbelief.

"You have no idea," he held up a hand in front of him.

"No idea? I thought you were dead! How do you think *I* felt?"

"How do I think *you* felt? How do you think *we* all felt? We've been here going through hell and you... you just left."

"I'm sorry," she said, tears welling in the corners of her eyes. "Is Rochelle, are you and Rochelle...?"

"Me and Rochelle are nothing that concerns you now." His voice was hard, the Sammy she loved was behind a brick wall of anger. She thought he'd be pleased to see her, to run into her arms and they'd be together forever.

"I'm so confused." She shook her head and looked up at him pleadingly. Why was he being like this?

"Lacey needed you. Ben and Janet needed you. *I* needed you." His blue eyes flashed with the truth. He was hurt. She'd hurt him. Of all the things she meant to do, hurting Sammy was not one of them.

"I'm sorry," she stammered.

"I'm…" he shook his head. "I just can't talk to you right now. I'm sorry." And he closed the door on her.

She staggered down his drive and continued to walk back into town. Her feet were sore, and her heart was breaking all over again, and she just felt so confused about everything.

She needed Janet.

When she eventually got to the payphone outside Super Pan, Peggy put the spare change she'd been carrying around for weeks into the phone and typed in the only phone number she had ever learned by heart.

"I'm so glad you came back," Janet said as Peggy slid into the front seat of the Escort.

"I don't know why I did," Peggy said, wiping her face with the back of her hand.

"Come on, let's get you home."

Home.

She wanted nothing more than to curl up in her very own polka dot covered single bed in her own room. In Janet's house. In 1983. And that was where they were going. And even though it felt painful as hell, it still felt a little bit wonderful.

FIFTY-ONE

Explanations

Janet threw Peggy's bags onto the floor by the door, took her hand and dragged her into the kitchen. "I'll make tea," she said.

"Tea is the last thing I want," Peggy said, slumping onto the bar stool.

"Coffee?"

Peggy nodded.

"What happened?" Janet asked when the kettle was on.

"I don't know," Peggy said, shaking her head.

"Well, the good news is Sammy's alive," Janet said as she got out the Bryan Adams mug and another plain blue one. "But I guess you already knew that, or you wouldn't be here. How did you find out anyway? Did I tell you?"

"Enough with the questions Janet." Peggy put her hands to her head, this time travel headache was going to be epic.

"Of course, you have a lot to think about." Janet poured some coffee, milk and one sugar into the Bryan Adams mug and slid it across the counter towards her along with a glass of water and some painkillers.

"I went to see him. Rochelle was there. I... I don't know. He told me to go away." She looked up at Janet, her eyes glistening.

"He's going through a hard time, I think you were the last person he expected to see."

"*He's* going through a hard time?" Peggy scoffed. "What about what I've been going through? I've spent the last month thinking he was dead! It's been complete torture."

"You don't know, do you?" Janet asked slowly.

"Don't know what?"

There was silence as Janet's face fell.

"What?" Peggy demanded.

"It was Nick."

"What was Nick?" Peggy shook her head in confusion.

"The accident still happened Peggy."

"No, he's alive..." Peggy said, looking up from her coffee.

"Sammy didn't die, but Nick did."

Peggy gasped.

"The report was wrong. The officers on the scene knew it was Sammy's car, everyone in town knew that car. They found a body and assumed it was Sammy. But Nick was driving that night."

"No," Peggy whispered.

"Nick was drunk, he was speeding and hit the tree. The whole town is in mourning Peg. He was well liked, he was a good kid who made a dumb mistake."

Peggy shook her head.

"You missed the funeral. Sammy spoke on behalf of the family. The cool and calm Sammy Ruthven we've all come to know and love has been a complete mess these last few weeks."

"I should go back and tell him I didn't know." She

jumped up from her stool and felt Janet's strong grip on her hand.

"No, not now."

"I have to tell him I didn't know, I never would have left if I had known!" She struggled to get out of the teacher's grip.

"Don't take this the wrong way, but right now you aren't his priority. Let him be."

"But I came back to be with him!" She escaped from her teacher's clutches. "I came back here for *him!*"

"Peggy," Janet said calmly. "In life you need to make decisions for yourself, not for anyone else. If you only came back here for some boy, then you might have made a serious mistake about your future."

"He's not just *some boy* Janet, he's the love of my life. But then, you wouldn't know anything about that." As soon as the words left her mouth, she regretted them.

"I know more than you think," Janet said.

"Whatever," Peggy rolled her eyes.

"I know you're upset. I know this isn't you."

Peggy pretended to ignore her.

"If you really love him, you'll give him what he needs right now, and that means not going over there and apologizing just so you'll feel better and he'll take you back."

Peggy stood up, grabbed the side of the bench with all her might and screamed.

"Why did you come back Peg? Was it just for Sammy? Or was it for everything? For all of this?" she gestured around the little kitchen.

"I don't know, maybe it was the dumbest mistake of my life." She fell to the floor and began to cry.

"Why are you *really* here? You need to ask yourself that."

But Peggy didn't have to ask herself anything. She

knew there was more to being back than Sammy. She knew it was Janet, Lacey and Ben, even Tricia. It was the Fire Station, Super Pan, it was the music, the clothes, the movies. It was having to call people on the landline. It was every single little thing.

"I'm sorry," she mumbled as she looked up at Janet.

"Your room is still made up, you should get some rest," Janet said.

"Where are you?" asked Lacey in a tone that was less than enthusiastic when she realized who it was on the other end of the phone.

"I'm back."

"For God's sake girl, where have you been?"

"I went back to my present," said Peggy.

"Why?" asked Lacey.

"I couldn't deal with it," Peggy said truthfully.

"Welcome to my awesome world where 'dealing with it' has become my daily past time."

"I thought it was Sammy."

"What?"

"In the accident. I heard it on the news and I just, I ran away."

"It wasn't Sammy," Lacey said.

"I know, I only just found out."

"It was Nick. Remember Nick?"

"Please Lacey."

"Our friend Nick, Sammy's best friend Nick. Nick who took Sammy's car home when Sammy went with you to walk you home?"

"You think this is my fault?"

"Yes… maybe, I don't know. But I am damn pissed that you freaked out and left us to deal with it all without you."

"I know."

"How could you possibly know?"

"Because for the last month I've been torturing myself and bleeding out of my heart every night because I thought it was Sammy. Every night I dreamt of him dying. Every day all I could think of was that I'd never see him again, and then I come back and all anyone can do is hate on me." Peggy felt hot tears stream down her face.

"I'll be right over." The phone clicked, and Peggy put down the receiver.

"I'm still so mad at you, but it's good to see you," Lacey threw her arms around her friend and held her tight.

"I'm so sorry Lace," she muffled into Lacey's hair.

"It's been really hard," Lacey said making herself at home by plonking down into one of the red armchairs in the lounge. "We've been staying at home for days at a time and not answering each other's calls and then someone will answer, and they'll say we should all go out, and we all go out and get drunk. We don't dance, we just sit there. Then we all stay home for the next few days not seeing each other again."

"How is he?" asked Peggy folding her legs up on the couch.

"Sammy? He's kind of a mess to be honest," Lacey shrugged. She looked exhausted. She was hardly wearing any make-up and the red shirt she had on washed her out completely.

"I want to talk to him, but Janet keeps telling me to leave him alone."

"That's good advice."

"I saw Rochelle at his house."

Lacey shrugged. "I don't know anything about that."

"Did he ask about me or anything?"

Lacey shook her head.

"What am I meant to do?"

Lacey shrugged again. "I can't tell you what to do, but I can tell you that things have been rough around here."

"How do I get him back?"

"I don't know if you can."

Peggy felt a new wave of tears building behind her eyes.

"He's messed up right now," Lacey went on, "and you leaving was a big part of why. You can't expect everything to just go back to how it was overnight."

Peggy nodded. "But I just need him to know why I left. That I thought it was him. That I nearly threw myself into the God damn Grand Canyon because I thought it was him."

"I'll tell him for you," Lacey promised.

FIFTY-TWO

The Fire Station III

Another night of being ignored by Sammy Ruthven in a bar was nothing new. Although this time the air was not filled with sexual tension but instead thick and heavy with grief.

It had been two months since Prom, and it was decided that everyone - friends, acquaintances, relatives and class-mates would have a drink for Nick at his favorite bar. It was debatable that the Fire Station was Nick's favorite as Peggy wasn't sure she'd ever seen Nick have a really good time, but nonetheless everyone was there. They were wearing white sweatbands around their wrists or upper arms with a simple blue letter N stitched on. The sweatbands had been stitched by June-Belle who was sitting at the bar looking very out of place. Horace was looking only slightly less out of place talking to some of his friends at the other end of the bar.

"Anyone need another drink?" asked Lacey.

Peggy and Sammy both shook their heads.

"I do," said Ben.

"Me too," said Tricia and the three of them went to

the bar leaving Peggy alone with Sammy for the first time since she'd seen him at his door.

"I talked to Lacey," he said, looking into his drink. He hadn't looked at her all night.

"I thought it was you..." Peggy began, "I'm not trying to give you an excuse." She shook her head. "I totally messed up, there is no excuse for running away. I should have stayed, but I wasn't thinking straight, at all."

"Yeah, what you did sucked big time." He looked at her for the first time since she'd seen him at his door the day she returned. His eyes were full of pain, there was no smirk on his lips, but he still made her heart flip over.

"I thought it was you," she said again, wanting so desperately to crawl across the great emotional divide that was now between them. Wanting him to take her in his arms and cry and laugh and just be together like they were before.

He looked away, back to the empty dance floor. No one was dancing tonight and even the music was a little quieter and slower.

Lacey returned and placed a tray of drinks on the table.

"I got bourbons and cokes, because that was his favorite drink. Not my favorite, but..." Lacey took a large swig and handed drinks over to her friends.

Peggy lifted a glass to her own lips and took a sip. She made a face, it was strong. She pushed it back into the middle of the table.

Rochelle stumbled over towards the table, clearly having had more than a few bourbons herself. She leant over the table, quite obviously presenting her breasts to Sammy who glanced at them but looked mainly in the direction of her eyes.

"Wanna dance?" she slurred.

"You should probably get a taxi Ro," Sammy said, standing up to help her.

"Ro?" whispered Lacey into Peggy's ear and giving her a knowing look.

"I'll dance with you," Peggy said.

"*You?*" slurred Rochelle.

"Sure, why not?" asked Peggy.

"Uh, I don't know... because you hate me." Rochelle looked confused and teetered slightly backwards on her heels.

"Come dance it off." Peggy squeezed past Lacey, taking Rochelle by the hand and onto the dance floor leaving Lacey slack jawed.

"Why are you doing this?" Rochelle yelled at her as she began swaying in time with the power ballad that was currently blaring from the speakers.

"Doing what?"

"Dancing with me?" Rochelle stumbled and fell into a woman dressed in a biker jacket who was standing near the dancefloor.

"Hey! You made me spill my drink!" shouted the woman.

"You got in my way," Rochelle shouted back as she nearly fell over again.

"Rochelle," warned Peggy trying to grab Rochelle and hold her up.

"Bitch," spat the woman, and before Peggy even knew what was happening, she was in the middle of a fight.

Peggy tried her best to hold Rochelle back, but her upper body strength was no match for Rochelle's fists of fury. The glass the woman had been holding smashed on the floor and Rochelle was in a frenzy, throwing random punches and flailing limbs in the direction of the woman who started screaming like a banshee and grabbing at Rochelle's long brittle locks.

Peggy grabbed the woman's wrist and dug in her pink nails before she even knew what she was doing. The woman let out a yelp and let go, causing Rochelle to fall back into Peggy leaving both of them in a heap on the sticky cigarette butt encrusted dance floor.

Seriously, how many times was she going to end up lying on the floor of this bar?

"Awesome," Jonas laughed as he held a stack of glasses above them.

"Hey!" called out Sammy as he ran across the dance floor, landing on his knees in front of them. He checked they were OK and stood up to face their attacker who was puffing up her hair and looking quite proud of herself.

"We've just lost someone," Sammy said to her calmly.

"You'll lose her in a minute," the woman said, her eyes narrowing in recognition at Sammy's face. "Hey, aren't you that guy that had to pay for Jonas' golden tooth?" She laughed. "I'm surprised you'd even show your face around here again."

"I paid my debt to Jonas," Sammy said. "And now I think you better leave." Ben and bartender Greg came to stand behind him.

"Or what? Are you going to hit a woman?" She put her hands on her hips, taunting him.

"He won't, but I will." Tricia appeared and stood next to Sammy folding her arms.

The woman looked thoughtful. "This place blows anyway," she said before walking off towards the door.

"This place is awesome, *you* blow," shouted Lacey after her as she helped Peggy to her feet while Ben helped Rochelle.

"No one talks like that about the Fire Station," Lacey said.

"You OK Ro?" Sammy asked.

Peggy winced, why wasn't he asking about *her*?

"I'm fine," Rochelle said taking herself back to the booth and sitting down.

Greg went to get her a water and returned with a tray of drinks for everyone.

"I'm on break," Greg said folding his arms and leaning casually against the table.

Ben looked up at him. "I could use some air," he shrugged and followed him out. After a few minutes, Peggy followed after them, she needed some air too.

She stood out the front of the bar looking across the road to the parking lot, to where Sammy's car had been that night before Nick had decided to take it home. Ben and Greg were nowhere to be seen, so she started walking towards Dee's when she heard Ben's voice down the alley behind the Fire Station. When she turned into the alley the last thing she expected to see was Ben and Greg kissing.

"Oh," she gasped as they looked over at her.

Ben let go of Greg, swore and kicked the dumpster behind him.

Greg grabbed his hand. "Ben," Greg said. "Peggy's cool."

Peggy walked towards them. "Sorry," she said. "You know I won't say anything."

"Maybe it's time people knew," Greg said looking up at Ben.

"No," said Ben. "Peggy, if my dad ever found out he'd kill me. He would *really* kill me. Please."

"I won't tell a soul," she said. "But Greg, you need to

tell Lacey *something*. I'm so over hearing about how much she loves you and I think it might be time for her to move on."

Greg laughed awkwardly. "It's a deal."

When Peggy went back in everyone was drunkenly dancing, except Sammy. She went over to him. She wasn't sure that she should, but she just wanted to be next to him.

"I never wanted to end it," Sammy said, swirling around his drink in his hand.

"Do you... do you want to get back together?" Peggy asked.

"I don't know," he said.

"Oh," she said.

"I really needed you and you were gone and that was really hard."

She nodded her head. She didn't know what more to say and so she looked for an escape.

Ben was standing at the bar talking to Greg who was showing off throwing around a cocktail shaker, Tricia must have been pretty drunk because she was talking to Horace at a table in the corner, Leigh and Rochelle were talking to the only other guys in the place and Lacey was dancing by herself on the dancefloor.

When the lights finally came on everyone groaned. No one wanted to leave and face the light of day.

"No!" shouted Lacey. "No not yet!"

When someone dies drunk driving, the last thing you want to do is drive home drunk. So the group stood outside the bar confused about what to do next. Usually someone would just drive everyone home. But not tonight.

"I'm going to call a taxi," Tricia said, walking off towards the nearest payphone.

"There is no way a taxi is coming tonight in this town, seriously, no way," Lacey said, sitting awkwardly with her legs in the gutter trying to light a cigarette.

Sammy took it out of her hand and lit it for her, taking a drag and then passing it back.

"No taxis," said Tricia, returning from the payphone.

"No surprise," said Lacey.

"I'm walking," Tricia said. "You wanna come with Ro? Leigh?"

Rochelle pulled Leigh along after her and followed Tricia down the street.

"What about us?" moaned Lacey, smoking her cigarette as Greg came to sit between her and Ben on the curb.

"Hey," he said, taking the cigarette out of her hand.

"Hey!" she smiled, letting him take it.

"You guys need a ride? I can drive you if you can wait about an hour."

"Yes," Lacey nodded, taking the cigarette back from him and taking a drag. "A hundred times yes."

"You guys?" Greg gestured a thumb towards Ben, Sammy and Peggy.

"Yeah, sure," Ben said, shoving his hands in his pockets.

"I'm good," Sammy said.

"Peggy?" asked Greg.

"Uh, yeah, I guess so," she was reluctant to take him up on the offer in case Sammy presented her with a better one, but that didn't seem like it was going to happen. That night they walked home together from prom was the most romantic night of her life. She wanted to re-live it. Have him walk with her again. Every night. But nights like that don't come around very often. They are kind of a once in a lifetime deal.

"I'll come help you clean up," Lacey said eagerly.

"Good, there's something I need to talk to you about," he said as she followed him back into the bar giving Peggy a wink.

"I'll uh..." Ben followed them both, leaving Sammy and Peggy alone.

Sammy Ruthven sat on the curb, cigarette in hand. He put his head between his legs and he did what Peggy thought was something like crying, but she never saw any tears, so she really wasn't sure, but in that moment, she couldn't have believed he was doing anything else.

"Hey," she said, sitting down next to him.

He looked up at her and then gently pushed her sweaty hair behind her ear. "I still love you," he said, leaning his forehead on her shoulder. She leant her head on top of his and they stayed like that for a long time. Not speaking, just being there together in that moment, until the moment passed.

He lifted his head and took her head in his hands and he kissed her. A long, hot, sweaty, bourbon, cigarette, sad kiss.

She gasped as he drew away from her.

"I think I just... I need to be on my own right now," he said. "I need to figure some stuff out."

And he got up and he walked away, leaving her still reeling from the kiss, cold and alone, but grateful. Grateful that Sammy was OK. Grateful that her friends were just inside, that everyone was getting home safe and that Janet was at home waiting for her.

FIFTY-THREE

Goodbyes

———————

"I thought I was never going to see you again," said Jack as they walked through the buzzing quadrangle on the first day of summer school. Jack couldn't help feeling a little sorry for them. As much as his life sucked right now at least he didn't have to go to summer school.

"You won't after today," she said, her voice catching as she squinted into the sun and blinked away the tears. "But I had to come and say a real goodbye, and I had to make things right with the parentals." She pushed open the main doors of the school and held them open for him to follow her. "I couldn't have left everything the way it was. Just disappearing like that. I don't want to be that person."

They walked slowly and silently down the hallway, navigating through summer school students, past the mural of Saint Christopher, past the portraits of the nuns and past their old lockers both knowing this was the last time they would do this together.

"I'm glad you came back, but it's a slow torture," Jack said, running his hand through his hair. His sneaker squeaked as he came to a stop just before the book room door.

"How's that?" Peggy asked.

"Every time I see you, I think it's going to be the last time, so I talk myself into it, being OK without you and then... Puff the Magic Dragon, there you are again."

"Well," said Peggy, hugging her duffel bag to her chest. "This is it. For real this time." She shrugged as the bell for first period rang and in seconds the hallway was empty, leaving them standing there staring at each other in the silence.

"Do me a favor," Jack said, breaking the tension. "Look me up when you get here."

Peggy forced a laugh over the heaviness in her chest.

"I guess you'll be old and middle aged," he said. "You probably won't even be hot anymore."

She playfully whacked him on the arm.

Jack looked at the door. "I'm kind of expecting you to just go in and then walk out again and laugh hysterically and tell me this whole thing was some kind of sick elaborate hoax." Jack looked down at her and his lip began to wobble, and he swore. "I don't want the last memory you have of me to be like this," he said, wiping away a tear from the corner of his eye.

She laughed. "Like you haven't seen me at so much worse?"

"What about your folks?" he asked, crossing his arms and trying to act normal. "I know they're not much, but..."

"Future me has got it covered."

"Uh, how exactly?"

"Middle-aged me sends them emails and leaves them voice notes," Peggy said.

"Emails and voice notes from the past?" Jack asked confused. "But that stuff hasn't been invented yet for you."

"Not for teenage me, but middle-aged me is out there somewhere doing it."

Jack gave her a look of disbelief.

"I know, because I got an email from my future self yesterday."

"You wrote yourself an email?"

She shrugged.

"Why didn't future you write me an email?" he pouted.

Peggy laughed. "I tell you that my future self sent me an email and all you can ask is why you didn't get one." She rolled her eyes, smirking.

"It's a very good question, and I'll be expecting an email soon."

"I'll try to remember," she smiled.

He grabbed her up suddenly in his shaking arms, squeezing her so hard she let out a yelp.

She pulled back and wiped her own face with a sweaty palm, laughing. His eyes looked so sad. Pleading. It was so hard to see him like this. She wondered why, now that she was at peace with the destiny she'd chosen, why was it still so hard to say goodbye to the past?

Feeling for the new silver chain around her neck she pulled the key out from beneath her t-shirt. She took off the necklace, put the key into the lock and turned it. Jack watched slack jawed as the door frame shuddered into life.

"It does that," she said.

"Now what?"

"Now I go in and I come out in 1983."

"Right," Jack said, his eyes wide.

She grabbed him again, embracing him urgently and awkwardly. She kissed him on the cheek and then opened the door.

"Bye," he said.

"See you later," she said, tears streaming down her pink-blushed cheeks.

"Not soon enough," he said, his own tears streaming down his cheeks.

She stepped into the book room, the musty air heavy with the smell of old books and dust. She flicked on the light switch, illuminating the hundreds of forgotten old books and just as she was about to step in and close the door behind her Jack jammed his foot in.

"Can I come with you?" he asked suddenly.

She smiled and kicked his foot playfully out of the way.

"You have to find your own destiny Jack."

She held up her hand and waved, feeling slightly stupid until he returned the gesture.

And Jack watched as the door frame sprung to life once more and as a weird multi-colored light flickered wildly, three times from beneath the door.

And then she was gone. Really gone.

FIFTY-FOUR

Destiny

"Are you really going to stay in Santolsa forever now?" asked Lacey excitedly as they chowed down on a ham and pineapple pizza in a booth up the back of Super Pan.

"Yup," Peggy mumbled through a mouth full of crust.

"I mean, where else would you rather be anyway? I know it's a bit boring around here, but we've got good pizza. And we've got the Fire Station... and we've got Dee's Diner. We've even got..."

"You don't have to sell it to me Lace, I'm going to stay," said Peggy, smiling at her as she chewed.

"Even though Sammy's still kind of ignoring you?" Lacey asked.

"He's not *ignoring* me, he's just taking some time out for himself. And yes."

"Yes what?" asked Lacey, reaching over the table for the chili flakes.

"Yes, I'm happy here, even without Sammy. I want to be with him more than anything, and every night I go to bed, and I curl into a ball and feel sick about everything. But there's still nowhere else I'd rather be." Peggy sipped on her 7UP and smiled as she caught a glimpse of him and her other friends walking into the restaurant.

"Finally," said Lacey, rolling her eyes and waving them over.

Tricia took a slice of pizza before even saying hi and Peggy watched while everyone else said their hellos. Sammy nodded in Peggy's direction and slid into the booth opposite her, grabbing a menu, focusing on it intently.

"What are we going to do with the rest of the summer?" asked Ben as he tried to get the attention of a mustached waiter.

"What are we going to do with the rest of our *lives?*" Lacey asked dramatically.

"Get jobs I guess," said Peggy, shrugging.

"That is the stupidest thing you've said," accused Lacey as she slopped another slice onto her plate before Tricia ate the whole thing.

"Well none of us are going to college, except Ben," said Rochelle, shrugging as she slid into the seat next to Sammy. Peggy made a weird breathing sound and Lacey elbowed her in the ribs.

"I know, and really, he's the stupidest one of us all," said Tricia.

"Thanks Trish," said Ben who had just ordered a large pepperoni pizza all to himself.

"Congrats Ben," said Peggy. "You're going out to California huh?"

Ben nodded, grinning.

"If mum and Roger can work it out, I might be free to go check out LA for a while," said Lacey. "I've got a cousin who knows a bunch of people down there." Lacey was staring out the last slice of pizza.

"I can totally see you in LA," said Peggy.

"Come with me!" Lacey grinned.

Peggy laughed. Hanging out with Lacey in LA would be quite the adventure. She looked over at Sammy. But maybe she'd had enough adventures for now. She couldn't just run off again. So, they weren't together, but she still wanted to be around. She wanted him to know she was here for him. And besides, she was loving living with Janet. It was in that moment that she realized for the first time that she loved Santolsa and it was the only place she wanted to be.

"I think we should just try to make the most of it," said Leigh, shrugging.

"The most of what?" asked Ben, looking around for his food and eyeing up the other pizzas as they went by.

"The summer," said Rochelle.

"Life," said Sammy picking up the ashtray and putting it on another table. It was a small gesture, but Peggy knew it was for her.

Tricia nodded. "He's right, life's short. Even when you get a long one, it's still short."

"To the summer," Lacey held up her glass of Pepsi for a toast.

"To pizza," said Leigh, taking the last slice of Hawaiian while Lacey glared at her.

"To life," said Peggy, holding up her 7UP.

"To us," said Ben, holding up his beer.

"To Nick," said Sammy, clanking his glass with Ben's.

"Anyone feel like the Fire Station?" asked Lacey after a pause.

"Lace," said Tricia, "I don't want to be the one to tell you this, but someone has to."

"Tell me what?"

"Greg."

"What about him?" she said, her eyes lighting up at the mere mention of his name.

Ben coughed and gave Peggy a look. "Yeah, what about him?"

Tricia rolled her eyes and stamped out her cigarette in the ashtray in the middle of the table. "Not. Going. To. Happen."

Lacey pouted, "Don't be such a stick in the mud Trish."

"Don't you think if it was going to happen it would've happened by now?" Peggy said gently as she watched Lacey's face fall.

"Last time I talked to him he said we should just be friends, but I *know* that's because he was just waiting until I finished school, and now I have!" she argued. "Tonight is the night, it has to be!"

"I saw him making out with Henry Nichols like last year," Tricia said bluntly.

Ben spat out a mouthful of the pizza that had finally arrived and watched dumbstruck as it landed in the middle of the table.

Lacey's mouth flew open. "Henry? *Henry?* Henry the baseball coach?" she squealed.

"Sorry babe," Tricia said, not seeming very sorry at all.

Although Sammy had moved the ash tray, there was still smoke blowing over at them from the other tables and Peggy sighed. She wondered when restaurants would become non-smoking. She made a mental note to Google it later, but quickly realized *later* would be much, much later.

"I don't even believe it for a second!" Lacey shook her head and elbowed Peggy.

"Oh Lace, I'm sorry," Peggy said, patting her arm. It was nothing compared to not being able to Google for twenty or so years, but Lacey still seemed pretty upset about it.

"I'm going anyway," said Lacey pouting. "Anyone wanna join?"

"I'll go," said Ben, shrugging.

"I'm not really up for it tonight," said Peggy. She was still reeling from her goodbye with Jack earlier that morning. She just wanted to be tucked safe and sound in her bed with some magazines.

"Can I give you a ride?" Sammy asked her, looking at her for the first time all night. "I'm heading home too."

Peggy's stomach flipped. "Yes. Thanks."

"I can drive you too Ro," he offered. Rochelle nodded, and Peggy felt her face flush. She was trying to not hate Rochelle, but she was also painfully aware of the fact that Rochelle and Sammy had slept together, whether recently or not it didn't really matter. They'd seen each other naked. It gave Peggy an intense sense of unease knowing that the three of them were to sit in the car together. Maybe she should have just said she'd go to the bar with Lacey. But she really did just want to go home.

And Peggy was right. It was so awful and awkward. As they got to the car Rochelle automatically opened the front door, obviously an old habit, and Peggy slid herself into the back of the brown Dodge, a loaner car Sammy was driving around. She wished that she could fall into the cracks between the seats and never be heard from again.

"You're so good at cars Sammy," Rochelle gushed, putting her hand on his knee and acting like Peggy didn't exist. "You'll have a new car in no time."

"I need to get some more cash. After I paid for Jonas' stupid gold tooth, I'm kind of broke."

Peggy listened to their conversation, feeling like a kid in the back, her parents giving her a ride.

"That's my fault," she said. She had to say something, or they were going to forget she was there. "I should have paid for it." Peggy realized for the first time, not only did she not have the internet, but she didn't have her credit cards anymore. She couldn't have paid for Jonas's tooth even if she'd wanted to. She really was going to have to get a job.

"It's not your fault he forced you to kiss him, the creep," said Rochelle before going back to the conversation across the gear stick and ignoring Peggy again.

She let out a small sigh of relief when she realized they were heading towards Rochelle's side of town and Rochelle let out a sigh of something else.

Sammy, who seemed to only just become aware of how awkward this whole situation was, turned on the radio.

It was their song. Peggy couldn't help but smile as she caught his eye in the rear-view mirror. They sat in silence and listened to the music, each of them preoccupied with their own thoughts.

There was an awkward pause when Sammy stopped outside Rochelle's house. It was as if Rochelle didn't believe it. Like she was waiting for him to keep driving towards Peggy's house.

"Later Rochelle," said Sammy, rubbing his forehead and pushing his dirty blonde hair back, only to have it fall back onto his face again.

"Later Sammy," Rochelle said reluctantly as she opened the door and stepped out.

"Sleep well," Sammy said with total indifference and then added, "jump in the front if you want, Peg."

Peggy said goodbye to Rochelle, waiting until Rochelle was walking towards her house before she got in the front.

He put his foot gently down on the gas and began driving, sticking to the speed limit back down Rochelle's street.

They sat in silence, getting closer and closer to her

house. She knew she was missing her chance to talk to him, but she didn't know what to say. She was willing him to say something first. Eventually he did.

"You can't ever do that to me again," he said after many minutes of awkward silence.

"No," she said, shaking her head. "I won't."

"I'm not good at this stuff," he said, hitting the steering wheel lightly.

"What stuff?" she asked.

"Talking about stuff."

"What, like feelings?" she joked.

He rolled his eyes at himself. "Even the thought of it... just..."

"You don't have to talk about your feelings," she said. "You said you needed time, I'll give you whatever you need Sammy, time, space, whatever you need. I *will* wait for you. I'd wait thirty-three years for you."

He seemed to be considering this fact for some time before saying, "Is that all? What about thirty-four?" he smirked tiredly at her. It was the same smirk she'd seen him do on that first day. Her body reacted like it always did. Racing heart, clumsy fingers, awkward words.

"How about sixty?" she asked.

"How about we just take it a day at a time," he said, pulling up outside her house. "I can't think too far into the future right now."

He leaned over towards her, the scent of his aftershave, pizza and car grease was intoxicating. Her heart pounded, and she was so sure in that moment that he was going to kiss her. Just like that night in the kitchen. Wild, passionate, out of control, because they loved each other that much they could get through anything.

But he only kissed her on the cheek.

She walked towards the door and felt a stinging behind

her eyes. Why wouldn't he kiss her? Would she really have to wait thirty-three years for him? He was waiting for her to go inside, and so she turned back and gave a little wave, trying to compose herself and act cool. But when she walked into the house, she kicked her shoes off so hard they left marks on the door frame.

"Everything OK?" Janet called from the kitchen.

"No!" Peggy called back before stomping into the kitchen, sitting at the bar stool and telling Janet everything.

But by the time she got into her bed with her magazine after falling asleep on the couch watching *Laverne and Shirley* with Janet, she felt happier than she had in a long time.

Because even though she had some work to do on getting everyone to forgive her, she was home.

FIFTY-FIVE

The Permanent Circle

―――――――――――――

"We will be persecuted again, thrown in jail again, we cannot continue to live like this," Helena cried. She was done with this desert, done with this life.

"There, there," Catherine said putting her hand on the girl's shoulder.

Helena shook her off.

"We will make a permanent circle," Maria declared.

"A permanent circle would leave way to accidents Sister Maria," said Catherine. "Someone may stumble by this place and step into the circle unknowingly."

"We will keep it hidden, keep it safe. Only allow it to open for those like us. Those who face persecution. Those who need help. No one will be able to pass into the circle unless they are of pure heart and good intent and need our help. And for extra protection, we will hide it within the walls of an abbey built around it."

"And what will we call this abbey?" Helena asked, slumping down onto to the brown-orange dust next to the circle drawn in the dirt.

"Saint Christopher's," said Maria.

"Saint Christopher?" asked Helena, squinting into the evening sun.

"Yes, my child," said Maria. "For he is the patron saint of time travelers."

FIFTY-SIX

Dee's Diner
_____

His jaw almost dropped right onto the sticky diner table. This was really happening. She was here. It wasn't her, but it *was* her. She was still the same person, just thirty-three years older. His heart skipped a beat as they made eye contact. She grinned and began to rush towards him. He stood up, arms slack by his sides, mouth hanging open.

"Jack!" she said as she took him in her arms and squashed him like a long-lost aunt probably would. She pulled back to take a good look at him, holding his shoulders in a strong grip. She had never been this strong before. Her hugs had always been limp and kind of pathetic and here she was squeezing him and gripping him and, quite frankly scaring the hell out of him.

"You're so *young*," she said, touching his face as water began to well up in the corners of her slightly wrinkled eyes. "I'm sorry, this is… maybe we shouldn't be doing this." She shook her head, blinked her eyes dry and let him go. "But here we are, and the universe still exists." She laughed nervously, just like she used to. The high-pitched awkward giggle she always did when she felt like a dork.

Her hair was different, lighter, straighter. Last time he'd seen her she was wearing it a lot bigger.

"Should we sit down?" She threw her purse onto the seat and sat down. Jack sat back down opposite.

"What can I getcha?" asked a waitress.

"Just a tea please," she said.

"And for you sir?" the waitress asked him.

"Just a coffee," he said, unable to take his eyes off Peggy.

"You know the coffee here is terrible," Peggy said when the waitress was out of earshot.

Jack shrugged.

"So how do I look?" she asked nervously.

She looked amazing. She still looked beautiful and it made Jack feel nervous. He did not want to feel this way about her. Not now. Not with her looking like this, like his mom's age.

Jack shrugged.

"I'm totally a cougar, right?" She winked. She was winking? She'd never winked at a boy before in her life. Why the hell was she so confident? What had happened to her?

Jack shrugged.

"Are you going to speak?" she asked.

Jack shrugged.

"You can't try to work it all out in your head. When you start trying to work it all out, that's when you get the headaches."

Jack nodded as she kept rambling and nodded at the waitress as she poured his coffee and put down Peggy's tea. He had no idea why he ordered coffee, he hated the coffee here, or why he was still nodding, or why she was drinking tea.

"The thing is with destiny, is that you just have to trust

your own choices," she said, sipping on her tea. "I just had to trust that turning up here was going to be OK."

Jack didn't even know you could get tea at Dee's. Here she was talking about destiny, drinking tea and she was fifty freaking years old. Destiny was a fine thing indeed! It had ripped the girl he loved from him and left him to be bullied and beaten at school and all alone on the weekends. Jayne wasn't talking to him since he'd cancelled so many of their plans and he couldn't even show his face at the coffee shop since Mindy had started working there. He didn't believe in stupid crap like destiny, especially if this was the sort of thing that it brought him. A fifty-year-old version of the girl he loved. Wearing a wedding ring no less. Jesus, when was he going to get a break?

"Do you want to know what your destiny is?" she asked.

Jack shrugged.

"Oh yeah, you don't believe in stupid crap like destiny," she said, teasing.

Jack added some more sugars to the disgusting coffee.

"I told you," she said.

Jack took a sip and although it was better, she was right, it was still horrible. He made a face and pushed the cup into the middle of the table.

"Are you going to talk now?"

Jack shrugged.

"Stop shrugging," she demanded in a motherly tone that weirded him out.

Jack shrugged and shrugged and then shrugged again.

"Stop," she said.

He shrugged again.

"Stop it!"

He didn't stop shrugging until they were both laughing hysterically.

"It's good to see you," he said laughing. It was good to see her. Damn good.

"It's good to see you too," she said.

"Why am I here?" he asked.

He'd received her email early this morning, six months after she'd left, asking him to come see her at Dee's Diner for lunch. The email had told him she would be old and not to freak out, but she wanted to see him and talk to him about his destiny. She said it was his choice to turn up or not. Well, of course, he was going to turn up. She knew he'd turn up.

"I have something for you," she said.

"More Twinkies?"

"Do I still need Twinkies to prove this to you?" She waved her hands around her face.

"I have so much I want to say to you," he said.

"Then say it."

"So many questions." He shook his head and ran his hand through the back of his hair.

"Then ask them."

Jack had thought of so many things over the last few months that he wanted to say and wanted to know, but in that moment, he couldn't think of any of them.

They sat in silence for a moment until she reached into her bag and pulled out a plain white envelope.

Jack had never expected his destiny to come in a plain white envelope. Jack had never expected his destiny to come at all.

She pushed it across the table like a secret document. He looked at it blankly.

"Finished with that?" asked the waitress as she pointed at the cold coffee. He nodded. Then he watched her as she picked up the cup and whisked the envelope into her hand, thinking it was trash.

"No," Peggy said, panicking and grabbing the envelope off the waitress. Jack watched as something fell from the envelope and landed right in front of him on the streaky table. He stared at it. If he believed in signs, he would've thought that this was a pretty good one.

"Is this...?" he asked, touching it with his finger and looking up at her.

"Yes."

His mind was running in all sorts of directions he didn't even know his mind could go in. Did he have a destiny after all? Was *this* his destiny? He looked again at the ring on her finger and allowed himself for the tiniest briefest smallest moment, to wonder if *he* was the man who put it there.

"It's up to you what you do with it," she said.

Jack looked up at her.

"Maybe I'll see you soon," she said, her bottom lip quivering only ever so slightly. She held up a hand and gave him a dorky wave.

Jack watched as she walked away and then looked back down at the key on the table. It was nothing special, just a regular brass key, like any other regular door key.

And then he grabbed it and shoved it into the pocket of his faded black jeans.

To be continued...

Author's Note

It has been an absolute honor to share the world of Santolsa with you and travel through time together.

If you didn't want *Class of 1983* to end, good news! You can continue your journey with the sequel *Summer of 1984* which follows Jack's adventures from this point onwards!

As an indie author, I have no agent, publisher, publicity or marketing team to help get the word out about these books, so if you enjoyed it, it would mean the world to me if you could share a review on Amazon, Goodreads and hey, take it back to the eighties and lend someone your copy!

If you would like to receive occasional love letters and updates from me about books I'm writing and books, movies and music I'm loving, head to: www.magicpizza.press and sign up for the newsletter.

And if you want to be friends on Instagram you can hang with me at: @victoriamaxwellauthor or drop me a line at: hello@magicpizza.press

Acknowledgments

This book is by no means a perfect work of fiction. As a self-published indie author, I have no editor, no agent, no publisher or fancy people to thank. But I have been very blessed with some incredibly talented and supportive people in my life who helped me to get this story out into the world. Thank you, Emma Lloyd, for being one of my first readers. Your kind words about this work supported me so much. Thank you, Helen Comerford, for reading this thing and helping me iron it out a little, it's nice to have a fellow traveler on this indie path! Thank you, Amy Morgenstern, for fixing up my American English and laughing at the bits that are meant to be funny. Thank you, Heather Blanchard, for helping me with my scrappy commas, terrible capitalization and my attempted overuse of the word "boredly". Thank you, Ian, for all the evenings sat in the pub or in bed late at night talking about time travel plot problems. Thank you for helping me to believe in myself, and for reminding me daily that the only way to really fail is not to try. Thank you, Mum, for giving me your love of words and stories and for paving the self-publishing path ahead of me! And thank you Dad, for always believing in me and my dreams. I wish you were here to hold this book in your hands, but I know you've been reading it over my shoulder. And finally, thank *you* for reading this book. You have helped my dream come true. I hope all yours come true too and that we all find our place in this world.

About the Author

Victoria is an indie author, tarot reader, ex-high school English, Drama and Autism teacher and a lifelong lover of magic and stories. Her interests include road trips, stone circles, book stores, pizza, sweet potato fries, rainy days, eighties movies and talking to cats. Class of 1983 is her first novel.

Made in the USA
Coppell, TX
11 January 2021